Also by Robert Kotlowitz

SOMEWHERE ELSE

The Boardwalk

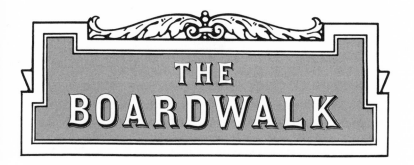

THE BOARDWALK

by
Robert Kotlowitz

Alfred A. Knopf · New York · 1977

THIS IS A BORZOI BOOK
PUBLISHED BY ALFRED A. KNOPF, INC.

Library of Congress Cataloging in Publication Data

Kotlowitz, Robert.   The Boardwalk.
I. Title.
PZ4.K8694Bo [PS3561.O846] 813'.5'4 76-13727
ISBN 0-394-49226-9

Manufactured in the United States of America
FIRST EDITION

For Dan and Alex

PART ONE

Hold fast in life to the nature of ordinary things, for they have the power to console. That was Gus Levi talking, sitting across from us at table number five at Sloan's, trying to urge us on with middle-class assurances. That was his way, direct and benign, inflated by a prickly loner's pride, full of persistent adult hope; and I took it to heart as I took everything he said. Consolation: it was almost as though we had already lost everything. He meant the classic events, essential matters; wedding tableaux, funeral rites, the ceremonies of birth; husbands, wives, children, and the dead; the apparatus of human continuity, the pursuit of the future. Also those sweet moments that return us to ourselves, when the whole world seems to breathe in as one; or other moments, less sweet.

It is 1920, Baltimore. A young woman named Beatrice Sandler stands under a purple velvet canopy alongside her groom, Jack Levin, while a clean-shaven rabbi blesses them with an unctuous smile. She cradles a bouquet of white roses against her white dress. He is in a cutaway, with a gold watch chain looped over his slim stomach. Their families and friends sit behind them. The couple look knowing and impatient. They were high-school sweethearts a half-dozen years before and had long ago blessed themselves far beyond the rabbi's imaginings. Now, at five o'clock in the afternoon, holding hands in the gilded ballroom of a downtown hotel, they cannot wait to get at each other.

Or 1925, again Baltimore. This time Jack Levin stands alongside
his father, Barney, in the maternity ward of Women's Hospital. A
nurse unfolds a blue blanket in front of them. Barney moans with
pleasure. He says something in Yiddish, adds a warning under his
breath against the evil spirit. He is missing the middle finger of
his right hand. And the name, he asks. There is a moment's silence,
a certain nervousness in the air linking father and son. Theodore,
Jack says. Theodore, Barney says. First Benedict, I never heard of
it before, now Theodore. They look at each other. Jack smiles at
his father. Barney retreats. He has no cards to play. He knows it.
Well, he says, can you afford another son? Did Haskel give you a
raise? Barney knows how to get at Jack Levin. But Jack brushes him
off. Come, he says, also thanking the nurse, we'll go visit Bea.
She'll like that.

It is 1928. Jack Levin faces his brother-in-law, Haskel Sandler,
across a desk. It is the end of a long working day at Haskel's lumberyard. Haskel, not looking up from his invoices, hands Jack a box
filled with five hundred newly printed cards. The cards read Jack
Lewin, Yard Supervisor and Construction Counsellor, Chesapeake
and Virginia Lumber. Beneath the name and title, there is also an
address and telephone number. Lewin, Jack says, staring at the
card. Where did that come from? Easier than Levin, Haskel says,
as though it means nothing. But Lewin's not my name, Jack says.
Levin's my name. Take my word, Haskel Sandler says, I know what
I'm doing. I been in the business fifteen years, don't fight me. You
want to be a success, you want a share of the business someday,
do as I say. It'll be easier for you as Jack Lewin. Jack hefts the box
his brother-in-law has handed him, weighing it all silently, studies
the card again. Lewin, he thinks, Lew-in, as a whole new sound
begins to create itself in his head, and thinking it, thinking Jack
Lewin, Bea Lewin, Theodore and Benedict Lewin, slowly takes
the first step on the way to becoming someone else.

1932. Sunday night. It is the weekend's end, nothing left beyond it. The brick rowhouse near the reservoir is quiet. So are all the identical houses on either side of it. In the living room Bea Lewin sits next to the radio, crocheting an antimacassar. All her friends are crocheting this year, pretending to save money by making their own household objects by hand. Next week, she will start to knit a dress under her sister Celia's direction. The prospect pleases her. Her hands are eager for the long needles, the endless yards of soft wool, the doing of it. Jack sits across the room, in the peach satin wing-backed chair, his own, flanking the fake fireplace, the marble mantel that Celia has found for them in the wreckage of one of the old houses being torn down on lower Eutaw Place. It is carved with a cherub's head and grapevines. Jack is working at his dreams. He holds a clipboard in his lap. Graph paper covers it. He designs houses on the graph paper, a new house each week or so for the Lewins, each tiny square on the paper representing one foot of living space. He has eighteen plans tucked away in a pigeonhole of the secretary in the dining room. Tonight he is working on a bungalow, something sweeping and long, to contain the whole family on a single floor. The radio is on. Music comes through the speaker. Upstairs, away from his mother and father, Ben Lewin finishes his homework in his back bedroom, facing the alleyway. Paper litters the floor, crumpled paper, clean paper, paper that is barely touched. It is the way he works, writing a few words, throwing the paper away, talking to himself. His bed is unmade. In the next room, Teddy, Benedict's brother Theodore, lies on the very edge of his mattress. He is straining to hear the end of the "Ford Sunday Evening Hour" floating up the stairs from the living room. He is dying to know who will be the guest next week. John Charles Thomas? Fritz Kreisler? Richard Bonelli? Some great pianist with a Russian last name who will make Teddy feel despair for his own beginner's technique and drive him to uncontrollable fantasies of an international concert career? The announcer lowers his voice, the message slips away. The orchestra begins to drone the theme song. "Abends, will ich schlafen geh'n, vierzehn Engel um mich steh'n . . ." And so on. It's too late. He has missed the announcement. The Hansel and Gretel prayer unwinds. It is almost over. Another week done for. Teddy hears the murmur of voices from downstairs, hears Ben slam his closet door on the other side of the wall. His mother and father talk quietly in the living room. Jack's design is put aside. Bea is pregnant. She is going to have another baby in four months. She tells Jack that she can feel a kick. Here, she says, placing her hand over her stomach. The "Ford Sunday Evening Hour" has run a bit short tonight. The orchestra has to fill another forty seconds with the Hansel and Gretel prayer. The Black Forest melody depresses Teddy. It is sad and unbearably sweet. Sunday night. The husk of the week. Jack and Bea downstairs in the living room, arguing mildly now about what they should listen to at ten o'clock. There is a buzz of insistent quibbling, neither willing to let go. Sunday night is radio night. Ben in the room next to Teddy's. Another baby coming. School tomorrow: Miss Waskins' temper again, Miss Lane, Miss Dorsey, Miss Dorsey's sister, all the young graduates from Towson State Normal and Goucher College. The orchestra stumbles on. "Abends, will ich schlafen geh'n, vierzehn Engel . . ."

Three years later. Jack and his second son, Teddy, sit in Miss Eversfield's waiting room in the Preparatory Department of the Peabody Conservatory of Music. No one in Jack's family, or Bea's either, has ever been inside the Peabody. Teddy wears a blue serge suit with knickers. It is the suit he wears when he plays in recitals in the waxed living room of his present piano teacher on Chauncey Avenue. Teddy and his father have been waiting for twenty minutes. Finally, Miss Eversfield's secretary invites them into Miss Eversfield's office. Miss Eversfield herself greets them. She has hair the color of ivory, tiny black patent leather shoes with heels precisely one inch high, scrubbed fingernails with perfect cuticles. Jack recites Teddy's accomplishments. They sound very serious in Jack's crisp tones, already include an early Beethoven sonata. Miss Eversfield smiles kindly, looks them over with light blue eyes that shine with boredom. For a second time, she tells Jack the cost of tuition. Where will we get that, Teddy wonders again. Jack persists. There is nothing left to do then but for Teddy to perform. They move into a second office, a studio with music racks and blackboards covered with chalked notes. In the middle of the floor stands a vast Knabe grand. Teddy sits at the leather bench. Too low? Miss Eversfield asks politely. It can be adjusted. No, it is all right, Teddys says eagerly, it's perfect, even though he feels as though he can barely reach the keys. He plays scales, called out by Miss Eversfield, arpeggios, a section of a Mozart sonata, a Moszkowski waltz. Miss Eversfield does not listen to music composed after 1900. He calculates a hundred mistakes, bears down too hard on the sustaining pedal, knows that all is lost. The piano keys have begun to sweat. He will have to go back to the waxed living room on Chauncey Avenue. It will cost three hundred and fifty dollars a year, Miss Eversfield says again. Sure, Jack says. We will let you know, she says, nodding that snow-white head, holding out the perfect hands, inviting them through the soft, reflective, late-afternoon stillness of the Conservatory offices, filled with a calm that is new to both father and son, something so strange and accommodating at the same time that they both take it at first as vaguely threatening.

Or finally this seasonal rite, 1939, in Atlantic City. It is a Friday in late August, lighted by the midafternoon Jersey sun and made nearly blinding by a speckled surf breaking on the Atlantic shore in low fragile rollers. On the beach sits a young boy, fourteen, in navy wool bathing trunks and a white canvas belt with rust marks on it. Just below the right buttock there is a clumsily patched mothhole. The boy has no chest. His arms are fishbone thin. He sits round-shouldered on the sand, squinting at the sea, hugging his knees. His rib cage can be seen from the water's edge.

Alongside him, his mother eyes the shallow water, where his sister is playing with a pickup friend. They scream in the water, arching their backs in shock when the cold surf splays over them.

His mother frowns, tugs at a shoulder strap. Sharing his mother's blanket, Charlotte Melnicov reads Gone With the Wind. Charlotte Melnicov is his mother's best friend, for the moment. She is three years late with the novel and she is now buried in it. Charlotte's blond hair is pulled tight into a bun, protected by a pink bandanna. The men on the beach stare at her in passing, stare at the boy's mother. The boy notices, becomes alert. It is his habit. Overhead, a blimp advertises rubber tires; everyone is bored with it. On the right, the Steel Pier reaches out to deep water, where a trained horse dives into the ocean five times a day. The little girls shriek in the water. Charlotte sighs; Atlanta burns. Mother and son exchange a word, pass along a Hershey bar. A swollen Rachmaninoff melody dimly snakes its way through his brain.

1

Two hours later, they were almost alone on the beach. His sister stood in front of them, wrapped in a seedy towel from the hotel. Her teeth chattered, her eyes were bloodshot, her fingertips like prunes. A chill lofted in like a knife from the shoreline. They all shivered.

"You look disgusting," he said.

"Teddy," his mother said.

"Well, I can't help it, she does."

His sister looked off at the Steel Pier. She couldn't keep her teeth from chattering. She kept moving from one foot to the other; she had to go to the bathroom. Her hair hung in strings, just below her ears. There was nothing to do about her, and everybody knew it. She had been an afterthought for Bea and Jack. They had thought that all those possibilities were over for them, were sure of it, and along had come Marion. They had teased each other about it with worldly jokes which they had shared with their friends. A daughter. Who had dreamed of it? But even Marion's barber didn't know what to make of the child, or how to try to shape her. She was six and hardly a beauty yet.

"You have a hole in your bathing suit," she said.

"I do not," Teddy said. Still, he reached for the patched moth-hole. He had once seen one of Walter Schultz's testicles slip through a hole in his gym shorts and the shock of that lonely, wrinkled humiliation, visible to everyone in the gym class but

Walter, had never left him. Marion laughed. She didn't even have half her teeth.

"Get your stuff together," Bea said. "Let's go, Charlotte."

Char-*lot,* like a pistol crack.

"I can't put this down," Charlotte said, looking up from her book.

"We always stay on the beach too late. We never learn. And I don't want to walk into the hotel looking like this while the old men are having services."

"They're not interested in you," Charlotte said.

"It's the idea of it. Out of some respect. For God's sake, Marion, stop shivering."

The child made an enormous effort. For three, four, five seconds, she went rigid, stood stock still. Then her teeth began to chatter again and her shoulders shook, out of control.

"If you listened to me, you wouldn't be freezing to death," Bea said. "I told you to get out of the water an hour ago. Now look at you. Nobody ever listens to me." She got to her feet. "Don't leave a litter behind. Wrap all your stuff in the towels."

They were walking up the beach now, toward the Boardwalk, into a powerful orange sun that was settling at the same moment behind every beach on the great coastal plain. They could still feel it on their faces, were greedy for it, in a last-minute, pure benediction made possible by daylight saving time. After only five days in that sun, carefully controlled by Bea with two kinds of lotion, Teddy and Marion had already turned brown. Teddy was excessively proud of it, had begun to admire himself in the bathtub each evening, white against brown, running his hand in the green water from stomach to skinny thigh. It was like milk and toast at breakfast. But the sun was almost gone now, down over Barnegat and points west. They walked on slowly, Bea and Marion, Charlotte and Teddy. Charlotte tripped over her robe, caught herself. Teddy gave her a hand, a touch on the elbow. A gentleman leaned over the Boardwalk railing, observing her. As they came closer, he tipped his straw hat, offered a half-smile that already seemed prepared for a rebuff, also paid attention to Bea. They both ignored him, fixed their eyes on the Surf Hotel's solarium, glinting in the sunset, and, behind it, Sloan's; then on the Hotel Cotswold across the street. In the Cotswold's white clapboard facade, Charlotte caught a glimpse of Scarlett's Tara, a grove of palmetto trees, a few soldiers in gray uniforms, lounging on the rambling portico in the late afternoon sun. Her imagination hung there a moment. Pillared Tara, high on a Georgia hill somewhere, a couple of hundred darkies in bandannas exactly like her own, and soft, yearning idealizations of southern gentlemen with Robert E. Lee beards and superbly vague Confederate manners. She had never been south of the District of Columbia, had never known anyone who had ever stayed at the Cotswold. None of them did. It was filled with Christian ladies from Virginia and Philadelphia, the last in the line of great hotels going north on the Boardwalk. For a moment then Teddy thought that Charlotte might fall asleep right on her feet. He had seen that look on her before, dim and full of dreamy deadweight.

The four of them walked into Sloan's through the street entrance, underneath the porch with the green rocking chairs. Upstairs, the old men were already praying in the sunroom, facing east over the Atlantic toward Jerusalem. They could hear them murmuring in unison, led by Rabbi Miller. There was a terrible damp chill beneath the porch. Sand was everywhere. Nothing could ever really dry out there; the sea owned it. Rabbi Miller's voice suddenly rose to a shout, then quieted down. The murmuring continued. Marion's teeth began to chatter again. Poor child. The last thing Teddy saw as he went through the screen door was the lady in the ginger wig sitting behind them on the extravagantly long veranda that ran around the Hotel Cotswold, high above the street. She was pretending as she always did to be reading the Philadelphia *Bulletin* while she examined all four of them, Bea, Charlotte, Marion, and Teddy, out of the corner of her eye.

Jack and Bea Lewin, as was sometimes their way, had made a lunatic arrangement between them, rationalizing it on behalf of the children, then acted on it. Bea, Marion, and Teddy were to spend seven golden days at Sloan's (formerly Solomon's, the hotel stationery read) in Atlantic City, while Jack stayed home in Baltimore. For ninety-four dollars and fifty cents a week, they shared a room that measured twelve by fifteen, in which Bea and Marion slept in a double bed and Teddy spent the night on a cot which he opened up for himself each evening. For the same money, they also had three meals a day. At the end of the week, on Sunday afternoon, Bea and Marion were to go home on the one-forty *Sunshine Special* and Jack would arrive the same afternoon for a second seven-day period. Teddy would move into the double bed with his father, while his older brother, Benedict, would come from New York and take over the cot. Ben was visiting the World's Fair on money he had earned delivering groceries for the Brookfield Avenue Market. Everyone benefited from the arrangement, but only Teddy, of them all, had two weeks at the seashore.

They had a single mirrored dresser in their room, with tiny blue flowers hand-painted on the front of each white drawer. One wooden chair stood in a corner and a night table on Bea's side of the double bed; there was also a dim reading lamp with a paper shade and an empty glass vase alongside it. Bea's dresses hung in a closet in which Teddy had discovered he could hear everything that went on in the next room. Their bags stood on the closet floor. Outside the window, a fire escape led to the ground, two floors below. Along with unoccupied rooms, fire was the nightmare of Atlantic City hotelkeepers. Sloan's had a brick front, added when it was still Solomon's, but the rest of it was made of white clapboard, like the Cotswold. So was the Surf, twelve feet away across an alleyway. The Surf sat between Sloan's and the Boardwalk. It faced the ocean. It didn't matter what was on the other, landward side of Sloan's. Teddy had never noticed; neither had Bea.

Charlotte was down the hall in a room just wide enough for a single bed. She shared a bath with Bea, Teddy, Marion, and two other guests. She was there to keep Bea company, while Jack stayed in Baltimore earning their living. When Bea left, she would stay a second week without her friend. The matter had been discussed for a full month, back and forth, urgently, while Charlotte changed her mind a couple of times before finally saying yes. It was how she arranged most things.

Charlotte was thirty-two, eight years younger than Bea, although they looked exact contemporaries. She had been passed along to Bea and Jack through mutual friends, her usual route from family to family. With each one, she stayed a year or two, sometimes a bit longer, as an "aunt" who came to dinner often. With this family, with Bea and Jack and their children, she was now in her second season.

She was beautiful in a soft, Chekhovian way. There was something in her face, beyond the heavy dreaminess, that sounded memories of languid nineteenth-century Russian estates and their isolated inhabitants. She wore light, pink, moist lipstick at a time when everyone else was trying to look as though they were on fire; this lipstick was imported from Paris. She dyed her hair blond, the blond of yellow roses or a child's crayon, then grew it long, down to the waist, against the fashion. In public, it was parted in the middle and gathered into a heavy bun by turtleshell pins that were two inches long. It thrilled Teddy and Marion to see Charlotte in the act of combing it out, loose over her shoulders and breasts like another layer of clothing, held by one hand, brushed by the other. It also thrilled them to smell the cold cream that littered her room, to catch her applying some oily white substance to her skin, massaging it vigorously with her fingertips, designed to soothe, cool, freshen, or even to remove temporarily the soft blond hairs that were barely visible on her upper lip or in her nostrils. Depilatory, the boxes read. Armored like that, sometimes glistening with unguents made in the south of France, Charlotte looked curiously vulnerable to the children—full of mindless expectancy and hope—and it softened their feelings for her.

Also against the fashion, Charlotte had become a lawyer. She came from a family of temperamental intellectuals—Melnicovs from Kiev—who challenged each other with their own racing intelligence and were barely able to remain on speaking terms from one year to the next. In that family, women who became lawyers were no surprise. Charlotte's cousin Sarah, in Boston, was a lawyer; so was Sarah's sister, Doris; her father's cousin, Estelle, who now lived in Annapolis, had gone to medical school for two years; and there was said to be a Melnicov in Cape Town, South Africa, who was a social work supervisor for an entire Bantu tribe. But Charlotte, hair dyed blond, lips a moist pink, images of Portia in her head, had taken the bar three times in Maryland and had failed each try. It was a humiliation for her among the other Melnicovs, the brilliant aunts, uncles, and cousins who straddled three continents like world conquerors, a source too, she thought, of secret satisfaction to her widowed father, who jealously wished her just enough success for security and continued to support her with the rents from some East Baltimore properties; and another urgent Melnicov matter, along with the embarrassing question of marriage, that she forced her friend Bea—all her families, in fact—to talk about incessantly.

They all took their baths, fifteen minutes apiece, first Marion, with her mother on her knees alongside the tub, scrubbing Marion's back, ears, and crotch, then self-admiring Teddy, clean as a whistle from the Atlantic before he even stepped into the tub, Bea herself, and finally Charlotte, who sank moaning into bath salts, bubbles, and a final, cleansing rinse. The two aging gentlemen whose rooms flanked Charlotte's had bathed between four and five, preparing for evening prayers. They had achieved among themselves a civilized cycle in which Bea's family and its needs were the chief impulse. The two aging gentlemen were kind; what the children needed the children got; as their mother and in her own handsome right, Bea also benefited; and Charlotte was too beautiful not to be indulged. Besides, when she was finished the bathroom smelled like a lilac paradise.

Teddy was almost dressed when his mother got back from her bath. Marion lay flat on her back on the double bed. She had fallen asleep with her one-eyed doll sharing the pillow; a faint snore fluttered through her nostrils. Bea lay down next to her. "I must have a five-minute nap," she said to the ceiling. "Or I will die." Teddy believed her. Each afternoon, after the beach, she slept for five minutes and woke up a new woman. Everyone in the Sandler family, she said, all her five brothers and four sisters, was famous for catnaps. It saved their lives. Marion had inherited the gift. Now, mother and daughter lay side by side as though in their tombs. Marion was wearing little pink drawers that weighed precisely one ounce. They were a size too large for her. Teddy had once picked them up and felt as though he were holding a nickel's worth of sweet cotton candy in his hands.

He tiptoed around the room looking for his shoes. His mother wore her Japanese kimono from Yokohama, green, black, and pink silk, with two flying herons embroidered on the back and only a tasseled sash to hold it closed. Underneath, she was naked. She almost always was. She walked through the hotel corridors to and from her bath that way and around their crowded room, as though the whole world was blind. Teddy could always tell when she was naked underneath. He could tell from the way the robe fell over her buttocks. A few days before, in this very room, her kimono had fallen open while she was scolding Marion, a swift, angry unfolding, an accident, and Teddy had caught for life the riveting, perfect geometry of the triangle darkly visible at the top of her thighs. For a second or two, it had moved in and out of his vision in the late afternoon shadows, while his stomach began to flutter in something like panic. Then, as Bea pulled the sash tight around her waist, Teddy had caught her watching him with a faint, bemused smile which, when he felt the worldliness in it, made him turn away stiffly to hide his agitation.

Marion snored again, twitched lightly, then jumped out of bed and began to dress. Bea awoke, checked her watch. "There's no point in rushing," she said, yawning at her daughter. Teddy himself was fully dressed now. White ducks, navy sports shirt, saddle shoes. The room smelled of talc; the whole top of the white dresser was dusted with it; you could leave your fingerprints in it. In a moment, Marion was starched and frowning in a stiff little dress. Like the furniture in the room, her dress had tiny flowers stuck onto it. There was still a light puffiness around her eyes, the residue of an allergic response to yesterday's salmon dinner. Seafood destroyed Marion. Salmon swelled her eyes, swordfish produced hives as big as quarters. Bea had been furious when she caught Marion eating her salmon; the child knew better than that. Two mouthfuls and, within fifteen minutes, her eyes were half closed. Teddy, too, was allergic. Each morning he awoke with his itching eyes caked with overnight crust. Bea boasted somewhat about her children's allergies. It gave them heroic stature in the Sandler family without the need to suffer heroically.

They were all dressed now, Bea in a navy blue skirt—navy was the family color—and white blouse, with navy-and-white spectator shoes, her dark silky hair cockily parted on the left. Marion watched her put on the last touch of makeup, coldly taking it all in, storing up future technique. To Teddy, she looked like the Duchess of Windsor or her sister-in-law Marina. It was one of the miracles of the family, sometimes resented by all of them, this contained gift of Bea's of looking like British royalty when Jack was not sure how they were going to pay for her clothes, or theirs, either. But she did not throw money around. She bought carefully, knew where the sales were on Charles Street, which ones counted; and she was good at it, had perfect confidence in her ability to shop without being taken advantage of. Everyone, in any case, said the depression was over. Those years were surely done with. She would now maintain herself intact until Jack became a success. It would happen, it was happening all around her to others. She would not give an inch until he, like her five brothers, especially like Haskel, had learned how to capture the future and dominate life. That was what she believed in, the future and its perfectability, and she had the trained stamina of someone who had patiently taught herself how to wait for it. In the meantime, she would try to look and smell like a modest English rose garden and continue to depend for monthly guidance on copies of *Vogue* borrowed from her sister Celia; there was a pile of them two feet high on the floor of her closet at home.

They were in no hurry to go downstairs before dinner. Bea checked Charlotte when she came by to pick them up, Charlotte checked Bea, a slow appraising walk around the other, hems examined, makeup, seams. You look stunning, one said. *You* look stunning, the other said. Stunning. It was the word they used to indicate acceptability. Then they asked Teddy to check both of them, while Marion sat on the bed and observed them silently. She was developing a perfect eye, that child, and so was her brother. Who was more beautiful, Teddy asked himself, while they turned in front of him. He could not find an answer. Charlotte wore a pink dress with a scalloped flower at her waist to catch the eye; delicate but not fragile. Her hair was pulled tight, her mouth was as pink as her dress. She did not look like a lawyer. Neither did Bea, who looked merely perfect. She always looked perfect, even in her Yokohama kimono, naked underneath. Pink. Navy blue. Long hair, marcelled bob. An unreserved Slavic fullness; American angles, full of snap. Which was more beautiful? Who could tell? The immaculate children reserved judgment.

2

They walked down the two flights in silence, through the vacant, early evening atmosphere of the hotel stairwell, through the astringent soap smell of the carpeting that Teddy hated, that they all hated, down slowly into the lobby that Bea and Charlotte despised without passion, thinking themselves too sensitive for the loud jokes and the sometimes coarse manners, too tasteful for the vulgar gossip and energetic malice, a little too good, all in all, for the other fifty-eight guests at Sloan's who shared with them the possibility of a temporary utopia made up of sea, sun, American air, and three meals a day cooked by somebody else.

At the foot of the stairwell, Bea and Charlotte clung nervously to each other, arm in arm. They seemed on the verge of withdrawal. Teddy and Marion remained alongside them. It was their first Friday night at Sloan's, the largest crowd of the week, the noisiest, the hungry moment of return for all the husbands who spent the week itself turning profits elsewhere, in Philadelphia, Baltimore, Pittsburgh, other cities. Teddy thought of his father, wished him there, alongside them for the moment. With his father around, he would not feel like such a stranger. Charlotte's hand tightened under Bea's arm. Marion was pulling at her mother. Go, Bea said, shaking her off. Don't nag me. Her daughter ran off to search for Gloria Goldman. Dinner was not quite ready. It was always ten minutes late, as though a fashionable deadline had to be met each night. There was a smell of roasting chickens everywhere, the sound of silverware still being set in the dining room in the back. They were too early, they should have waited upstairs. Then, in an instant, Larry Bernard appeared, reached for Bea's hand and kissed it. Teddy blushed. Larry Bernard then did the same with Charlotte, holding onto her hand for half a minute. That was part of his style, kissing hands with a kind of ironic good humor, pretending to pay equal attention to everyone. Teddy slipped away, he always tried to slip away from Larry Bernard, lost himself in the crowd, wandering around the lobby as though he had no place to go. Every now and then he looked back over his shoulder to spy on his mother and her two friends. Irritable now, full of impatience, Teddy checked the dining room, eyed the sullen college boys waiting alongside their tables to serve dinner. He was very hungry, always was in the evening lobby smell of brisket or poultry cooking in its own hot juices. Someone was listening to the radio on the cigar counter. Pearl Sloan, formerly Solomon, was trying to turn the volume down. She was the owner's wife. She ran everything, while her husband, Hy, trotted at her heels. Danzig, Teddy heard, as the radio suddenly blared, then went silent. There were too many guests in the lobby, too much noise, too few places to sit. The air was already stale. Everyone kept sneaking glances at the dining room and checking their watches.

Something brushed Teddy, a fresh scent, gardenia, an elbow. It was Mrs. Talles passing swiftly by, like a full-bodied angel with black wings, smiling at him with the reddest lips in the world. Mr. Talles was right behind her, smoking his before-dinner cigar. He had just arrived by car from his Baltimore factory. Mrs. Talles was wearing a black dress to set off her complexion. Her skin was dead white, the family treasure, always protected by an elegant parasol which was raised on the beach even when there were clouds overhead. She had a green one, a mauve one, a third the color of eggshell. No sun ever touched her face. Teddy liked Mrs. Talles. How could he not? She captured him daily with her smile. There was something hearty there, something cheerful and full; a crimson mouth, sharing laughter. She liked to play bridge at night in Sloan's cardroom, when her husband was away during the week, and always won enthusiastically, startling the guests with her spontaneous gaiety. Once he arrived at Sloan's for the weekend, Mr. Talles, smoking his cigar, never let his wife out of his sight.

Over his shoulder, then, Teddy heard Marion scream with laughter. Gloria Goldman always did that to her by making herself cockeyed. Marion's laugh was like fingernails scraping over a blackboard. Her own eyes, he saw as he turned, were still a little swollen. She certainly was no beauty. Gloria Goldman was laughing with her. To get away from them, what they looked like, how they sounded, Teddy moved closer to the cigar counter, leaned on the glass, began to listen to the radio. Stalin, Lowell Thomas said, as though he were talking about an old friend; static broke in then, an electric interruption crackling over the air. There was a new boy, Teddy saw, standing alone on the other side of the lobby. He looked at Teddy nervously as the crowd opened for an instant; their eyes met, broke away; no acknowledgment. The boy wore glasses, a tie and jacket: overdressed at the beach. He seemed to know it, shying from Teddy with self-consciousness. Then he disappeared into the crowd.

There would be no *Anschluss* in Danzig, Lowell Thomas said calmly. He read a somber quote, translated from the French. It was a message from Daladier. Teddy paid attention. There would be no Sudeten-style takeover. The British said it and the French said it. The West would fight for Danzig.

Larry Bernard was suddenly standing alongside Teddy then, listening to the radio, too. He was the baldest man Teddy had ever seen. There wasn't a hair on his head, he was all bare-skinned skull, but his shoulders, Teddy knew, were covered with thick tufts of it. He looked ridiculous in a bathing suit, all his hair was in the wrong places. "Hiya, kid," Larry Bernard said, as though Teddy had just handed him a million dollars. Teddy looked up, smiled despite himself. Larry Bernard was easily the tallest man in the room, thick, too, like his shoulder hair, thick and fleshy, two hundred and forty pounds, it was claimed, maybe more. He had once played varsity football at the University of Maryland and still talked about it. The women said he was handsome, bald as he was. Bea said it. Charlotte said it. But it was power they meant, the strength and presence, the threat as well, that comes with size. Larry Bernard liked to say what was on his mind. Why not? People had been listening to him all his life. Looking up at him, they had always paid attention. He compelled it. Even Teddy Lewin was subject to Larry Bernard. A few days before, he had sneaked a look at a postcard Larry Bernard had left for mailing, message up, on the cigar counter. It had rested just about where Larry Bernard's fist sat tensely folded now.

"Darling," it said, "Atlantic City is A.C., the same old *dreck*. It never changes. But you might have made the whole difference. Big L."

Dreck. Crap. A thrill of sophistication had run through Teddy at the sight of the word. It was wonderful to speak with such ease, such freedom. He sensed certain shared assumptions between Larry Bernard and the woman he was writing to, some sweet secret current that ran between them; they clearly understood each other; and Larry Bernard, in all his sudden worldliness, Larry Bernard, the Big L, like Bea Lewin herself, had instantly seemed larger, more formidable than ever.

On the other side of the counter, Pearl Sloan sighed at the news. Larry Bernard shook his head angrily. "They're sure as hell gonna fight this time," he said, slamming his fist into the palm of his hand. "I hope they get that son-of-a-bitch." He was not kidding around. His face was getting red. Charlotte and Bea, Teddy saw, were standing on the other side of Larry Bernard, watching him silently. They had all come together again, Charlotte and Bea, Teddy and Larry Bernard, over the evening news. They always seemed to be standing near him, resting, like iron filings waiting to be polarized in the magnetic field surrounding his powerful bachelor's bulk. They were all silent now. No one

had anything to say. Lowell Thomas was talking about Musso-
lini. The Italians had been warned to stay out of the conflict, he
said. "Let's get that one, too," Larry Bernard said, slamming his
fist again. There would be a showdown. Every European capital
said so. The world could depend on it. That was the news, Lowell Thomas said. That was the news for tonight.

Then Larry Bernard quieted down as the commercials came
on, more or less returned to himself, turned to bend down and
whisper something into Charlotte's ear. As he talked, she looked
up at him in her querulous, is-that-all? way, the way she looked
at all men who showed an interest in her, and whispered something in return. On they murmured, the whispers hissing past
Teddy's ear. He couldn't make out a word they were saying.
From time to time, a faint half-smile appeared on Charlotte's face,
and once the blood rose to her cheeks. It was Larry Bernard's
assurance again, his air of formidable success. He had once run
for Baltimore city councilman, Charlotte had told Teddy several
times, and nearly won. He could make Charlotte Melnicov, he
could make all women, blush at will.

"Hello, my darling, hello."

It was Dr. Lazarus, the pediatrician from Pittsburgh, who
made a point of crossing the entire lobby to talk to Bea. He
would walk a mile to talk to Bea Lewin, he always boasted to
everyone, as though she were a Camel cigarette. He sounded to
Teddy like a machine gun going off at full clip. Rat-a-tat-tat, Dr.
Lazarus said, and out came a few thousand words. He was full
of feistiness and optimism, was famous for it at the hotel, and
Bea was his favorite of all the guests. His wife now stood behind
him, hair braided around her head. She was a full three inches
taller than the doctor and always gazed at everyone over his
shoulder. Bea paid particular attention to her, acknowledging
her docile grin, her patient attendance on her husband.

A bell finally rang for dinner. Dr. Lazarus was telling Bea that
she was a sight for sore eyes. It was what he always said, turning
each time to his wife for confirmation. Alongside them, Larry

Bernard was paying close attention, in his deft, effortless way, to Charlotte. They were holding hands, listening to the doctor compliment Bea. Teddy stood in front of them, feeling sorry for Mrs. Lazarus, watching his mother blink her eyes with pleasure and pretend to be put off by the doctor's cheerful words. Then the dining-room doors opened. There was a movement in that direction, a slow, irresistible response from the crowd, as though the sun were finally shining in there after a week of rain. Gloria Goldman's mother took her off. The Talles boys, Thelma Talles' sons, Joseph and Tibor, spit their gum into a potted palm and scrambled off into the crowd. They were black as Spanish olives. Tibor was Teddy's age, Joseph two years older. On the Sunday he had arrived at Sloan's, Teddy had seen their father, who was twice their size, smack Tibor across the face with an open palm, right in the middle of the lobby. The crack could be heard for thirty feet in either direction. While everyone froze, Tibor had recovered with a crooked smile and the imprint of five fingers on his dark, blood-mottled cheek. Teddy had never learned what Tibor had done to deserve that; it was buried forever inside that flushed head. The Talles boys kept threatening to take Teddy to Chalfonte Alley. Tibor had been talking about it all week long while Joseph grinned knowingly behind his brother's back and thrust his middle finger into the air. All Teddy would need was five dollars and a rubber.

The bell rang again, the lobby stirred with good cheer. Larry Bernard went off to his nightly table that was filled with other successful lawyers. Charlotte insisted that they sit apart at dinner; the presence and talk of successful lawyers were unsettling to her. They saw enough of Larry Bernard between meals, she said defensively, and so each evening he left them alone for an hour, not unwillingly. Bea, Charlotte, and Teddy drew together. Marion stood in front of her mother, Bea's hands on her shoulders. They would wait another minute or two before going into the dining room. They would be sure to separate themselves from the crowd. Dr. Lazarus was finally ready to move off, finally able to leave Bea alone. His wife smiled passively behind him as they turned to go.

In a corner of the lobby, meanwhile, the old lady Eisen was being helped off her high-backed upholstered chair by her nurse, who was in white uniform and oxfords. They struggled together like a ward and her governess. Bea and Charlotte watched them, Teddy watched them, Marion's salmon eyes opened wide. The old lady Eisen had been coming to Sloan's for thirty-three years, before the owners had changed its name and theirs from Solomon, long before her husband had invented his chocolate laxative. She was eighty-two now and a widow with two million dollars. With her nurse, she occupied the entire second-floor front of the hotel, with two baths of her own, one of which ran real salt water. She wore a ginger wig like the woman on the Cotswold veranda across the street. She groaned as the nurse pulled her to her feet—Marion winced at the sound—and held tight to her silver-knobbed cane as she moved off.

There was another news summary, Teddy discovered at the cigar counter, one final one before dinner. In London, the radio said, they were building air-raid shelters in front of Buckingham Palace for the use of the royal family. Schoolchildren were being evacuated to the north. On the continent, the Polish cavalry, the nation's glory, was on its way to the Prussian frontier. So were a thousand German tanks. Teddy listened with Pearl Sloan, watched the old lady Eisen's nurse walk her across the lobby floor to the dining room as though she were a soft-boiled egg. Europe, the radio said again. Always Europe. Teddy's grandfather came from Europe. He was born in Warsaw, or somewhere near there, a town called Lomza, he thought. Danzig was near Warsaw. Teddy still had cousins in Warsaw. They all had unpronounceable names. He felt a tremor of sympathetic excitement for them, for all the Poles, all the continent. Thank God for the Polish cavalry. Thank God for the Maginot Line and the British navy. *Vive la France*, God Save the King, *à bas les Boches*. In Poland now, at this very moment. . . . Pearl Sloan turned off the radio with an irritated snap of her fingers, moved toward the dining room with everyone else. Teddy turned to the lobby, saw the new boy pass by, stiff in tie and jacket, all the husbands who had arrived for the weekend, Thelma Talles in her black dress. The new boy had ruddy cheeks, a high color that seemed a little strange, a stance full of dignity and constraint. Gestures, voices, a hundred attitudes simultaneously perceived, they were all frozen in Teddy's mind, frozen together like that for life. Dr. Lazarus rising on his toes to charm Bea, the old lady Eisen caught shuffling in her own rich amber, the Big L, the connoisseur of *dreck*, fastened to pink, yearning Charlotte, the watchful Talleses tracking each other through the lobby of a strange hotel, even the somber baritone, the unsuccessful attempt at a tragic intonation, of Lowell Thomas' famous reverential voice. It was how he would remember them all, how they were placed forever in memory, as though there were nothing else to them, as though they had no other lives, no other selves beyond this moment.

Bea's hand touched Teddy's elbow. "Come on," she said, already moving in another direction, an iridescent dragonfly suddenly and aggressively on the wing. "It's time to call your father."

3

In the phone booth, Bea waited for the call to come through. She was perfectly cool, perfectly marcelled. The children clustered outside the folding door, Charlotte behind them. Bea touched the back of her hair with a single finger, poked at a dipping wave. There at Sloan's she might be susceptible to Larry Bernard's or Dr. Lazarus' spirited flattery, but she was also ready for another life, ready to reach for it without hesitation, perfectly prepared for a Windsor garden party, a five-day crossing on the *Normandie*, New York to Le Havre, or a suite at the Shelburne, perhaps, facing the sea ten floors up, with steamer trunks stamped with international insignia littering the floor: six weeks' worth of clothes, each outfit repeated only once. A simple, honeyed dream, common to the century, sunk deep in her consciousness by the obsessive ambition of her five successful brothers and nourished there by the visible evidence of their new money. It was something she would never give up.

The door caved in as Marion fell against it. Bea scolded her, shoved her back into Teddy's arms. There was a flutter of arms and legs, some whining, an impatient silence. The phone rang. "Jack," Bea said into the mouthpiece, a languid smile on her face, a bemused greeting, full of expectation and experience, which Teddy recognized, knew as well as his own name. "Honey . . ." She closed the door in the children's faces. A minute passed, the door opened. "Say hello to Daddy. Quickly. It costs a fortune." Marion slipped into the booth, stuck her face close to the phone, said "yes" four times, with a pause between each. Then it was Teddy's turn. Give your father my regards, Charlotte said hurriedly.

"Daaaaad."

It was hot in Baltimore, his father said, slicing each word cleanly. One hundred and three at noon. Teddy was lucky to be where he was. Was he having a good time? Was he enjoying every minute of it? The seven-year locusts were back, chewing the foliage off the trees. A terrible sight. Nothing would help. Pause. Teddy's father would arrive on Sunday. So would Benedict. Pause. Teddy's father was bringing his own father. Teddy blinked. "Grandpa?" he said. How would they all manage in one room? Jack's tenor voice sang over the wires. He was full of explanations. He sounded eager and high-spirited, like a man expecting a gift. Teddy could see his neat little moustache through the mouthpiece. He would arrive on Sunday, he told Teddy again. There would be a two-hour gap between his mother's departure with Marion and Jack's arrival. Teddy had heard it all a hundred times before. Teddy was not to bother to hang around the hotel waiting for him, he was to go to the beach as though it were any other day. Did he have a friend he could play with? Ben would be there for dinner. If, Jack said, he didn't get lost on his way from New York. Father and son laughed. It was an old joke, Benedict's cherished chaos. So, his father said, suddenly slow, suddenly sweet, we'll have a week together. Yes, Teddy said, wanting to hear more. Yes. Pause. You'll like it here, Teddy said, waiting. It's nice. Had he touched a piano all week, Jack asked. It was important not to let too much time go by, not to go stale, not to let the fingers grow stiff. But I'm on vacation, Teddy said. Bea opened the door. "Hurry up," she said. "Daaaaad. Don't forget to bring the *Dick Tracys*."

Bea grabbed the phone, pushed Teddy out. She and Jack spoke for a full minute then, irritability suddenly crackling in the booth. It was visible to all of them through the glass panes. Bea was talking loudly, interrupting Jack. Then he interrupted her.

Back and forth. They were both masters at interrupting the other, at interrupting Teddy and Marion; if they had it in mind, they never let anyone finish what they had to say. Four words from Bea, very firm. A silence, then several more. Finally, it calmed down. There were a few seconds of reasonable farewells. When Bea hung up, Teddy said to her, "Grandpa's coming." Bea gave him a mean look, tapped her foot. "So I just heard," she said. She didn't know what to do with the energy her husband had just touched; she never did. It was time to go to the dining room, Teddy decided, time to have their dinner, like everyone else. He was an old hand at this. "I'm hungry," he said brightly. Then Marion said the same thing. He took his sister by the shoulders, old friends now, old collaborators, moved her along playfully from behind. Gradually, he got them out of the way of Bea's anger and left her to Charlotte Melnicov. A few minutes later, he was seated comfortably in the dining room between Marion and Mr. Levi, waiting politely for his mother and her best friend to join them at their round table.

The boy with the ruddy cheeks was sitting directly opposite him, at the setting that had been empty all week. Mr. Levi made the introduction, speaking up clearly so they could all hear him. A new guest, Mr. Levi said, in his neat formal way. Just arrived. The boy looked to the right and left, then up at the ceiling. Teddy nodded vaguely in his direction. His name was Erich Kessler. Alongside him sat his father. His name was Frederick Kessler. They were from Germany and lived now in New York. Mr. Levi said it as though it were the most natural thing in the world. Alongside Teddy, Marion was all eyes, staring at Erich Kessler. She always fell in love with Teddy's friends. Frederick Kessler flashed a practiced smile at her. "You are the sister?" he asked across the table. Marion froze, remained silent. "Well, Marion, are you or aren't you?" Mr. Levi asked, leaning in her direction. "Answer," Teddy said. Poor mute little girl, faced with strange new guests, foreigners. She was saved by her mother's arrival. Bea and Charlotte were just sitting down. Mr. Levi held

Bea's chair for her, not quite making it to Charlotte, while Bea smiled gratefully at him in return. She liked to have her chair held for her, liked even better Gustav Levi's touch of open gallantry.

Mr. Levi then had to repeat the introductions. Again, Erich Kessler looked to the right and the left. His color heightened; he made a little pyramid of his silverware, pretending to be absorbed elsewhere, mumbled a greeting to Bea and Charlotte; but he looked very neat in his tie and jacket. His father smiled ingratiatingly at the two American ladies, full of appeal and soft sympathy. It was beautifully done, well rehearsed and irresistible, the smile that he had discovered over the years could help batter down the thick, bureaucratic walls of immigration offices, foreign consulates, and alien registration halls. The American ladies smiled back shyly, had no choice, but Teddy could tell that before Mr. Levi had finished saying the Kesslers' names, Charlotte Melnicov had made a decision to discard them. He had seen that before, the instant decision, for whatever reason, not to pay attention, to pull away. She was touchy about people, Bea had once explained, she was afraid, and her fear made her look like a snob. Bea herself, however, nodded firmly at Frederick Kessler, swiftly appraised Erich in terms of Teddy, then looked around impatiently for their waiter. He was busy serving the old lady Eisen and her nurse, who had a table to themselves. "Saul's never here when you need him," Bea said. "He has two tables to serve and he's always at the wrong one." She began to tap her water glass with a spoon. She had already forgotten the Kesslers. "What does she think *she's* doing, wearing black this time of the year?" Bea said to Charlotte. Together they stared at Thelma Talles across the room, two beauties of the night turning on a third.

Teddy decided to get out of the dining room as soon as he could. He had seen this before, too, knew this tone, Bea's anger and irritation snapping in her voice, knew how Charlotte would try to feed it, inflate a minor family disturbance for the excitement it gave her. His mother was angry with his father about Teddy's grandfather; she was telling herself that Jack's father was being given what was rightfully hers, another week in Atlantic City. "Don't let him get away with that," Charlotte would say reproachfully, "don't let him take advantage of your good nature," and Teddy would have to stay out of his mother's way all evening.

Then, as Saul served them all dinner, served Bea and Marion and Teddy, served Charlotte Melnicov, served Frederick and Erich Kessler, served Gustav Levi, Bea began to calm down, to forget herself and her anger. The food was not bad, it never was: finely chopped liver with onions and hard-boiled eggs embedded in it, a light consommé topped with floating parsley, roast chicken, carrots, peas from Iowa, dietary laws observed. Sloan's was proud of its kitchen. Pearl Sloan ruled there like Catherine the Great, and her husband, Hy, was her Tartar slave. Only Saul's service lacked a certain grace. He did myopically what had to be done, that was all. Everything was in place, almost. At each meal, at least one guest was missing a fork or a knife, or a piece of china or a glass; and sometimes an entire course. But they were too fond of him to really complain. It was his pigeon-toed clumsiness that endeared him to guests, that and the knowledge that he needed their tips to become a lawyer at Temple University; and they all loved the ambitions of young men.

A reserved gaiety took hold of the table. Marion, who had been half in love with Saul all week, now could not take her eyes off Erich Kessler. He had hardly said a word throughout the meal, had yet to meet the gaze of another guest with his own. She stared at him, mildly transfixed. His glasses reflected the light as he looked down at his plate; every now and then he smiled at a remark. Teddy wanted to poke Marion with his elbow. But Erich Kessler refused Marion's worshiping stare, gave back nothing, his shyness becoming a palpable presence at the table.

His father, meanwhile, was telling Charlotte and Bea about Germany. Frankfurt, he told them, had been their home. Frank-

furt am Main. Main was a river, he explained. Bea nodded as
though she knew where it was. A city of great poetry, he boasted,
birthplace of Goethe, cradle of vigorous philosophical discourse
and all the arts, although not so great in music, he admitted, as
some others. For music, one wanted Berlin, or Munich, or Bay-
reuth; but for verse, for the art of Polyhymnia, Thalia, and
Calliope, there was no city so great in central Europe as Frankfurt, home of the first Rothschild bank and capital city of the
Holy Roman Empire. Gustav Levi nodded appreciatively at the
recitation, pointed his long, thin, intellectual nose at Mr. Kessler
as he ticked off his points. When one found oneself a citizen of a
city like Frankfurt, Frederick Kessler said with quiet excitement,
one knew that the heart of Western civilization, its very nerve,
its essence, lay at one's fingertips. That was what he had always
known and what his son had assumed from birth. Bea hid an
embarrassed yawn. There was a silence. No one, not even Gustav
Levi, really had anything to say to all that, it was so incontro-
vertible. His name, Mr. Kessler then added with an uneasy smile,
was really Friedrich. It was pronounced like Erich. Like so. He
shared the same thick glasses as his son, the same square, heavy-
boned build, *echt deutsch*, the same high color and something
of the same dense reticence; it was the German peasant they suggested, two generations from the soil.

"Friedrissssh," Charlotte said, mimicking him. "You're lucky
to be here when you think of what's happening to the German
Jews."

Yessss, he said, still trying to be polite. He had beautiful
manners. Erich had beautiful manners, too. So still, so quiet.
Who would ever guess that he was even at the table? Teddy
watched him handle the silverware, manipulate his fork with his
left hand, his knife with his right, shoving peas onto the one with
the other; no waste motion there. It was all under perfect control,
gesture and speech, all power of decision relinquished to the
adults. When they spoke to him, he replied. When they spoke to
each other, he listened. Otherwise, he was silent, patiently mak-

ing his way through dinner, course by course, with the style of a somber young *Graf*. Where was his mother, Teddy wondered.

"Have you ever thought about the revolutionary events leading to the destruction of the Second Temple?" Mr. Levi asked at the end of the meal, out of nowhere. It was clear that the question was meant for the two boys. Mr. Levi turned from one to the other, eyes full of sociability and calculation, waiting for an answer. "Have you?" he said. Teddy and Erich looked at each other at last, smiled. One head was as empty as the other.

Mr. Levi always asked questions like that. Erich would have to get used to it. It was what was on Mr. Levi's mind. He had once been to Palestine, he had told them all, had lived in Jerusalem for three months, considered himself an expert on Jewish history. He also knew a lot about culture, was old friends with Polyhymnia and the others, with music, poetry, and philosophy. He liked to play a Socratic role at the dinner table, passing his knowledge along by asking questions. By asking only one question, he had already made Teddy and Erich friends. "Consider," he went on dutifully, "how long the oral tradition lasted before the rabbis decided to embody it in a written context."

What was he talking about?

"Oh, Gus," Charlotte said, "you're always way over our heads." Teddy had a stupid smile on his face. Erich looked blank.

"I'm trying to get the boys to learn how to think historically," Mr. Levi said, pushing his teacup away. "Do you know how to think historically?" he asked Teddy.

"I don't even know what it means," Teddy said.

"Don't they teach you anything in school?" Mr. Levi asked. "It means being able to think about the world," he went on, without waiting for an answer, "with the authentic conviction that it didn't just begin the day you were born."

Teddy thought for a moment, glanced at Erich Kessler. "I can do that," he said.

"It's very rare, that ability. Most young people—"

"I'm sure I can."

"Well, if you can, you're one in a million."

"Sonja Henie's one in a million, that's who's one in a million." It was Larry Bernard, who had come over to the table to be close to Charlotte. "What did I interrupt?" he said.

But they were finished. The question of thinking historically was done with. Sonja Henie. One in a million. Gustav Levi took a final sip of tea, frowned at Larry Bernard. The conversation was over. Ignoring Mr. Levi, Larry Bernard leaned over Charlotte's shoulder, confirming a date in his deep, resonating voice. Gravity pulled at his stomach. The football player was getting fat. Charlotte almost disappeared inside his huge enfolding arms. She was protesting self-righteously. Bea would have only two more nights in Atlantic City, she was saying. It wasn't right to leave her friend. Everybody listened in on the conversation. Frederick Kessler sighed in sympathy. Gustav Levi looked contemptuous. For God's sake, Bea said, I can take care of myself. Go ahead, have some fun. It was an old game with Charlotte. Bea had no patience with it tonight. Nevertheless, Larry Bernard needed Bea. Judge Aaron was in for a couple of days from Trenton. They were old legal friends, Judge Aaron had helped Larry with advice in his one and only political campaign. Not that he had to apologize for Judge Aaron, Larry said, he was a brilliant man, well known up and down the seaboard. He was staying at the Ritz. Maybe Bea would join them for a cup of coffee.

Teddy sat up straight, became alert. Judge Aaron's wife, Larry said matter-of-factly, was in an institution, had been, on and off, since her father had killed himself after the Crash. She was somewhere in Bucks County now, near Lambertville. The four of them would have a cup of coffee together at the Ritz. Judge Aaron was really a brilliant man, he knew everybody, was somewhat older than they, maybe fifty-five, fifty-six. Larry Bernard tossed the facts around as though they didn't count, as though he didn't expect them to have any influence on Bea. He waited a moment then, standing behind Charlotte. All right, I'll come,

Bea finally said, lowering her eyes demurely, softened by dinner and the invitation, almost swallowed alive by the hollow bass column of Larry Bernard's voice. He knew how to talk, where to put the right emphasis, how to say things. Teddy's back was stiff. He felt something powerful in the air, something that came from inside that voice and from Bea's easy response. It was without definition or recognizable nuance, beyond himself and his sister, something that excluded them. He threw Marion a look. Her face had gone sour. She would have to entertain herself all evening, have to put herself to bed.

Charlotte Melnicov and Larry Bernard were now bantering with each other. Everything seemed settled. Teddy could see the black hairs on the back of Larry Bernard's hands as he gripped the arms of Charlotte's chair from behind. His stomach fell over his belt. He caught Teddy's eye, there was an instant's pause. "Little Pad-a-roos-ki," he crooned across the table. Someone was laughing, Charlotte or Bea. Little Pad-a-roos-ki. Why didn't they object, why didn't they stand up for him? Then Larry Bernard laughed too, and winked at Teddy to show that he was only joking. Teddy's mouth pulled down. He turned away, loathing his talent—as they all called it—for the moment, the miserable little gift that left him vulnerable to Larry Bernard and others like him, while his mother sipped her tea and said something agreeable to Frederick Kessler, something about Teddy and Erich being company for each other. She looked pensive and immensely satisfied at the same time. Why not? After dinner, she would go down to the Ritz with her friends, the Big L and Charlotte Melnicov, and have a cup of coffee with a decrepit old judge from Trenton, who had a crazy wife locked up somewhere. She was faithless, he thought, always ready for a betrayal. It was as simple as that, as bitterly constant.

They were saying grace now at table number one. Larry Bernard had to shut up. Bea had to sit back in silence. There was no more talk about coffee at the Ritz. How pleased she looked, full of that calm sense of herself that Teddy knew was absolutely untouchable. He couldn't resist that calm, couldn't bear the need to share it. On the other side of the room, Rabbi Miller was on his feet, mumbling rapidly in Hebrew. For doing this at Sloan's on Friday night and ostentatiously hovering in the kitchen to check on the dietary laws, he got room and board for the summer. The women made jokes about him, Bea and Charlotte, clucking away about his scrappy little beard, always badly cut, about his peculiar accent, his terrible English. Bea smiled patronizingly, glanced at Charlotte, who smiled back. By now, Gus Levi had joined in with his benign, friendly voice. He pronounced each word distinctly. He didn't mumble. He never mumbled, Teddy knew. He gave everything its due, Polyhymnia, Calliope, the five books of Moses, and all the rest. They were all trapped until the prayers would be finished. "When the Lord turned back the captivity of Zion," Gus Levi recited, "we were as in a dream." After a moment, Frederick Kessler joined in. The words rang out in Gus Levi's unembarrassed voice. His partner was more diffident. Everyone else at the table was silent. Larry Bernard stood at a kind of attention behind Charlotte. Bea's face had taken on a saintly expression, full of self-imposed purity. Charlotte gazed spiritually into space, over the heads of the other guests. Teddy hated that look. He saw it all the time in the synagogue during the High Holidays. At the final Amen, he knew, it would snap in two under the brittle edge of its own falsity. "Then was our mouth filled with laughter," the two men said. "And our tongue filled with joyous song. . . ." Gustav Levi's voice spiraled through the psalm, taking its own measured time, accompanied a single beat behind by Frederick Kessler's low Frankfurt echo. Everyone paid attention. Like Larry Bernard, Gus Levi demanded it; but he was not running for office, nor was he interested in affability. It was all on his own terms. The price for that at Sloan's was that, along with the old lady Eisen, Gustav Levi was considered the house eccentric. It was his pleasure, and Teddy Lewin's. Little Pad-a-roos-ki's.

4

Within ten minutes, dinner was over, grace said, the dining room half emptied. Gus Levi's voice had faded; so had Rabbi Miller's and Frederick Kessler's. But all their spirits were momentarily lifted by the Friday evening dinner, the presence of ritual, the effects of communality, and even, in some cases, true belief. They would enjoy it for a few hours, then sleep it off. Tomorrow was the beginning of the real Atlantic City weekend.

In the corner of Sloan's lobby, the old lady Eisen was already seated in her high-backed chair. There she waited after dinner every evening for the guests to come up and talk to her. She expected it. Not for nothing was she a rich widow, eighty-two years old. Behind her stood Nurse Chernichowski in her white oxfords; while nearby, Charlotte was putting on her pink lipstick, cocking her head self-consciously at herself in her compact mirror, working her lips together, moistening them to get it just right. Larry Bernard was still at her elbow. Charlotte caught Larry's eye in the mirror, gave him a half-smile in the glass, played with him that way for a few seconds. He grinned back into the mirror, took her around the waist, tried to tickle the palm of her hand with his index finger. She blushed, pulled away. "You're impossible," she said. "You never give up." Nothing would embarrass him. All of Sloan's would know.

Teddy saw it all, heard Charlotte scold Larry Bernard, caught his confident grin in response. While Bea recited boring directions for the evening to his sister and himself, Teddy kept an eye on Charlotte and Larry Bernard. Their little byplay stirred him pleasantly. He wanted them to go on touching each other with quick, flicking gestures. He thought of Dr. and Mrs. Lazarus together, thought of Charlotte and Larry Bernard, of his mother, flushed, turned away. If Bea wasn't back by ten, she was saying, Marion was to go to sleep. Teddy would take her upstairs, sit with her if she was afraid of the dark. But that wouldn't be necessary. She would be home early. She was only going to have a cup of coffee with old friends. That was what she said, old friends. She had never even met Judge Aaron, wouldn't know him if she fell over him. Teddy looked her straight in the eye. She didn't bat a lash.

Charlotte had moved in to say good night to the old lady Eisen, to perform the evening lullaby. It was a song she liked to sing. Like Bea, she was seduced by the scent of fragrant wealth the old lady gave off, by the presence of a sturdy professional nurse, in white, who had learned her work in the spas of Poland and risen through great bourgeois households from Lomza to Ciechocinek, London to Leeds, New York to Atlantic City, more stylish now, more snobbish, than any of her employers in a long, prosperous career; by the range of fabrics, too, of the old lady's dresses, an occasional seersucker, high-necked voile, summer chiffons, light as butterflies, that she wore down to her ankles, dotted swiss and chintz, and even hot, clinging silk; as well as her collection of flashing European tiaras, the three finest from old St. Petersburg itself, studded with antique diamond chips and tragic aristocratic histories. The old lady nodded to Charlotte, gripped her cane by its silver knob. She wore spots of rouge on her cheeks, had her ginger wig on. At eighty-two she was the acknowledged Empress of Sloan's, beyond ordinary life, with a broad, triangular nose, flattened cheekbones, and tipped eyes from the Baltic, as Slavic as the sandy Kurzeme Plain.

"Tell me," she said to Charlotte, leaning forward slowly to take her hand. "Didn't we meet in Riga last summer?"

Standing behind her, the nurse went "tsk," gently warning

Charlotte off. The old lady lost her memory like that every now and then. Sometimes she thought that she was still living in Latvia. She had once reminded Bea of a holiday they had taken together in 1881 at a Baltic resort. She recognized Teddy as her nephew from Vilna. Charlotte withdrew, moved back to Larry Bernard. Nurse Chernichowski shook her head from side to side in wonder; on her way from Poland to England to America, she had seen everything there was to see and continued to be surprised by all of it. Then, forgetting Riga, the old lady took a piece of her husband's chocolate laxative from her handbag and tried to thrust it on Marion as an after-dinner treat. This time Nurse Chernichowski actively interfered, moving in quickly on her white oxfords. She managed to get the chocolate into her own hands without fuss, changed the subject deftly, distracted the old lady. The old lady Eisen, everyone knew, had little to do with reality anymore. Every evening, it was said, she insisted on taking a bath in salt water, then flew into a rage at Pearl Sloan because her soap wouldn't lather.

They stood together in the lobby now in a kind of family cluster, Charlotte and Larry Bernard, Bea, the children, killing time, waiting. The adults would be ready to leave for the Ritz soon, ready for a cup of coffee. For the moment, they had nothing to say to each other. Meanwhile, Tibor Talles had begun to circle around them, trying to get Teddy's attention. His shoulders were slightly hunched, his head thrust forward, waiting for an opening. Beneath his olive skin, he was sunburned pink. Behind him, his father sat on a sofa counting out dollar bills for Joseph. Each time Mr. Talles peeled off a bill he wet his thumb. Seven, eight, nine, he counted, pausing a moment to take a sip from a glass of seltzer. Ten, eleven, twelve. Tibor signaled Teddy, pointing over his shoulder with his thumb, but Teddy was watching Mr. Talles. So much money, so much new prosperity, like Teddy's own uncles, all the Sandlers. He would have liked some of it for himself. Back home in Baltimore, Mr. Talles manufactured army uniforms and spent a lot of time at Fort Meade.

He looked like his sons, brooding, morose faces full of ancient suspicions; but when he smiled, when they all smiled, a curious Persian sweetness, thick as honey, softened their faces.

The cluster broke up, Bea moved off with Charlotte and Larry Bernard. "Mother," Teddy called. She waited for him. What did he want to say? "Will you be back late?" he asked. He could barely meet her eyes. Bea hesitated a moment, looked as though she had just forgotten something, looked a little foolish.

"I'm only going out for a cup of coffee," she said. It was as though she were counting out the words, one by one. "I told you that before. I'm surprised at you, Teddy."

Then she turned, they were gone, the three of them, exactly as planned, and Tibor was at him, hissing in his ear: "We're going to Chalfonte Alley to get blown. Me and Joseph. If you got five bucks, come on." Teddy's whole frame began to shake. He nodded something or other, comprehension, acceptance, he wasn't sure. He was afraid to turn them down; they might never ask again. Five dollars. Where would he get five dollars? Mr. Talles, whose spirited wife grew very subdued when he arrived for the weekend, was making a fortune out of the draft. His sons had a blow-job every Friday night. Five dollars. "I can't go with you tonight," Teddy said, trying to keep the excitement out of his voice, trying to sound ordinary. "Some other night when I don't have to hang around the hotel with my sister." Then they too were gone. He was left alone with Marion. She would be stuck to him like a burr for hours. She was already at his side, walking in step with him like a faithful dog. Little Marion, her father's darling, with hair like string and a fishy pair of swollen eyes.

"Well," Teddy said irritably. "What do you want to do?" They played checkers, then two games of double solitaire, slapping the cards down on the table in a fury. Marion was faster than Teddy at it, won both games, always did. He could hardly stand it, began to grow sulky at the superior look on her face. But they soon became bored with games, bored with each other. Finally,

Teddy sent Marion off to look for Gloria Goldman; she and Gloria could listen to the radio together in the sunroom, and he would have himself to himself. His friends Tibor and Joseph were off prowling the streets behind the Boardwalk for experience, with pockets stuffed with dollar bills. It was nine o'clock. Nurse Chernichowski and Saul the waiter were helping the old lady Eisen to the elevator. Bedtime for royalty, curfew for the court. Pearl Sloan watched them from the cigar counter. They each had hold of an elbow, propelling her forward step by step. Her silver-knobbed cane dangled from her right hand.

Sitting in a corner, his back to the room, Frederick Kessler was reading the English translation of *The Forty Days of Musa Dagh,* a thick, elegant volume, with a red binding. Mr. Kessler kept a little pocket dictionary on the table alongside him, referred to it impatiently every few minutes. A couple of feet away, Gustav Levi was writing postcards. He used a heavy black fountain pen, thick as a cigar, with a gleaming gold point shaped like an arrow, wrote in a practiced, flashing hand full of artful loops and arcs. He was always writing postcards, or preparing to. The clock dully sounded nine times. Pearl Sloan rang up the cash register, left to check the kitchen one last time. Her husband, Hy, who got up every morning at five, was already asleep. At last, agonizingly slowly, Erich Kessler and Teddy approached each other.

"Oh," Teddy said, looking surprised. "I didn't know you were here." Erich nodded solemnly. "I was going to take a walk. Want to come?" "Yes," Erich said. "It's boring here." Erich laughed at his own words, a brief Teutonic bark that shot over Teddy's head. That was the entire negotiation, twenty words and a humorless laugh. Then Teddy told Marion they were leaving, while she mooned shyly at Erich and Gloria crossed her eyes again for their benefit; and together they listened to five minutes or so of cautionary tales from Mr. Kessler relating to seaside resorts. Finally, he quietly returned to his book, and the two boys, first passing Gustav Levi at the writing desk, his black pen gleaming in the lamplight, headed out the main door for the Boardwalk. High above the street, the huge Cotswold veranda loomed like a pair of arms threatening to encircle the world; but the boys, moving out of its vast shadow and out of sight of Sloan's, quickly put it behind them.

Teddy acted as guide. It was his Boardwalk. He had been in Atlantic City a week longer than Erich Kessler; he would force him to see it through his eyes. He assumed a faintly priggish, didactic tone. He gave a sermon, as though he was sure of everything, somewhat holy, full of false emphases. For that, he could be forgiven. The salt air buoyed him, the company of a new friend challenged him. He would do it right. Over there, he said, striding along, hands in the pockets of his white ducks, in that dinky-looking store, books could be bought dirt cheap, forty-nine cents, fifty-nine cents, eighty-nine, and ninety-nine cents, thousands of them. There were a lot of great bargains inside, piled up in huge bins. You had to scramble to find them but they were there. Teddy had his eye on a couple, a Garden City Press edition of *Personal History* by Vincent Sheean, which Benedict was pushing him to try, and a fake-leatherbound *Nana* he had found himself, illustrated with voluptuous silhouettes of naked women and printed on paper that felt like satin. Erich Kessler grunted approval. "Who is Vincent She-an?" he asked.

Then, a half block farther on, Teddy pointed out the hole-in-the-wall in which the Boardwalk's famous gypsy foretold all human events and solved every riddle. During the day, she stood in the beaded doorway, Teddy said, and invited passersby in. She wore a purple dress down to her ankles, like the old lady Eisen, seductive gold earrings, smoked long blue cigarettes. Her bare feet were always filthy, and you could see the nipples of her breasts through her dress. Only gentiles, Teddy said, repeating what he had heard at Sloan's, went in there to have their fortunes told. God knew what really went on inside; the future in a deck of cards, clouds of blue cigarette smoke, other dark, gypsy things. The boys exchanged a glance and, despite themselves, shied away superstitiously. They lingered then at a miniature golf course, bought ice-cream cones, ate them in front of the colored fountain at the Claridge. Soft mauve and green lights rose higher and higher on the hotel's deep lawn. A spotlight wavered in the air. The water hissed noisily. The crowd sighed with pleasure. There was no sight quite like it in the whole city, no lawn so even, so perfect, so deep.

A million visitors, two million, strolled in both directions. Wicker carriages rolled by, pushed by Negroes who charged their passengers by the hour. Candystands lined the walk, peanut brittle, salt water taffy, sour balls, and popcorn like pebbles; the air reeked with it. On their left, the sea was invisible, but the sound of the breaking surf split the night air. Massive piers thrust into the ocean. Stars were everywhere overhead, dense creamy galaxies that overlapped without boundaries; lovers below; husbands in for the weekend; tired children and wan mothers; a dim moon offshore; and on their right mammoth hotels styled to the vagaries of their builders: a hallucinatory Tudor, faithful romantic Gothic, Victorian, Edwardian, Moorish, twenties boom, the willfully eccentric, pridefully bizarre, turreted, towered with frosted stucco, minareted like Islam, open to the sun, closed, timbered, bricked, and some, here and there, mortared in honey-colored stone.

That, Teddy said, is Haddon Hall, and *that* is the Marl-borough-Blenheim and the Morton, and *that* is the Traymore, and down there is the Shelburne and the Dennis, and you just saw the Claridge. They're all like the Cotswold. Fifteen dollars a day, without food. Lots of Baltimore people, Teddy said, stay at the Shelburne. You can sit on the porch at the Shelburne, he said, pointing in its direction, and watch the horses race on the big electric sign over the Million-Dollar Pier. They could just make them out from where they stood, jittery electric bulbs combined to look like jockeyed horses, jumping erratically across an electrified track to an electrified finish line. Six horses, each a different color. Then back to the start again and another race.

The Shelburne porch wasn't as big as the Cotswold, Teddy said, but it was big enough. You could sit there half the night on rocking chairs and bet the evening away. Some of his aunts and uncles stayed at the Shelburne, Teddy said; they were all rich.

It seemed to Teddy that Erich Kessler was hanging on every word. He appeared quietly staggered by the incoherent vistas, intimidated by the crowds. He looked for his cues, grunted appreciation. He kept taking off his thick glasses and polishing them. Without them, he looked like a frightened child. Every now and then, a piece of information slipped through his reticence like grass through a cement crack. He lived in Washington Heights, he told Teddy at one point. That was in Manhattan. It was nice in Washington Heights, he said. Everywhere you went in Washington Heights, you could see the Hudson River and the George Washington Bridge.

Teddy had to listen to Erich Kessler with care, had to pick his way through his sentences syllable by syllable, sound by sound, transcribing sound into sense as he went along. He was familiar enough with the German accent, had been hearing it in Baltimore for almost five years. There were dozens of Germans in Baltimore like the Kesslers, old, young, middle-aged, they just kept coming, like imported delicacies; but often their accents set up an instant antagonism, a need for special, tense attention that bred resentment out of feelings of strangeness, out of all those uncontrollable, unthinking alien signals that make themselves known through language. There were Germans Teddy had met who could barely get a dozen English words out in comprehensible order. Others sounded as though they had been trained to speak English in phonetic syllables. Their diction was so impeccable it was almost deranged. Erich was somewhere in the middle, neither fluent nor frozen, struggling courageously in a war on two fronts against an erratic Yankee syntax and the middle Atlantic vernacular. He spoke slowly, treading the cobblestones of American speech with well-made, thick-soled boots that were built for sturdiness, not grace.

He and his father, he went on, measuring it out carefully, lived in a flat on the second floor of a new apartment building. That was the word he used: flat. They had a view of New Jersey from the living room. Erich shared the bedroom with his father. There were a lot of Germans in Washington Heights, a lot of Viennese, too. Some of the Germans were from Frankfurt, a few old acquaintances. It made his father happy to be with them. Then Erich had nothing more to say. He began to scrape at a spot of ice cream on the front of his shirt.

"Joseph and Tibor Talles went to Chalfonte Alley tonight," Teddy said after a moment. Erich nodded, examined the chocolate spot. "You know where that is?" Teddy asked. "No," Erich said. Teddy pointed inland, vaguely. He couldn't tell whether or not Erich knew what he was talking about. "You know what I mean?" Teddy said. He heard a new note creep into his voice, something nervous and tight. Erich didn't answer. It was just as well. You really couldn't push those things, Teddy knew. He thought a moment of Chalfonte Alley, of Joseph and Tibor, vile images.

The conversation stopped dead. Then picking up suddenly, his energy on the alert, Teddy began to offer Erich a few statistics about Atlantic City. Like music, statistics were one of Teddy's strengths. They existed in his head like printed clusters of black notes waiting to be translated into performance, into something public and useful. The populations of each of the forty-eight states, the number of times *Tobacco Road* had been played, the height of Mt. Everest and a dozen others, all gathered inside Teddy in a single undiscriminating embrace with the scores of the *Pathétique* or the "Minute Waltz" or the *Aragonaise*. They were sometimes coequal, obsessively sprung from a shared number-driven impulse, or nerve, and, like music, they had their own compulsively seductive sound. All the information Teddy had about Atlantic City he had picked up from little promotional booklets scattered around Sloan's lobby. His mind clicked down the pages now. Ten million people, he said, came to Atlantic City every summer. Erich nodded once again, impassively. Most of them came from Pennsylvania, it was so close by. Teddy made up a figure: 28 percent. Summer visitors came from as far as Michigan, which was halfway across the country. There were about two hundred thousand rooms for rent every night in Atlantic City. You could get a room for two dollars, you could get a room for ten, you could get a room for two hundred. It all depended on where you wanted to stay, Sloan's, the Cotswold, the Shelburne, or a dump four blocks from the beach.

It seemed to be going down well enough. Erich was giving him brisk, satisfied nods; he was taking it all in. Anyway, Teddy said, the Convention Hall, which he signaled lay just ahead, covered seven acres of ground, in all, and could seat forty thousand people at one time. He let that sink in before going on. There was not a single supporting column in the main hall, he said. The whole damn thing was held up by the world's biggest trusses. It was one of America's wonders, like the Empire State Building. At the same time, the roof of the Convention Hall contracted more than three inches every winter when the temperature dropped. Also, he said, a whisper at one end of the auditorium could be heard all the way down at the other end, the acoustics were so spectacular. Beyond all that, he remembered that 200,000 tons of sand had to be removed to leave room for a foundation for the Hall. After all, when you got right down to it, Atlantic City was nothing but a long skinny sand pit, shaped like a broken toothpick.

They could now see Miss America pennants hanging outside the Convention Hall. Forty-eight girls posing in one-piece bathing suits that fit them like satin girdles. One of them would be Queen of the whole U.S.A. soon, Teddy told his friend. He felt a surge of unexpected pride as he said it. It was the biggest, most important competition in the whole country. Only the most beautiful could enter, only the most pure, only the most truly American. The whole world paid attention to Miss America, it was like being a movie star. For the moment, as he spoke, he believed himself, fell half in love with the idea, wanting it to be true. But some wicked sense of irony rattled his words. He began to laugh a little, examining Erich's quiet profile, thick, serious glasses, his heavy Central European look of common braininess so conscious of itself. There was not much beauty there, no sense of purity. It was not at all American. Well, Teddy said, still laughing, it helped in the Miss America contest if you weren't Jewish, Jewish girls never won, Jewish girls probably couldn't win, he didn't even know if they could enter. Erich gave him a quick, tiny smile of comprehension, shrugged good-naturedly.

Anyway, Teddy went on, the Boardwalk beneath their feet was more than four miles long and cost two million dollars to build. It went as far as Ventnor, he said, pointing straight ahead. Then he finally remembered to tell Erich that there was a horse that was trained to dive into the ocean five times a day from the deep end of the Steel Pier. Erich opened his eyes wide. Can horses swim? he asked. How deep was the ocean out there? A diving horse almost in the middle of the Atlantic? It was the most interesting fact of all, a triumph for Teddy, and they both silently turned it over in their minds for a moment or two, concentrating on it.

But Teddy forced them along again, picking up the stride this time, the Boardwalk crowds a little thinner here, easier to move through. He was full of purpose, energy piled on energy. New statistics hovered in his mind, questions and answers formed behind them. There was a second glimpse of Joseph and Tibor Talles, dim, flickering images now which disappeared almost instantly. The sea alongside them was a steellike blur. Salt foam broke hissing at the shoreline. The boys marched in quickstep unison, the smell of cotton candy souring the air. He was up to something, he knew. He recognized the symptoms, knew this restlessness. An eyelid trembled, an old tic. Everything seemed to wait for expression. He couldn't stop talking. He wouldn't shut up.

Would there be a war? What would happen if the Germans

won? What would happen to the Jews then? What would happen to all of them? And so on. Erich remained silent, eyes fixed on the black depthless horizon ahead. He didn't have any answers for Teddy, he didn't have any answers for himself. Could the Germans break the Maginot Line? That wasn't possible, was it? No one could break the Maginot Line. It was ten miles deep, sunk fifty feet into the ground. And so on. The words flew out to sea like hungry gulls. Ma-gi-not Line, a flap of Gallic syllables. Say, Teddy said then, brought up a little short. A kind of slow huskiness filled his voice, the sound of oncoming duplicity. Say, he said again, pulling the word out, why don't we take a look at that place. I mean, Jesus, it's really something. He slowed down, so did Erich. Look at that, Teddy said, pausing in wonder. Let's walk through. Let's take a couple of minutes. Why not? Erich was agreeable. That was his temperament, trained by events. It was simple. They turned off the Boardwalk without further discussion and made for the entrance to the Ritz. As they hurried along, Teddy began to talk about the Reds and the Yankees, about the races for the pennants and the coming Series, a hopeless jumble, all gratuitous, as though someone had asked him, Europe now forgotten, Europe already dead. He couldn't wait to get inside the hotel, pushed his way blindly through the revolving doors, waved Erich on.

Once inside, standing amidst the almost silent lobby traffic, amidst the guests of the Ritz and their deskmen and servants, he had an instant sense of another life moving beside him on a noiseless, parallel track. It was different from his own, as foreign as Erich Kessler's accent, a rich, deferential, rapt pulse against which the slightest tactless move on his part would bring immediate retribution, immediate disapproval. He must not intrude. He must not disrupt. He must behave himself. No one must recognize him for what he was. Bland-faced and wary, he forced himself to move, lifted one soundless foot, then the other. There was a bar on his right, Merry-Go-Round it said over the door canopy, blue neon lights shining mistily somewhere in the dark, a formal dining room on the other side already set in blinding white for breakfast. He could hear an organ playing "Deep Purple" in the bar. He moved on ten feet, twenty, Erich alongside him, stopping when he stopped, precisely paced to keep from making an error. Whenever they stopped, Erich took off his glasses and polished them. He seemed very nervous, seemed to have no idea where they were.

At last, step by step, they arrived at the heart of the lobby. They saw a vast rectangle stretching an entire block to the west and another toward the sea. They now stood amidst a reflected paradise of chrome, plate glass, and deep-piled beige carpeting. A convention hall of a lobby, broken up by mirrored pillars. The biggest room in the world, filled with the familiar scent of money everywhere, the overpowering fragrance of luxury. Squat, contemporary chairs, with squared-off backs and crushed velvet upholstery six inches deep, chandeliers the size of baby grands, and bellhops who looked Teddy's age and wore pillbox hats like the Philip Morris midget. Where could you get a cup of coffee in such a place? "Irving Berlin stays here," Teddy whispered out of the side of his mouth. "With his three daughters." Erich looked startled. He knew who Irving Berlin was.

Around them, the contemporary chairs were filled with guests of the Ritz. Suntans like cream, dresses of summer rainbow colors, white suits. The chandeliers over their heads shone like diamond suns. To the rear, there was a library filled with best-sellers, and a writing room with a dozen teak desks; nearby, a florist's with orchids in the window, a perfume shop, a French hairdresser, an arcade of sweet-smelling grandeur. Someone was being paged, someone was wanted on the telephone. A bellhop moved across the carpet, a small silver tray extended in his hand. Could Gustav Levi feel at home here, could the rich Victor Talles, his wife Thelma, could even the old lady Eisen with her silver-knobbed cane? Who at the Ritz would understand about Riga?

Then a kind of restlessness set in. The boys welcomed it. There was nothing here for Teddy Lewin, nothing for Erich Kessler. Erich was squinting through his glasses, as though he were afraid he was going to lose his vision. He wanted to escape, they both wanted to escape. They moved around delicately, politely, following each other's spoor on the balls of their feet, as though they knew where they were going. They were looking for a way out, a blessed exit to the Boardwalk and a world they were comfortable in. What had Teddy thought he would find here? He tucked the question away. Let it rest for a while. He'd deal with it later, create an unforgettable coincidence over a cup of coffee when he was better prepared, force fortune in his own way, surprise Bea and her judge another time.

He felt better, though. He felt better as soon as they hit the Boardwalk and began to head for the north side of town. He was positively overcome by cheerfulness, was full of smiles. For some reason, Erich seemed to have loosened up, too. He emerged from the Ritz with his powers of speech fully restored, and on the way back it was Erich who did most of the talking. Teddy didn't mind. He was in a sudden benign state, filled with a pleasant giddiness and the languors of music. Rachmaninoff occupied half his head, long, slow, meandering melodies that opened and shut like the swelling pleats of an accordion. He could listen to Erich and Rachmaninoff at the same time, it was one of his tricks. He also knew how to practice the piano inside his head; he didn't need a keyboard. Erich was talking on in his heavy way, releasing the words as though there were a price on each. A strange language was expensive. He was telling Teddy about how he had come to the United States a year before his father, alone, about how he had lived on West End Avenue in New York with a family that wanted to give German refugee boys a start, about how he had grown to hate them.

"Hate them?" Teddy said, suddenly distracted.

"They never changed the bed linens."

"Never changed the bed linens?"

"Yes."

"You mean just yours? Or theirs, too?"

"Mine, yes. I don't know about their own."

"You mean they never changed your sheets?"

"Yes."

"Was that because they were poor, or was that the way they lived, or what?"

"Every month they were paid for me by the Jewish Agency. It was to make money from me."

Then Erich told Teddy that the family made him say a prayer to President Roosevelt every night at the dinner table. What kind of prayer? Teddy asked. "To say I was grateful," Erich said. He paused a moment, stared at Teddy without expression, then walked on. Things were different now that his father was here, he said. His father managed a lady's hat factory on Thirty-sixth Street for his American cousin. Felt and straw. His father was lucky to have a rich cousin with a hat factory. He and his father were happy together in their three-room flat in Washington Heights. His father did the cooking; they had dinner together every night. Without prayers. "Where's your mother?" Teddy finally asked. An agonized look washed over Erich's face, vanished like a sudden squall. He looked away. "My mother is in Frankfurt," he said. "She waits for a visa." "Ah," Teddy said, expelling his breath. They slowed down then, made the second half of the trip at a half-hearted pace, window-shopped, poked their heads into a couple of auctions. Teddy decided that he liked Erich Kessler. He liked the stolidity, the way he placed himself on his two feet as though he were made of granite. Teddy would like to lean into that. There was nothing flighty there, nothing agitated, no trembling of an eyelid. Erich Kessler would never be able to practice the piano in his head.

Later that evening, while Teddy and Erich sat alongside each other in the lobby at Sloan's, Bea came in. She was alone. No Charlotte, no Larry Bernard. Marion was upstairs asleep. She hadn't missed Teddy at all. She had taken care of herself. Bea chatted with the boys, seemed pleased that they were together. She told them that she was tired. Judge Aaron had walked her all the way back from the Ritz, a goodly distance, as they all knew. It was almost eleven. An early evening. Bea had lost her edge. There was no anger left over from her long-distance phone call, no resentment, everything was as it should be. Teddy said nothing about his walk along the sea, did not mention his visit to the Ritz. He wanted to hear about his mother's evening. She acted as though it had all been perfectly ordinary, summed it up in a few words. Coffee with old friends. Old friends. She was tired, she said again, moving off. Teddy said good night, watched her as she started up the stairs. She never took the elevator at Sloan's; climbing the stairs helped to keep her in shape. She looked comfortable, at ease. Her spectators were scuffed in one spot, the cocky little part in her hair somewhat crooked. Navy and white, trim as the British fleet. Tonight she looked especially like Wallis Warfield. She smiled back at Teddy over the bannister, sharing something. That smile, in that way, could bring him close to tears; and it did now. Then she disappeared up the stairwell. It was almost silent in the lobby. Erich stirred, sleepily emerging from his own journeys, yawned into the stale empty air. Teddy began to hum Rachmaninoff without knowing it. One more day was finally over.

5

On Saturday, the porch across the street at the Cotswold filled up with new guests. Old ladies from Richmond and Roanoke, Confederate dowagers from the Tidewater, rocked back and forth alongside new friends from Bala Cynwyd and Bryn Mawr, treating themselves to the clamorous sight of Sloan's Jews holding their Saturday services in the sunroom, directly facing the Cotswold veranda. Rabbi Miller led the prayers gutturally. A dozen or so old men, a handful of devoted women, responded. There was some business with a Torah, an unfolding, a lifting, a few psalms in Hebrew. It was over in an hour or so. Then they all dispersed. Meanwhile, as the morning rose toward noon, the Cotswold porch turned its attention to Sloan's lobby, in which the cheerful guests called indelicately to each other across the room, shouting loud cries of surprised greetings, as though they had all been forcibly separated from each other all these years, as they waited for lunch, then after lunch itself, settled down for the short parade to the beach, up Virginia Avenue, due east, loaded with comforting gear. A stout pair, husband and slow-moving wife, a family of three following on their heels, folding chairs, comic hats, bathing suits so tight that the jellied flesh billowed out of their buttocks, a robed woman, here and there, in street shoes. It was not a bad show and worth an occasional laugh.

Half the guests at the Cotswold never went to the beach. It was the same at the Marlborough-Blenheim, the Dennis, the Traymore, the Claridge, and the Shelburne; and when they did it was to sit inside a canvas cabana that cost fifty dollars a week and play rummy all afternoon long. But what the old corseted ladies observed from the veranda across the street provided an uplifting reward they could never find quite so easily at home, where they all lived, cut off, in the same restricted neighborhoods, one that made them tremble pleasurably from time to time with a sense of the superiority of their own lives. They could not take their eyes off Sloan's. It forced their attention, confirmed them to themselves. It was the other side of the moon, an insistent, foreign, harassing mystery which would never quite reveal itself fully, orbiting darkly in the reflected light of the Atlantic City sun.

But all was calm in the dining room at Sloan's this morning. Teddy had had breakfast with Marion, prunes again, soft, Saturday bread, eggs, milk. Bea was still asleep, lying flat on her back upstairs just as she did when she napped in the afternoon. It was the only way she could be comfortable, mouth open, head leaning slackly to one side, the bottom half of her handsome, symmetrical face slightly awry. Teddy was afraid of the way she looked when she was asleep. The strong scent of mortality seemed to come from his mother's bed then, a potent, nearly irresistible stillness from which he always wanted to flee. He had left her like that a half hour before, tiptoeing nervously out of the room. Half the dining room was now empty. They ate in shifts on Saturday morning, to the despair of the kitchen. It was Pearl Sloan's edict; on the weekend, the guests could sleep late.

Across the round table, Gus Levi was finishing his orange juice. He was reading *The New York Times* editorial page at the same time, had it folded in quarters. A deep rumble came from somewhere inside him, an unconscious hum, a profound response to the words he was reading. Finally they became too much for him. He put the paper down. He no longer knew what to think of the world's future, no longer was sure how to deal with it. It seemed to Gus Levi that to deal with the world's future meant making a decision to prepare for one's own doom. There seemed to be no escape from that. Already, half of Europe was living underground. In China, the war was in its eleventh year. The Italians had just massacred the Ethiopians, the Spanish had eaten each other alive. All moral authority was gone, all authority as he recognized it, the West was done with, the East struggling over the bones of its own dim past. And Gustav Levi, veteran of the Great War, skinny doughboy from Fort Dix, onetime Palestinian pioneer with socialist notions of farming collectively with others just like him, expert on the history of the Jews, eight thousand consecutive years of it, lover of culture, thin-nosed intellectual, was finally making a good steady living for himself wholesaling ladies' underwear from Paterson, N. J., after a couple of decades of relentless struggle. In a war that grandiosely scaled the whole world, in a war that with one shot severed Asia from Africa, Europe from America, all the parts from the whole, it would all be instantly plowed under, buried like an archaeological treasure that time itself had forgotten. Nothing would be left, nothing remembered, nothing visible, not the past, not Jewish history, neither culture nor profits, not even a moment's echo of historical irony. Mr. Levi folded the paper neatly, listened a moment to the harsh echoes inside himself, looked across the table over his bifocals.

"I'm glad you made friends with the Kessler boy," he said to Teddy.

"Yes."

"He seems like a nice boy," Mr. Levi said. "You'll be good for each other."

He peeled his soft-boiled eggs, partially scooped them out, admired the remains of each shell. Mr. Levi had romantic feelings about eggshells. Their aesthetic perfection stirred him. The sense of their function softened him. They were ever consistent, ever the same, one egg seemingly like all others, which was somehow best of all. He felt that, properly understood, they might go a long way toward helping to explain the world's mystery. But what was the world's mystery? Eggshells were simply another mystery in themselves, in a never-ending chain of mysteries. This morning, Mr. Levi was wearing a flowered sports shirt. Teddy could see the grizzled hair on his chest at the top of his open shirt. Teddy could tell that it was harder for Mr. Levi to smile at breakfast than at dinner. Putting down the twin shells, he tried to smile now, but the effort showed. "The question of friends is really very important," Mr. Levi went on. "In fact, essential. They are a kind of protection against the steady chill of daily life. Do you have a sense yet, Teddy, of how cold the world can be?" It was another of Mr. Levi's rhetorical questions. "Of how little it cares, how it makes strangers of all of us, even in our own homes? Friends close the distance, fill up the spaces. Without them, it's hard to connect with life. They help us to face the prospect of oblivion, to share that destiny."

Such a labored speech, so feeble and gratuitous in the face of his eager young friend. Clearly, his heart wasn't in it. Gus Levi and Teddy Lewin looked at each other for a moment in perfect understanding. Then, eating his breakfast, Gus Levi said: "The news looks very bad."

"I know."

"Do you know how bad?"

"There's going to be a war."

"Yes. And the whole world will be in it."

A scrap of fear touched Teddy. All the grownups talked about a war, all the grownups accepted it. The whole world was waiting for it, as its due. There was some pleasure in the fact, some sense of heady anticipation; it would change Teddy's whole life, of that he was sure.

"If Russia stays out," Teddy said, "we'll win."

Mr. Levi looked at him in surprise, then made a disgusted sound. "They've tricked us. I always knew they would. It's the same old tsarist Russia, no difference, only without a crown now, without a Romanov. Socialist pieties today instead of divine right. They've allowed themselves to be neutralized. For that, they'll pick up half of Poland, and Germany will take the rest."

Again, there was the scrap of fear, the familiar hangnail at the edge of the heart. Half of Poland. What would that mean? "Well . . ." Teddy began, looking for words.

"You think about all this?" Gus Levi asked.

"A lot," Teddy said. Then he added abruptly, "Erich Kessler's mother is still in Germany."

Gustav Levi scooped out the last of his egg, pushed the plate aside. He lighted a small cigar, eyed the burning end thoughtfully. "Rabbi Samuel bar Nahmani," he said, crooning a little, "in the name of Rabbi Jonathan said, and I quote, 'Catastrophe comes upon the world only when there are wicked persons in it. . . .' Do you know that one, Teddy?"

"No."

" '. . . only when there are wicked persons in it. And it begins with the righteous first.' "

"What does?"

"Listen and I'll tell you. Rabbi Joseph taught: 'Once the Destroyer has been given permission to destroy, he does not distinguish between the righteous and the wicked. . . .' Do you follow me, Teddy?"

"Yes."

"And what is more," Gus Levi said, "he not only doesn't distinguish between the righteous and the wicked, he begins with the righteous first. About that, Rabbi Joseph wept. 'Are the righteous as nothing?' he asked. Abayyi said to him: 'They are the first for their own good. It has always been so. The righteous are taken away from the evil to come.' "

They stared at each other again for a moment. This time Teddy didn't know what to say to Gustav Levi. Adult tricks, adult rationalizations, justifying their own faithlessness to themselves and each other. His own rabbi in Baltimore talked like that from the pulpit, clenching his hands over the words, Rabbi Miller talked like that at Sloan's in broken English, and now Gustav Levi himself was lost with the rest of them on the dizzying heights of abstraction. It always forced him into silence. "Well,"

Teddy said nervously, "I just don't believe that. With all due respect. I just don't believe that has anything to do with Erich Kessler's mother. Or anybody else. All you're saying is that maybe it's okay, maybe it's all for the best, if she doesn't get out of Germany."

"That's not what I'm saying," Gustav Levi said, without conviction.

". . . . . ."

"It's not," Gustav Levi insisted.

"Then what do you mean?"

"All I'm trying to do," Gus Levi said, "is to give you a way to think about unimaginable things without having to slit your throat."

"Unimaginable things," Teddy repeated across the table. "I think I think about unimaginable things all the time but I don't think about slitting my throat."

"What can you know about unimaginable?"

Teddy blushed under the question, threw his friend a resentful look. "I know," he finally said.

"Okay," Gus Levi answered miserably. "You know."

The exchange lay there between them like a loaf of stale bread; neither wanted to touch it. Teddy began to scrape the crumbs in front of him with his knife. Gus Levi smoked on, dropped ashes into a saucer. He would go to services soon; he would share the Torah; he would pass the morning that way. Across the room, Teddy saw Mrs. Talles having breakfast with Joseph. Mrs. Talles was all in white this morning, her hair the color of pitch, her mouth like strawberries. She was alert to the whole room, eyes flickering across each table as she took it all in. She smiled when she saw Teddy, a beguiling flash that was over and done with in two brilliant seconds. Teddy waved. Alongside his mother, Joseph ate in silence, contained as an olive grove. Chalfonte Alley seemed far away. He kept his eyes riveted to his cereal, steadfast to himself. He always let his brother Tibor do the talking, always placed himself somewhere in the background.

He was always the same, without emphasis. Just then, Teddy saw Charlotte enter the dining room. She paused at the door, searching the room as though she couldn't remember where her table was. Her mind always seemed to be somewhere else, just a beat behind reality. Then, after a moment full of dimness, she came over to Teddy and Mr. Levi.

"Is Mother here?" she asked as she sat down.

"Still asleep," Teddy said.

Charlotte was already discussing her breakfast with Saul. She had not put on her makeup, was as pale as sand at dawn. Her hair was pulled back in a sloppy bun. Teddy could see a half-dozen bobby pins stuck into it. It was a lazy job. She had not even said good morning to Gustav Levi, who picked up *The New York Times* again as soon as she joined them.

"You can have hot cereal if you want," Saul said, shrugging his shoulders. He couldn't wait to get back to Temple to work on his torts. Charlotte glanced at Mr. Levi's plate, then at Teddy's. "What I want are two scrambled eggs, scrambled hard, with toast. Light toast, Saul. And orange juice." Saul headed for the kitchen. Charlotte would have her two scrambled eggs, light toast, juice, all of it perfect. It was the same every morning. Finally, settled in her chair, she acknowledged Mr. Levi. He nodded back silently. They always played this perfunctory game together, were always a little wary of each other. Charlotte pretended that he was over her head, that she couldn't follow him, that he was "too deep." She, on the other hand, was not fastidious enough for him. In his bachelor pursuit of cultivation, that was something he could not forgive. For a woman with a law degree, she seemed to be careless about intellectual matters and worse, about the way she sometimes looked. Part of her hair was coming loose now. "Would you like the second section of the *Times?*" he asked.

Charlotte yawned desperately. "Oh, I couldn't read anything this morning. I was up until three o'clock with that book."

So be it. They had touched, fingertips only, no chance of a

wound. Mr. Levi retired, murmuring courtesies. Teddy sat there with Charlotte for a few minutes, to keep her company, then, when Larry Bernard arrived, left the dining room for the lobby. Larry Bernard looked disgusting, he hadn't even bothered to shave for breakfast.

6

By midafternoon, most of them were at the beach, implanted in gravelike plots which they had staked out hours earlier. It was jammed with the Saturday crowd, half of it in from Trenton and Philadelphia for the day. How grateful they all were, how lucky, they said. Hot sun, cold sea, shuddering opposites. Iced water in milk bottles. Cocoa butter and creamed lotion. Moth-eaten blankets, beach towels, rubber caps, pink earplugs. Wax paper, Coke bottles, bread crusts—prole refreshments. Two lifeguards on a white wooden stand eight feet high looking directly out to sea; a wheel of rope; first-aid equipment in a metal box bearing a red cross; three young girls at their feet, breasts heavy with adolescent fat. Buttocks, armpits, stomachs, genital outlines, navels, multiple cleavage.

Teddy watched Larry Bernard rub cocoa butter onto Charlotte's shoulders. She had Nordic skin that went from white to painful red and never tanned. She had to be careful in the sun. Larry Bernard used an even, circular motion, thirty seconds to the left, thirty to the right. Taking his time. Easy and with a certain discretion. A few feet away, Bea sat watching the shoreline. Marion was in the surf again with her pickup friend. They were both screaming. The sun shifted behind them; a cloud scudded in from Asbury Park; overhead the advertising blimp floated slowly to the north. The girls were in six inches of water, flat on their stomachs, pretending to swim. Marion's hair was in her eyes.

Larry Bernard was working on Charlotte's back now, a deep, slow half-moon to the base of her spine, the massive flat of his hand first, then softly again with his fingertips to spread the cocoa butter evenly. *Gone With the Wind* lay in Charlotte's lap. Larry Bernard still hadn't shaved. His bald head was covered with a colorless lotion that glistened in the sun. He was on his knees behind Charlotte. His stomach sagged over his wool trunks, his heavy buttocks rested on his heels. Charlotte moved her back under his fingers. Teddy watched him work, waited for signals to pass between the two. Bea sat alongside Teddy, humming "Lover, Come Back to Me." It was Bea's favorite song, had been for more than ten years. The sky was blue, hm, hm, hmmmm. . . . The Kesslers sat directly in front of them, their backs to the sea, facing the sun. Mr. Kessler wore a white bathing cap, like an Olympic swimmer. Its bottom edges were turned up over his ears so that he wouldn't miss any of the talk. It made him look strangely virile. Erich's glasses glinted in the sun. Father and son looked even more alike in their bathing suits, shared a Teutonic thickness heavy with the promise of force. They each had a hammertoe on the right foot, a family bond that went back three hundred years. The father had Gustav Levi's *New York Times* with him. Twenty feet away from them all, Thelma Talles' egg-shell parasol spun in the dense light.

There was no conversation. There was nothing they wanted to talk about, nothing for Frederick Kessler to miss. The afternoon stretched for hours behind them, for hours ahead. They had all the time in the world on the longest day of the week. Charlotte, skin now shielded, went back to Miss Mitchell's South. Larry Bernard relaxed, borrowed the sports page from Frederick Kessler. A tanker appeared on the horizon, hovered immobile at the edge of the world. Bea lay down on her blanket, closed her eyes. Sweet boredom settled around them; the day languished; nothing could hurry the sun.

Teddy saw Joseph and Tibor Talles, twenty feet away, begin to head for the water. Their mother called something to them.

Teddy would think about it for a minute, then join them with Erich Kessler. Erich Kessler and his father were going to see a new Hedy Lamarr movie after dinner. *Lady of the Tropics* it was called. Robert Taylor was in it, too. The Kesslers had invited Teddy to go with them but Teddy had turned them down. In an advertisement for the movie, he had seen Hedy Lamarr wearing a headdress that looked like a pagoda. That wasn't Teddy's idea of a movie, and Robert Taylor bored him. Erich's father told them that he remembered Hedy Lamarr from Europe. She was Viennese. She had made a dirty movie called *Ecstasy*. In it, she had floated naked in a lake and had her breasts rapturously kissed by her aging costar. They had all heard of it. It was notorious. Mr. Kessler said that the movie was not without seriousness. He claimed that it said something about frigidity and the possibilities of a cure. At that, Charlotte had said, oh, come now, lifting her head for a momen from *Gone With the Wind*. It's true, Frederick Kessler insisted politely, the movie was really about a serious subject. He had trouble with his *r*'s, he always did, another Frankfurt problem—*se-wious, twue, fwigidity*. Teddy and Erich were suddenly all ears at the word, but the exchange quickly died down, scorched by the sun, done in by lethargy. It's going to be a great Series, Larry Bernard said, turning a page in the paper. I wish we had a major league team at home, he said. Let's go in the water, Teddy called to Erich.

They raced each other sluggishly to the shoreline, then joined the Talles boys in the surf. Teddy had to fight his way in, the water was so cold. He saw Erich gasp alongside him, wince in actual pain. Teddy stood for a moment or two, shivering, his arms raised limply out of the water, the water breaking just below his waist. Behind him, Marion was screaming in the shallow water. She tried to splash him, was too far away. He shook his fist at her. Then he ducked, holding his nose, came up, began to swim out, rolling over on his back so that he would not get the water in his eyes. The salt was terrible for his allergy. Erich was just behind him. Ten feet out, both Talles boys came in on a wave. Tibor was yelling, Joseph had his head down. When the brothers swam out again, Tibor surfaced alongside Teddy. He had small, supple muscles in his upper arms, real biceps which formed themselves in perfect mounds when he crooked his elbow, his body compact, all of a piece from head to toe. Teddy envied him. He was laughing and flailing at the water to stay afloat, the soft wet brown of his shoulders reflecting the sun. He told Teddy that the ocean was so cold it would make his pecker disappear inside his head.

They stayed in for twenty minutes, yelling most of the time. Even Joseph yelled as they sailed in on a wave. Once Teddy was slammed into shallow water on his left elbow; when he surfaced, he could see bloodmarks just below the surface of the skin. A minute later, farther out, Erich was somersaulted onto his back. He looked terrified when he finally came up, panicked without air. He wasn't even sure for the moment where he was. Without his glasses, he couldn't recognize a face three feet away.

Teddy floated briefly, watching the sky as it dipped in and out of his vision, examining the vast backdrop of the Boardwalk and the thin slice of real estate behind it. From the sea, Atlantic City looked a hundred miles distant, a remote skyline of behemoth hotels, flying pennants, and a million open windows. The light was so clear that Teddy could see the hotel window curtains blowing in the offshore breeze, fluttering in and out like tiny handkerchiefs. It looked gala from the sea, a white flapping happiness caught in the midafternoon sun. Then the current shifted, there was a sudden cold pull. Teddy was turned on his side, his vision shunted. The wave pulled him in a few feet, drifted closer to the Steel Pier. He let it carry him, gazed placidly at the mammoth pilings. One day, he wanted to try to swim under the Steel Pier to the beach on the other side. It was like night under there, the sea as black as squid's ink, the iced air foul with unchanging shade, untouched by the sun. It would take a couple of minutes with a good, fast crawl, trying all the time to avoid being smashed against the pilings and torn apart by barnacles, then out of the grotto into God's clean air. He wondered if anybody had ever tried it; it was supposed to be against the law.

A neat, rhythmic series of waves cradled him. Up he rose for a second or two, then sinking, he began to kick his legs energetically. A few minutes later, the sea changed again. Teddy hardly had to do anything to stay afloat. The water had turned to velvet, supported him like a taut bed sheet. He stretched his arms out to make a cross, shut his eyes, spouted water like a baby whale. Bliss: it was nearly insupportable. He moved his little finger in the water, then a foot, set up a beat between them, quickly grew bored. The waves were moving him slowly toward the shore, angling him on the diagonal. All four boys floated in the same way. Six feet in, three feet out, six in, three out, an identical rhythm, the same easy rise and fall. A jellyfish sailed by, then another; hundreds of poisoned stingers waved weightlessly just below the surface. Teddy reached for the bottom, tried to stand up. Erich too was trying to touch bottom. He had spotted a second cluster at the same time. Then the Talles boys did the same.

Son-of-a-bitch, Tibor cried. He beat at the water, cried out angrily. Jellyfish took over the Atlantic coast late every summer, drove swimmers crazy with their slow, bobbing progress in to shore, then out again with the tide. The boys moved off, decided they had had enough. They swam out for one more ride, let three perfectly good waves go by, unwilling to relinquish the sea, finally rode in together on a fourth, and, dripping with salt, went back to their families.

The crowd had begun to thin out. The sun was down over Absecon, there were more clouds coming in from the north. Don't get me wet, Bea said from the blanket. Charlotte looked up from her book. Larry Bernard was gone. Dry yourself, Mr. Kessler said to Erich. He handed him a towel from Sloan's. Teddy lay down on the blanket. He closed his eyes, felt enclosed by exhaustion, welcomed it, began to purr in the weak sun, a peculiar, tentative sound that came from the base of his throat. Bliss again. Lying there on his back, he began to finger a two-part invention on the blanket, curving his fingers and giving each note full value. He liked to play Bach. It made him feel that he counted for something, made him sit up straight at the piano. On the melody went, passed from one hand to another, swift triplets hammered out on the sand. The sun was suddenly hot again. The air was still, dead, without a breeze. There was a murmur of voices around him, Charlotte to Bea, Bea to Charlotte, soft woman's laughter, then Marion asking for a cookie, the tide moving slowly up the beach, the one sound that was contained within every other sound, the beginnings of another Bach invention, the notes in the very bones of his fingers, barely under way, then Teddy was asleep.

When he awoke, his shadow stretched another foot toward the sea. The pilings beneath the Steel Pier gave against the breakers, swaying like sea reeds. The day had changed; it was suddenly cool everywhere; a mauve light hovered over them on the beach. Teddy turned his head, saw Thelma Talles make her way toward the Boardwalk in a white terry cloth robe. She no longer needed her parasol, still spun it overhead for the walk to the hotel. Victor Talles followed her, carrying blankets, beach chairs, towels, and a racing sheet. He was in a green slack suit, one he had given up manufacturing for army uniforms; he never put on a bathing suit. Joseph and Tibor were a hundred feet ahead of them, snapping wet towels at each other. The Kesslers were gone, too. And Bea?

"Where's Mother?" Teddy asked, sitting up. The tanker was still in sight, way off to the left now, on its way to a northern port. Charlotte was sharing the blanket.

"She's washing her hair," Charlotte said. "Marion's, too." The words came out in a slow, reluctant singsong; she was still trapped in her book.

"There's not many people left on the beach."

". . . . . ."

"There really was a crowd this afternoon."

Charlotte marked her place, closed the book. "When everybody goes is the best part of the day," she said.

Teddy leaned back on his elbows, saw his own ribs mark his torso like the rungs of a ladder. "I really slept," he said.

"You were snoring," Charlotte said. "Why don't you put on your shirt? Look, you've got goose bumps."

"Are you going to marry Larry Bernard?"

". . . . . . ."

Teddy smiled like a conspirator.

"Don't overstep now."

"Come on, Charlotte. Tell me. Are you going to marry Larry Bernard?"

"Do you think I should?" she asked, after a moment's hesitation.

"It doesn't matter what I think."

"With me, it matters what everybody thinks. That's the trouble. If it's not my father, it's the rest of the Melnicovs, and if it's not them, it's my friends."

"You can do what you want, it's a free country."

"That's what the books say, but when it comes to real life . . ."

"From what I can see, everybody does what they want, Charlotte."

"That's how it may look to you. And how would you know anyway?"

"Has he proposed?" Teddy asked.

Charlotte was suddenly all business. She stood up, gathered her things. "What am I talking to you like this for? It's none of your business. A kid half my age."

"Less," he said, smiling again. She always ended up like this, a mistress of mock indignation. He knew that she took everything he said seriously. He stood up, folded the blanket. "Wait for me," he said. "I'll walk with you."

They set off together, Charlotte trailing her robe in the sand. "Carry my book," she said. On they walked, making a terrific effort. Charlotte dropped her cocoa butter. Teddy picked it up.

They both tripped on the blanket, began to giggle. "For God's sake," she said, as Teddy dropped his shirt, "you're all butter-fingers." They climbed up the Boardwalk and down the other side. They were like the exhausted survivors of a lost caravan. A deep chill filled the street, automobiles, shadow, mud and sand, hotel signs, city noise. The horizon lay almost at their feet. But the evening was coming on, Saturday night. The hotel guests were in their baths; the sun was almost down; there was the sound of kitchen noises in the alleyways.

They entered Sloan's through the street door, under the porch, pausing for a moment to clean the sand off their feet. They were so tired they could hardly stand up. It was another form of bliss. Then, against his will, like a somnambulist, Teddy took one look around, raised his eyes. He found the lady in the ginger wig, in a line with a hundred others, caught the hungry, appraising look, sighed. His mouth turned down, he brushed nonexistent sand from his trunks.

"So you think I ought to marry Larry Bernard?" Charlotte asked.

"I never said that," Teddy answered. He looked around one last time at the veranda behind him. It was irresistible. A hundred old ladies rocking away before Saturday dinner, cooling themselves with souvenir fans of Atlantic City, watching the goings-on at Sloan's. It was all great sport for them. Charlotte was holding the screen door open. "Come on," she said. "Before every fly in town . . ."

He scooted in. "I never said you should marry Larry Bernard." He was unable to leave the subject alone. "How do you know he doesn't have a girl friend back home?"

She gave him a suspicious look. "What do you know about that?"

"I don't know anything."

"You sure? Not that it matters."

"Honest, Charlotte. I'm just kidding."

" . . . . . ."

"You know I'm not serious."

"What difference does it make? The whole story is no story. There's nothing there, nothing between us."

"You're taking it too seriously. I never said you should marry Larry Bernard in the first place."

"Don't worry your little head," Charlotte said. "It would never work, anyway. One lawyer in the family is enough."

Then, before they started up the stairs, she threw him a look that was not without its own humor. There was something self-deprecating in it, something modest. It pulled Teddy close to her for the moment. You don't have to believe all that, Charlotte seemed to be saying, just because I insist on it.

7

Midway through dessert that evening, it became clear to Teddy that something was being withheld from him. There was a certain amount of whispering, more than ordinary, between Bea and Charlotte, sudden silences, lapses in attention, some sharply overdone scolding of Marion, who sat at table number five in her thin, flowered dress again, hair washed, sulking. Every now and then Larry Bernard would escape from his own table between courses to visit them briefly, talking out of the side of his mouth to Bea and Charlotte as he squatted between them. He too didn't want to be overheard. This went on for twenty minutes or so, a rustling of secret activity, mild blushes, a word picked up here and there around the table, not entirely vague, not specific either, while Gustav Levi and Frederick Kessler, who had each discovered in the other something to admire, tried to keep civilized conversation going. It didn't work. They had lost their audience for the evening. They had only each other to talk to: the threat of war and the future of Europe. Finally it all came clear. Charlotte and Larry were off to the Ritz again for a cup of coffee and so was Bea. With Judge Aaron, from Trenton, whose wife was stuck away in an institution in Bucks County. Marion's eyes filled with tears.

"Teddy's going to stay with you," Bea said, looking to Teddy for confirmation. He gazed back at her steadily, a splinter of steel. "You'll play with Gloria," Bea then said, suddenly sounding unsure of herself.

"Gloria went to Hackney's for dinner," Marion said.

"Well," Bea said, "maybe you'll go around the corner to the St. James and see the show with Teddy." Teddy drummed the table with his fingertips.

Larry Bernard was at their side, then, he always had everything perfectly timed, holding their chairs, helping them to their feet, not rushing them precisely, but making it impossible for them to waste time, to stall. Mr. Levi was already on his way to the lobby, grace after meals being the preserve only of Friday night, while the Kesslers had apologetically fled the hotel to make the early show with Hedy Lamarr. Almost everyone, in fact, was moving toward the lobby, getting ready to flee Sloan's. In the middle of the crowd, Larry Bernard had Bea and Charlotte on each side of him, walking just ahead of Marion and Teddy. He held Charlotte by the elbow, left Bea untouched. Fumes of self-pity rose from Marion. Teddy was like a bead in their wake, three feet behind them.

All around them, meanwhile, clusters of satisfied guests made plans for the evening. Boardwalk auctions, the chance to pick up a diamond cheap. Night clubs. Miniature golf, shooting galleries. The show around the corner at the St. James. A walk to the north, a walk south, following the sea. Somebody knew a place where they showed stag movies. The Talleses were on their way to the Harlem Club with Dr. and Mrs. Lazarus. It was famous for a great chorus line and dirty comedians. Instead of applauding the show, the customers at the Harlem Club pounded the tables with wooden gavels. Mrs. Talles was giving last-minute advice to Tibor and Joseph, who were going to play the pinball machines on the Boardwalk. In a corner of the lobby, leaning forward in her high-backed chair, the old lady Eisen puffed on a Turkish cigarette. It didn't matter to her what day of the week it was. Saturday night could be Monday, what difference would it make? She held the cigarette between her forefinger and thumb, blew smoke out through her pursed lips without inhaling it. The attendant Clara sat behind her. Teddy examined the broad, flattened nose, the triangular Baltic face, the faintly red wig, the tiara from Russia. The old lady Eisen examined him back through her inquisitive Lapland eyes, gave him a wicked smile of recognition. He felt as though his mind had been read.

Bea turned to say good-by. It was the same routine as the night before. She would not be late, she said. Keep an eye on Marion. Everything would be all right. Meanwhile, her own eyes restlessly avoided Teddy's. She was all in white tonight, white dress with blue-and-white belt, with white beads supposed to look like jade, a fake ivory bracelet, her blue-and-white spectator shoes freshly polished by her own hands. She had oiled her hair into fluent, liquid waves. Through his rage, Teddy could see how beautiful she was, how clearly she was aware of it, how meticulously she had placed each decorative piece, real or faked, on her body, how controlled she was, how objectified, outside Sloan's, outside her friends, her family, outside even herself for the moment, perfectly intact.

Teddy became quiet for a moment. He stood there watching her. A bracelet clacked, Bea ran her beads through her fingers. "Good-by," Teddy said sharply.

She turned to him then and gave him a plaintive look that was unworthy of her. It was filled with appeal, asked for favors. It suggested complicity. They both understood it. Then she turned again with an impatient gesture and walked off with Charlotte and her boyfriend.

Within a half hour, a little more, they were all gone. The lobby was nearly empty. In her corner, the old lady Eisen had fallen asleep with one eye half open. Teddy could hear her snoring. Nurse Chernichowski sat dozing behind her. What did the old lady dream about in her high-backed chair? What was on her mind? Chocolate laxatives, perhaps, boxed squares of them piled a mile high, the liberating success of a lifetime. Or Latvia, across the sea somewhere, as real in her consciousness as the silver knob on her cane. Or Moscow during the Great War, Tsar

Nicholas and his father, Alexander, before him, Clara Chernichowski, a bathtub filled with intractable salt water. A million
dollars, two million, more. She was no fool, even though she
couldn't remember what day it was. But when you were rich,
Teddy knew, it didn't matter whether you were a fool or not.
One day was as good as another. Life became simple, rich people
knew what to expect. For them, for the old lady Eisen, for
Teddy's uncles, the whole world snapped to, came to attention.
The smell of their money was like an aphrodisiac. Everyone welcomed it, everyone liked to sniff at it, wherever it grew, looking
for nourishment, for sudden vigor; nobody complained.

Up front, Gustav Levi sat in a wicker chair overlooking the
street, musing like a Catholic counting his beads. Teddy knew
that while he kept an eye on his sister, Gustav Levi kept an eye
on him. Gustav Levi liked Teddy, liked to show it, preferred
Teddy's opinions to those of half the guests at Sloan's. And Teddy
on his part fed on the respect Gustav Levi bestowed on his
skinny frame, listened as a result to what Gustav Levi had to
say, followed the direction of his thought far beyond the extent
of their conversations. Gustav Levi beckoned to Teddy now, curl-
ing his middle finger exaggeratedly, like a movie villain. Sometimes a little bit of the clown surfaced in him.

"What are you up to?" Gus Levi asked as Teddy approached.

"Nothing. I have to stay with my sister." His voice sounded
sour in his own ears.

"You want to take a walk, I'll stay with her."

"That's all right. Maybe I'll take her around to the St. James."

"I'd be glad to watch her. I have a little dyspepsia tonight, I'll
be here."

"It's okay."

"I should watch my diet more carefully. I eat too much at this
place. I have heartburn all the time." He paused a moment.
"What's the matter with you?" he asked, looking Teddy up
and down.

"Nothing's the matter."

"What are you jumping around that way for? You're like a Mexican bean."

Teddy made an effort to stand still. "This place is so quiet," he said pointlessly.

"Thank God," Gus Levi said, under his breath.

"I should have gone to the movies with Erich."

"Go. It's not too late. I'll watch your sister."

"Nah," he said. "I'll take her around to the St. James. She'll like that."

"It's not a show for kids."

Teddy's eyes widened.

"It's not fun, I mean. It's not good taste. It's all noise. A *gehenna*."

"If it's no good, we'll leave."

"Do as you like. I warned you. Don't come complaining to me." Mr. Levi then swallowed two pills, made a face, drank half a glass of water, gently burped twice. "Have a good time," he said. "Don't stay out late."

There was no need to worry. Within an hour, they were back at Sloan's, out of breath, having run hand in hand all the way from the St. James.

"How was it?" Gus Levi asked from the depths of the wicker chair.

"It was a gyp," Marion said.

Gus Levi smiled with satisfaction.

"It was nothing," Teddy said. "The worst."

That was, in fact, the general opinion in Atlantic City. Everybody rushed once to the Saturday night show at the St. James because it was free. It was a hangover from the early days of the depression, when the management had created it as a come-on for bargain-hunting guests. The institution had stuck. Now amateurs signed up to perform. The management leavened them with a professional or two and opened up the lobby to the world. Hundreds came on Saturday night, a different crowd each week. It had made the St. James famous and it filled the hotel, early and late, for two shows.

There was such a mob, Teddy told Mr. Levi, sitting down next to him, that they had nearly been crushed to death. People were standing in the street and watching the show through the screen doors. Teddy and Marion had gotten inside through a side door and once inside couldn't get out again. They had moved through the sweating crowd inch by inch, nearly asphyxiated by the scent of body powder, and shoved their way up front to get a good look at the entertainers. They had to find a place on the floor under the nose of a three-piece band—saxophonist, upright piano, and drums. The piano was out of tune. It hurt to listen, Teddy said.

"I know, I know, I've been there," Gus Levi said.

A comedian had come out and told jokes about his wife in a loud voice. His saliva had rained down on Teddy and Marion, convulsing them, disgusting them, too. They sat there with their hands over their heads, trying to keep dry. The comedian thought they were laughing at his jokes. He kept playing to them, Teddy said, for encouragement. One of the buttons on his fly was open. The man was an amateur from Chester, Pa.

Then a blond woman in a dress made of orange satin had come out and sung "Lullaby of Broadway." She was fat like Sophie Tucker and carried a long chiffon handkerchief which she waved in time to the music.

"A shouter," Gus Levi said. "Yes," Teddy said. "A shouter."

When she sang the words, "Come on along and listen to . . .," she tried to growl like a tiger. Some of the people in the audience, some of the young people, had growled back. "Let me, let me," Marion then insisted, and growled a few words professionally at Mr. Levi. Marion had talent, she opened up her mouth and out came a huge voice made of pure metal. "Not bad," Mr. Levi said.

He had never seen hair bleached so yellow, Teddy said, it was
like a tulip, and all the time the woman kept pulling at her
skirt to make it shimmer in the lights. While she sang three songs,
everybody out front greeted old friends and talked to each other.
Did they think she was deaf, that she couldn't hear? Teddy had
never seen an audience like it before. There was even some
hooting and boos, the real thing, as though they had all paid
good money for what they were getting.

It's not like that at the Ritz, Teddy heard himself saying. It
couldn't happen at the Ritz. He paused, momentarily disoriented,
tried to find himself. Marion began to sidle away then, tired of
the story, her part over with, drifting slowly to the other side
of the lobby. "Go on," Mr. Levi said, a little peevishly, "I'm waiting." Anyway, Teddy said, hurrying to finish, somebody had
then stepped on his hand while they were sitting on the floor,
and when an entertainer made his entrance in a derby hat and
a black bow tie, spouting Yiddish, not a word in English, they
had gotten up and sneaked out. Who understood Yiddish? Who
wanted to? It was, as Marion had said, a gyp. It was, as Mr. Levi
had promised, not fun, all noise, a *gehenna*. It was terrible.

As Teddy finished his report, Gus Levi moved down in his
chair onto the base of his spine, folded his hands over his stomach, looked disapproving first, then gloomy. Asperity singed the
air. Mr. Levi had a tumbler of neat Scotch on the table next to
him. He sighed, reached for the tumbler. "You're superior to
all that?" he finally asked. "You and the Ritz?"

Teddy looked at his friend questioningly. "I don't understand," he said.

"You're so much better than they are?"

"Than who?"

"The St. James, the people there."

"I didn't say that."

"It was implied."

"But what does the Ritz have to do with it?"

"I'm talking about you. It's not good enough for you?"

Teddy took a breath, steeling himself. "You yourself," he said, "you yourself warned me. You said it was all in bad taste."

"Never mind what I said. You were making anti-Semitic remarks."

"I was making anti-Semitic remarks?"

"The whole time you were talking."

"That's impossible."

"What's so impossible?"

"How could I? I'm a Jew!"

"You're a Jew! What a piece of news! The whole world should hear. You American children! You're all alike. Thin as paste. No blood. You can't even imagine an anti-Semitic Jew."

Teddy blushed again, hesitated. Rabbinical quotes at breakfast, harsh inquisitions at night. "It was just the crowd at the St. James," he said. "You know what I'm talking about."

"You wouldn't care if they were gentiles," Gus Levi said, bringing himself up in his chair. "Then they could do anything they wanted."

"But I *don't* care," Teddy said.

Mr. Levi looked as though he had had enough. "Sit still," he said. "You're still jumping around. What's wrong with you tonight?"

"Nothing."

"You want a Coca-Cola?"

"No. Thank you."

"You want an ice cream?"

"No."

What did he want? He didn't have the slightest idea. Some pressure kept him in motion, some tension caused his fingers to twitch against his thighs, made him tap his feet on the floor, cross one leg, then the other, try to break away from Gus Levi's steady, virginal, adult gaze to peer nervously into the dim corners of the lobby, where Marion sat almost alone, drawing stick figures on hotel stationery. "Any news on the radio tonight?" he finally asked.

"There's never any news on Saturday night," Gus Levi said. "The news always sleeps until Monday morning." Teddy laughed. "You'll have to be patient for at least another twenty-four hours."

"I can wait."

"You have no choice. So you might as well learn. It's not so bad to know how to wait. In the meantime, why don't you take a walk and get rid of your heebie-jeebies? Go out and get some good free American air. I'll keep an eye on Marion."

"Are you sure?"

"Did I just say it or didn't I?"

"Okay, okay," Teddy said. "It'll only be for a couple of minutes." Still, he sat there without moving.

"I'm not myself this evening," Gus Levi said. "When I have dyspepsia, strange things come out of my mouth." He gave a little belch, as a joke, sipped the Scotch, looked more cheerful. "I'm very sensitive these days to certain kinds of talk."

" . . . . . . "

"You understand that not only is Erich Kessler's mother still in Frankfurt, but so is Frederick Kessler's."

"Ah," Teddy said, mindlessly. He did not want to hear about Erich Kessler's mother tonight, he did not want to hear about Erich Kessler's grandmother. He had heard such stories before, heard them all, more than once.

"And those things are much on my mind," Gus Levi said. There was a moment's silence. Then Gus Levi said, "I thought you wanted to take a walk."

"I do," Teddy said.

"*Nu, mein kind?*" Mr. Levi gave him an agreeable smile. The air was cleared, the game played out. "I promise you," he said again, "there'll be no news until Monday."

He rushed along the Boardwalk, sidestepping the crowds, past the gypsy fortune-teller and the taffy stand, past the bargain bookstore and the Steel Pier, past the Dennis, the Morton, the Marlborough-Blenheim, past the sickening colors of the fountain at the Claridge, past the Traymore and the Shelburne, past the gaudy electrified horse race atop the Million-Dollar Pier, talking to himself silently, ticking off with the speed of light an improvised encyclopedia of gorgeous facts, each designed to destroy the gnats of emotion that stung him so irresistibly. Already he had a hive on his chest, hot and swollen, nearly an inch wide. He fingered it through his shirt as he strode along, moving his lips almost invisibly.

As an island with southern exposure close to the Gulf Stream, he told himself, Atlantic City had a most popular natural advantage called "equable climate." Calm as the waters of a lake. Reliable as Old Faithful. Pleasant as a warm bath. Mean annual temperature: 53 degrees. Not hot, not cold. Sixty percent better than the U.S. average. Avg. fall temperature: 56.8 degrees. Avg. winter temperature: 35 degrees. Avg. spring temperature: 48.6 degrees. In the summer, when it really counted, the avg. was only 72.8 degrees. That was what equable was all about.

In 1938, Teddy recited, the inside of his head shifting like an abacus, more than $100,000,000 in personal income was earned in Atlantic City. This represented an annual growth rate of about 10 percent. It was expected that this rate of growth would be maintained, if not increased, during the next decade. By 1950, when the world of tomorrow would arrive, annual personal income would be at $200,000,000, going up to $300,-000,000 by 1960 and $500,000,000 by 1970, when Teddy would be middle-aged and maybe rich. Teddy paused, took stock. Climate. Geography. Growth. Money. The underpinnings of life, the amazing heart of prosperity, the way to the future. He would have to share all that with Erich Kessler, pass out the data piece by piece. He would feed the endless information into his alien ear. He would stuff that cautious, reticent head, full of Teutonic admonitions from his father on how to behave properly in a strange land, how not to attract attention, how to avoid pain, with beautiful, irreplaceable facts about America, designed painlessly to transform even a Patagonian into a Yankee, the whole rainbow mosaic of incomparable testimony about the United States of America, all forty-eight of them, to say nothing of Atlantic City and its surrounding townships, listed, as always in Teddy's head, in alphabetical order: Absecon City, Brigantine City, Buena Borough, Buena Vista, Corbin City, Egg Harbor City, Folsom Borough, Hammonton Town, Linwood City, Longport Borough, Margate City, Mays Landing, Northfield City, Pleasantville City, Port Republic City, Somers Point City, Ventnor City, and, finally, Weymouth.

Did Erich Kessler know that the snowfall in Atlantic County, in all those towns, villages, and turnpike crossroads, was less for the entire winter than in any one month in either Philadelphia or New York, or Trenton, Wilmington, Baltimore, and Pittsburgh? That was because of the salt air. Was he aware that the average humidity at noon in Atlantic City was 68 percent and that the offshore breeze blew at 14.8 miles per hour? Also, that the temperature hit 90 only twice each summer? (Could that be possible?)

Then Teddy went to work on the Boardwalk, a truly substantial subject, horizontally monumental, consisting entirely of three-dimensional objects accessible to human touch. The supports, he reminded himself, were made up of eight-by-eight timbers, structural steel, structural steel encased in concrete, and reinforced concrete columns, both round and square. The joists, on the other hand, were of yellow pine, heavily creosoted against termites. All in all, there were 8,079,368 lineal feet of decking, or some 1,530 miles; about 12,464,578 nails of all sizes and varieties, or 1,270 miles of them stretched end to end. To keep the Boardwalk in repair required the steady, uninterrupted work—in rain, meager snow, or shine—of forty carpenters, and all together they used twenty miles of longleaf pine and Sitka spruce to replace decking that had rotted. Ten million pedestrians a season tested the results. By 1970, there would be twenty million.

There had been two previous Boardwalks, the first only eight feet wide, laid flat on the sands and taken up section by section each year for the winter. The second was sixteen feet wide, also laid flat on the sand. Two horrific storms tore it up in the eighties. Apparently, the climate was not so equable then. The latest, the elevated one beneath his own feet, had been accumulated, extension by extension, over five decades. It was started in 1890 by the Phoenix Bridge Co. of Philadelphia. For its dedication, a golden nail was driven into the first section by Mrs. R. P. Stoy, whose husband was the mayor of Atlantic City. The Boardwalk now reached 4.13 miles from Absecon Inlet to the southwesterly boundary of Atlantic City, where Ventnor's own Boardwalk, which had a history of its own, picked up the trail.

Teddy was past the Convention Hall now, nearly past all the forty-eight panels of Miss America contestants, smiling out at him and the rest of the world through mouthfuls of nearly identical teeth whitened with expert brush strokes. Teddy slowed down a bit, emptied his head of facts, began to examine the panels. Linda Sue Wofford, he read. She was from Tennessee. Her head in the picture was tilted at forty-five degrees, her eyelashes were an inch long. Teddy came as close as he could, peered at that perfect smile. Close up, the picture disintegrated into a million dots; Linda Sue Wofford atomized; it was the mystery of still photography, a wonder. Still, at a distance she was adorable. She wore a gardenia in her hair and a gold barette, a bathing suit with a halter. And Grace Monoghan from New England, alongside Linda Sue. She stood with one knee posed in front of the other, her chin tucked under a chilly smile. Anne Troxell, Dorothy Barnes, Margaret Ann Morris. Frances Marie Howard from Ohio. She had a single snaggle tooth. Gertrude (Trude) Beauchamp. Lenore Ault. And others. They all began to merge in his mind, the perfect Union, forty-eight million dots come together to produce the miracle of photography. America, he thought; America the Beautiful; his own shining sea out there, beating against the Jersey shore. Turning impatiently, he hurried on.

He felt another hive on his chest, just below the first. They always came like that, never less than two. He checked its width, scratched at it, walked even faster. The Ritz was in view now, that was how far he had walked, closer every minute, sitting there alone a few blocks away, like an elegant, immobilized ocean liner facing out to sea. Inside, he knew, there was no place where you could buy a cup of coffee. Should he pay a visit, should he wander urbanely past the Merry-Go-Round Bar while the organ played "Deep Purple" or a new Irving Berlin tune in honor of the Ritz's famous guest and his three daughters? Should he confidently enter the main lobby, see himself reflected in plate glass, distorted in chrome, observe the midget bellboys with pillboxes on their heads delivering telephone messages? What awaited him inside the Ritz, what was there?

An echo sounded then, breaking the suspense. It cost $121,-000, he suddenly remembered, to maintain the Boardwalk each year. $121,000. He must feed that to Erich, add it to the total, watch the expression on his face when he took it all in. He must tell Erich about Linda Sue Wofford, too. He must bring him back to the Convention Hall to look at her photograph, and the forty-seven others, all yearning to climb the throne, to be Miss America, shoulders rounded in the fashion of the day, everything contained in the long smiles, the hidden brassieres and the swelling thighs, and the knees as dimpled as Shirley Temple. Could Erich Kessler understand American girls? To understand them, you had to be thin as paste. That's what Gus Levi would claim, that's what he would insist. American children, American boys and girls, were all alike. Thin as paste, and bloodless. Erich Kessler wasn't like that. He was full of invisible European substance, of centuries of inherited character. Then, in the next moment, trying to fix his eyes straight ahead, pretending to be thinking of other things, Erich Kessler and Linda Sue Wofford and Gus Levi, Teddy willed himself to walk past the Ritz, without even turning his eyes to look at it, his nerves as tight and hard as Tibor Talles' biceps. He made himself walk with a bounce, jaunty, like his father, ready for anything, and continued that way along the Boardwalk a few blocks beyond the hotel, beyond the sleek brick facade that stood behind him now. Within a few minutes, he reached the Ambassador. There he faced for a moment or two the great beached whale of stone, studying the last monstrous guesthouse before Ventnor and Margate, the Ritz's archrival, then turned his back on it for another moment to gaze out to sea. He steadied himself in the crosswind, then became as suddenly becalmed, as stranded, as the vast gray hotel behind him. His pulse quieted. Flags flapped in the wind somewhere to the right. Out to sea there was a single light and the Boardwalk's metal railing was cold to the touch. He shivered once, then, moving at a reasonable pace like everyone else, a mere stroll, he turned north again and headed back to Virginia Avenue.

Marion was in bed, the light flannel blanket tucked up to her chin, her thin straight hair thinner than ever, freshly washed tonight, colorless. A comic book lay on the blanket next to her.

"You all right?" he asked. He was busy unfolding his cot, pulling the sheets tight, hefting a blanket into the air. It came down like a parachute.

She nodded. Alongside her, the one-eyed doll shared the pillow.

"I don't want to go home tomorrow," she said. "You're so lucky."

"Well, I didn't go to day camp like you."

"I didn't want to go to day camp. I hated it there."

"Well, you went."

"Rosellen Klein stole my sourball candy every day."

"Her brother steals, too. All the Kleins steal, don't you know that? Anyway, you had two weeks there. All I get is one more week."

"I want to stay," she said. She pretended to make her doll comfortable.

". . . . . ."

"I don't want to go home."

"Come *on*, Marion," Teddy said.

"I don't."

"Just go to sleep, will you?"

"I didn't do anything tonight, like you. You're always so lucky."

"You got to the St. James. You saw the show."

"You're going to see Daddy tomorrow. You're going to see Ben. I haven't seen Ben in a whole month."

"You'll see him week after next."

"I don't want to go home. I want to stay at the beach."

"Well, you can't. There isn't enough money."

"There's enough money for you."

"I told you before, you went to day camp."

"I didn't even go to the World's Fair."

"Did I? Did Daddy?"

"Ben went."

"On his own money."

There was a knock on the wall. The children froze. "You see," Teddy hissed. "You're keeping the whole hotel up. Now go to sleep."

"I can't sleep with the light on."

"Since when?"

". . . . . ."

"You are really a pain when you want to be. You know that?"

". . . . . ."

"You always sleep with the light on. You slept with the light on last night before I got back." He threw his bathrobe around him, turned his back on his sister, undressed clumsily, slipped on his pajama bottoms. Marion watched him carefully.

"I saw," she said.

"Saw what?"

"Your thing."

"*Go to sleep.*"

"I played rummy with Mr. Levi."

"Yeah?"

"I won."

"Mr. Levi plays terrible rummy."

"I schneidered him."

Teddy turned off the light, slipped into the cot. The foot of the double bed was only six inches away, and now, lying on his side, he began to trace with his forefinger the flowers that were hand-painted there.

"You know why else I hated day camp?"

"Why?"

"They made me sing every day."

"You like to sing. You have a voice."

"They made me."

Teddy could see the back wall of the Surf, twelve feet across the alleyway, shining white clapboard that faced the fire escape outside their window. A light was going on and off somewhere in the street, throwing a dim shadow onto the wall every few seconds. Teddy turned on his back, folded his hands beneath his head.

"I want to see Ben," Marion said. "I want to see Daddy."

"You'll see them week after next." Teddy yawned at the ceiling.

"You're going to be here with Grandpa, too."

"Go to sleep. I turned the light off just for you."

"I never went to the Steel Pier, either."

"Nobody did. It didn't rain, that's why."

"I never went."

"Next time."

"I want to see the horse jump in the ocean."

"Next time."

There was a full minute's silence, another, then a light snore came from the bed. Marion's dress lay on the floor, alongside her cotton candy underdrawers. Bea wouldn't like that. Neatness and order, no mess, that, along with a few other things, was his mother's heart's desire. Teddy yawned again, turned on his side, thought of Baltimore, home, their harmonious brick rowhouse near the reservoir, with six more like it on one side, three on the other, his mother and father in their own tidy bed, together, their wedding picture with the cradled white roses and the unctuous rabbi, standing on the chifforobe. In the picture, they looked like their own ancestors. Tomorrow, his mother would be home; and his father would be here, in this room.

The shadow on the Surf lightened, went dark. Teddy could hear their neighbors next door moving around slowly, abstract domestic sounds, faceless sources; then silence. Tomorrow Bea and Marion would get into a taxi in front of Sloan's. Almost at the same moment, his father would do the same in Baltimore. Step by step they would proceed on their journeys in opposite directions, taxi to train, train to taxi, taxi to home, or hotel. Ordinary journeys, a million others exactly like them repeated every day of the year, travelers like Bea and Jack and Marion unthinkingly trusting themselves to the skills of strangers who were sure to deliver them safely, on schedule, and to the right place finally. And at some unknown point on the journey, they would pass each other in time and space, pass within sight and touching distance almost, then move on. But they would pay no attention to the moment, neither anticipate it nor recognize it. It would pass as though it had never happened. They would not care, no one would care. They would not even know. It would be as though they were already dead to each other.

Marion's snore ceased; a little gurgle and it was gone. Her doll fell off the bed. Next door there was still another hollow sound. Inside Teddy's head, Thelma Talles' parasol twirled dizzily, held in her own white hand. No sun ever touched her. She had skin like snow. Her two sons held her beach robe for her, helped her into it adoringly. They surrounded her like courtiers. Blow-job, Tibor said, into his mother's ear. Joseph hid his face. Their father raised his hand, took aim. Teddy shifted in the cot, a nerve jumped in his leg. Vile images. He thought of Linda Sue Wofford again, Dorothy Barnes, Frances Marie Howard with the snaggle tooth. She didn't stand a chance as Miss America, not with that sharp, intelligent look, smart enough for anything. Miss America. Could Bernice Sinsky or Sally Abrams from Baltimore ever become Miss America? Anne Troxell, Margaret Ann Morris, Lenore Ault. Wonderful immaculate Protestant names, before which even life itself cowered, like the names of the girls from Roland Park he met at the Peabody, studying piano and music theory on behalf of Western civilization and Miss Eversfield, in their day-school grays or blues. Demarest and Backer, Corner, Lipscomb, Hutton, Fotheringill, Miles, Steele, and Coursey, girls with tight little smiles and no talent, as remote and inexpressive as a newfound star; but beautiful nonetheless, beautiful because of it, full of unfamiliar and stirring assumptions. He would see them all soon, share their classrooms on Mount Vernon Place, give them the answers during music theory quizzes to help them to cheat, applaud conspicuously when they performed on the piano during public examinations, hoping to buy their applause in turn and bind himself to them.

The door to the room opened slowly, a thin rectangle of light beamed in from the hallway. He heard his mother's whisper. Charlotte responded. Hissing back and forth pleasantly. Soft laughter. The rectangle widened. Bea slipped into the room. Teddy closed his eyes, breathed evenly. He heard his mother begin to undress. She was humming her favorite song. It must be nearly midnight. A shoe came off, dropped; another. There was a whispered noise again, her white dress. Jewelry, piece by heavy piece, bobby pins, wristwatch, earrings, a clatter on the white dresser. Slowly all sound disappeared; it was quiet again in the room. Something brushed against Teddy's face. His mother sidled through the narrow corridor between his cot and her bed. He could smell her toilet water, still fresh, too sweet. It was the smell of English roses in late bloom. Opening his eyes, he saw Bea sitting at the window, elbows leaning on the sill. She was staring out into the dark through the screen. She had her kimono on. Two herons flew across her back. She hummed her favorite song, sat deathly still. Her chin was cupped in her hands.

The fever came over Teddy briefly; disappeared. He waited patiently, waited some more. Bea arose, turned, walked to her bed. She was naked inside the kimono. Teddy recognized it, he knew it by heart. He wanted to call her name. Bea . . . Still humming, she got into bed; she would sleep in her kimono tonight. It became absolutely still again, as though a shade had been drawn in the room. Bea fell asleep, almost on the instant. Going under at the same time, Teddy was trailed by a swelling Rachmaninoff melody again, borne aloft by it momentarily. It carried his thoughts of his own mother first, then others, an exhausting demi-dream of a maternal Charlotte, his friend and confidante Miss Melnicov, sitting at an open window facing out on a strange cobblestone street. She was unembarrassedly naked. Her blond hair hung loose to the waist, clothing her breasts. To all passersby, she shouted the same thing: "I await my visa. I go to America, to Washington Heights. Meanwhile, I live as I please." Her son Erich held her gently from behind, trying to soothe her, massaging her shoulders. He wore his thick glasses, averted his eyes. There was Frederick Kessler, too, somewhere deep in the shadows of the room, tiptoeing back and forth deferentially so as not to disturb anyone. Mr. Kessler's own ancient mother was seated alongside Charlotte at the window, puffing amateurishly on a Turkish cigarette. At eighty-two she was as one-eyed as Marion's doll. They were all waiting there, in full open view of Frankfurt's furtive citizens, the elite of the old iron city, peremptory, placating, and regretful, each of them, as Teddy finally fell asleep.

8

They woke him at seven, Bea and Marion, both frantically racing around the room, bumping into the furniture. "We have to *pack*," Bea said, a terrific urgency in her voice, as though their train were leaving within the hour. Actually, they were going on the one-forty *Sunshine Special*, along with everyone else heading for Philadelphia, Baltimore, Wilmington, and Washington.

"Can't I sleep a little bit more?"

"The cot's in the way," Bea said. "I have to get the small valise down from the closet shelf and I need your help." She was already dressed, or half-dressed, in a pink slip and stockings. "Come on."

"I just woke up."

"Get up, Teddy," Marion said.

He closed his eyes but his mother and sister were too much for him. He knew that energy, respected it, was no match for them in their present mood. They wanted him up, they needed the floor space to maneuver in. There were clothes and bags to be brought from the closet, they repeated. Every drawer had to be checked twice. Everything that was to be put in the bags had to be folded within an inch of its life, as though it were going to be preserved for posterity or examined by a harsh judge, with life or death as the stake, for neatness, compression, order, symmetry, discipline, those things, at the far end of the journey.

"How many dresses do you have there?" Bea asked.

Marion counted the folds slowly, trying to keep them in order. "Four."

"How many underpants?"

"Five."

"Socks?"

And so on, checking themselves, each other, counting, recounting, making piles of clothing, placing piles within bags, then replacing them, once, twice, three times. It was as though they were going beyond recall, making a final, irrevocable move toward which they had better not act casually for a single moment.

A few minutes later, when Teddy got back from the bathroom, he found Charlotte with his mother, helping her pack handkerchiefs. There were two dozen of them, each identical. Charlotte was in her bathrobe, her hair hung to her waist, overnight cream glistened on her face. Without makeup, her lips looked the color of her skin. It was very peculiar, pale and unassertive. Teddy preferred her that way. "You're going to wake everybody on the floor up," Teddy said. Charlotte had the aura of early morning about her, sleep-heavy, full of yesterday's remnants.

"Mind your own business," Bea said. She poked at a pile of clothing. "Why don't you keep this blouse for the week?" she said, turning to Charlotte.

". . . . . ."

"I won't need it at home."

"You don't mind?" Charlotte said.

"It looks better on you."

"You know, if your father-in-law weren't coming . . ."

". . . . . ."

"I tell you what I'd really like instead of the blouse."

"What?"

"Your jade necklace. The white one."

"Take it."

"You're sure?"

"What am I going to do with it? Where would I wear it?"

"What should I do about Larry Bernard?" Charlotte asked.

"Marion, darling, run down and see if they're ready with breakfast. Go with her, Teddy."

"Should I marry him?"

"Marion. Teddy."

"Where's my doll?"

"You're *holding* it," Teddy said.

"Do you have to make a decision now?" Bea asked.

"There's nothing to make a decision about. Not yet. Not quite." Charlotte stood at the doorway, her hair falling over her shoulders. Already her cheeks were beginning to show a new plumpness, a fruit-ripe softness, something heavy and overfull. She no longer looked like a girl; the grave Slavic maiden was being transformed. She ran her fingers through her hair, tossed her head to help shake it out. She caught a glimpse of herself in the mirror across the room, pulled herself up. "Sometimes," she said, "my hair looks ridiculous to me."

"It's beautiful," Marion said, reaching out to touch it.

"No. Sometimes I think it's all wrong. Badly designed. Out of the wrong century. It reminds me of my mother's hair in a picture taken just before the war. Nineteen twelve. Nineteen thirteen. A few years before she died. She used to look just like this. I'm too mature for it." She turned her head from side to side, examining the angles.

"It makes you an individual," Bea said. "All the rest of us running around with the same bobbed style . . ."

"I'm going to cut it off," Charlotte said.

"Please," Marion begged. "No."

"I have to do something about myself. I can't go on like this. I'm going to be an old maid in a few years." She held her hand up as Bea began to protest. "It's true, isn't it? Another five years and I'll be a spinster. Then I'll talk to anybody who talks to me. I'll be one of those."

"You'll never be an old maid," Teddy said

"The question is, what is it I want," she said, disregarding him.

"Larry Bernard." The querulous look came over her. "Can I really want Larry Bernard? Is that what I want?"

"Don't eat yourself up," Bea said.

"I'm going to take the bar again. That's where my independence is. This time . . ."

"You're crazy if you marry Larry Bernard," Teddy said.

"Did you hear that?" Charlotte said.

"Nobody asked you, Teddy," Bea said.

"Why don't you think I should marry him?"

"Don't encourage him or you're liable to hear something we'll all regret. Don't say anything, Teddy. Don't say a word." Bea delivered the words in a scolding tone, full of mockery. Charlotte made a move into the hallway. "Teddy," Bea ordered, "tell them we'll be down for breakfast in five minutes. Marion, go with him. Let me get dressed. Give me some peace." Within thirty seconds, she had the room cleared.

They had the dining room almost to themselves. A few old people, scattered at other tables, ate their breakfasts slowly, as they did at eight o'clock every morning. Saul was able to give the family all his attention, and Marion, watching him with passion renewed by a sense of leave-taking, came close to tears at his teasing before she had finished her milk.

"You gonna come back and marry me?" he asked.

Yes, yes, she nodded, blinking into her glass, while Teddy was assaulted by the feeling that, once gone, they would never see Saul again. He hovered over them, slack, serious, brooding. "Maybe when you grow up, you'll be my secretary?" he said. "Would you like that?"

Would she like that? Teddy could almost see her heart pounding in her chest. Secretary Marion, Attorney Saul. He looked like Paul Muni, ready to argue his first case. Marion would hand him his brief, stand by his side in court, waiting for the judgment. Then they would embrace when they learned that he had won.

But Bea would have none of it this morning. She would not let them fool around at the table. There was too much to be done, they had to get organized, she didn't want to be rushed. No last minute fuss, no final chaos. She arranged—for the third time—for the bill to be held for Jack, for the linens to be changed in the bedroom, for all tips, including Saul's, to be properly distributed by her own hand. She loved to tip. It suited her dreams, touched her aspirations, an act of giving that unequivocally defined all roles. No, they did not waste a minute. Teddy had hardly finished his own milk before Bea was rushing them back upstairs.

"What do you need me for?" he complained.

"I want you where I can get my hands on you."

Upstairs, while Charlotte, Marion, and Teddy sat around impatiently watching her, Bea unpacked the valises once more, counting articles of clothing, examining them as though she had never seen them before, testing for runs in her stockings, fingering the texture of underwear, blouses, skirts, handkerchiefs, even, at one point, draping a blouse over her torso in front of the mirror, eyeing it from one angle or another, as though she were shopping at Hochschild's or Hutzler's. Then she packed again, making room for Marion's odds and ends, a pound-and-a-half's worth, perhaps, a makeup box of her own, and a cardigan she had bought for herself at the last minute on the Boardwalk.

"That's smart," Charlotte said.

"It was a good buy."

"I think I'll get myself one."

"Try a green. You look better in green than you think. It brings something out in your eyes."

"You think so?" Charlotte tried to get a look at herself in the mirror. The friends talked on, dropping the loose change of their conversation as though the supply were limitless. On and on, clothes, hair styles, the rising heat in the crowded room, when to leave for the station, what time they would arrive in Baltimore, the question of whether Jack would remember to leave any food in the house, circling back craftily from time to time, as though on tiptoe, to Larry Bernard, to his virtues and intentions, especially his intentions, then on to Ben, whose well-being Charlotte was to keep an eye on.

"But I don't know how I'll be able to put up with your father-in-law," Charlotte said.

Teddy was embarrassed. His mother let Charlotte complain about his grandfather as though Teddy were deaf. Charlotte didn't like the old man; the old man reciprocated. Teddy felt the discussions were disloyal. He resented Charlotte for them, resented Bea for allowing them. By disassociating herself from his grandfather, she also separated herself from him, and he did not like the sense of distance it established, the remoteness, however brief and passing. But today Bea did not pick up on Charlotte's remark. She was silent for a moment, looking deep in thought, then alighted on her own family, her five brothers, four sisters, each of them ticked off in a summary recitation. First Jenny, then Rosa, Sylvia, and finally Celia, above all Celia. She might be at the Shelburne next week, Bea said. Charlotte was to watch for her. So was Teddy. Celia. Everyone called her the dowager duchess. She was the oldest of the sisters. It was Celia, Bea always said, who had taught her everything after their mother had died, how to walk, how to dress, set a table, furnish a room, who had seen her through childhood and adolescence, then through college, or two years of it before the money had failed; Celia, who had even saved Baby Bea's life during the great Baltimore Fire. Teddy yawned at the very thought of Aunt Celia. The first thing Aunt Celia did whenever she saw Teddy Lewin was to check his fingernails.

But Bea didn't even have time for her own family. "Teddy," she ordered, writing on a sheet of paper. She was putting down a list of things for him to buy for her at the corner drugstore. A ten-cent Hershey bar to hold Marion on the trip. The *Ladies' Home Journal*, make sure it was the new issue. One small bottle of Bayer's. One small bottle of suntan lotion for his father; it would be Teddy's responsibility to see that Jack used it, he had skin like parchment. And change for a ten-dollar bill. Take Marion.

So it was done, the minutes passed. Spun by Bea's energy, the morning circled in on itself again and again, spiraling down finally to the point of noon. Where had the time gone? The baggage was brought downstairs, there was a next-to-final colloquy with Pearl Sloan about the bill, then they were in the dining room having early lunch alone at a deserted table. Nothing however was quite ready. Bea tapped a glass with her spoon, checked her watch, looked distracted.

"You don't go until one forty," Charlotte said.

"There'll be a mob," Bea said.

"Relax."

"Teddy, Daddy won't be here until after four. God knows when Ben is coming. I want you to take care of yourself, no monkey business now."

"For God's sake, Bea, what do you think he has in mind?"

"It's a city of strangers."

"*I'm* here."

"I'm going to get drunk," Teddy said.

"Saul," Bea called over her shoulder. "I arranged for an early lunch. We have to make a train. You know that."

"Coming."

Then lunch did in fact actually come, all of it, hot, fresh, at one serving. They were finished in fifteen minutes, Saul thanked, saying gloomy good-bys to Bea and Marion, hugging the little girl, being hugged, taking his glasses off and wiping them in a surge of emotion. They were all surprised by it. In the lobby afterwards, Bea made a promenade, a quick circular acknowledgment of her week, a gracious handshake with the old lady Eisen, who made a last attempt to remind her of Riga, a pleasant exchange with Nurse Chernichowski, hasty, mouthed, falsely cordial good-bys to Victor and Thelma Talles across the room, a full five minutes with the Lazaruses, who were driving home to

Pittsburgh later in the day, during which the appreciative doctor again told Bea how beautiful she was while his wife smiled approvingly over his head; then Frederick Kessler, back from a quick morning swim in the Atlantic, his bathing cap still on his head, bending over in his terry cloth robe and kissing her hand, Erich solemnly clicking the heels of his saddle shoes as he shook Bea's hand, and Gustav Levi, wearing a sunhat with a celluloid visor, embracing her paternally. "Maybe you'll come visit me in Paterson," he said. "Who knows? It's not so far."

Teddy carried their bags outside. Someone had already called a taxi. Others were getting ready to leave for the station, too. There was a certain amount of confusion on Virginia Avenue, Bea and Marion seventy minutes early, across the street the Cotswold jitney, which met all trains coming and going, backed diagonally into the curb, almost blocking the street, getting ready to take its Philadelphia guests to the one forty; up above on the veranda a long line of Sunday matrons gazing down at the small family straining to say good-by without causing too much stir. At the last minute, Pearl Sloan came running out of the hotel and thrust a package into Bea's hands.

"What?" Bea said.

"It just came," Pearl explained.

Bea unwrapped it: a Whitman Sampler, sixty chocolates, a king's ransom of creamy riches. She looked at Charlotte curiously, examined the card. "Sam Aaron," she said to them all. Teddy stowed the bags in the taxi, hugged Marion furiously. "You're hurting me," she said. "I guess you won't need that Hershey bar I bought for you," he said to his mother. For a moment, Bea clutched the box of candy to her breast, looked helpless. "You take it," she said to Teddy. "Oh, no," he said. "It'll make my face break out." Then they pecked at each other's cheeks, like harried lovers. "Wait a minute," said Charlotte. "Here's Larry." He came rushing out of the hotel, freshly shaved this morning, wide awake. "I almost missed you," he said, striding over to them. His bald head was burned red. He kissed Bea. "I wish you were staying," he said. He had his hand on top of Teddy's head at the same time. "Don't worry about this one," he said. "He won't get to the beach until he practices two hours every morning." Teddy squirmed out of his grasp. Larry put his arm around Charlotte's waist. She stood there without resisting. It made them look married. "Well," Bea said. "Do we have everything?" Gloria Goldman strolled out of the hotel. The girls screamed at each other, pretended to weep. Gloria crossed her eyes. Marion became hysterical. "Well," Teddy said again, "I guess you won't need that Hershey bar." "Here," Bea said, thrusting it into Teddy's hand. She clutched her Whitman Sampler, kissed Charlotte on the cheek, kissed Larry Bernard, pulled Teddy to her, hugged him. "Take care of Daddy," she said. "Take care of Ben." Toilet water, powder, cotton skirt, the corner of the candy box snagged against his chest momentarily, his mother's lips, the impress of her lipstick, the flesh remembering its shape, retaining the scent. A lifetime in a farewell, a glimpse of a Virginia lady leaning over the veranda railing across the street taking their photograph, Larry squeezing Charlotte's compliant waist, Sam Aaron's card, his adorable sister, made more adorable by imminent departure, a recurrent fury. Good-by, he called. He thought of Wallis Warfield again. He was glad they were going, he couldn't wait for them to leave. Take care of my fish, he said angrily. We'll write to you. Daddy and I. Ben. Grandpa.

PART TWO

1934. Baltimore again. It is six o'clock, Sunday evening, dim with the late fall dusk that descends on the city in October like a dying hawk, feathered shadows everywhere, the air chilled by a stabbing breath of ice. Teddy Lewin leaves the Rialto Theater, having seen the feature film twice, his Sunday habit, makes his way home up Linden Avenue. He is fighting the sense of flattened reality that always overcomes him outside when he leaves a theater. It is the sudden loss of beloved phantoms, the renewed onslaught of banality. Linden Avenue, deep in Sunday lethargy, is not Sunset Boulevard, it is not the Champs-Elysees or Pall Mall, it is not even Eutaw Place, elegantly strung along a block to the west. It is merely Teddy Lewin's own familiar, meager street, where the number 32 streetcar runs heavily in front of skinny red-brick row-houses, inhabited up and down their narrow floors by ordinary lives. For the moment, Teddy moves slowly, sings to himself. A few minutes later, he approaches the grammar school up the street, glimpses a familiar sight fifty feet ahead, a furtive, moving body scurrying out of his way, hustling into a hidden areaway of the school. It is Eddie Glazer, aged sixteen. Eddie Glazer's IQ is said to be eighty or less. His spinster aunt, who teaches English at Western High School and boards with his family on Brookfield Avenue, has painfully taught Eddie the alphabet. Eddie's eyes are set a half-inch apart, he can barely articulate language, his emotions burst through the muddy surface of his mind like small, thick lava eruptions. Teddy pulls up short, considers the possibilities. He has seen Eddie Glazer almost every day of his life. Eddie wanders the streets near his home, has nothing to do. He seems never to grow older. He talks to everyone, repetitive, daily phrases, "got a date, got a date, going to the dance Saturday night?", has painful, blushing crushes on half the children in the neighborhood. Sometimes he follows Teddy. He smiles dubiously at him, catches at his coat sleeve, begs for attention, for a touch. Now Teddy decides to move on. As he passes the areaway, Eddie thrusts himself forward, encircles Teddy's small body with his own, presses him into the shadows, against a wall. I love you, he says hurriedly, pressing himself against Teddy. A fever sets in. Teddy flails at Eddie Glazer, breaks away. No, he cries, running. Don't touch me. Did I hurt you? Eddie says, his voice filled with fear. Did I hurt you? Eddie Glazer groans. He is inconsolable. Don't tell, he calls after Teddy. Please don't tell.

1937. It is eight o'clock on a Monday morning. Benedict Lewin races through the front hall of the Lewin rowhouse, gathering books, sweater, lumber jacket. Along the way, he swipes his brother Teddy lightly on the behind. It is the middle of his freshman year at the Johns Hopkins University. He lives at home as a day student and dreams of a room of his own at Brown or Cornell or the University of Michigan. Meanwhile, outside at the curb, Buster Kahn, who picks Ben up every morning, blows his horn irritably. They are five minutes late. First class is at eight thirty, and Buster, who pays for his gas with the car pool contributions of Ben Lewin and a wizened rabbinical student who is studying the archaeology of ancient Palestine with Professor Albright, still has to make a delivery for his father on his way to school. Buster's father is a tailor. Ben, looking anguished, looking distraught, a growing, characteristic look that he is still unaware of, rushes for his lift, yelling at his buddy to lay off the horn, for God's sake, the neighborhood is still half asleep.

A year later. Four o'clock in the afternoon, near the end of Yom Kippur. Teddy Lewin and his friends stand outside the synagogue, lined like lemmings on the steep flight of steps that leads to the prayer hall. It is where they stand every holiday, on the steps and on Eutaw Place below, on Yom Kippur, on the New Year, at Passover. The talk is of baseball and other things. The holiday is almost over. Everyone is in new clothes today. Everyone at the beginning of the service last night looked bathed thrice over, shaved clean to the bone. Yom Kippur is an immaculate holy conception. They would all go through the day, through the whole twenty-four hours, in stony piety, carving it out as though it were a piece of granite. Suddenly the door to the synagogue bursts open. There is a commotion. A cluster of three or four men makes a path through the crowd outside. They are unshaven now, late in the afternoon, wearing dark suits, like all the other men. In the center, in a moment in which time seems to splinter once, then again, Teddy sees his own father. He walks curiously. He is carrying something that demands all his strength. A body is curled in his arms. An arm is thrust around his neck. Teddy waits a moment, hears his name being called. In his father's arms lies his mother. That is what he sees. It's nothing, Jack says soothingly. It's the fast. She'll be all right. One of the men surrounding them passes a small yellow bottle under Bea Lewin's nose. Bea is awake, the color of ancient, fragile ashes. Don't worry, Jack says. Teddy accompanies his father down the street, off Eutaw Place. Bea smiles wanly. I guess it's not for me, she says. Teddy smiles, fights a rising hysteria. He has never seen his mother in his father's arms. Jack is breathing hard now. There is a look of fixed strain on his face. They climb the stairs to the house, twelve of them, up the steep rise. Inside, it is filled with deep shade, a wonderful early fall coolness. Haskel sits in the living room, his ear stuck to the radio. It is World Series time. He has spent the holiday listening to the game in his sister's house. What? he says abruptly as they come in. He rises to his feet. They all calm down. Teddy gets some orange juice for Bea. Dr. Fensterwald is

called, just in case. Jack takes his wife upstairs. Bea in his father's
arms, like Elizabeth Barrett Browning being swept off to Italy by
Robert Browning, Norma Shearer enfolded by Fredric March, in a
boring old movie Teddy saw a year or so ago.

Or this, late winter, 1939. The Lewin family speeds along
Gwynn's Falls Parkway in their new Chevrolet, on the way home
from Friday night dinner with Bea's sister Celia, in Windsor Hills.
The earth is glazed with frost. In the woods on either side of the
parkway patches of clean snow fill the hollows. The family is singing, in close harmony, the latest hit tunes. Nobody, however, can
remember all the lyrics to the songs. There is a lot of fakery and
cheerful improvisation. "I didn't know what time it was, you sang
along. . . ." Marion carries the melody in her huge, round voice,
with the sound of pure metal at the center of it. As her voice fills
the car, Jack's eye is caught by the sight of an endless series of
flatcars braked for the night on the Western Maryland railroad
overpass a quarter of a mile ahead. "Then came my heartburn time
of it, and it's time you were through. . . ." Jack slows down, tells
them all to look. Bea purses her lips, frowns. She says nothing.
Teddy's heart thuds. There is a brief silence. The world, Ben finally
says in his knowing way, is catching up with us. Or vice versa. Each
flatcar is loaded with four small tanks, their gun snouts lifted at an
exact, unvarying thirty-degree angle. They are lined up against the
winter moon, east and west as far as the eye can see, in perfect
black silhouettes. There is a silence again. Teddy thinks of grimy
newsreel pictures he has seen at the Rialto of Japanese soldiers in
old-fashioned puttees snaking their way through Manchukuo, of
Spaniards in knickers running through the streets of Madrid with
their hands covering their bare heads as the bombs fall. A German
officer comes to mind, entering the Rhineland on horseback in a
picture on the front page of the Sun papers, wearing a spiked
helmet that looks like a weapon in itself and an old army over-
coat that hangs halfway to his ankles. Other Germans then, Germans into the Sudeten, into Prague, Germans into Austria, into

Vienna, into Linz and Salzburg. Germans everywhere. Hmmmmm, Jack says. Hmmmm. We'll soon be exactly like everybody else, Ben says. Soon we'll all be in the same boat. Something in his voice sounds satisfied. Marion starts to sing again. Bea shh-shhs her. Teddy's heart again beats heavily. Ah hate wah, Ben drawls. Ah hate all wahs. Yesss, ah do. . . . They are now beyond the overpass. Teddy takes one last look through the rear window. He cannot resist it. He has never seen an actual tank before. None of them has.

And finally 1939 again, spring. It is another evening, six o'clock, midweek. Teddy Lewin, on his way home from the Peabody, climbs the steep hill from St. Paul Street to the apex of Mount Vernon Place, hugging his schoolbooks and music scores against the west wind. He has finished a half-hour class in theory, has cheated again by passing Barbara Demarest the answers in a surprise quiz, unable to resist her stricken appeal, signaled by a calculated, shamed look thrown two or three times in his direction, then had a second half hour in piano, privately, taught by Miss Mabel Johns, a tall, sharp-boned Scotswoman with hands like claws and a humped, predatory Edinburgh nose. Chopin fills his head, a slow, morose waltz, some Haydn he has overheard from another classroom. The Washington Monument now rises alongside him. The Peabody itself is behind him, the Walters Art Gallery, as enclosed as a fortress, down the hill to his left. A thin keen of culture fills the cold evening air. There is nothing like this in his own neighborhood, a few miles to the north. He crosses the top of the hill, heads for the number 32 streetcar. The living rooms at eye level, the salons, the huge high-ceilinged conversation pieces of the homes that line Mount Vernon Place are now open to the evening. Inside one or two of them, through huge, floor-length windows, Teddy sees small clusters of people standing together in amiable groups. They drink amber liquids out of shapely, stemmed glasses, listen to each other intently. The women are in formal dresses, the men in black ties. They laugh easily, do not hurry. Damask draperies frame them, paintings, candelabra, grand pianos fit for the stage of the Lyric Theater uptown, and light that is like a material, a luxurious fabric in itself, a soft, clinging ambience through which the guests move like swimmers in slow motion. This is Teddy's Wednesday night habit. He is a voyeur of social manners, a greedy thief of other people's worldliness. He is addicted to it. Outside on the street, he pauses a moment, watches a small party that is taking place in a living room paneled in dark wood. Bronze sconces line the walls. A manservant paces the room as though he owned it, offering a tray filled with glasses. Generous lives, Teddy thinks, wanting it for himself, warm intelligence, elegance, and wit. Nevertheless, the young woman who catches his eye through the great six-foot window, who spies him spying on her, who resembles Barbara Demarest and all the other girls in his music theory class, freezes him in an instant with a look of disapproving temporal authority. There is not a moment's doubt in that look, no tentativeness, no shyness; it is beyond anything he has ever known in a stranger. For a second, he cannot move. Only Bea Lewin has that power over him. But it is only temporary, it doesn't last. He hesitates in embarrassment, clutches his books, tears the cover of his Czerny exercises by accident, then quickly turns in the direction of home and moves on toward the squabbling excitements of his mother's dining table.

1

Standing severely behind the registration desk, Pearl Sloan was momentarily put off by unexpected problems and visibly unhappy about it. A sunny Sunday morning had turned cloudy by early afternoon, just as the one-forty *Sunshine Special*, bearing away Bea Lewin and her daughter, Marion, among hundreds of others, had pulled out of Atlantic City's terminal station for North Philadelphia. Pearl's guests, eyeing the sky in disappointment, eyeing Pearl accusingly, had resisted the beach, stayed home at Sloan's and thronged the lobby at a time when all the new incoming guests were expected. Some had already arrived. Pearl handled the desk alone, a grim look of overwork pinching her mouth, while her husband, Hy, stood ineffectually alongside her. He was no help with administrative work. His place was with the kitchen workers and the cleaning women. There he was an authority, full of threat and knowledge, a master sophisticate in matters of plated silverware and soap. As for account books and reservation lists, he was not, as Pearl Sloan sometimes said, "much in the head."

She had an impatient line in front of her now, seven brusque new people standing amidst their cheap luggage. She was having trouble checking in Lewin. "I have Levin," she kept saying. "J. Levin, but no Lewin."

Teddy started at the sound of the name. He was hidden behind a potted palm twenty feet away, listening in and watching the desk in a shy effort to sharpen the sweet anticipation of welcome. He could see Pearl Sloan, but not his father.

"That's me," Jack said. "It's Lewin. I don't know where you got the Levin."

"I'm Levin," Barney said, over his son's shoulder.

"Let me handle it, Pa," Jack said.

"No Lewin," Pearl said stubbornly.

"My wife . . ." Jack said, and at the word, something familiar finally rose in Pearl's mind. She sighed in recognition. "You must be Bea Lewin's—" she said.

"Yes," Jack answered and moved to sign the register that Pearl Sloan shoved in front of him. Twenty feet away, Teddy eyed the back of his father's head as he concentrated on his signature.

There was further confusion then about the room arrangements. Should Jack share a room with his father and let Teddy and his brother Benedict sleep together? He should but he wouldn't; not with Barney's midnight washboard rasp. Not with the notorious early-morning wheeze that came from six decades of cigarette smoking, a half-million European and American cigarettes in all, Chesterfields, Rothmans, and a heady Turkish brand that together had produced the heavy chest whistle that started its long ascent through Barney's lungs and esophagus, then noisily forced its way into the larynx and throat, emerging finally, thick with sputum, through his mouth or nose in a wavering, half-hysterical shriek. No, he wouldn't sleep a wink alongside that.

"Pa," Jack said, "I'm getting you your own room. You'll like that."

Pearl Sloan would put him on the same floor, she said, next to his daughter-in-law's old friend Charlotte Melnicov. Miss Melnicov would be pleased, Pearl offered. The Lewins, father and two sons, would share Bea and Marion's old room in the old arrangement, slightly rearranged, Jack and Teddy in the flower-embroidered double bed and Ben isolated at their feet in Teddy's cot.

"That's what your wife reserved for you," Pearl said, smiling at last.

"Have you seen my son?" Jack asked, smiling back.

Behind the palm, Teddy made a move.

"Teddy? He was here early in the afternoon seeing your wife off."

"And Miss Melnicov?"

"Miss Melnicov went fishing with Mr. Bernard," Pearl Sloan said. "In the Bay. Maybe your son went for a dip. I'll ask around. But first a word about the dining room."

There was a problem. If they simply substituted Jack, Barney, and Ben for Bea and Marion, table number five would be left with only one woman, Charlotte Melnicov. That wouldn't do. Pearl Sloan looked put off again. She checked the list of incoming guests, running her finger up and down the register, searching for a single. "I'll tell you what," she said. "I'll open up the table and give you one more. A lady from Philadelphia. Sukenik. That way, let me see, you'll have Miss Melnicov, Miss Sukenik, Mr. Levi, the Kessler men, you, your sons, your father." She was counting on her fingers. "Nine people. Very congenial, very friendly, very nice. The ladies will like it."

"I don't want to eat with a bunch of old Jews," Barney Levin said.

"Pa."

"I got enough *alte cockers* at home."

"You're eating with us," Jack said, "at our table. Now don't make trouble."

"Why don't you go upstairs and get comfortable," Pearl suggested quickly. "Saul will bring your bags up." She gave Jack two keys, sent Hy off for Saul, called for the next guests, tried to keep the line moving. Bad weather. It could ruin everything.

Then Teddy finally emerged from his palm. He seemed to be slightly oblivious to Sloan's lobby as he approached his father, a little absent-minded. A spume of guilt trailed him, an air of false innocence. He was wearing his navy-blue trunks with the patch, sneakers, T-shirt.

"Daaaaaad!"

Jack grabbed him, held him to himself, clasped his head between his hands. "Look at you," he said. "You're taller in one week. This place must agree with you." He shook his son by the shoulders, held him out at arm's length.

"I didn't expect you so early," Teddy said.

"Look at you."

"It's great here," Teddy said. "I really like it."

"Look at your tan."

"I'm on the beach all day practically."

They began to murmur to each other, standing in front of the desk, a perfunctory question each about Bea, Marion, and Ben, a few words about Teddy's angelfish, something about the piano, about the weather, the heat. Jack's thin moustache twitched with pleasure. Teddy couldn't stop talking. To each question, he offered a long, slow response filled with irrelevant detail. No, he hadn't practiced the piano, he was just taking a few days off, what difference would it make? The piano at Sloan's was terrible, anyway. The sounding board was cracked and some of the black keys got stuck when the weather was damp. The food inside was good, there were a lot of choices every day. Their waiter's name was Saul. Saul was studying to be a lawyer. Jack would like him. Also, he said, they had to share a bath upstairs and the bathtub itself had some rust marks on the bottom. He was encased in dreaminess as he confronted his father, barely touching him, hovering at the very rim of reality like a hummingbird dizzy from the beating of its own wings. Father and son looked so alike standing there, slim as Sinai reeds, small-boned, straight, with thin aristocratic noses and strange, unexpected blue eyes, a Nordic resonance sounding faintly beyond them, something exotic to that lobby. Face to face there, perfectly self-contained, they seemed like near-identical reflections in a genetic mirror that showed no visible flaws. Then Barney, too, wheezing with impatience, grabbed Teddy, held him by the wrists, a powerful muzhik's hold, even though his right hand was missing the middle finger, holding him there as though he were a calf or a newborn foal, piercing him with a peasant's inch-by-inch examination. There was no resemblance between grandfather and son. "Skinny," he said contemptuously. "Like a rail, like a marink."

"Grandpa, you're hurting me."

Barney let go, pulled roughly at Teddy's ear. That was his way, a hug here, a yank there, a little pinch when nobody was looking; inflict a touch of affectionate pain and no one would ever be able to forget you. They all laughed. It was the oldest routine in the family. "I'm glad you could come," Teddy said, not knowing whether he meant it or not, and shyly clapped his grandfather on the shoulder.

"Well," Jack said, pleased at the exchange. "You're the old hand around here. Show us where our rooms are."

Teddy guided them upstairs, through the midafternoon crowd sleepily milling around the lobby. They were waiting for the rain actually to start pouring, looking for a little conversation or a bridge game while they waited, a few of the men trying to put a pinochle hand together, or some rummy, two- three- four-handed, it didn't matter.

"It's too many people," Barney complained, looking over the lobby from the stairwell.

"They're usually at the beach," Teddy said.

"Where are the young people?"

". . . . . ."

"I don't want to spend all my time with a lot of old Jews. I told you."

"Pa."

"I want some life around me. It's like a funeral down there."

Jack rolled his eyes, led the way. "Which floor?" he asked.

"One more," Teddy said.

"So, where's the ocean?" Barney asked.

Teddy pointed east with his thumb.

"It's far?"

"About a hundred feet."

"A-ha. And the waves, a man can stand up?"

"It's not bad. There are plenty of lifeguards," Teddy said. "Down the hall now, Dad."

They crowded into the room. The cot stood unfolded in its usual place, already made up for the evening. Jack sat on the bed, bounced up and down, checked the closet, looked in every bureau drawer. "Your mother didn't leave a message for me by any chance, did she?" He slammed a drawer shut.

Teddy thought a moment, looked for a signal. "Well, you know they had to rush to make the train," he said.

"So?"

"There wasn't much time."

"What are you trying to tell me, that she didn't leave a message?"

"Yes."

"Nothing?" Jack asked. "Not even her love?"

"Oh, Dad," Teddy began. "You know that. Nobody has to leave a message." But his voice had taken on an edge: let Jack ask Bea herself for her messages and leave Theodore Lewin out of it.

Jack smiled. "They have a good time?"

"Marion didn't want to go home. She's mad at me because I'm staying."

"Next year," Jack said vaguely. "We'll all come together. You'll see." He was staring at himself in the mirror, cocking his head from one side to the other, making little moues, flirting. "I need some sun," he said.

"You'll be tan in a couple of days," Teddy said, watching his father. He was as vain as Bea, as comfortable in front of a mirror as his wife, giving back gaze for steady gaze, with as sure and passionate an eye for his own qualities, his own virtues. He smiled into the mirror then, slightly embarrassed, turned his open self-admiration into an examination of his teeth.

"Everybody thought your wife was the most beautiful lady in the hotel," Teddy said blandly.

"They did?" Jack grimaced at the mirror.

"She was, too." Teddy paused. Then: "She could have had a date every night."

"Is that so?"

"Yes."

"A date with whom?"

"All kinds of people."

"You don't say?"

"She was the center of everything. You can ask anybody."

"And what does the center of everything amount to around here?"

"Well, there are a lot of people—"

"Never mind," Jack said, snapping it out. "I'll find out soon enough." He sat down again on the bed, plumped a pillow. "I brought your *Dick Tracys*."

"Oh, Dad, that's great."

"You can have them as soon as my bag comes up."

"So, where do I sleep?" Barney finally asked from the doorway. He sounded testy.

"I'll show you," Teddy said.

Teddy took his grandfather down the hall, unlocked the door, gave him the key. They both walked in. "If I bend down to tie my shoes, I'll be out in the hall," Barney said. "What's that out there?" He headed for the window.

"That's the Surf."

"A hotel?"

"Yes."

Barney was checking the back wall of the Surf, the fire-escape that lay just outside his window. "The screen has a hole," he said.

"The bugs won't find it in the dark," Teddy said.

Barney laughed, a cracked, phlegm-filled chortle that died almost as soon as the sound broke in the room. He reached for

Teddy's ear again, but Teddy slipped away, sidestepping his grandfather neatly. "Is the Melnicov holding her breath for me?" Barney asked.

"She can't wait. She talks about you night and day."

"She's got a boy friend?"

"She's seeing someone."

"A rich man?"

"How would I know?"

"Don't get so huffy-puffy. I asked a simple question."

"It's none of my business."

". . . . . ."

"Ah, Teddy, just because your grandfather likes the blondes, especially . . ." Barney cupped his huge hands in front of his chest, pretended to squeeze.

"Come on, Grandpa."

"Don't worry. The Melnicov got no use for Barney Levin and Barney Levin got no use for her."

Saul appeared then with Barney's bag. Teddy introduced them. Saul nodded myopically. "My son will give you a tip," Barney said. "Down the hall." He began to unpack, three sports shirts, three undershorts, four pairs of socks, a second pair of slacks, a back corset, a toilet kit, five bottles of medicine, for coughs, for open gum sores, for flatulence, for headache, and the fifth unidentified. He examined each bottle as he unpacked them, read the labels aloud to Teddy. One spoonful each four hours until condition clears. Once every twenty-four hours, do not continue without prescription. One after each meal, with water. Two every four hours, keep out of children's reach. The fifth bottle he set on the bed without comment.

"What's that for?" Teddy asked.

Barney sighed. "That's for old men," he said. "Ask me no questions. Now, do me a favor, put my clothes away."

Teddy arranged his grandfather's clothes in the two drawers, huge undershorts, big enough for a horse, lisle socks with arrows running up the sides, green slacks, sports shirts with flowers on them six inches in diameter, ugly back corset, set his medicine neatly on top of the bureau alongside his toilet kit. "Come, I'll show you the bathroom," Teddy said.

Then Ben arrived as they walked into the hall, unexpectedly staggering up the stairs with an army duffel bag slung over his shoulder, somebody's serial number stenciled onto the canvas, a reject picked up on Ninth Avenue in New York. "Ben!" A yell from Teddy Lewin. Jack stuck his head out of his room, pulled back in surprise. Then he walked into the hallway, clapped his first son on the shoulder, embraced him clumsily on his free side, pulled away, examined his height, weight, growth, embraced him again. He was a little more diffident with this arrival, slightly more self-conscious, wore a guarded look that seemed prepared for any response. Ben was not Teddy, never had been. Meanwhile, Barney was on top of his grandson with a good, solid slap on the back that shook Ben and almost threw him off balance.

"You'll kill me one of these days," Ben said, swinging his duffel bag onto the floor.

"Ben," Teddy said again.

There was a jabber of men's voices, grandfather, father, two sons, a willful crosspurpose of questions and answers, a mindless attempt to assert the new reality in the small hotel room in which they now stood, their own presence momentarily enclosed by Ben's, by Ben finally there and accounted for. He was reunited with them at last, after a summer in the strange, threatening bog of Manhattan. There he had lived on the money he had earned delivering groceries at home for the Brookfield Avenue Market, testing a new life, or lives, in the heart of an unknown city, rehearsing his own future in a cheap room filled with metal furniture at the William Sloane House, courtesy of the Christian Association. Four hundred other young men, all on the loose, lived at Sloane House in midtown Manhattan at the same time, chasing the same thing. Ben would tell his family all about it when he was good and ready. It might be tomorrow, it might be next week, or never. That's how he would keep them jumping. In the meantime, they could hardly wait. It had been the subject of Baltimore family conversation all summer, between Jack and Bea, between Marion and Teddy, between them all, Jack and his father, Bea and her sisters as well, Ben's adventure, Ben's journey, his adolescent daring, his life.

"It's muggy in here," Ben said.

"It's going to rain," Teddy said.

"What's the weather been?" Ben asked.

"Sun every day. Perfect."

"Just when I come," Ben asked.

"It'll be all blue skies tomorrow. You'll see."

Ben hefted his duffel bag onto the double bed, sat down alongside it, ran his hands along the inside of his thighs. "This room's not much bigger than the one I had at Sloane House. Is the cot for me?"

"Yes," Jack said. "Teddy and I are going to share the bed."

Teddy felt a moment's shock. He hadn't slept in a bed with his father since he was four. What had he expected, that Ben would share the double bed with his father and he would remain in the cot? He should have known better. He sat down on the bed now, taking his brother in. Ben looked like his mother, like her family, had the same black hair, silky and full of waves, the same even, unmarred features, a Sandler look of fixed assurance and self-involvement out of which a certain kind of excessive expectation is sometimes bred. He needed a shave now, his clothes looked a little dirty, his loafers were unpolished, white wool socks dusty with travel and perhaps a day's wear too much. To Teddy, Ben seemed full of weary sophistication, full of knowledge, experience, full of lived-out youth. His lazy, curving posture said it, his voice, his impatient bored eyes, his restlessness. One summer in New York.

"Did you have a good time?" Teddy asked.

"A good time? Sure, if a good time's the test."

Teddy snagged on that for a moment, then rushed on. "What'd you do with yourself all the time?"

Ben yawned. "I wouldn't know where to begin to tell you."

"At the beginning."

". . . . . ."

"What was it like?"

". . . . . ."

"Come on."

"Well, I guess it was a little like traveling around Europe."

"You mean it was so strange? New York is so foreign?"

"I mean being on my own."

"You liked that?"

"That was the whole point."

"Were you always alone?"

"A lot of the time."

"Didn't you have any friends?"

"Here and there."

"Who?"

"You wouldn't know if I told you."

"Come on, Ben."

". . . . . ."

"Try."

". . . . . ."

"Then tell me about the Fair."

"It's junk. I only went once."

"Come on."

"I'm not kidding you."

"Tell me about it."

"It's all a junkyard."

"Oh, Ben."

"There's not an acre of authentic imagination in the whole place."

"You just want to criticize."

"You asked."

"There must be something good."

"There's nothing there that connects with the life of real people."

"What about the Futurama?"

"Fu-tu-ra-ma," Ben said, exaggerating disgust. "All you see are what the big corporations want you to see. It's all propaganda, brilliant propaganda on behalf of capitalism. It's all an expression of the Fascist imagination at work. There's absolutely no difference between the big corporations in this country and the Fascist states. Power, strength, control, that's the way the game's played. Screw everybody, that's the way it's played. Christ, the Italian Pavilion looks like the world's biggest hard-on with a waterfall running down it."

Standing in the doorway, Barney snorted.

"I saw pictures of it," Teddy said, laughing. "It doesn't look so bad. I wouldn't mind the chance to see it for real."

"You'd hate it once you were there."

"Maybe I wouldn't."

"Take my word for it. The best thing at the Fair is the bobsled run."

"You're kidding again."

"Quit doubting everything I tell you. Why should I kid you? The bobsled is really the best thing at the Fair. It's simple, direct, and to the point. It has a beginning, middle, and end. Also, it provides a universal thrill."

"Come on, Ben."

"I told you, I'm telling you the truth."

"But everybody says the Fair is wonderful."

"Who's everybody?"

"All the magazines, the newspapers. *Life. Look.* Everybody."

"For God's sake, Teddy, that's nothing but publicity. Where's your head? You really are a gullible kid."

And that was that, for Benedict Lewin, for the moment. He wanted a bath, so did Barney and Jack. They went back to the business of settling in, of arranging themselves for the week.

Ben unpacked his duffel bag, put his stuff away. Barney ran his bath, complained that there wasn't enough hot water. Jack, meanwhile, wandered around the room, opened the bureau drawers again, one by one, then the closet door. He stuck his head in. There was a pause. Teddy and Ben watched him. "I can smell your mother in here," Jack finally said. "I thought there was something when I came in."

They were all silent. Jack moved around the room with a distracted look, then lay down on the bed. "Everything smells of your mother," he said.

"You want to take a nap?" Teddy asked.

"Maybe," Jack said.

"I can go downstairs," Teddy said.

"In a few minutes."

Then, as he spoke, Charlotte drifted in, like a strand of seaweed beached by the late afternoon tide. She was exhausted from fishing in Barnegat Bay, she said. They had worked hard, caught nothing. It had been something of a bore. She and Larry Bernard had grown tired of each other's company, especially in the face of failure. Now she kissed them all in the bedroom, pecking Jack's cheek, hugging Ben to herself.

"You're almost a man," she said, half smiling. She gripped him by the upper arms, looked him in the eye, her head tilted admiringly. "Wait'll your mother gets her hands on you."

Ben reddened pleasantly. "Good to see you, Charlotte," he said.

"I'm glad you're here," she said. "I'm glad you're all here." Then, pulling the pins out of her hair, letting it fall suddenly shining to her waist with an uncharacteristic, brisk shake of her head, Charlotte too went off to bathe and take a nap before dinner.

Within a few minutes, Jack began to snore lightly on the double bed. At his father's feet, waiting on the cot for a free bath, Ben lay on his back and read *The Good Earth* in paperback. The room was silent. The conversation was finished. Teddy changed his clothes then, careful not to disturb his brother, careful not to move too fast or too hard, careful even about his breathing. After a final glance in the mirror, one last attempt to make his part straight with his middle finger, he headed for the lobby, pulling the door to with the faintest of clicks. There he sat for an hour or so watching the card games. Pinochle. Rummy. One table of contract bridge. There was nothing else to do, no place else to go. His friends were everywhere in the lobby, Gus Levi writing cards again in his perfect handwriting, squinting at a desk in the corner, Erich Kessler somberly coaching his father over a hand of solitaire, the Talles boys politely flanking their mother on a couch, sitting upright on either side of her like courtly Spanish pageboys. It was true what his father had said upstairs, you could smell his mother in their room, you could smell Bea in the thin-walled closet and the bureau drawers, sweet talc from England, toilet water, something else pervading it, something domestic and private and essential, her very self. She would be at Sloan's with them for the week. She would be an invisible, unpaid guest at the hotel; they would not be alone.

Outside now, it had started to rain. A heavy steam settled in the air, and inside Sloan's the guests began to sweat with uncontrollable human humidity. It was the same across the street at the Cotswold, the same for the corseted lady in the ginger wig and all her Virginia and Philadelphia friends, the same at the Marlborough-Blenheim, the Shelburne, and the Ritz, an indisputable hothouse fact about Atlantic City in the rain that had never made its way into any of the promotion brochures.

2

Sunday night supper at Sloan's was Pearl and Hy's own tribute to the National Recovery Act, a depression extravaganza formulated in economic despair six seasons before, back in the first year of FDR's reign, experimented with then for two seasons more until it became clear to the proprietors that it not only pleased their guests but helped to attract them. It was finally fixed forever, in terms of menu and style, in the summer of 1936, when Pearl Sloan grew bored with the planning of it, and that was how it had remained. By then it had grown into a thirty-foot shivering buffet of silver herring, whitefish, carp, and bony salmon, all refrigerated in golden aspic. Alongside the fish rotated lazy susans of shredded cole slaw and green lettuce salads, black olives with pits like bullets from the hills of California, sweet New York pickles, and fat bursting Jersey radishes; plates of soft finger rolls and moist crackers; and iced tea and coffee, brackishly standing in urns two feet high. For those who needed a little warmth, who could not subsist for the evening without one steaming dish, there was a huge square of three-inch-high macaroni, stone-heavy with baked Italian cheese, egg noodles from Manischewitz, durum wheat, and sodium additive. Later in the meal there were pale sponge cakes out of Pearl's own ovens, pastries and fruit, and ice cream made that afternoon on the other side of Atlantic Avenue. Two bouquets of Ventnor roses flanked the table at either end, a dignified, long-stemmed profusion of reds and deep yellows that cost a small fortune. The long table at the head of the room was planned like a major still life. It contained Pearl's entire aesthetic credo—an elaborate, nourishing watercolor, rich in carefully mixed pastels and sweeping, therapeutic brush strokes that had made the early evening dinner, the special sustaining Sunday night supper, irresistibly novel, irresistibly festive for more than half a decade; and at the same time also released at least half the college boys, including Saul, for the evening so that they could momentarily escape the damp sponge of hotel domesticity and take in a movie.

At table number five, Charlotte Melnicov set her plate down and examined her supper companions. Everything seemed in reasonable order, although not everyone had arrived as yet. Charlotte stood there for the moment as sole authority for the table's etiquette; in her hands, she seemed to suggest, reposed the good manners and mutual respect of her male companions, some of whom were already seated at the table. Charlotte had washed her hair before supper, an elaborate, difficult operation, lasting a half hour, then brushed it wet against her scalp. Her part was now arrow straight and gleaming, right down the middle. "Well," she said, "how shall we arrange ourselves?" There was a pause, a long silence, before she went on. "Gus, do you want to stay where you are? Jack, you come alongside me. Teddy . . . all right, stay where you are. Has anybody seen the Kesslers? My God, the humidity in this place."

They all remained where they pleased, Jack and Ben flanking Charlotte, Teddy next to Gustav Levi and, without a word, began to eat their cool buffet delicacies. Barney was still in the supper line at Pearl's grand table. "The heat," Charlotte said.

"It's terrible," Jack said. "It was just like this in Baltimore this morning."

"Poor Bea," Charlotte said. "To get home on a night like this."

"Marion's probably under the hose right now," Teddy said.

". . . and the Good Humor man's tinkling down the street with six kids riding on each running board," Ben said. The brothers forced a laugh.

"I was in Baltimore once in August," Gustav Levi began.

"You don't have to say it," Ben said.

"Actually, it wasn't so bad. I was taken to the country club every day. I went swimming, I was even able to play a little golf."

"When you're with the rich, it's always easy," Ben said, forcing a laugh again.

"It made it bearable," Gus Levi said.

"Where were you?" Teddy asked. "The Woodholme?"

"That sounds familiar."

"There are two clubs," Teddy said. "And they're both different."

Gustav Levi shrugged. "I'm not sure. Is one of them yours?"

"Not really," Ben broke in.

"All my aunts and uncles—" Teddy began.

"It's nothing to brag about," Ben said to his brother. Then he turned back to Gus Levi. "But in fact, if you could remember the name of the club, Woodholme or Suburban, we'd be able to instantly tell you the kind of people your hosts were. We'd be able to identify their politics, how they felt about the world, how they felt about themselves, how they felt about each other."

Gustav Levi laughed. "That's all?"

"It's true," Teddy said. "We could."

"Well, then let's say I was at the Woodholme. In fact, I think I was."

"Eastern European Jews," Ben said, popping a radish into his mouth. "Mostly second generation, some first. Still very hungry for everything, still scared of the past. All Democrats, politically, with perhaps a half-dozen exceptions for patronage reasons. Judges, that kind of thing. All Zionists. All on the make."

"Ben," Jack said.

"It's all verifiable, Papa. You know that."

"It's true," Teddy added. "All my aunts and uncles—"

"Not yet quite at home," Ben went on, "with the symphony or art museums or literature, but beginning to cast flirtatious looks in those directions, beginning to get a crush on culture and other aspects of Anglo-Saxon life in our Anglo-Saxon world. Also beginning to corner the money in town."

Gus Levi looked impressed. "And the other club?" he asked.

"Germans," Charlotte said. *"Deutschen."*

"Very sure of themselves," Ben said, "but as Jews full of self-hatred. Old mercantile money, mostly, a couple of outstanding collections of contemporary art, one or two, some interesting eccentrics, sexual and otherwise, and probably more family idiots than inbreeding and the law should allow. Mixed politics, conservative practices, liberal instincts that go back to the 1848 revolution. In general, anti-Zionist and fiercely so. Terrified of being accused of double loyalties. Also terrified of the Woodholme and that gang which they see as the wave of the future. Which it is. Yet still a home to a small core group of outstanding families, outstanding in the community and among themselves."

"And if one were to choose?"

"One never chooses. One is not allowed to choose. One goes where one belongs."

Gustav Levi poked at the aspic on his plate. "And you know where you belong?"

"He makes too much of it," Jack said, smiling reluctantly. "Don't take it too seriously."

"You take it seriously enough, Pops," Ben said.

"You always blow it up."

"It's the way he says it is," Charlotte said. "There's no way of getting away from it."

"Well," Jack said. "Two country clubs. Who cares?"

"You care," Ben said. "So do we. So does everybody else. Despite themselves. The whole business says something about the fate of the Jews in this country."

"There you go again."

"It does. I can't help that."

"Since when are you so worried about the Jews? I thought it was capitalism that bothered you these days."

"Oh, Dad," Teddy said. "We're just having a discussion."

"It's a common enough social phenomenon, especially in old cities like Baltimore," Gus Levi said, equably. "And it's interesting in itself."

"When you think of everything that's going on in the world," Jack began irritably, then subsided. "Where is Grandpa?" he asked, after a moment. "What's he doing?"

"I think he's coming now," Teddy said.

Jack peered anxiously over their heads, found Barney, who had been slowly making his way along the buffet table, testing each dish. "I want to be sure he eats the right food."

"He's all right, Dad. Don't worry so much."

Barney now approached them, silverware in one hand, food in the other. When he reached the table, he nodded at everyone, lingering a moment over Charlotte. "Miss Melnicov," he said, exaggerating the courtesy. "Mr. Levin," she said, almost inaudibly. Then he found a place across the table from her, began to eat as soon as he sat down.

"Mr. Lewin," Gus Levi called to him heartily. "If these are your grandsons, I congratulate you. They're highly intelligent young men, a pleasure to be with. Already I count Teddy among my close friends, as I did his mother before she left."

"Levin," Barney said.

"We're Lewin," Teddy said out of the side of his mouth. "He's Levin."

"Either way, what's the difference, we're all from the same tribe."

Barney threw Gus Levi a suspicious look, as though Gus were trying to sell him a piece of questionable merchandise. Then he took a mouthful of macaroni, began to chew the noodles without responding.

"We are, you know," Gus Levi persisted. "There's no getting away from it. It's the same tribe, maybe even closer than that. Levi, Levin, Lewin. It's all the same, it all comes from the Hebrew name Lewy."

"I never thought of us having the same name," Teddy said. "You mean we might be related?"

"It's not impossible," Gus Levi said. "If you tracked it down, who knows what you'd find?"

"That would really be funny if we were related."

"Who knows?" Gus Levi said. "Especially among Jews. Actually, the etymology of the name itself is ambiguous, no question of that. In Hebrew, the root *lwh* can stand for three totally different things. And all of them have been associated with the name Lewy at one time or another " They all sat in silence then, suddenly mulling the possibilities of a shared familial destiny, waiting for Gus Levi to go on. "One meaning," he continued, "is whirling around, like a dervish, spinning so fast that you lose your senses. I think that has to do with getting carried away by ecstasy while worshiping God. That's all that could mean."

"Sounds pagan to me," Ben said.

"It probably was. Religious emotion was very uninhibited then."

"So was religious belief," Ben said.

"Exactly," Gus Levi said. "Compared to the modern world, well, there's no comparison, it's beyond our imagination. And in that it's just like everything else. We can't grasp the power of that imagination, it was wholly without inhibition."

"There are things like that now," Teddy said.

"In our world?"

Teddy nodded mildly, looked to his brother for confirmation.

"What would you call Nuremberg?" Ben asked Mr. Levi.

"That has nothing to do with God," Gus Levi said.

"It has something to do with religion," Ben said. "It has something to do with ecstasy."

Gus Levi thought a moment, looked serious. "Yes, you're right," he said slowly. "But it's the blood side only. It's the side that has foreclosed on its own humanity, the side where the enemy always lives."

"Well, what about the Lewys?" Jack asked impatiently. "Let's get back to them."

"The Lewys, yes. Well," Gus Levi said, making a conscious effort to sound more cheerful, "one meaning of *lwh* is whirling, losing your senses. Another meaning is attachment, the act of staying with someone, the decision to be faithful. In the Bible, Leah named her son Levi because she hoped that his birth would keep her husband at her side and renew their marriage. It was taken very seriously. But at the same time it had a religious meaning, too. It could also mean being attached to God, the act of staying with Divinity. That meant someone holy, someone with ordained religious duties, like a priest, which in fact is what all the Levis actually were."

"I know that," Teddy said.

"Don't interrupt so much," Jack said.

"And since the priesthood was hereditary," Gus Levi continued, "the name Lewy and all its variations stuck through the generations. It became almost a genetic thing. Every Lewy father passed the name and all the religious obligations that went with it down to his sons, and they in turn passed it down to theirs, and so on and on and on across continents and through centuries. If the written records survived, all of us could probably trace our families back three thousand years."

"If the written records survived," Teddy said, "couldn't everyone?"

"They probably could. But *we* would know exactly which road to take and none of it would look strange to us. You can be sure we've all been Lewys all these years."

"I'm not Lewy," Barney said. "I'm Levin, from Lomza, Poland."

"I understand," Gus Levi said. "But your family didn't just spring up in spontaneous generation out of Polish soil."

Barney then threw his son a look so accusing, so foul, that Jack visibly pulled himself up in his chair at its force. Teddy and

Ben felt it, too; so did Charlotte. They understood its impulse, recognized all the murderous ingredients of that deadly glare. It was notorious in the family. Everyone ran from it. Tonight, its spirit had been summoned by an incomprehensible trinity made up of something called *lwh*, etymology, and spontaneous generation, and exacerbated by Gustav Levi's high-minded manner; and Barney would not let his son forget it. In revenge, he belched loudly. Ben tittered, Teddy turned red. Across the table, Jack exchanged brief signals of oncoming panic with his sons. It was another family habit. Then he pretended to relax, along with Teddy and Ben, and turned away from his father disapprovingly as Pearl Sloan came up to pay their table a visit.

"Everything good, everything right, everything okay?" Pearl Sloan said, her voice rising with the question in an attempt to be solicitous. She was like that only on Sunday night, already knowing the answer to her question. Now she examined each plate at the table as her guests murmured their enthusiasm at her. "Did you ever see such a picture?" she asked, turning to a woman standing behind her. "Look at that plate. This is what you have to look forward to. When people say Sloan's, this is what they mean. Anyway," she added, turning back to table number five, "I bring you Miss Etta Sukenik, your new table partner. Mr. Levi. Mr. Lewin. The boys. Mr. Levin . . . you see, I remembered. Miss Melnicov." She nodded at everyone, extended an authoritative hand as she mentioned each name. There was a minute's general relief, everyone's attention shifted painlessly, and all the men, with the exception of Barney, made an attempt to rise to their feet. Miss Sukenik thanked them, urged them to seat themselves, sat herself down across from Charlotte. Pearl Sloan whispered a few words in her ear, patted her shoulder, offered encouragement.

"You're not eating my fish," she said to Teddy, straightening up.

"It makes me break out."

"It's fresh from the Bay. It was swimming in the saltwater this morning."

Teddy gave her a hapless look. What can I do? it said; in a perfect world, I'd die for your fish.

"Where else can you get fish like this?" she asked, moving off to the adjoining table without waiting for an answer. "Hello, my friends," she called to table number six. "Everything good, everything . . ."

"What kind of glasses is that?" Barney asked Etta Sukenik from her left.

"Pince-nez," Etta Sukenik said, holding them up on a black ribbon made of fine grosgrain. "Like so." She placed them over the bridge of her nose, gazed at Barney affably. "They give me something to play with," she said. "All children, of whatever age, need toys." She took the glasses off and let them dangle from her neck. She had beautiful diction.

"Sunday night is buffet," Charlotte said. "You'll have to serve yourself. Over there." She tried a cordial smile that might still suggest certain unstated limits.

"Ah, so," Etta Sukenik said, getting to her feet hesitantly.

"Try macaroni," Barney said. He, too, got to his feet. "Macaroni and the herring."

"Pa," Jack said.

Barney mumbled something under his breath, something soft in Yiddish, to protect an old man from the follies of his children, while Etta Sukenik headed safely for the buffet table. He then sat down and glowered at each of his dinner companions in turn. The table became silent again. Finally, Ben began to squirm in his chair. He cleared his throat a couple of times, spoke. "Weren't you saying," he called to Gus Levi, "that in Hebrew the root *lwh* has three separate meanings?"

"That's right."

"Well," Ben said, "I think you forgot one."

"Let's see." Gus Levi began to count on his fingers. "There's whirling. That's one. There's being attached. That's two. And then the third is to pledge, to give one's self over, the act of being vowed to Divinity. That's the third."

Ben considered it for a moment. "I think maybe the order should be reversed," he said.

"I don't understand."

"I mean there's a logical progression if you reverse the order you listed them in. That way, they're not three separate meanings at all. See what I mean?"

"That's very clever," Gus Levi said. "You mean pledging, first, then attaching, finally passion, ecstasy, devotion. It makes sense, it makes a human process. I never considered that."

"Well, it's a thought," Ben said. "And not much else. Anyway, what does it all come to?"

"How do you mean?"

"What does it all add up to?"

"You mean what does it have to do with our lives?"

"With our world, now."

"More than nothing," Gus Levi said drily, "and less than something, perhaps."

"Seriously."

"What should it add up to?"

"I'm asking you."

"Ben," Jack warned.

"It's all right," Gus Levi said. "I've heard these questions before."

"And I've been asking them for years," Ben said good-naturedly. "And all I ever get, naturally, are the same old enigmatic answers."

"But every question doesn't have to have an answer. It's enough sometimes just to ask them."

"There's not much satisfaction in that."

"Only when you're young. Forgive me for saying that, but it's true. You want me to give you an answer that will be the answer to all questions. You want me to state revelations that will explain everything, clear up all mysteries. Nothing less will do. But for me, it's a losing game. My goals are too modest for you. I'm just trying to ask a few questions, look for a few answers."

"Then what is the answer to this one?"

"To the business about *lwh?*"

"What does it all come to?"

"It comes to a way of connecting," Gus Levi said impatiently. "It adds up to a way of learning how to link your life with others, now and then."

"At last," Ben said, his good-natured tone vanishing. "The face of humanism. I knew it was coming. It always does. Gentility, human relationships, culture. Doesn't all that seem inadequate to you, almost obscenely inadequate?"

"Next to what, may I ask?"

"Next to what is at stake in the world today."

"Which is?" Gustav Levi asked, shrinking a little.

"Survival."

". . . . . ."

"Life or death for all of us, in an age when those are the only real choices."

"With you it's everything or nothing?" Gus Levi asked.

"At this point in history, yes."

"There's no room for small victories anymore?"

"Small victories?" Ben asked. "Is that what you think the world is waiting for? Is that what you think they're going to allow you?"

"The world . . ." Gus Levi began. But the exchange broke down under its own weight. They were all uncomfortable with it, wanted it over with. It was a losing game, as Gus Levi had predicted.

"I think," Teddy said, a little too eagerly, "that you really both think the same thing."

"Don't get so nervous just because we disagree," Ben said.

"I'm not," Teddy said.

"Mr. Levi and I understand each other very well, disagree or not. Wouldn't you say so, Mr. Levi?"

"I would have to agree with that, at least," Gus Levi said, laughing politely.

"Well, it's too much for me," Charlotte said. "I'm not used to such deep talk. I don't want to think about all that. I don't want to think about survival. That's not what life's about, anyway. Animals survive. Men live."

"I must agree with that, too," Gus Levi said, sounding surprised. They were all quiet then for a few minutes, silently working away at their fish, their salads, their heavy macaroni.

Then Etta Sukenik and the Kesslers arrived at the same moment, carrying silverware and dinners. There was an amiable moment or two of social confusion at the table; everyone was introduced, Etta Sukenik to Frederick and Erich Kessler, the Kesslers to Jack and Ben Lewin, then to Barney Levin; everyone was seated, everyone was finally dining together. The air began to clear. There was the sound of laughter; even Barney joined in. At a question from Charlotte, Frederick Kessler told them about the Hedy Lamarr movie. He rolled his eyes in dismay. Erich confirmed his father's opinion; it was a waste of time and the theater had been half empty. Charlotte talked about fishing, about the boredom of it, about sitting out in the middle of the Bay in a tiny boat that didn't move. All the time she talked she kept looking over their heads at the lawyers' table across the dining room. The subject of etymology came up again. The Kesslers were asked by Gus Levi about the meaning of their name and discovered that they had no ready answer. It had never occurred to them to wonder about it. There had always been Kesslers in Frankfurt, in all of Hesse and the Rhineland. There were Kessler cousins in Bremerhaven, Lübeck, and upper Silesia; a branch of the family lived in Berlin and there was a bachelor uncle living alone in Bonn; the name had been in Germany forever.

What did the name mean? Ben asked. Father and son looked

at each other. Maybe, Frederick Kessler said, thinking it out slowly, somebody who makes a . . . *Wie heisst das?* he asked Erich. Kettle, Erich said. Somebody, Frederick Kessler explained to the table, who makes a kettle. That is a *Ketzler,* Erich said softly. *Ketzler, Kessler,* his father said, it's the same thing. Kettle makers. Somebody probably once made kettles in my family hundreds of years ago. He looked astonished at the idea. Then, while Jack asked her leading questions, Etta Sukenik explained herself to her table companions.

"An opera singer?" Jack said.

Etta Sukenik nodded. Jack Lewin had never met an opera singer; neither had anyone else at the table, not even Gustav Levi. There was a moment's dark silence, darkest at Charlotte's place, where Charlotte assumed a brooding look full of wariness, an attempt to assimilate the information. But Teddy's eyes opened wide. An opera singer, another musician, a professional. There were not many opera singers at the Peabody. Meanwhile, Etta Sukenik waited; she knew the refrain. She sat there totally at ease, her pince-nez resting on her high pigeon chest, an imposing woman in her late thirties, with a strong, tapered soprano's body and an assertive mind that wholly accepted everything that came its way.

"Have we ever heard of you?" Jack asked hesitantly.

Etta Sukenik laughed. "That's for you to say. Have you ever heard of me?"

"I don't think so," Gus Levi said. "No offense meant."

"Actually," she said, "I sing with the San Carlo in Philly, all the lyric spinto roles, and I do the Easter show every year at Radio City Music Hall."

"Are you a star?" Teddy asked.

"Sometimes, when I sing at Radio City, people ask for my autograph. At the San Carlo, nobody's interested in autographs. What they want is a big sound, a good top, and a performance that moves."

"What's a good top?" Jack asked.

"Strong high notes."

"A-ha," Jack said.

"Philly's got a lot of Italians and they all come to the San Carlo. The Protestants go to hear Stokowski's orchestra under the new man Ormandy."

"What do you do at Radio City?" Teddy asked.

"Have you ever seen the Easter show?"

"No."

"I stand on a platform in a white dress, holding white lilies in my arms, and I sing about Jesus. I get fresh lilies for each performance."

"Are you a Jew?" Barney asked.

"Of course I'm a Jew. What did you think?"

"What should I think?" he said.

"I went to the opera very much in Frankfurt," Frederick Kessler said. "We had a whole new Ring two years ago. Furtwaengler himself conducted. He came all the way from Berlin. Do you sing the Ring?" This short speech, full of quiet excitement, almost lost Frederick Kessler his battle with the letter *r* once and for all. "Opewa," "Fwankfurt," "Do you sing the Wing?" is what his friends heard him say. They all looked down at their plates.

"I don't touch Wagner," Etta Sukenik said, meeting his eyes to answer him. "It breaks down the voice."

"Did you know Rosa Raisa?" Gus Levi asked.

"No."

"She was a Jew, too."

"So is Alma Gluck," Teddy said.

"In Frankfurt," Frederick Kessler went on, "there are no Jews left in the orchestra. It's the same everywhere, in Berlin, Munich, all the cities. They're all in London or New York."

"I never sang in Germany," Etta Sukenik said. "But I went to Salzburg once. For the Mozart. To hear a *Figaro*."

"That's not Germany," Frederick Kessler said.

"Well, it is now," Etta Sukenik said.

"How do you manage all that?" Charlotte said, finally bringing herself to speak.

"Manage? Manage what?"

"A life in music, travel, the demands of a career."

"I'm alone. The thing to manage is to make sure my life is filled."

"I thought you mentioned a family."

"Me? Never. I only have myself."

"I envy you."

"There's nothing to envy. I assure you."

"An independent life like yours?"

"I'd give you all of Puccini and Verdi for a husband, children, and a home. Half of Mozart, too."

After waiting a moment, as her words sank in at each place, Etta Sukenik went on, taking in the table with a dramatic sweep of her arm. "And which one of these gentlemen is your hubby?" she asked.

"I'm single," Charlotte said, blushing. "I take care of myself, too."

At this claim, Jack, Teddy, and Ben threw her an identical look, full of query and doubt. Barney snorted. He knew precisely how much Charlotte relied on her father for support; he knew too about her struggle with the bar. They waited for her to go on. "You know," Charlotte said, "most women dream all the time of what you have."

"How would anybody know what I have?"

"You have freedom. What everybody wants."

"And you don't have the same thing?"

"I have a father at home to take care of. I have daily responsibilities."

Again, Barney snorted.

"Ah, so," Etta Sukenik said. "Daily responsibilities. Remind me to tell you a thing or two about freedom when we have a little time together, just you and I, sisters under the skin."

"You sing about Jesus?" Barney interrupted.

"It's just an act, just words. I pretend."

"I've never been to Radio City," Teddy said.

"Our young friend here plays the piano," Gus Levi said.

"Is that so?" Etta Sukenik said.

And so the conversation began to sink, stern first, with an end-of-meal heaviness. No one regretted it. They had all talked too much, they were all ready to go down with the ship. Yawns sifted through the air like distress signals. Barney's eyes closed for a full half minute. Silence then, under the limp clatter of china and silverware. At the buffet, dessert was now being laid out. Huge pastries, filled with cherries, blueberries, and pineapple, ice cream, sponge cake, and a bowl of strawberries three feet wide. Etta Sukenik, who seemed perfectly self-contained, returned to herself as soon as the talk stopped. She was undaunted by silence, just as she was undaunted by conversation. She fooled with her pince-nez for a moment or two, rose, brought herself some ice cream and coffee; everyone else at the table did the same.

Within a few minutes, after a final gurgle of coffee, tea, and ice water, dinner was over. Table number five had done all it could on its own behalf. Frederick Kessler stood up, patted his stomach without thinking. Barney Levin surveyed the room, a long, dark, raunchy look that appraised everything in its path, then coughed his ancient tobacco hack. A busboy brought the news that the rain had stopped. The air was clearing, the humidity thinning. Jack Lewin rose to his feet, stretched lazily, gazed at his two sons: Woodholme and Suburban, *lwh* and etymology, politics and religion, they were *smart*, no doubt about it. They could hold their own, even better, with anybody; they could outargue him, their own father, they always could, even while they were half asleep. Jack smiled then like a simpleton with pure, momentary happiness. Two sons, double images. A few feet away, separating himself from the rest of them, Ben was already moving in the direction of the lobby. He seemed less languid than when he had first arrived, moved with a snap that was a result of his dinner exchange with Gustav Levi. That was what always released Ben's energy, a little opposition. He was going to take a walk alone, make his first exploration of the new city, evaluate the terms, taste the Boardwalk at his own solitary pace; it had now become, after a full summer's indulgence in another place, a habit to last a lifetime. Teddy waited for an invitation to join him, then waited some more, flashing his brother soft, beguiling looks that brought no response. He thought he might hear about New York, about the Fair, details about Ben's summer, but Ben was gone, smartly sidling his way between the tables in the dining room on his way to the front of the hotel.

Then the old lady Eisen, supported by Nurse Chernichowski, passed by, moving at a crawl; then the Waldmans, newly arrived that morning from Englewood; Zalman Stern, who cultivated a handshake that would crush bones; Bertha Wolf, her cheeks spotted with rouge, whose husband was in a Pennsylvania jail for embezzlement; the Friedmans, the Spectors, the Ullmans, the Lewises; then Maurice Pearman, the Hebrew school principal from Pittsburgh, whose brusqueness cut through good and bad manners with equal sharpness; the Sindlers, the Krakowers, the Rosenbergs; Ida Kahn, Sarah Cooper, Frieda Davidson, three widows; dozens of others, deep thinkers and lovers of pleasure, tribal chieftains, desert warriors, inheritors of history, gnomic wanderers in search of milk and honey, even several beauties with a look of the Old Testament about them, men and brothers, bachelors and philanderers, the beginning of the processional end of Sunday evening.

Soon they were almost alone in the dining room, a cluster at table number five, a few others here and there. Teddy stood alongside his friend, Erich Kessler, vainly trying to muster some talk, but Erich would not listen. On Teddy jabbered, mindlessly, afraid of being enveloped by a cloud of silence, while Erich stood there foursquare and stolid, opening up his belt a notch and hitching up his pants. From across the room then Tibor Talles sent them a hand signal. Wait for me outside, it said. Something was in the wind. He flashed it again, for good measure. He had something urgent to share. With Tibor it was always urgent; nothing could ever rest there. Meanwhile, Larry Bernard, who had left them alone all evening, looked as though he was heading for their table. He made a clear start in their direction, then changed his mind and moved away, throwing one last look over his shoulder at them all. Teddy turned questioningly to Charlotte. She gazed back at him, a disappointed light at the center of her eyes.

"We've decided to take a vacation from each other tonight," she said.

Finally the whole Talles family began to parade single file past them. Victor Talles leading the way, concentrated on his Sunday night need to get away from Sloan's, to rev up his Chrysler and head again for the Newcastle Ferry and Route 40, to make his way home for another week of manufacturing cotton fatigues while enjoying a sales trip or two to Fort Meade or Washington, D.C., where life these days could provide a pleasurable surprise or two for any man willing to accept it. God bless the U. S. Army. God bless the draft. Joseph followed his father, yawning. Then came Tibor. He gave Teddy and Erich the high sign again, winked at them like an old voluptuary, pink and confident under his honeyed Persian skin.

Thelma Talles followed them all, moving slowly, white on white, dropping a hello here and there, smiling brilliantly at the few guests who remained in the dining room. She would go back to her bridge game tomorrow night, might even have a chance for a game tonight if all went well, if Victor did not procrastinate or get any urgent last-minute notions about going upstairs before he left for Baltimore. As she passed by the Lewins, Jack perceptibly came to momentary attention, an alert straightening of the shoulders, a sudden, quick flickering of the eyes, focused briefly on her white flesh, red mouth, black hair. She laughed aloud at something Tibor said to her over his shoulder. He always made her laugh. For the moment, Jack's eyes locked on hers. It lasted hardly a second, while she was still laughing at her son. Then she looked away modestly. She called something to Tibor, looked back briefly. Then she was gone. Jack cleared his throat. He put his hands in his pockets, turned to make comfortable small talk with Gus Levi and Frederick Kessler and their new friend Etta Sukenik. Frederick Kessler was describing *Die Walküre* in Frankfurt. Gus Levi's dyspepsia was on him; he stood with one hand over his heart. Furtwaengler, Frederick Kessler said, as Jack pretended to listen to his new German friend.

Barney Levin had noticed. So had Etta Sukenik, who smiled with Italianate pleasure. So had Teddy Lewin, who turned now to watch Thelma Talles trail her family through the doorway for a last gathering in the lobby before she lost her husband for another week.

3

They were sitting under the Boardwalk, Tibor's idea, as though they had to deal with the forces of the law, as though they were oldtime bootleggers in hiding or on the run. Teddy had never been beneath the boards before. It was like a great, tunneled grave, miles long, like being buried under a filthy avalanche. Above his head, there was an empty echoing of leathered feet. It never stopped, he could almost reach up and touch it, millions of callused soles walking away the Atlantic City evening, stomping out echoes of the weekend's adventures, exercising on behalf of sanity and physical well-being. Between the pine boards there were slices of open air: topside. They could see the night sky, lighted pink by Boardwalk concessions, and an occasional rain cloud, scudding off to sea like a crab. It was grisly to Teddy sitting there; it was grisly to all of them, except Tibor.

The sand was like ice to the touch. It was like that on the beach in front of them, too. Five minutes after the sun went down all its heat disappeared into the earth while the surface of the sand became as cold as a corpse. It always took Teddy by surprise. Sand could not hold heat, but the earth itself, real soil in which life grew, coddled it. Meanwhile, a hundred yards away, the sea beat in at the Jersey shore. It was the one constant, like the sun, in and out, in millennial thrusts. The moon would pull at it forever. It reassured Teddy. It calmed him sometimes. What could be important in the face of that?

Tibor now passed around his pocket flashlight. It was a new invention, as big as his pinky, a little yellow cylinder that came on with a click and sent a slender column of light straight out into the night. Fifty-nine cents at Woolworth's. It lasted a month, then was supposed to be discarded for a new purchase: a neat cycle. Erich Kessler tried it, sent its beam wavering above their heads, caught briefly the blurred motion of a thousand feet moving on the Boardwalk. "Shine it up their giggies," Joseph called. Tibor laughed. Erich handed the flashlight back. He had no idea what he was doing there, couldn't figure out what Tibor had in mind, what he needed them for, why they were gathered on their haunches in a solemn, straggling line facing the sea.

Then Teddy tried the flashlight, following Tibor's nagging directions. "Flick the catch," he said. "Flick it. Like this." It finally caught on the third try. Teddy shone the beam at his side, then behind him. He was sitting in a garbage dump, he suddenly realized. They were surrounded by candy wrappers, beer bottles, used condoms. A broken trash basket lay on its side somewhere behind them. There was a discarded sweater, moldy with damp, a pair of sunglasses without lenses. He swept the beam along a midget dune. The sand was black. An ancient pile of dog shit rested on top of the dune. Three petrified stools, entwined like a pretzel, a nest for a family of huge green flies. Teddy shuddered, clicked off the light. Why had he come? Tibor gave them their orders and they snapped to like yokels taking basic training.

"For Christ's sake," Teddy said. "I'm freezing."

"Me, too," Joseph said.

"In a minute, in a minute," Tibor said. He was struggling with something in his pocket, pulling at it awkwardly from his squatting position, finally yanking it out in a single fierce gesture. "Son-of-a-bitch," he said.

"I'm going back," Erich Kessler said. "It's too cold under here."

"Not yet," Tibor said. "I went to a lot of trouble for this."

Joseph yawned, lay back, folded his arms beneath his head.

"Watch out for the crap," Teddy warned.

"Hurry up," Joseph said. "I have to take a leak."

"You got time," Tibor said.

They crept around each other on the hard sand, like the green flies behind them, hissing their dissatisfaction between their teeth. Joseph stood up and turned his back on them, sending out a stream of piss in the direction of the Steel Pier, as though he were watering his father's lawn on Strathmore Avenue on a late summer afternoon, watching it steam briefly as it hit the cold sand, tracing a circle before he was through. The boys waited for him.

"Come on," Tibor called.

"Hold your horses," Joseph said.

"He's got a bladder like a piece of Swiss cheese," Tibor said. "He'd piss all day if you let him."

The talk was making them restless. The contrived toughness, the strained vocabulary, seemed to release in them a whole new source of energy; and the setting, Tibor's own choice, was transforming Teddy and Erich in an identical way, helping to prepare them for Tibor's performance. Like them, he fed on the black excitement he was creating. His own voice quavered a bit. He stood up, sat down. He could hardly wait; none of them could wait.

"For Christ's sake," Teddy said.

"I'm going home," Erich said.

"Okay," Tibor said. "Joseph first. Take the flashlight."

Joseph did as he was told, sat cross-legged on the sand, spread out in his lap the shredded pages of the book his brother handed him, lighted the Woolworth flashlight. Alongside him, Erich stirred, tried to read over his shoulder. "You're breathing down my neck," Joseph said prissily. "Whyn't you wait your turn?"

"What is it?" Teddy asked.

"Something I picked up in Chalfonte Alley," Tibor said.

"It ain't all you picked up in Chalfonte Alley," Joseph muttered.

"Don't listen to him," Tibor said. "He's just jealous 'cause I came twice Friday night."

"You wish it," Joseph said.

"I know it," Tibor said, kicking at the sand.

"It's one of those books," Teddy said.

"I wanted to share the wealth with you guys," Tibor said.

"Hurry up," Erich said.

Joseph sat in silence, turning the pages slowly, almost five minutes to each page. Every now and then the cheap little flashlight went out, while Joseph cursed, sputtered on, sparkled there underneath the Boardwalk, as its narrow beam lighted the pages on Joseph's lap. Halfway through, Joseph began to mumble to himself. He pulled at his crotch, turned another page. A lifetime passed.

"Hey, Joseph," Tibor said, "got a hard-on yet?"

"I'm going back," Teddy said.

"What's your rush?" Tibor said.

"I'm freezing my ass off."

"You'll be hot soon enough. Move, Joseph. There're two more waiting."

Joseph was almost finished. "Jesus Christ," he mumbled. He smoothed the book out. "How much did this cost you?" he asked.

"Five bucks."

"Where'd you get five bucks for this?"

"I've been saving it."

"From what?"

"A little here, a little there."

"Jesus Christ," Joseph said ruefully. "I've got to piss again."

"Don't try to piss with a hard-on," Tibor called. "You'll infect yourself."

Then Erich Kessler, too, sitting cross-legged on the frigid sand, spread out the folded pages, smoothed them gently, and shone the yellow light into his lap. Using his index finger as a pointer, he followed the light word by word, pausing every now and then to lift his head and peer thoughtfully into the darkness. At the same time, he released a little sigh into the thin night air that he was unaware of, a breath that came from deep inside himself. He read even more slowly than Joseph, stopping at length whenever he came to a photograph.

"What are you doing back there?" Tibor called.

There was no answer from Joseph. "Hey," Tibor called. "That's some piss."

"Leave him alone," Teddy said.

"Jesus. The man has no shame."

"Come off it, Tibor," Joseph said over his shoulder. "I'm just pissing."

"Leave him alone," Teddy said. "Let him do what he has to do."

"What do you care?"

". . . . . ."

"You know what he's doing back there?"

Teddy stared into the dark, remained silent.

"Believe me," Tibor said. "I'm telling you."

"Then it's his business. Who cares?"

"You know, you sound like you really been around, like you know a lot more than you act like."

"What do you mean?"

"What I said."

"I don't know anything."

"I know all about you quiet guys."

"What's to know?"

"Still waters."

"I'm getting bored down here. I'm going back."

"Come on, the kraut's almost done. You'll have it in a minute."

"I don't know if I want it anymore."

"What are you, some kind of fairy?"

"Yeah, I think maybe I am."

"Yeah? You do that kind of stuff?"

"Come on, I'm kidding you."

"I don't know about you, baby. If I could only see your face in the dark, I could tell. You want to try something?"

"I told you, I'm kidding."

Tibor had his hand suddenly on the inside of Teddy's thigh, a neat, swift, firm thrust, then just as suddenly pulled it away. He laughed. "Okay, okay. You're kidding. So am I. You never know. . . . Jesus Christ, Kessler, move your ass. We haven't got all night."

There was a final sigh from Erich Kessler. He lifted his head, took off his glasses. There was a look of absolute impenetrability on his face. Everything had been absorbed quietly; it was all crammed into that Teutonic fortress, locked up now for life, a capital hoard for old age. He handed the flashlight and book to Teddy in a formal way, acknowledging his friend's turn with a nod of his head. Then he got to his feet and, arching his spine, began to rub the small of his back.

Teddy sat for a moment without moving, holding the thin, tattered paperbacked book in his hand, fooling unthinkingly with Tibor's new flashlight. He had lost all desire to participate, was no longer interested in Tibor's game, was afraid that by joining with the others he would inescapably become one of them forever. A dirty book, a hideout under the Boardwalk, Tibor Talles and his arrogant assumptions; what could he have been thinking? He despised himself now for all the side-of-the-mouth talk, the bleating dead-end locutions, for willingly playing it all Tibor and Joseph's way. It was an ordinary adventure, conventionally crass, conceived without imagination; that was what embarrassed him. And while his resistance mounted, while his mind indignantly tooled away at all the arguments with itself, Teddy's right hand flipped open the book and his left shone the flashlight onto the first page.

He knew what he had, thirty-two grimy pages filled with misprints and misspellings, the kind of book that was sometimes passed around the boy's side of his high-school classroom, a hustling narrative about a naked man and two naked women who liked to watch each other make love. Each one spied on the other two, in turn, that was the story, then they all spied on themselves in a mirror. Six photographs illustrated the text. In the photographs, the man wore socks, like Barney Levin's, with arrows running up the sides. The women both had bobbed hair and small, sagging breasts. His name was Herman; they were Claire and Mignon. The setting was a mountain cabin by a lake; it was winter and the snow outside was six feet deep.

On page eight, Teddy let the flashlight dim and go out. He took a slow, deep breath, exhaled. What was happening to him he had known would happen from the beginning. Some familiar mechanism in him had been sprung at the book's opening words, some agitation set trembling by the first photograph. He could not give it up now. He would make the experience last as long as he could, stretch it out page by page, like Joseph Talles before him, like Erich Kessler. Around him there was the murmur of adolescent voices, soft, winning combinations of Oriental slyness and Germanic presence, Talles and Kessler, an odd, hothouse mix that seduced him at some level beyond the book he held in his lap. In front of him, the surge of breakers, folding in on themselves, seemed closer now. The tide was on its way in. Teddy rested like that for a few minutes. Human voices and sea became one; footsteps above him pounded without end. He wanted Tibor and Joseph and his friend Erich Kessler to leave him there alone, to finish the book in his own good time, leave him to brood on the heavy blood that ran through him now. The book had mesmerized him; they always did. It amazed him. He did not understand such power.

"You gonna take all night?" It was Tibor, rushing him.

He snapped on the flashlight, went back to his reading, shifting from one buttock to another. Like his friends, he sat cross-legged on the sand, hunched over. On he read, page by page, sometimes going back to reread a paragraph out of incomprehension or to fix a memory, to groove it once and for all in his brain so that he would never forget. He studied the pictures the same way. The force of those pictures could not be resisted for long. Breasts, belly buttons, open mouths, swollen genitals, pubic hair, the clash of naked adult bodies in outrageous positions that had to be traced inch by inch to be completely understood and, once understood, assimilated. Teddy paused again, flicked off the light. His vision blurred for a moment. He blinked, caught a glimpse of a cloud moving in swiftly to cover the moon. The light of the moon spread behind the cloud like spilled milk. Teddy shivered with the cold, thought uncontrollably of the three lovers. They filled his brain, hazily changing shape at will. Herman's almost hairless body became transformed. Tufts of black hair grew out of his shoulders. His stupid, callow face turned slowly into Larry Bernard's, remaining there like that for an instant, Larry Bernard's huge bald head stuck on top of Herman's skinny neck, those two massive, hairy hands holding from behind in their full palms the two meager breasts that belonged to either Claire or Mignon. Then, while the cloud scudded like a rat toward the east, the moon emerged as opaque as ever, its brilliant light refocused on the beach. There was another slow transformation, Charlotte Melnicov for Claire, blond hair down to her pelvis, legs spread wide, her own hands holding Larry Bernard's in place over her full Slavic breasts, and then, almost at the same time, Mignon, adorable, feckless Mignon with the thin lips and perfect spit curl became on the page the aristocratic face of Bea Lewin, Bea Lewin from Baltimore, Md., lasciviously watching her friends. . . .

"For Christ's sake," Tibor yelled, "move your ass."

Teddy snapped to, relief flooding him. That was what he needed, a sharp order. He finished the book in five minutes, hurrying himself along the text, barely able to pay attention, taking in the final two photographs with perfunctory glances. He closed the book, smoothed it out, handed it back to Tibor.

"Well?" Tibor asked.

"It's all right."

"All right?"

"I mean, it's not the first one I've ever seen." Teddy yawned with a great, soul-shuddering effort.

"What's wrong with you, Lewin, you too good for the rest of us?"

"No, I'm not too good for the rest of you."

"I didn't notice you hurrying any while you were reading."

"No, I didn't hurry any."

"Your asshole buddy here says he never saw anything like it." Tibor looked to Erich for confirmation.

"In Frankfurt there are no books like that," Erich said huskily.

"You heard that?"

"Well," Teddy said, "I've seen more than a couple at Forest Park High School." Then he, too, exactly like Erich Kessler, got to his feet, arched his spine, and began to massage the small of his back.

"Let's go," Joseph said.

"For what?" Tibor said. He had begun to sulk.

"What are we gonna do under here? The whole world's walking on our heads."

But still they sat, only Teddy on his feet, depression settling over them like a soft, smothering wave. They were all helpless in the face of it, Tibor suffering worst of all. None of them was sure what had happened to them, none of them understood. But as they all came to their feet then, to stand alongside Teddy, they could read in each other's eyes the sense of failure the evening had produced, the disgust with themselves, the dim realization of the hoax they had enacted upon their own susceptible bodies.

"I'm going to walk on the beach," Teddy said. "I'll see you all later."

"You won't see me," Tibor said.

"What are you gonna do?" Joseph asked.

"I'm going on my own."

"Where you going on a Sunday night?"

"I don't have to go any *place*."

"Well, I'm going back to the hotel."

Then Erich hesitated, looking from Joseph to Teddy, back
and forth. But Teddy didn't respond; he would not invite his
friend to walk with him. "I'll go back with you," Erich said
quietly to Joseph. They all actually separated then, without
another word, Tibor disappearing down the Boardwalk, one
among a million, his shredded book rolled up in his pocket,
Joseph silently crossing over to Virginia Avenue under the
Cotswold veranda, declining as always to comment, with Erich
walking firmly at his heels, making each step look as though it
counted for something.

Teddy headed for the shoreline. It was a calm sea now, calmer
than it had seemed from under the Boardwalk. He was not supposed to be on the beach; no one was supposed to be on the
beach after dark, it was like the law against swimming under
the Pier; but who would know? The incoming tide had formed
tiny lakes here and there, silent estuaries three inches deep in
which soft ripples ran back and forth with the current. The pools
were filled with noiseless, thick, nearly invisible life, echino-
derms, arthropods, annelids, and tough, valved pelecypods, the
sea's palpitating nightwash, beached by the moon, long-spined sea
urchins half hidden in foam, purple starfish, huge female sand-
bugs laden with eggs, basket stars like lace, amethyst gem clams,
stinging Obelias and Tubularia, and tiny pink coquina shells
spread along the mud bottoms like severed butterfly wings. Teddy
skirted them delicately, walking on his toes, eyeing the sand for
dry shells he could bring back for Marion, something she could
show off at home. The air still smelled of rain; an astringent
odor of salt rose from the edge of the beach like a cloud.

On his right, Teddy could hear the sound of a band coming
from the Steel Pier, a dense wall of overarranged music to which
five hundred vacationers might be dancing at that very moment.

He stopped, listened. A pinched clarinet solo, four sandy trombones sliding underneath the melody with a repetitive accompaniment, shivering percussion; swing, jitterbug, Lindy; pompadoured girls from Philadelphia mindlessly whirling on their wedgies like ancient *lwh*'s. They would really make the black barnacled pilings shake. There were lights everywhere on the Pier; three movies inside; vaudeville; a fun house with glorious mirrors and a vast, inexorable barrel that rotated slowly and threw you off your feet. At the very end, way out where the water was fifty feet deep, the trained white horse was probably getting ready to dive into the sea for the last time that day, in front of a tired, freezing audience huddled together on steep bleachers. Turning away, Teddy leaned down and took off his shoes. He rolled up his pants, waded into the water. It was like ice, like the sand beneath the Boardwalk. He stood there like that for five minutes, the music still coming at him in brassy waves, dipping his toes, holding up his pants legs like a middle-aged gentleman, full of fastidiousness and giddy pleasure. Foam broke against his shins, fat, glistening bubbles white with salt. A starfish quivered off to the right, broken shells littered the water's edge. The moon disappeared again, shone out a few moments later, shafting a beam diagonally across the beach from shoreline to Boardwalk. Teddy thought he could stay there forever, wading invisibly in the freezing water, but even as he thought it he began to grow bored with the sea. There was the sudden sound of the whole band playing together, a single note reinforced twenty times over. It resonated a few seconds, then cut off. Bending down without another thought, Teddy picked up his shoes and turned to make the walk back to Sloan's.

Later that night, he awoke to the sound of his father undressing. Leaning on his elbow, he saw that Ben was already asleep in the cot, turned on his side away from the double bed. He was snoring. Jack put his finger to his lips. Teddy lay back, wrapped in his sheet. When his father got into bed, Teddy pulled into himself, contracted like a reflexive turtle, pulled his knees up, turned on his own side toward the wall. He was trying to sleep on six inches of mattress. Nevertheless, his left foot accidentally touched his father's, a touch like an iceberg. His foot jumped, he pulled back again. He felt the bed sag under his father's weight. "Good night," Jack whispered. Teddy whispered back. Night quickly buried them then, memory pierced their shroud. Herman, Teddy thought. Claire. Daredevil Mignon. They were freer than Teddy Lewin. They were freer than he would ever be. They chose to do what they did, then did it. That was real freedom. Sleep came up then like the earth opening. Falling, going sweetly under, hearing at the last moment Barney Levin's phlegmy cough hack its way down the hallway, Teddy took to turning the pages of Tibor's dreambook again, patiently stalking the scented, old spoor of love, love given, love received.

4

By morning every drop of rain had moved east, every dim gray cloud had gone sailing slowly over the Atlantic, to be dispersed somewhere in the direction of Portugal and the rest of the Iberian peninsula, leaving the great skinny American city by the sea scorched by a new sun, hot as an oven-baked copper plate, as glinting, orange, and round, a perfect, solemn circle full of foreboding.

Teddy could already feel the threat of a powerful heat at the breakfast table. It touched his flesh, raised a thin film of perspiration on his forehead. It hovered near the ceiling like an aura, floated down below along the sweating woodwork, hung over the table and over Saul himself as he served the orange juice, the eggs, the fresh, creamy bread, so soft it came apart in Teddy's hand, and the good coffee, percolated under Hy Sloan's own baleful eye, in the vast kitchen in the rear of the hotel.

Teddy had caught sight of the kitchen one evening through the swinging doors in the dining room, when a stupid new waiter, down from N.Y.U. for four weeks, had made an entrance through the exit door. He had been blissfully preoccupied with Platonic classroom ideas as he came in, carrying in the palm of his hand, over his head, an oval tray laden with flank steaks, mashed potatoes, string beans, and several boats of steaming gravy. Heading into the kitchen through the same door, at the same moment, was a colleague from Hofstra, doing his job correctly. The collision still echoed in Teddy's mind, the sudden white-aproned face-to-face smashup, the womanly shrieks of terror from both waiters, the unbelieving Yiddish curse from Hy, which hung in the air a full five seconds, the breaking plates, dripping gravy, potatoes falling like Niagara, the heart-thudding crash of bone on bone, crockery on linoleum, glass on the floor. It was glorious, after the first instant, a moment of pure shocked joy for all the guests in the dining room, who couldn't help themselves, who were both embarrassed and delighted at the same time and began to titter nervously at the mess that spread at Hy's feet. Then there was a weak cheer from the back of the room and, when it was discovered that no one had been hurt, a great simultaneous outburst of good-natured kidding from all the diners; and at that moment, the guilty door still swinging slowly back and forth on its hinges, the two waiters on their hands and knees mopping up in front of it, Teddy had seen into the depths of the workroom back there, into all that hidden, clamorous labor, black iron ovens as big as walk-in closets, vats like bathtubs, pans, pots, steel basins, drainers, detergents, mounds of peeled carrots and limp celery, a scurrying of faceless busboys and cooks, aproned waiters yelling at each other, bare bulbs hanging over-head, steam rising like smoke signals to the damp ceiling. He had been momentarily electrified by what he had seen. Then, as he sat erect in his chair, staring, the doors had swung closed and the dining room returned to its normal drone.

At Teddy's side now, Saul had begun to sweat. It dropped from his forehead onto the tablecloth, made two furrows down either side of his nose, gave his skin a peculiar oily cast that was a unique glandular mix, an aged Semitic compound all his own. He could hardly see, wiped his eyes with a napkin, wiped his forehead, cheeks, the back of his neck. It would be an endless day, a purgatory filled with the usual deadly repetitive effort, tables set, served, and cleared three times, each meal a heavier burden as the day went on, today's made totally unbearable by the warning they were all receiving, at that very moment, of heat that would enter their bodies, their bloodstreams, their very skulls, like the bubonic plague.

"Already I miss your sister," Saul murmured. He wiped his eyes again.

"She'll be glad to hear that," Teddy said.

"It's not the same without her. It's not the same without your mother, either."

"We'll all be back next year. My father says so."

"Next year," Saul said, musing a bit. "Next year maybe I'll be on the road to Timbuktu."

"You mean that?"

"Maybe Miami Beach. I'm looking around for a good place to find a practice."

"Come to Baltimore."

"I already got that, in Philadelphia." He wiped the back of his neck again.

"Whyn't you go to California, to Hollywood?"

"Yeah. Maybe Hollywood . . ."

"It's nice out there."

"I hear."

"The sun's always shining."

"It's like Florida."

"Anyway," Teddy said, "I'll tell Marion."

"Tell her. Tell her it's not the same."

Saul moved off like a swimmer under water, squinting against the light. As he watched him go, Teddy drank his juice in one gulp. That helped. The neat citrus taste pinched him awake. There were vitamins buried in all that liquid pulp, good, sound, health-giving, invisible beings that would spread through his system and heal all wrongs. His eggs were another matter. They were full of water, soft as sponge, always were. No one in the whole kitchen knew how to scramble an egg. Teddy pushed them away, closed his eyes wearily. Where was everybody? He was

still alone at table number five, had sneaked out of their bedroom upstairs, unwilling to disturb Ben and his father, afraid
they might miss a half hour of cherished vacation sleep, somehow
made doubly valuable because it was stolen from real, everyday
time. At home, Teddy's father opened up Uncle Haskel's lumberyard at seven thirty in the morning, every day but Sunday, and
he was out of the house each morning before Teddy was up;
except on weekends and holidays, Teddy had not seen his father
before dinner in ten years. His grandfather was sleeping late, too,
rasping lightly through his nose, and there had not been a
sound in Charlotte Melnicov's room next to his when Teddy
put his ear to the door on his way to the bathroom.

He counted six people in the dining room, the Waldman
family and Bertha Wolf, new arrivals. They were having breakfast together, the Waldmans, Sam and Irene, and their children,
Ralph and Nan, a family of wholesale jewelers who specialized
in senior class rings in Bergen County, had staked out the annual
take for themselves each spring, who knew their way around
every high school in north Jersey and into eastern Pennsylvania;
and across from them, Mrs. Wolf, dreaming lazily of her husband
sitting in a Harrisburg jailhouse, her wounded eyes supported
by two pouches like grocery bags. She had six more months to
wait. It was silent at their table. Everything moved in slow
motion. There was a whole week ahead of everyone, all the
time in the world to get it all in.

The temperature rose another five degrees. It was going to be
over ninety, whatever the statistics in the brochures claimed. It
was going to climb to ninety-six by one o'clock in the afternoon,
even though it was only a week from Labor Day and the prospect of some sort of equinox, a slight tilting of the earth's axis
away from the sun, an increasing slant on behalf of the polar cap
and the slow icing process that would eventually take them all
into the dead heart of winter. But they would have to wait for
that. It would take some patience. First, they would have to get

through the day's solemn baking atmosphere. Thank God the
sea lay two hundred feet nearby. Thank God for the cooling
breakers which split on the flesh like iced shards—the hotter the
day, the icier the water. Thank God for a surf upon which a
human body could sustain itself almost without effort, while the
thick velvety waters of the Atlantic spread beneath one's back
like a gift of heaven, a salt-sprayed bed distilling life from itself
and passing it on. Yes. Teddy loved it here. There was no better
place in the world. He pitied all those who could not be in
Atlantic City. All those at home now in New York, Newark,
Philadelphia, Pittsburgh, Washington, even Sam Aaron from
Trenton, the judge with the crazy wife, most of all Marion Lewin
and her mother, the beautiful Bea Lewin from Baltimore, Md.,
who was undoubtedly sitting now in the deep shade of their
red-brick rowhouse near Druid Hill Lake, far back in the tiled
kitchen, alongside the massive, old-fashioned stove with the
chimney pipe that ran into the wall, reading the morning funnies
in the *Sun* or the gossip from Hollywood, probably waiting for
an invitation to the Woodholme for the day, where they could
have lunch and swim in the pool with all of Teddy's rich cousins.
He would have to find something nice for Marion, something
special, better than a seashell or a doll that might be dismem-
bered in a day, a Japanese flower, maybe, that would bloom when
drowned in a glass of water, a makeup kit like Bea's or a
Monopoly set of her own.

The room was slowly filling up. The Spectors were now at
their table, only a few feet away, the Krakowers, the Lewises,
white-haired Zalman Stern, Maurice Pearman, acknowledging
everyone with the same tight smile. Ben slipped in then, looking
as though he had not slept a wink. He yawned, settled himself
at the table, asked Saul for a menu. They discussed breakfast
together like two gentlemen of leisure, five minutes of highly
specific chat, as though Ben were a crown prince whose every
wish had always been fulfilled. Why not? Finally, the precise

brand of cereal agreed upon, the correct amount of toast, the variety of jam, the need for cream, Ben acknowledged his brother, threw him a tired, not unpleasant glance of recognition. It said: Oh, yes, I remember you, you're the dippy kid who sleeps in the room next to mine in Baltimore, and didn't I catch you sharing a double bed with my father last night upstairs in this dump?

The games they played with each other, the games they had always played with each other. Maybe I recognize you, maybe I don't. Tell me how wonderful I am, how smart, or I'll take the chess set back. Tell me *again*. I am older than you, therefore the steak leftovers are mine. You wash the dishes, I'll scrape; washing is more fun, everybody knows that. Or, I'll wash, *you* scrape, scraping is a big deal. The brotherly con, the everlasting race for first place, the never-buried resentment of the new arrival, then the sudden access of tenderness, old for young, big brother for small, the painful start at a recognition of similarities, shared interests, equal talents, the subtle, interlocked, swimming genes, a little bit mine, a little bit yours. Where did the color of your eyes come from, how did your nose acquire the Sandler shape and mine the Lewin, or the other way around; and the urgent demand from one to the other, younger to old, or the reverse, that respect be laid out between them like a fine-woven carpet on which one might openly place one's self-regard like a precious gift that would be snatched away at the first menacing gesture.

"Christ," Ben said. "Is it always like this?"

"What?" Teddy answered.

"This heat. I might as well be home."

"You'll go swimming, it'll cool you off."

"I didn't sleep so well," Ben said. "The room was like an oven. It's really not big enough for three people."

"It's as big as they come here."

"It's like the Y."

"What'd you do last night?" Teddy asked.

"Wandered around."

"Where?"

"Just up and down the Boardwalk."

"Pretty nice, isn't it?"

"What's nice about it?"

"The life, the crowds. It's interesting."

"You find that junkyard interesting?"

"Junkyard?"

"It's ugly."

" . . . . . ."

"The American bourgeoisie in full flower."

"Oh, Ben."

"What's wrong?"

"It's too early in the morning to start that again."

"If you don't want to hear, don't ask."

"You're in one of your grouchy moods. I could tell as soon as you sat down."

"You asked me a question and I answered."

"You've been grouchy ever since you got here."

" . . . . . ."

"First, it's the World's Fair. Then it's Mr. Levi, now it's the bourgeoisie again. You're always knocking the bourgeoisie."

"What better?"

"It's like knocking yourself."

"That's right."

"What's wrong with you?"

"Us, baby. Not just me."

"What's so bad?"

"What's so bad. Now let me see. Mmm. All right, I'll ask you a question. You want to be like the Sandlers?"

" . . . . . ."

"Do you?"

" . . . . . ."

"Well, I think maybe you do, Teddy bear. I think you better think about that. What they want, you want. Agree? When they talk, you listen. You're like putty in their hands. You, with your talent and your head. You want to be just like them."

"If you mean rich . . ."

"I mean rich and all the values that go with it."

"And all the money," Teddy muttered.

Ben ate his breakfast, deposited dish by dish by Saul, stealthily examined the room, hid his shyness as though it were a physical defect. That was how he did everything, how he had to do everything. To walk into a strange room meant to feel the slow, heated, familiar rise of his own self-consciousness, the undiminishing sense of being the object of other people's attentions, appraisals, harsh judgments. He was too smart, too brainy, too intelligent. He was out of their class in every sense in the dining room; yet he felt like a slave in their presence. Middle-class values, the excesses of the rich. He ached for both, moved at the same time arrow straight in another direction. He'd show them, he'd pay them back for leaving him high and dry the way he was, not quite poor enough to be able to forget it. "Pass the sugar," he said, stretching his arms above his head, yawning lazily, a huge, vacuous, rude, hypocritical yawn, designed to be heard fifty feet away. Teddy laughed. Ben often made him laugh like this, made him envy his independence, his sly nose-thumbing, his need to set himself apart from them all, while everyone else, Teddy included, swam together in a tight little school, wiggling their identical tails in unison, shifting mercurially from left to right, depending on who was calling the signals, like tadpoles a hair's width apart.

"Say," Ben began slyly. He was unable to leave well enough alone. He stirred his coffee, then tasted it, taking his time. Teddy instantly grew wary.

"Say," Ben said again. "How do you think your mother and father are doing?"

"What do you mean?" Teddy said. A slow reply, lasting almost half a minute.

"I mean how are they getting along these days?"

"Same as always."

Ben threw his brother a sharp look. Their eyes locked resentfully. "You know better than that," he said.

"I do not," Teddy said. "They get along fine." He could hardly swallow his toast.

"Just thought I'd ask," Ben said, sipping his hot coffee. "It's not the Garden of Eden with them, you know, it's never been with those two."

"They get along perfect," Teddy said, between his teeth.

"All right, all right," Ben said, turning away.

Through the heat, the guests had begun to gather in force. Thirty-eight people were now at breakfast, having slid into the room silently, while Ben and Teddy were pecking away at each other. They sat wherever they pleased. Breakfast was a kind of open house, a generous-hearted custom established by Pearl Sloan to make her guests feel at ease with each other, make them say hello to perfect strangers and bind them together in the clutch of her five-storied nest. Gus Levi wandered by wearing a transparent sports shirt, freshly shaved, two sharp purple nicks on his chin already scabbed. The morning's *Times* was under his arm. He complained to the brothers about the heat, sat down, wiped his brow. He looked tired, a residue of sleeplessness shadowing his eyes. Heat and insomnia, they totally distracted Gustav Levi, wore him down, eroded his brain, took away all his energy, physical, mental, and whatever sexual starts were generated within that intellectualized body. Teddy could see the grizzled hair on his chest through his shirt, the two fleshy nipples, fat as fifty-cent pieces, the creases beneath them. Exercise, that's what he needed, five-mile walks on the Boardwalk, a half-mile swim every day in the sea. His neck was lightly powdered, freckles spotted his high forehead like bird droppings. Gus Levi ordered breakfast, asked after their health, asked after their night's sleep, perfunctory talk underlined by quick, shafting smiles that came out of an essential sweetness that Gus Levi could not help, that was part of his fate, his doom. That sweetness would undercut all his dealings with the world, force him to keep the peace, avoid scenes, whatever the cost. He was ruled by it, it fixed his character; and he was unaware of it the way some men are unaware of high blood pressure or a susceptibility to alcohol. Sweetness: he would have laughed ungenerously at the idea.

Against the window screen, Teddy could see heat waves rising in the early morning sun. Someone had set up a small electric fan on the sill, a whirring disc with four blades that swiveled slowly from right to left, then back again. Put your finger into that and you'd lose it in an instant. Teddy shuddered; his severed thumb, leaking blood and nerve ends, already lay on the floor in front of him. Then Larry Bernard crossed the room, hesitated at their table, sat down without being asked.

"Anyone seen Charlotte," he asked heartily, as though he had just eaten a huge steak.

No one answered.

"Sleep half the day if you let her," he went on. "They call it beauty sleep," he said to Teddy. "All beauties have to have their beauty sleep."

Gus Levi handed him the sports section, settled back with the editorial page.

"You must be Ben," Larry Bernard said, turning to Bea Lewin's oldest child.

"Yes, I am."

"A-ha," Larry Bernard said. "Easy to guess. You look just like your mother.

Ben raised an eyebrow, gave him his bust-my-ass look.

"Saul," Larry Bernard called. He ordered breakfast, turned to the sports news. Teddy glared at him from the other side of the table. Who had invited Larry Bernard to have breakfast with them? Sluggish currents of contempt and cherished hatred of the Philistines ran through him. Then, within seconds, Miss Sukenik and the Kesslers arrived, as though they all belonged to the same family, mother, father, and son. Erich sat down without saying hello, avoided Teddy's eyes, avoided everyone's eyes. One dirty book; a night under the Boardwalk; Herman, Claire, and Mignon, unexpected morning presences at table number five. Erich went to work on his breakfast. So did his father. They hardly spoke, a mere dollop of courtesy offered to their American friends, good morning—*gut* morning it sounded like—and without hesitating they were at their pancakes and syrup. Miss Sukenik, her pince-nez swinging from her neck, ordered hot water and lemon, that was all, her regular morning meal, she explained. Hot water and lemon, Saul repeated in his flat voice. It cleared her throat, she said, helped the membranes around the larynx, opened up the voice box, created a little activity in her stomach, stirred things up. Real food would wait until noon. She might have a piece of toast, might not. Her voice emerged from her throat like liquid, with a soft soprano purr that suggested, even through all the morning banalities, the beginnings of a sleek Puccini melody, something sung by Cio-cio-san or Floria Tosca to a waking lover. And while she explained her diet in her impeccable diction, Barney showed up, almost the last at the table, wearing baggy pants ten years old, huge pleats at the waist, old black-and-white golf shoes with tassels, first seen during Herbert Hoover's administration, a knit shirt a size too small. Ben and Teddy looked at each other, smiled, Hand-me-downs from one son or another. Barney lighted a cigarette as he sat down, his third of the day, turned his attention briefly to his grandsons, muttered to them under his breath. Someone had stained the toilet seat in the bathroom, he complained. Then he turned once more, this time to Etta Sukenik, and, burying the hand with the missing finger in his lap, began to court her through the purple smoke of his cigarette.

"Wonder what's keeping Charlotte," Larry Bernard said, looking around as though he had lost something. Then, interrupting Barney, he introduced himself to Etta Sukenik. "Better keep your eye on this bunch at table number five," he told her. At his words, Barney stuck his chin out, blew smoke across the table. "They give you any trouble," Larry Bernard went on, "you just come to me."

Etta Sukenik put her pince-nez on the bridge of her nose and considered Larry Bernard for a moment. "I think I'm in very good hands," she finally said, sipping hot water. She turned to Barney, acknowledging him, then, on her other side, to Frederick Kessler, to whom she nodded as though they were sharing a curtain call.

"Wolves," Larry Bernard said good-humoredly. "All of them. Just remember who your real friends are."

"And what's the news, Gus," Larry Bernard then asked, cutting the exchange. Teddy became half alert at the question, waited for his friend's response.

"Nothing good," Gus Levi said. He finished reading a sentence, put the paper down. "Another ultimatum from Germany," he said. "More tumult in Danzig. The whole continent is mobilized and Daladier is ready to move." Gus Levi turned to Teddy. "It's just where it was on Friday. Told you," he said, "that nothing ever happens over the weekend."

"It'll happen soon enough," Ben said. "A sure thing, if there ever was one. Can't be stopped now, not that combination of necessities, not that kind of energy. Maybe London or Paris or Berlin won't even be there by Labor Day. Wouldn't surprise me. They're all getting what they asked for."

Frederick Kessler grunted. "And the Jews in Europe," Etta Sukenik said in Yiddish, surprising them all. "What will happen to the Jews?"

Gus Levi threw a look at the Kesslers, each of whom impaled a pancake at the same moment, folded it neatly in two, then lifted it dripping to his mouth. It was as though they had heard nothing, as though the rest of the table were speaking an incomprehensible language. Europe was suddenly a forgotten fantasy that lived only on the front page of *The New York Times*. The real world, their world, lived elsewhere now. Frederick Kessler grunted again as he finished his pancakes, pushed his plate away. A moment later, Erich finally looked up at Teddy, for the first time, nodded inscrutably. Sudden pity filled Teddy as he accepted that opaque, inexpressive, foreign greeting. He wasn't fooled by it for a minute. Where was Mrs. Kessler's visa, what would happen to Erich's mother in Germany?

"Well," Larry Bernard then said. "No use kidding ourselves. It looks like bad times. We're all going to have to dig our own bomb shelters." He lighted a cigar, examined the flaming tip, puffed on it studiously, gazed across the room. A silence followed. Everyone considered what he had said. Gus Levi folded the *Times* into quarters, began to read again, his stomach rumbling. Larry Bernard shifted uncomfortably in his chair. Etta Sukenik squeezed another drop of lemon into her hot water.

"What's got into your old man?" Larry Bernard said to Teddy.

"Who?" Teddy said.

"Yours."

"What do you mean?" Teddy said.

"What's he doing over there?" Larry Bernard said. "Too good for us?"

"Where?"

"There," Larry Bernard said, pointing with his cigar. Teddy and Ben looked across the room at the same time, a quick, shared, classic look, full of the same resentment. Their father was seated at the Talleses' table, they saw, alongside Thelma Talles, eating pancakes this morning like the Kesslers. He was talking a mile a minute to his breakfast partner, laughing at his own jokes, unconscious of table number five, which was now silently watching him in action behind his back; and facing on the other side of his table, Thelma Talles' own sulking sons, the quiet Joseph and Tibor himself, the champ of Chalfonte Alley.

5

By early afternoon, a languor, a soft dispiriting lassitude, had settled into Teddy's bones. He knew the feeling, recognized the sudden loss of energy, the irresistible slowing of the blood. When he turned his head at lunch, as Ben called to him across the table, his whole consciousness witnessed the process. His eyeballs moved slowly to the left, the muscles in the back of his neck strained to follow. He turned a mere half inch at a time, his eyelids fluttering helplessly. When he finally made it, he saw Ben frowning at him in perplexity, looking as though he had already forgotten what he wanted to say. Teddy reversed the gesture, turned his head in slow motion back to Charlotte Melnicov, sleepily picking at her cucumbers alongside him, then to the Kesslers, Erich and Frederick, then to his friend, Gus Levi. Gus Levi still wore his transparent sports shirt. The razor cuts on his chin had shrunk since breakfast. His sallow skin was sweating in the heat. Over at another table, on the other side of the room, Jack Lewin was entertaining Thelma Talles again, in the company of her two sons. At number five, Barney Levin looked sour as he spied on them and tried to court Etta Sukenik at the same time. Teddy broke a roll in two, picked away at a leaf of lettuce, ate a half dozen vanilla cookies, thick with cheap dough. Gus Levi forced a glass of milk on him.

After lunch, he found himself wandering on the Boardwalk. How had he got there? He should have rushed upstairs with Erich and Tibor and Joseph, put on his bathing trunks, and made a run for the beach. Instead, he had left the table without a word, hefting a thoughtless sigh in the direction of the four-bladed fan that sat on the window sill, the sound of which brought Gus Levi's eyes up to his own. Are you all right, they asked, full of concern. On the Boardwalk a few minutes later, Teddy counted a dozen tourists out for a walk. One, he said to himself slowly. Two. Three and four. Dragging the count out, part of his brain ludicrously observing the other part at work. The tourists seemed to be strolling a foot off the ground, rigid as sleepwalkers. The noon sun scoured the planks all around them. Shimmers of midday heat floated in the salt air. Pale blue reflections came from the sky. But nothing really moved, neither the tourists nor the weightless clouds, nor the sun, nor the sea beneath it. The stillness suited Teddy. The surface of his body ran slow. Inside, a cacophony of Bach, Rachmaninoff, and Chopin filled his head, a simultaneous dissonance which he tried to sort out as he sluggishly moved along. Inventions, great, hammered chords, long, sinuous melodies, the same swift triplets he had practiced in the sand two days ago, the same urgent, descending rush of ten-noted Russian modulations, the same identical tunes without end out of the salons of Warsaw and the midnight boulevards of Paris. He mustered them note by note. That assured his reality, made him believe that the day actually existed. The venerable gray-bearded Bach, suave, urgent Rachmaninoff, swooning Chopin.

He knew Bach from old engravings, curls to his shoulders, jowls like pale jelly, with a long, nasty nose and a look of dour confidence. Another German, *echt deutsch*, this one from Leipzig, son of a cantor, a cantor himself. Orphaned at ten, the books said. Two-part inventions, three-part, poured from Bach's head without a beat between them, without a quarter-note rest. Billions of black-and-white notes, triad-obsessed. Preludes and fugues, cantatas for births, weddings, and other matters, partitas, sonatas, concertos, masses, passacaglias, passions. Passions according to this and that. New Testament narratives of betrayal and redemption, sob stories that went on for three hours about the Christian God hanging from his cross on Golgotha. When Teddy heard them, followed their endless flagellating lament and bittersweet exchanges in a German text that instantly became comprehensible through the music, he wanted to weep.

But Rachmaninoff and Chopin were somewhat more elegant. Rachmaninoff and Chopin were of this world. Chopin's mistress wore trousers, smoked cigars, and bore a man's name. What did that make Chopin? Tibor Talles would know. Chopin's music was as thin as Bea Lewin's smile. Thin and unbearably sweet, full of nostalgia and womanly longing. You could trace a lifetime of hopes in those endless melodies. They rose unresistingly in the mind like a morning mist, waiting to be dissipated by the full light of midday. They were like Rachmaninoff's, full of the same shapeless yearning, the same heavy, embroidered romance. Nothing would ever satisfy them. Teddy had once seen Rachmaninoff himself from the side balcony of the Lyric Theater, a mere fifty feet away. He had walked out onto the stage to play his own music with the Philadelphia Orchestra and Leopold Stokowski. That was his annual custom in Baltimore. Together, the pianist and the conductor had looked like two ravenous lions who had both stepped on a thorn somewhere. The stage below was heavy with Slavic pain, Slavic egocentricity. Stokowski stood in a spotlight and led the orchestra with his beautiful hands illuminated from above. Rachmaninoff sat stooped over the piano a few feet away, lower lip slack. His fingers worked the keys like massive pistons. He was round-shouldered and thin, an unsmiling neurasthenic Russian with brooding eyes and austere cropped hair who cast distant looks from time to time at his conductor and the audience. At the end of the performance, a great roar had come from the house out front, as though they were all sitting in Oriole Park, watching a baseball game. That night, Teddy Lewin discovered that there was a heady charm in being at once remote and passionate, detached yet beloved. It was something he would want for himself. People rose to their feet and cheered you for it.

It was too hot now. He should have tried to take a nap upstairs after lunch. He should have changed to his bathing suit and rushed to the beach for a quick dip. He should have hidden out in a dim corner of Sloan's lobby and written a couple of postcards to Marion and his mother. Overhead, the veranda at the Cotswold was empty. The early afternoon, the day's dreadful Jersey sun, was too much even for the ladies from Richmond and Bala Cynwyd. They were probably in their beds now, slip-clad, fans whirring gently overhead, thin cambric handkerchiefs bathed in toilet water folded over their foreheads. That was how they would pass the hour or two after lunch. With luck, they would also sleep for a few minutes. It was what the old lady Eisen did, what all the old ladies, all widows of whatever age, did in the early afternoon when it grew too hot.

The dozen tourists had grown to fourteen. A man in an orange shirt with short sleeves, a box camera hanging from a strap around his neck. His wife in a print house dress, without a girdle. Her buttocks rose and fell as she walked. Sometimes her dress rested a moment in the crease there. A porter from one of the hotels, carrying a message to another. Two soldiers in light khaki, their overseas caps snapped down over their foreheads. But Teddy lost interest. It was too ordinary, too commonplace. The man in the orange shirt was wearing sneakers. He should have been on the beach with his wife, sunning himself or swimming to escape the heat. They should have had the good sense to get out of the afternoon cauldron, this ninety-six-degree broil, this painful thickness of sun and still air. Teddy wandered on, practicing the piano in his head, thinking, through the music, of his brother, his mother, his sister. Ben seemed such a stranger. But they all did after a separation. By the time he got home to Baltimore next week, Marion would be a different person. It was always like that. It would take them a full day to become reacquainted, twenty-four hours to become brother and sister again. By the next morning, they would be fully related once more, her face like a thin memory of his own, her blood his. It would be the same with his mother, the same with Ben. His thoughts moved on like caterpillar legs, one smoothly eliding into the other, Marion becoming Bea, a long, multiple, tracklike fugue of family feeling, family thoughts. But like the tourists around him it began to grow tiresome. Ben was lost. He had disappeared into New York's summer. Remnants of him remained somewhere in mid-Manhattan and at the World's Fair. Something else had shaped him anew, something had changed him. But nothing had happened, nothing had changed. It was all Teddy's invention. Ben was the same. Ben had already proved it. And how, he had asked, are our mother and father getting along, Mr. and Mrs. Jack Lewin? Their life together isn't exactly a garden of Eden, he had said. No. Not exactly. Teddy had hated him for that, had hated Bea and Jack, too, for allowing such a question to exist. Teddy's hands moved at his sides, running scales now.

At the Peabody, Mabel Johns didn't think that Teddy was ready to play Rachmaninoff. She told him so every time he asked. It required too much technique, a hand as big as a gorilla's, fingers like rifles, biceps too. Sometimes he fooled around with the scores at home, on the Chickering that filled half the living room; but he couldn't span those octaves with comfort, he couldn't hammer out those chords at that speed. Halfway down the page, his technique came apart, his wrists began to ache. Mabel Johns was right about Rachmaninoff, but she had hopes for Teddy, nevertheless. She talked to him about "lyricism." Lyricism—that was when you couldn't play loud and big. He would play Haydn and Mozart, she decided, Schumann, Schubert, Chopin. He had the touch, he could make them all sing. Impromptus, fantasies, nocturnes, waltzes, that was his style. He knew it, too. Let somebody else fool with Rachmaninoff. Let another talent conquer the world with Beethoven and Brahms.

When Miss Eversfield had assigned him to Mabel Johns—

"She's most splendid with young boys," she had said to Jack—
Teddy's first hope was that she would be pretty. That was always
his first hope about a teacher. I hope she's pretty, he had said to
himself as he went through the thick, soundproofed door into
her classroom for the first time. As simpleminded as that. But he
had miscalculated. He was a minute early and Mabel Johns still
sat with a pupil at one of the two concert grands in her studio.
She cut him dead with a wintry smile bred in Scotland, told
him to sit down in the corner and wait his turn. Then she went
back to her lesson. She wasn't pretty, either. She was a tall, bent
woman with huge knuckles and knobby bones. She called him
Theodore. She wore her hair like a dandified man and shared a
house in the country with Monica Eisel, whose own studio at
the Peabody was right down the hall. Monica Eisel was a soft,
passive woman with enormous benign breasts. She was still pretty,
even in middle age, but, unlike Mabel Johns, she was not so
good with young boys. She shied away from Teddy in the hall-
ways at the Peabody and could hardly manage a greeting without
blushing up to her eyes. Mabel Johns, lecturing Teddy in a husky
voice, told him that she wanted him to play the piano with "expression." All his teachers before the Peabody, the whole long
line of bored, depression-priced ladies who had come to the
house once a week for two dollars a lesson, had always talked
about "expression." He finally understood, long after he first
heard the word, that when they said "expression" they were
talking about their own meager, sentimental feelings.

He could hardly keep his eyes open. He should have worn
his sunglasses on the Boardwalk, should have taken a nap,
should have told his brother to shut up when he started to talk
about Bea and Jack at breakfast. Ben had no right to talk about
their parents like that. It was a happy family. They were a happy
couple. They pleased each other. They loved each other. They
loved their children. It had always been that way. What could
be wrong in all that?

He was back at Virginia Avenue, back in the shadow of the

Cotswold veranda. He had no sense of having arrived there, no sense of having walked elsewhere and returned. The sun still blinded everything, the sun sucked up the ocean's water and evaporated it. Taffy odors came from down the street, the poisoned scent of cotton candy. Sugar and syrup, a flood of both. Teddy nearly drowned in it. All the blinds were down in the solarium at the Surf. Music disappeared, all thought. He wandered into Sloan's, snaked through the lobby mindlessly, headed up the stairs. He arrived at the room, paused, knocked. A premonitory fear held him. There was no answer. He tried the knob, shook it. It was locked. But he had forgotten to ask for the key, was too dumb today for even that. He had to walk down the stairs, had to ask Pearl Sloan for the key. She gave him a peculiar look. "You're not at the beach," she said. "How come you're not at the beach?" He didn't answer. Then again upstairs, up the stairwell one flight, two, slowly, deliberately, down the hall then, the key in the lock twisted to the right, and finally into the room. It was dusk inside. The bed was made, the cot folded up in a corner, the shades drawn. It was like a sweet empty cave. Ben's copy of *The Good Earth* lay on the dresser. The tiny hand-painted flowers on the furniture floated lazily in the twilight. Ah, he thought with relief, falling heavily on the bed. He was asleep instantly.

He awoke to the same dusk. He rolled slowly onto his side. Slow, powerful yawns came, a distant sense of his pulse. He lay there for a few minutes, staring at the drawn window shades, staring at the dresser. He put his thumb on his pulse, counted. It was there all right, slow and firm. He sat up, unbuttoned his shirt. Then he kicked off his shoes. Finally, he stood up, dropped his pants, dropped his shorts, and standing there in the dark vaguely began to admire himself in the mirror that stood on top of the dresser. There was a clean line at his waist separating white skin and tan, another at a diagonal across the top of each thigh. Down there, he was virginally pale. He stared at himself, touched his crotch. He was all awake now, body and mind in phase. A stirring began. He took his pulse again, waited a moment, staring into the mirror. A window shade flapped, a bare sound as arid as a fly swatter. Quickly then he reached for his trunks, slipped into them, smoothed down the front. He checked himself in the mirror for the last time. He thought he could smell his mother everywhere in the room.

Again he walked downstairs, past Pearl Sloan and her suspicious glance, through the empty lobby, out into the sun, into the city they had chosen above all others. It had no trees, no grass, no vegetation or landscape, just people, stone, sand, and sea. It was enough for Teddy Lewin, it was enough for all of them, worth ninety-odd dollars and change each week. He crossed the Boardwalk then, walked down the steps onto the beach, paused, shading his eyes with his hand. He scanned the beach, turning from left to right, caught sight of Ben, sitting back to back with Charlotte. Larry Bernard sat alongside them. They were all hugging their knees. Larry Bernard's head was covered with lotion. Ben looked meditative, a little bored. Charlotte was pink and beautiful in her bandanna. A few feet away, the Kesslers shared a blanket. Mr. Kessler wore his bathing cap, had his face raised to the sun. Flat on his back, Erich looked asleep. He was as solemn as a whale. Teddy swept the beach again with his eyes. Something familiar hovered in the foreground. It wavered there a moment, flickered in his vision. Then he lost it, turned another few degrees to the right. He saw the Monday crowd, slack and unhurried. There was plenty of room for everyone, plenty of sand to sink into. The lifeguards sat on the ends of their spines on high white chairs, eight feet over everyone. By now, the end of the summer, they were the color of honey, the hair on their arms and legs bleached a fine yellow. A hundred and fifty feet away, the Steel Pier thrust into a sea as calm as the cobalt sky above it. The air was without current, without sound. All the Steel Pier pennants lay dead on their masts. As Teddy watched, a single gull sailed in serenely, plucked something invisible from the water, rose into the air again. That's what Sloan's guests all came for, a calm as binding as eternity. Then the gull returned, aimed for the same spot, circled it before diving.

Teddy blinked in the sunlight. His eyes were tearing with allergy. Ben and Charlotte and Larry Bernard were all talking at the same time. Teddy moved up onto the first step. Ben's contemplation was gone. He sat up straight, alert. They were laughing together, Charlotte with her beloved book now clasped in her hands. Nearby, the Kesslers were storing up energy, absorbing ultraviolet rays to take back with them to Washington Heights for the winter. Erich Kessler still looked asleep, breathing deeply on his back, as even, as measured, as a clock's pendulum. Something familiar emerged again. Teddy straightened, stared ahead. Behind his mother, behind Thelma Talles, a few feet from Erich, Tibor Talles was digging in the sand on his hands and knees. He was scooping out great handfuls of wet sand, excavating a foundation, pausing every now and then to eavesdrop on his mother. As he worked, his brother Joseph watched him. Thelma Talles twirled her mauve parasol in the air, sat in light shade in front of her sons, her skin an arctic white. She was listening carefully to Jack Lewin, still listening to him as she had listened at breakfast and at lunch, while Jack sat hunched over, facing her as he talked, burying his stiffened legs in the sand down to the ankles, his curving spine so visible to Teddy standing on the Boardwalk steps that he could count the discs that ran down his father's back. The sun beat down. The gull sailed in a third time, this time parallel to the shoreline. A lone breaker finally crashed on the beach.

Teddy watched them for a while. Jack was shoveling sand against the side of his legs. He would take a handful of sand and cover his knees. Then, within seconds, it would slide away. Teddy could almost see each grain of sand as it fell. Six feet from Jack Lewin, Tibor Talles dug furiously between his own knees. Joseph was trying to give him advice. Teddy saw Thelma Talles smile, a brilliant, welcoming smile, one he knew, then extend her hand to emphasize a point. She waited for Jack's response. Her smile seemed to go on forever. Her hand hovered in the sunlight. They had a lot to say to each other. They had a lot to talk about. The minutes bore on. The sun shifted to the west. Ben Lewin headed for the water. Charlotte and Larry Bernard followed him, holding hands. She had taken off her bandanna, her hair hung to her waist. The conversation on the beach seemed to lose energy. Jack Lewin was wiggling his toes in the sand. Thelma Talles was laughing. Every now and then, Tibor glanced up from what he was doing, listened a moment, then went back to his digging. He ignored his brother. Teddy waited a few minutes longer. No one beckoned to him, no one saw him. He was alone on the stairway to the beach, fingering the patched mothhole on his bathing trunks. His brother Ben was splashing in the sea. Charlotte was holding on to Larry Bernard for dear life, standing in water up to her hips. Teddy's friend Erich Kessler was asleep on a seedy blanket. He didn't even know Teddy was nearby. Standing there on the step, Teddy thought a moment of his mother, imagined her at the Ritz having a cup of coffee after dinner, while she entertained Judge Aaron from Trenton. Judge Aaron couldn't take his eyes off her, hung on every word. He was worse than Dr. Lazarus. She knew how to talk, too, just like her husband Jack, knew how to manipulate a waiting world, make it sit up and take notice, come back and ask for more. They were like a vaudeville team, those two, Bea and Jack Lewin, with their small, neat, graceful bodies and thin, clean-cut smiles, dancing away in the spotlight on opposite sides of the stage, putting on the charm for an audience of enchanted strangers.

6

By six o'clock the swelling in Jack's feet was so painful that there was no question about going downstairs for dinner. As soon as he had tried to stand, in a gesture of absurd courage, they all knew he would have to stay in bed for at least twelve hours, just as the doctor had suggested when he had been called in by Pearl Sloan. Jack had swung his bare legs over the side of the double bed, had come down lightly on his feet, then groaned with a sound of agony that shook Teddy as he watched his father from the other side of the room.

His feet were swollen, insteps and ankles. So were his toes. His shoulders were already blistered; so was the base of his neck, where the skin looked raw in patches; the skin of his upper arms was taut and rubbery, a shining, mottled red. The pain was everywhere, a vast bodily emanation, nearly visible, that steamed in heated, rhythmic waves. They could hardly believe it, Ben stunned by his father's ineptitude in the face of a simple problem like how to avoid sunburn, Barney distraught first, then suddenly angry at his son for forcing him to act like a parent on his own Atlantic City vacation, Jack himself moaning in pain, humiliation, and self-pity. As for Teddy, he was the guilty one. Who else had a bottle of suntan lotion for just such occasions sitting in his bureau drawer, unopened? Who else was responsible? What would he tell Bea Lewin?

At five thirty, Thelma Talles had knocked discreetly at their door, asking how Jack was. Teddy had answered her questions.

She looked concerned, standing there in the hallway, trying to
see into the room over Teddy's shoulder. Her son Joseph hovered
in the background, prowling the carpet. Their own rooms were
on the floor above. After listening nervously, she had flashed one
of her white smiles at Teddy and was gone. By then, Jack was
soaking in a hot bath filled with Epsom salts. The doctor had
prescribed a hot bath three times a day. He could not go to the
beach for at least forty-eight hours, and when he did he would
have to wear pants, hat, and long-sleeved shirt, and even then
the doctor wanted him to sit under the Boardwalk. "You've got
skin like parchment," the doctor had said. He sounded affronted.
"You should know better." Then in an effort to soften the
asperity, he had added, "I see this all the time."

It ended with Teddy bringing a tray to his father after they
had all had their own dinners, with the crowd at table number
five parading upstairs one by one for a glimpse of the patient,
for an honest attempt to offer solace, peace, advice. In Germany,
apparently, they used baking soda for sunburn, or so Frederick
Kessler said, as he sighed with Central European pity at the foot
of the double bed. You put the soda on a wet plaster, he said,
gesticulating, then let it rest on the wound. Thank you, thank
you, Jack said, letting another groan escape. Gus Levi brought a
book, brought two, offered himself as a pinochle partner, anything. He had the dyspepsia tonight, stood in the room trying
to smother his belches, one eye on Teddy. Then, without anything to say, he left. Charlotte hung around waiting to be told
that she was essential, could find nothing to do, hung around
some more when no one said anything. Barney kept bumping into
her in the small room, glaring at Jack in the bed, saying between
coughs: "Look what you did to yourself. At your age." "Pa," Jack
pleaded. A half hour later, Barney excused himself. He was taking Miss Sukenik for a walk. She was waiting for him now
downstairs, had asked for Jack at dinner, had showed she cared.
She was going to tell Barney about the opera. Then Ben went
off, too, with hardly a look over his shoulder. He couldn't get

away fast enough, couldn't wait a moment longer. As though he didn't give a damn, as though Jack's suffering meant nothing, as though he were not a part of it, still a resident of the Christian Association in New York, as though he were detached from the whole business, a tourist in the Lewin family. Teddy found himself mumbling aloud, a few curses, exclamations of disbelief, the first small flames of a neatly banked furnace of pique.

Charlotte disappeared, too, wringing her hands as she left. She was wearing her wet pink lipstick, the dress with the rose at the waist, her hair combed tight to her skull like a second skin. Larry Bernard awaited her. She had to leave so that she could deal with her future. She had to make a decision. Should she marry Larry Bernard? The question of the day. Teddy shook his head. Should she marry him? As though the question really existed. Larry Bernard would never ask her. That much Teddy Lewin knew. No matter what she said, how she talked, that much Teddy Lewin knew as well as Charlotte Melnicov, wet lipstick, scalloped dress, and clinging blond hair, knew it. She reserved herself to herself, she always had, it was like her failures at the bar; and he had learned that those who reserved themselves, who kept their distance, who said no, were instantly welcome to the right by an indifferent world. For the rest of their lives. For eternity.

It was quiet in the room, quiet in all of Sloan's. Downstairs, Teddy knew, the Monday night bridge game had begun. Thelma Talles was probably just bidding two no-trump to a partner she had never played with before. All the husbands were gone, home now on their five-day round of profits and God knows what else. Only a few bachelors, like Gus Levi and Larry Bernard, or an odd family group, like the Kesslers and the Lewins, or a half dozen old men, shipped off for the summer by their families and led by Rabbi Miller, hung around downstairs. Teddy had seen the old men pray together in the morning, pray in the evening, tell dirty stories to each other, hold on to their canes and walking sticks, like the old lady Eisen, whose money they envied, and suffer phlegm. Now they sat together in a circle in the lobby, wearing felt carpet slippers, sleepy and flatulent from dinner.

Jack lay back in his bed, sunk into two soft pillows, wearing pajama tops, at the doctor's suggestion. It would make him a little more comfortable, the doctor had said, allow him to stretch himself a little, keep the sheets and pillow cases from rubbing his worst wounds raw. He was hardly burned at all from the waist to the ankles, where he had sat buried in the sand for hours. Tonight he wore no pajama bottoms. He could move his legs without trouble, moved them now restlessly, pulling at the bedcovers. The only light in the room came from the reading lamp next to the bed; it threw a dim pale circle onto the wall above it, but the rest of the room was in deep shadow. Sitting there next to the window, staring at the white clapboard wall of the Surf, twelve feet away, Teddy could hardly keep his eyes open. His buttocks ached on the hard chair. A tic began on his cheek. It was only seven thirty.

"Why don't you go out and get some air?" Jack said.

"I'm all right," Teddy said.

"Go on."

"No."

"Please."

"You want to go to sleep?"

"I just don't want to ruin your fun."

"You're not ruining my fun."

"I certainly ruined my own."

" . . . . . . "

"Come on now, you can't sit around here in the dark like a registered nurse."

"I don't mind."

"Jesus Christ."

"What's wrong?"

"I can hardly move. My back. My shoulders. I can't believe I was so stupid."

"It's my fault. I had a bottle of suntan lotion for you. In my drawer. It's my fault I didn't give it to you."

"Don't be silly. It's not your fault."

"Mother made me buy it especially for you before she left."

"Don't worry about it."

"Will we have to go home now?"

"Of course not." Jack lifted his head a moment to get a better look at Teddy. "I'm not sick. I'm burned. Every minute makes it better, every second the healing goes on."

"But what kind of good time will you have lying around like this?"

"I'll be up tomorrow."

"You won't be able to swim."

"I don't swim three hundred and fifty-eight days a year, another seven won't hurt me."

"If you want to go home, I'm willing."

"I told you. No."

They were silent for a few minutes, then Teddy spoke up. "Didn't Mrs. Talles see what was happening?"

Jack looked at Teddy uneasily. "How should I know? We were engrossed in a conversation."

"Seems to me she should have noticed."

"We were busy talking."

"She should have warned you."

"It was my fault. My stupidity. Nobody else's."

"But she was sitting right in front of you."

"She wasn't paying that kind of attention."

"Well." Teddy arched his back, stretched. "Should I give Mother a call?"

"Certainly not. She'd worry herself to death."

"I think she should know. You can't hide it from her."

"She'll know soon enough," Jack said fretfully. "Hand me the Noxzema. And just dip that poultice a little in the water. See if it's still warm. Not too wet now."

They worked together for five minutes, poultice, water, soothing cool lotion, a tender white smear across Jack's shoulders. Teddy could see tiny crisscrossed·blood vessels on the surface of his father's skin. They looked as though they had exploded. His upper arms, as he dropped the pajama top, were half again as round as they usually were. Just below the shoulders, over his vaccinations, masses of pinprick blisters had formed. Teddy could see thousands of them. He shuddered, blinked back tears. Such pain, such ugliness. He had never seen his father like that. He had never expected to. From his own self-involved stupidity, too. A sudden contempt rose in Teddy, a sour, ironic humor. It was the end of Thelma Talles, that was for sure. How could she care for Jack Lewin with all those ugly blisters and flesh that screamed at the touch? What could Jack Lewin do now? They had what they deserved, the two of them.

An hour or so passed. There was the sound of a saxophone from somewhere, the same old band playing on the Steel Pier, momentarily caught on an inshore breeze. A light blinked on and off on the Surf's wall. Their neighbors began to move around in the room next door. Shoes dropped; there were hawking noises; a toilet flushed. Jack dozed fitfully in five-minute stretches, moaning in his sleep. Teddy helped him again with his medication, making small talk. At one point, Pearl Sloan knocked at the door and handed Teddy a note. "This just came," she said. "For your father." When Jack opened it, he bit his lips. "Your Aunt Celia is here," he said. "At the Shelburne." Without even knowing it, Teddy checked his fingernails. "We're expected to make an appearance," Jack added. "Is she alone?" Teddy asked. "She's never alone. Somebody's in attendance. One of your perfect cousins, probably." "Hmmmmmmm." Then, a little later, Gustav Levi stuck his head in the door. He was just making his rounds, he said, taking temperatures, checking conditions in the wards. They were all too weary to smile. Was everything all right? What did they need? Everything was all right. They needed nothing. Ah, Gustav Levi said, they knew where he was; don't hesitate. Then he was gone, back to his books. The dimness returned. The room filled with yawns. The smell of Noxzema was everywhere, cutting through another, unpleasant odor. It was getting late. At last.

"What's your brother up to these days?" Jack asked.

"How should I know?" A quick, unwilling answer.

"He seems very surefooted." Jack paused a moment. "He seems to know his way around."

"That's Ben. You know him."

"What'd he do all summer in New York?"

"Ask him. He doesn't tell me anything."

"He doesn't talk to you, his own brother?"

"I told you, no."

"Nothing?"

"Practically."

"That make you feel left out, like a little kid?"

". . . . . ."

"You're the one with the talent, you know. No reason for you to feel less than Ben."

"I don't feel less than Ben."

"You're just as smart as he is. And you've got the talent."

". . . . . ."

"You have, you know."

"So what's talent?"

"What's talent? You think it comes a dime a dozen?"

"What difference does it make?"

"You don't think Ben would give his left arm for your talent?"

". . . . . ."

"The world worships talent."

His father's words made him nervous. There was something formidable there; they were too insistent. Miss Eversfield told him that he had talent, too. So did Mabel Johns, with certain qualifications, of course. They were all beginning to share the same expectations of him, Jack, Bea, the Sandlers, his teachers;

and he hardly resisted. He glanced out of the window at the bland clapboards a few feet away. "I don't feel like talking about it tonight," he said.

"Nothing wrong with talking about it. All brothers—"

"Where'd Grandpa go?" He turned to face his father.

"Hm. With his girl friend."

"He doesn't have any girl friend."

"He went with that soprano. Miss Sukenik. At his age."

"Grandpa's too old. So don't even think about it."

"Nobody's too old."

"You should see the medicine he brought with him."

"Nobody's too old."

"Stuff I never heard of."

"Look, hand me my pajama pants."

"What for?"

"I'm not going to sleep half-naked with you."

"You think I should share the bed, the way you are?" Teddy flushed at the question. "Suppose I roll over in the night?"

"You won't roll over. Don't worry about it. Just hand me the bottoms. Also, open the cot and get it ready for Ben so he won't wake us up when he comes in."

So he won't wake us up when he comes in. So he . . . Teddy began to mutter to himself as he went to work. Ben this, Ben that. Who cared? He could hear Jack struggling into his pajama bottoms inch by inch behind him, cursing and yelping the whole time. Teddy turned irresistibly for a split second, saw the familiar, skinny, dead-white legs, black hair like wire filigree, Lewin and Levin hair, holy *lwh* hair, God-loving *lwh* hair, turned back again to the cot. The blood filled his head. He flapped a sheet in the air. It settled slowly on the cot. He was too tired. It was too late. He should be asleep. Behind him, his father was making sounds like an animal, he was really in pain, and some part of Teddy was enjoying it. Goddamn fool, he said under his breath. Damn fool, damn fool; not knowing whether he meant his father, his brother, or himself.

7

The question now was how to get to the Shelburne.

Jack had come downstairs for dinner, having spent most of the day and the previous night in bed, bathing down the hall from time to time in Epsom salts, cooling himself in the deep shade of their enclosed room, receiving visitors, recovering with a hungry speed, an avarice, that took them all by surprise. The body was a miraculous thing, they all agreed. Sunburn could produce cancer, char flesh permanently. It could kill a man. But Jack's healing moved relentlessly along, a swift, sweet process in which pain quickly began to lose its force and disappeared for entire minutes at a time. Nevertheless, he could not bear to be touched. In the middle of the night, awakening to his father's slow moan, Teddy had brushed Jack's upper arm, a brief, caressing swipe that brought them both fully awake on the instant, Jack crying "Good God!" as Teddy pulled hastily away. He had been afraid that would happen. He had warned his father before they went to sleep. He would have to be more careful, have to watch himself, lie absolutely still alongside his father; and for the rest of the night, pinched by his own willpower, and guilt, he hovered in dim, fearful nightmares on the very edge of wakefulness. But by morning, it seemed, with the light streaming in from the alleyway, Jack was able to smile once more, and he had learned to keep his distance. The swelling in his feet had gone down, a few huge blisters had already burst, the Noxzema was working, whatever the doctor had put on the poultice had

had its effect, and the baths, all three of them, were most wonderful of all. But he let no one near him.

Everyone made way for Jack. Everyone was solicitous. Pearl Sloan relayed messages to and from the doctor. Larry Bernard stopped in right after breakfast, bringing an extra order of toast wrapped in paper napkins. He was full of sports news and windy cheer. Charlotte bustled about, Florence Nightingale, Martha at her duties, Bea Lewin's dear friend. How wonderful to be able to act on that, how wonderful to be visibly good. Some spring of fresh hope seemed to run through her as she changed the water in Jack's bedside pitcher, smoothed the sheets, pulled the window shades just so, each one even with the next. She was blissful in the placid grip of domesticity. Then, arranging Larry Bernard's extra toast on a plate on the end table, she made a shopping list of Jack's needs—bottle of aspirin, pack of Chesterfields, fresh jar of Noxzema—and went off with Larry Bernard, all smiles.

That was how the day passed. Ben spelled Teddy without having to be coaxed, without complaints. Barney was in and out, between meals. Gus Levi stopped by, bringing the morning's *Times*, black with headlines about the Polish Corridor and the fate of Danzig; and Frederick Kessler, dancing nervously on his heavy feet, afraid that he would say the wrong thing. Thelma Talles arrived too, later in the day, looking shy this afternoon. When Teddy answered her hesistant knock, Jack asked her in. He pulled the sheet up to his neck, smoothed the folds over his bare legs, smiled diffidently. Thelma Talles stood at the foot of the bed, rocking back and forth almost imperceptibly in her high heels, pressing her thighs against the footboard. She talked about her bridge game, five tricks here, a couple there, who won, who lost, about the heat, about the boys, about Teddy, Tibor, Joseph, Erich Kessler. It was God's blessing that the boys had each other. What would they have done otherwise? God's blessing. It was her expression. Jack laughed at everything she said, clutched the sheet like a maiden. Thelma Talles' voice was like her smile, full of brilliance and high, dazzling lights. She wore a simple green dress, smoked one cigarette after another with slow, deliberate gestures, blew the smoke out, sighing. Teddy waved his hand energetically behind her back to clear the air, while she slowly swayed forward and back at the edge of the mattress. She stayed a few minutes more, left the scent of plain talc behind when she left. It was sweeter than Bea's, floated everywhere. Again, Teddy waved his hand to clear the air, while Jack settled back into the pillows, suddenly serene.

Late in the day, Barney wanted to bring Etta Sukenik up, but Jack objected. "Enough, Pa," he said. "I'm tired." But it turned out that Barney couldn't find her in any case. She was somewhere with Frederick Kessler, he was told. They were not downstairs, not in their rooms. They had gone out somewhere together. "Tomorrow," Barney said, sounding disappointed. "She'll come tomorrow. You'll see." Chagrin filled his voice. And the afternoon and the early evening wore away, while Jack's scorched flesh began to regenerate itself, the fouled layers already peeling like ashes from his shoulders, making something of a mess in the bed, but leaving in its place a delicate, pink epidermal shield that Jack examined in the mirror with careful absorption. No doubt of it, he was better. No doubt, by late afternoon the pain had eased. Still, he could not bear to be touched. He walked around the bedroom in slippers whose insteps had been cut open. He took his three baths, used up almost the entire new jar of Noxzema that Charlotte had brought him, rested with poultices on his back, read the news, napped. Suggestions of yesterday's intense suffering returned, briefly. Teddy watched Jack screw up his face; his moustache twitched; he groaned. Teddy could hardly bear the sight. For the moment, it was as though his father were dying. Ben watched him, too. Then the brothers looked at each other with shocked faces.

But it didn't last long, once at noon, once again maybe an hour later, then it was over. They both even managed momentary escapes to the beach. Teddy swam for a half hour or so in mid-afternoon and lay alongside Erich Kessler on the hotel blanket, while Erich sought an easy way to ask Teddy about his father. But it was too much for him. He couldn't raise the subject, the question of pain was beyond him. Like his father, he was afraid he would say the wrong thing. So they talked about Washington Heights again, about the millinery business, about Frederick Kessler's rich cousin, bearable subjects. In the end, it was Teddy who felt like consoling Erich Kessler, like soothing the vague, heavy anxiety that seemed to lie everywhere on his new friend, camouflaged by clumsy chatter about the Palisades in New Jersey and the newly built laundry room in the basement of the Kesslers' apartment building. Then Tibor wandered along, looking sly. He stood over them, stretching his long, brown arms to the sky, legs spread apart. Teddy turned on his back, looked straight up at him. His belly glistened like a fat salmon's. "How's your old man?" Tibor asked. Their eyes met, a single, instantaneous fleck of comprehension passed between them, then quickly died. A sharp sense of self-betrayal settled over Teddy. There would be no understanding of that kind between them, no acknowledgment between Talles and Lewin that could mean anything. Teddy would see to that.

At table number five that night, sitting tieless and without a jacket at dinner, the object of sympathetic murmurs and soft, compassionate glances from the rest of the room, Jack had decided that they would visit Celia tonight. Now, he said over dessert, in a few minutes. Ben had been dispatched to make the phone call, over Barney's objections, over Teddy's. Jack wasn't well enough, they said, anyone could see that. It was enough that he had come downstairs for dinner, why rush things? I am not sick, Jack muttered. I am not sick. He should return to bed, Barney said, keeping his eye on Etta Sukenik, he should rest for the night. With enough rest tonight, the world would be his oyster tomorrow. But no, Jack had decided that they would go to the Shelburne after dinner, and that was the way it would be. Some perverse need to show Bea's sister his wounds before they healed, some solemn desire to play the martyr, drove him on. It always did with the Sandlers. They were always just out of reach of Jack Lewin and he reached for them, had always reached for them, for Celia, for Haskel, for all the others, above all Bea, as though the chance would be withdrawn forever if he didn't act on it instantly. Celia would tell them all of his travail, again and again, and for the rest of their lives, Jack Lewin's sunburn would be talked about whenever the subject of Atlantic City came up in family conversations. Despite himself, he liked the idea, to be at the center of Sandler talk. Now, to Barney he said, "You don't have to come, Pa. I'll just take the boys." They acknowledged each other across the table, Barney relieved and trying to hide it.

A few minutes later, Jack and the boys stood on the Board-walk, arguing feebly with each other. It was clear that the only way Jack could get to the Shelburne was to hire a rolling chair and be wheeled there. His feet were too tender, he did not want to be bumped by the crowd. That was all right with Ben as long as Jack understood that he would have no part of it, would not ride in a rolling chair, hire another human to perambu-late him in front of the whole world as long as he, Ben Lewin, had two good legs under him. "No man should have to push another man in a chair," he said.

"That's their living," Jack snapped.

"It's beneath a man's dignity."

"What would they do if everybody felt the way you do?"

"Other things," Ben said. "Like other men."

"You have a job for them?"

"You really think they should be parading the Boardwalk in Atlantic City like oxen?"

"For God's sake," Jack said. "You'd take away a man's liveli-hood, just so you could be right."

"Come on," Teddy said. He had begun to twitch. "Dad can't walk. You know that."

"I am not going to ride in one of those things. You can both do what you want. I'll meet you at the Shelburne and I'll be there before you will."

So Ben had strode off, walking a little more briskly than he might have, determined to arrive at the Shelburne before his father. Jack waved over a chair, hustled Teddy into it and, stiff-legged with discomfort, climbed up himself and settled in. Off they moved, without a sound, passing the same old sights, the same old candy stands and secondhand bookstores, the gypsy fortune-teller and the auctions, the sand sculptors working below the Boardwalk, the littered beach and the slow incoming tide, Larry Bernard's same old *dreck*. Past the Steel Pier, past the Cotswold, the Marlborough-Blenheim, the huge castle of the Traymore, right through the thousands of tourists who strolled easily along and hardly gave Teddy and Jack a second glance as they sat on their moving throne. No matter. Teddy assumed a dignity that came without exertion, a sudden victim of wicker affluence, rolling along on flowered cushions, feet up on the little metal rest on the floor, viewing the world without lifting a muscle. Some awful feeling of ineffable superiority rose in him. He recognized it instantly, let it lift him for the moment. How easy it was for it to surface. Behind them, the grizzled old Negro pushed them evenly along while Teddy stole glances at him over his shoulder. He was talking to himself in incomprehensible syllables, his graying hair set like iron filings on his scalp, his white coat immaculate, nodding like a courtier to all his colleagues who passed him going in the opposite direction. What would happen to him if everybody felt the way Ben did?

Jack was silent the whole trip, sitting fretful and tensed with his arms folded over his chest. That was how all his exchanges with Ben left him these days. His older son wouldn't allow him a moment's pleasure, wouldn't allow any of them a moment's pleasure. Everything had to be probed, analyzed, redefined, then set into another context and condemned. It all sounded false to Teddy. Who had asked Ben for his opinion in the first place? If he wanted to walk, let him walk. But it was typical, perfectly representative, that every little decision, every simple move, all the ordinary things that everyone else took for granted, had to be the subject of an Emancipation Proclamation, a Ten Commandments, a doctrinaire Manifesto handed down willfully, spitefully from above, in the prevalent spirit of killjoy cultivated by Benedict Lewin. It had always been that way. It was now getting worse. And these days, while he was being educated at the Johns Hopkins University, they were helpless in the face of his arguments. Even Gustav Levi had been a victim.

"Shelbine," the colored man said, standing at attention for his money. Then they went through the revolving door, which spilled right onto the Boardwalk, into the green-and-beige lobby filled with plants, ferns, moist potted trees, a touch of Africa, Teddy thought, an arboretum nourished day and night by dozens of paid hands, carpets so thick that Teddy's and Jack's heels left a horseshoe mark in them, bulging *vitrines* that held precious jewelry, green emerald clips highlighted by diamonds, a necklace resting on a black velvet cushion, wedding rings, engagement rings, one huge window somewhere in the back for sports clothes, a pink mannequin standing like a piece of waxed fruit, ready for golf. Jack was speaking to the man at the desk. House phone, Teddy heard, as his father moved off. It was like the Ritz in here, as soft and silent as the other hotel a mile down the Boardwalk, with another life going on just beyond reach, something invisible and desirable that had nothing to do with the life at Sloan's. There was something pliant in the air, something tactful and controlled, something none of them, not the old lady Eisen with her gift boxes of chocolate laxatives, or Bertha Wolf, waiting for her husband to get out of jail, or the imperious Mr. Pearman from Pittsburgh, who had the entire Talmud at his fingertips, or the Waldmans, who had a monopoly on senior class rings in Bergen County, or even his father's own Thelma Talles or his grandfather's Etta Sukenik, with her superb diction and carmined operatic sophistication, something that none of them would understand or even recognize.

"Come on," his father said, heading for the elevator.

It was the old trap, Teddy knew. It was like the spying expeditions he made twice a week on his way home from the Peabody, climbing the hill on Mount Vernon Place past the great homes lighted by the teasing glow of invisible money. There, at the Peabody, he left his adorable blue-eyed girls, in gray, green, and navy day-school uniforms, left them in classes in which he was their willing victim, so acquiescent, so submissive, so much wanting them, that he would cheat on their behalf, cheat at any opportunity, and then share their laughter in the face of the teacher's disappointment. The Shelburne surfaced it all. So did the Cotswold. And the Ritz. He was captivated by those other lives.

A door opened. A familiar figure stood there, plump, soft from bath oil and special scents. "Hmmmm," he heard his aunt say, appraising them, taking them in from head to foot. "Look what the wind blew in."

8

She leaned down, brushed Teddy on the cheek, pecked at Jack. They were not really a kissing family, did not like to touch. Celia held back now, resistant as ever. Teddy could smell his mother's perfume in the air. All the sisters wore it. Teddy inhaled, stood against the wall inside the door. "Your brother's already here," Celia said to him, backing into a narrow corridor. Jack and Teddy followed her. They were always following Celia, all of them did. She was used to it.

She led them into her sitting room, a huge square, twenty by twenty, one of the Shelburne's cubic prides. Teddy had it fixed in his mind almost before they were through the door: three huge windows looking out to sea, eight floors above the Boardwalk, Louis XVI furniture spread around in cool colors, the atmosphere somehow tinged with the beige of the fabrics, on the floor a couple of baskets of fruit, sent up by the manager at the beginning of each stay to make his aunt feel at home, a small inlaid writing desk somewhere in a corner, tasseled floor lamps softening everything with pink light; then through a door to the right, Celia's immense bedroom, with a pair of windows open to the Atlantic and two or three upended steamer trunks visible near the closets. A wind whipped through the suite. The curtains blew into the room in great floating pockets. Finally, swimming into Teddy's vision, there was Benedict Lewin himself, sitting with his legs crossed on a satin-covered chair, nonchalantly smoking an oval English cigarette, as though he came with the furniture, and Teddy's cousins, Hermine and Gideon, Gideon calling a hello from the bedroom and Hermine in a chair alongside Ben, smoking the same brand of cigarette, her own, through an ivory holder.

The family tableau. The Duchess' palace retinue. The rich kids at their ease. They might as well have been at home in Windsor Hills, Celia and her two elegant children, at home in their dustless Tudor living room with the unplayed miniature harp from Belfast, Ireland, standing in one corner and the dim view through the casement windows of Gwynn's Falls Valley, the skinny river rushing stonily downhill a hundred feet below; and on the opposite side, beyond the river, climbing at a sharp thirty-degree angle, a hillful of Maryland sycamores, fat with greenish seedballs, that held together the loose, rich, fertile earth. Teddy sometimes came uptown with his friends on Saturday afternoon to hike Gwynn's Falls Valley early in the spring. Together, they dipped their feet in the cold river, stone-hopped, ate mealy white-bread sandwiches. Along the way, Teddy could catch a glimpse of his Aunt Celia's house from a certain spot, a thin clearing amidst the sycamores. When he looked up and saw the long, low, brick-and-stucco house, timbered to perfection, he felt safe that she was there, that Hermine and Gideon and their father Sam were around, but he never took his friends up the steep hairpin-curved road to the house, even when they were dying of thirst.

"So, you got here all right," Jack said, sitting down across from Ben and Hermine.

"We're here," Celia said. "In one piece."

"And how was the trip?"

Celia made a face. "A line at the ferry, as usual. Forty-five minutes. Otherwise . . ."

"Is Sam coming?"

"For the weekend," Celia answered. "On Friday." She thrust a box of chocolates at them, making the choices for them even before they had a chance to look inside. Marshmallow for Jack, caramel for Teddy. There was a moment's exchange then about Barney, his health, his vigor, the satisfaction of giving him Atlantic City for a week. Celia stood with her hands clasped in front of her, her short neck arched aristocratically, a sweet smile responding to Jack's description of his father. She was only five years younger than Barney, treated him like a parent. How wonderful, her smile said, not to be an orphan, how lucky Jack was, how dear Barney. Mothers and fathers, she sighed. That other generation, the one that remembered Europe, she worshiped them all. Ah, Barney must come to the Shelburne, he must have dinner with them. Jack must see to it. "And you," she said, "look at you. Look what you've done to yourself."

"It's not so bad."

"Ben told me," she said, coming over to examine Jack's burn. "You might as well set yourself on fire."

"Don't make it worse than it is, Celia."

"You're all alike. Sam. Haskel. All of you. Bea turns her back for one minute . . ." But while her voice still spoke sympathy, she was already bored with Jack's sunburn. She stirred fretfully in front of her brother-in-law, turned to Teddy. "And you," she said, reaching for his cheek. "Such a face." But Teddy pulled back. "Look at him," Celia said, cocking her head. "Like a nervous puppy." Teddy chewed on his piece of candy. "Where did you get that face? Look at it. . . . He's ashamed. Did you ever . . . Don't be ashamed of the way you look. A face like yours. Such a *schön*! Your mother should be bursting. . . . Now let me see your fingernails. Come on, I won't bite."

Teddy came closer, held out his hands. Behind him, his father smiled knowingly. Celia took each of Teddy's hands in her own, examined them. "Not bad." She gave a short, powerful nod. "You use a finger brush daily? You have a cuticle scissors?"

"Yes," Teddy said.

"The fingernails count. Everybody looks." She dropped his hands. "Finish the candy," she said, "with your mouth closed. Don't talk while you're eating."

"Mo-ther."

Smoke drifted languidly from the other side of the room. Ben tittered at his cousin. Celia threw her daughter a slightly pained look, practiced and insincere. Then she turned swiftly, told Teddy where to sit, took the center of the sofa herself, alone there in a long chiffon dressing gown the color of pink roses, pinker now in the light of the floor lamps, the oldest daughter in a family with no parents, the richest, most powerful of them all, prideful and a little sour now at the thought of all her responsibilities. A few feet away, Hermine ignored her mother, slowly folded one long leg over the other, tucked an ankle inside an ankle, held her cigarette holder in the air between thin, tapered fingers. Teddy watched her out of the corner of his eye. He liked the way she moved. He liked the unhurried steadiness of it, the self-absorption. She had moved that way when she was twelve, even younger. He remembered her then, sitting long-limbed and contained on her parents' terrace, overlooking Gwynn's Falls Valley. She was more like Bea than Celia. Sleek as a Gibson Island debutante, sharp-boned and full of edge, like Brenda Frazier, full of movie manners and bodily ease. Teddy had once heard Bea say that she owned a dozen and a half cashmere sweaters. She was Ben's age, nineteen, looked five years older.

Then Gideon walked in. He was actually five years older, nearly twenty-five, and looked it, the back of his head already bald, a perfect circle of bare skull visible there. He had the same bony elegance as his sister Hermine, as his Aunt Bea, the same preserved air of detachment. But he was really like his father, like Sam, wholly without the appraising quality of his mother and his sister. They greeted each other. There was a virile gasp as Gideon had a look at Jack. "Good Lord, Uncle Jack," he said. "I heard from Ben but I never dreamed . . . ."

"It's not as bad as it seems," Jack said.

"It hurts just to look at you."

"Sorry," Jack said, smiling plaintively.

"And Teddy," Gideon said, holding out his hand to his cousin. "All my old pals are here."

"Hello, Gideon," Teddy said.

"By next year you'll be taller than your brother."

Teddy shook his head: maybe, maybe not. But he was pleased. Gideon always pleased him. He called him old pal and meant it. He smiled without thinking. Not many in that family smiled without thinking. There was a moment's flurry then as they all settled down again, a brief silence.

"Uncle Jack," Hermine finally said, "where are you all staying? I forget the name of your hotel."

"Sloan's," Teddy said.

"Sloan's. Where is that?"

"It's in Trenton," Ben said, smiling fiercely at his cousin. "We commute to the Atlantic City beach every afternoon by intercity bus."

"Don't be so sarcastic," Jack said.

"Come on," Hermine said. "Tell me."

"It's on Virginia Avenue," Jack said.

"Where's Virginia Avenue?"

"In Norfolk," Ben said, blowing smoke at Hermine. Across the room, Gideon stifled a laugh.

It was the same exchange they always had, the same back-and-forth lancing to draw a little blood, while Celia sat in the background without objecting for the moment, pretending that she was arranging flowers or plumping up the sofa cushions. It was like that at family celebrations and parties, at Thanksgiving dinner and at the Seder, the first Seder, that was held in Sam and Celia's house every spring. Once a year, a thirty-foot table was extended the length of Celia's dining room right through half the living room, with the Sandlers and their husbands and wives at the top and the children, the cousins, at the bottom, where they were wholly out of phase with the dinner that was being served to their parents, always a course behind, fish, hard-boiled eggs, and chicken being mixed together from one room to the other. Celia never really got the massive Seder in order, never had, a delectable chaos, in which the Haggadah narrative fell apart, settling over the whole family during the annual meal which the children adored. During those evenings, Hermine picked away at the poorest of them, Teddy and Ben Lewin, especially Ben, who was her born adversary, as though she were feeding on bones, trying to ask them questions that might embarrass them, trying to find a vulnerable point of malicious entry, then exploit it. She was good at it.

"What does the doctor say?" Celia asked, dutifully returning to Jack's burn. She passed a basket of fruit around.

"Stay out of the sun," Jack recited. "Rest. Take three hot baths a day."

"I wish the doctor would tell *me* to take three baths a day," Celia said.

"Would you like to use our bath?" Hermine asked. "We have two."

"For God's sake, Hermine," Gideon said.

"All I meant was whether Uncle Jack has a *private* bath," she said. "Not all hotels have private baths. If he has to take three baths a day, he should have a private bath."

"Thank you, dear. I'm all right," Jack said, in a soft, obsequious voice.

"I just thought," she said with a half smile.

"Didn't Bea tell me that Charlotte Melnicov is staying with you?" Celia said.

"Staying with me?" Jack asked, pretending astonishment.

"I mean at your hotel."

"She was with Bea last week. She's staying on for another."

"She has a boyfriend?"

"Larry Bernard," Teddy said.

"He's at the hotel?"

"Yes." Teddy said.

"I'm glad to hear that," Celia said, in a tone of exaggerated relief. "I didn't think it was such a good idea for the two of you to be staying together." She held up a hand as Jack began to protest. "It doesn't matter now," she said. "It's not important. Never mind. So . . . ."

She drifted off then, as she often did, into a long story, this one about a divorce, old friends from Baltimore, old acquaintances rather, gossip that had been going on for a year or more. Jack had heard the beginnings of it before. There was an only child involved, Celia explained, an eleven-year-old girl, a daughter so attached to her father that she had desperately fought the divorce, fought her mother, to keep them all together. Teddy sat up straight, was suddenly all ears; they all were. Celia relished the attention, telling the story well, telling it to Jack, as though it were for his ears alone, but telling it slowly and distinctly, episode by episode, pitching her voice so that they could all hear. Teddy knew the family, knew the girl. They had lived three blocks away, on Callow Avenue. Her name was Johanna Rosenstock. She wore glasses and plaits, never smiled, had small, square teeth.

"Take him back," she had screamed at her mother after they had separated. Celia looked amazed as she said the words. Take him back! From a child. The whole neighborhood heard the exchange. Everyone talked about it. A cry of passion. But the mother had paid no attention. The troubles had been going on too long. The mother was finished with the father. For good. And she was glad for it.

They began to live that other kind of life then, the mother and daughter in a three-room apartment on Whitelock Street, where all the neighborhood shopping was done, the father downtown, alone, in a hotel. Each Sunday, the girl had lunch with the father in the hotel dining room and then went to a movie with him. She adored him, adored their Sundays together. This had been going on for a year, Celia said, perhaps a little more. Then she paused, lowered her eyes. They all waited for her to go on. What was she going to tell them? Well, she said, raising her eyes, her cheeks flushed as pink as the lamplight, a few months ago the father had told the daughter that he was moving to Philadelphia. A new job, more money. All that. The child had listened carefully, had finished her lunch, gone off to a movie with him. That night she had repeated the news to the mother, as though it didn't matter, as though it were of no importance. A few months passed. The father moved. The Sunday afternoons, the lunches, the movies ceased. Then late in June, without warning, the girl was rushed to Sinai Hospital. One minute she was well, the next she was in critical condition. . . . Again, Celia paused. This time she looked up at the ceiling, as though she had to get herself under control, as though her instructions were written there. It had looked like peritonitis, Celia went on, like a burst appendix, or a stomach infection that takes weeks to diagnose. But what it was was her ovaries. Celia had begun to whisper. They were discharging pus, she said, were destroying her uterus, her womb, passing poisons into her . . . into her vagina. Jack frowned. There was another pause. The doctors had removed the ovaries, Celia then said. Imagine! Here she raised her voice. An eleven-year-old child!

Ahhh. . . .

Well, Hermine said, she had seen to it that she wouldn't have any children of her own.

Jack threw her a sharp look.

That's the way those things often are, Hermine explained. She had shown them, had paid her parents back for their selfishness. It was not uncommon. Revenge. Unconscious self-destruction. She had made it impossible to conceive, wounded herself forever. . . .

Celia heaved a long sigh. They all sat in a silence like death, Hermine inhaling a new cigarette, Teddy in wonder. He thought of Johanna Rosenstock, remembered her thick glasses, like Erich Kessler's, her twin plaits hanging to just below her shoulders. She had always looked so calm, so unexcitable. He couldn't remember her ever saying a word. Ovaries. What exactly were they, anyway? Ben stirred in his chair. Gideon was shaking his head. Take him back! Teddy tried to imagine himself shouting the words. At Bea. Or at Jack. At his father. Take her back!

Celia blew her nose from exhaustion, sat back in the sofa, limp. The curtains alongside her lifted gently on the breeze. The room suddenly filled with the smell of salt. There was another sigh, from Jack this time. Celia's story had demoralized them all. It was too fantastic and too believable, all at once. They could hardly move on their satin chairs. Finally, Celia stirred again, turned to her brother-in-law.

"Life is full of terrible things," she said.

"You should know that by now," Jack said.

She passed around the basket of fruit, shook her head in despair. "I'm never ready for it," she said. "I'm never prepared."

"There is no way to be prepared."

She sighed again, pulled at her chiffon robe. "Hermine, darling, pick me a nice peach."

"It's getting too gloomy in here for me," Teddy heard himself say. "When you're our age . . ." his aunt began, waving his words away. "The old folks at home," Hermine muttered.

There was another silence, broken by the guillotine sound of Ben Lewin biting into an apple. "You'll break a tooth," Gideon said. They both laughed. Teddy joined them. The sound of Ben and his apple filled the room.

"Benjy," Celia said, unable to control a smile.

"A pair of jaws," his father said.

Two more bites and it was almost done. "I always think I'm the only one who can hear myself," Ben said, chewing fast now.

"You should hear him with celery," Teddy said. Then it was over.

"How is Elsie Smirnoff doing?" Jack asked, after a moment. "Poor Elsie."

"Is she all right?"

"I saw her a couple of days ago," Hermine said lightly. "She seems fine."

"Fine," her mother said, mimicking her. "As though she could be fine."

They had finally arrived at the subject they could never avoid, the cherished obsession, never out of mind, the death of old friends. This time it was Jesse Smirnoff, Elsie Smirnoff's husband. Jesse Smirnoff, a corpse at sixty-seven. Jack Lewin's aging pal, somebody he knocked around the Woodholme golf course with from time to time. There was a death every week, it seemed to Teddy. Bea's friends, Jack's friends, funeral descriptions back and forth, Bea to Jack, Jack to Bea, Celia on the phone, all the sisters. It was everywhere in Baltimore. Next week it would be someone else, someone they all knew, passed on, passed away, gone, another deceased one, as they all said.

Every now and then it was someone in the family, a cousin, an in-law, someone's grandparent on the other side, someone like Barney, who when his time came would surely have to be buried, nine fingers and all, in a coffin specially vented with a smoking chimney. He must be more than sixty-seven himself by now. Outside of chronic emphysema, outside of a hacking cough that almost tore his larynx and his insides up every day, he was the picture of health. A little back trouble, maybe, something with his teeth, nothing that counted. But if Jesse Smirnoff could die, so could Barney Levin. So could anyone. So could Teddy Lewin's own parents. Both of them. Soon Bea and Jack would be laid out side by side at Sol Levinson's funeral home on North Avenue, while the old men from the synagogue, who smelled like stale bread, like ancient musty books, who devoted their lives to such deeds, such blessings, washed their bodies and prepared them for burial in the good earth. Just last week, they had done the same for Jesse Smirnoff, trying to make him look alive in death.

Celia was telling of the widow's grief again, describing their old friend Elsie Smirnoff with heavy, solemn gestures that embraced them all, one by one. She seemed to grow larger in the face of death, sitting there in the center of the sofa high above the sea, recounting every detail, seemed to expand with renewed breath and defiance. Celia: nothing daunted, despite her distracted expression, the edge of fear in her voice. As she spoke, Teddy thought of the one funeral he had gone to, Hermine and Gideon's grandmother, their father Sam's mother, a crumbling, wizened body, like the old lady Eisen, finally dead after decades of inflicting misery on all her daughters-in-law, whom she treated like unprincipled rivals. No one had wept at her funeral, not Sam or Celia, not all Sam's brothers and their bitterly relieved wives, not Hermine or Gideon. The gravediggers had cranked the coffin into the hole in the ground and everyone had gone home for a shot of whiskey. Teddy had gone with them to Sam and Celia's house, the seat of official mourning; it had the biggest living room in the family. The mirrors were all covered with sheets, prayerbooks were piled on a table in the hall, the rabbi smelled like the old men who prepared corpses for burial. Then they all ate sponge cake and sat on miniature chairs in the living room in front of the gleaming imported harp. It was not so sad, Teddy remembered; they had all started telling jokes to each other a few minutes after the rabbi left and the living room overlooking Gwynn's Falls Valley was filled with laughter that went on for the full week of mourning.

Then Gustav Levi's dyspepsia suddenly came to mind, his friend's post dinner posture each evening, slumped in a chair, hand over his heart, a tumbler of neat Scotch set alongside him. Sounds came from Gus Levi's intestines, terrible doom-ridden rumbles. From there, it was a single clipped step to Gus Levi's own corpse, flattened on the wicker couch on Sloan's front porch, laid out like an old suit, wrinkled, liver-spotted, skin appropriately the color of death itself, a couple of fresh shaving scars on his chin. The talk went on around Teddy, Aunt Celia solemnly eulogizing the Smirnoffs, her Elsie, their Jesse, as Teddy traced his friend's funeral procession down a strange New Jersey street. Teddy would bury Gus Levi in Paterson, where he lived, would see him into the ground himself, pack him in a coffin lined with

old copies of *The New York Times,* huge black volumes of philosophical Jewish history and biblical commentaries, Graetz, Philo,
Rashi, Maimonides, thick anthologies of English poetry and
complete leatherbound sets of the Russian novelists, with beautiful illustrations. That would keep the cold wind out, that would
keep the worms busy for a while, distract them from what they
were really after. It would be the end of culture, the end of
western civilization. Into Gustav Levi's coffin would go the accumulated spirit of twenty centuries, the poetry and music of
Thalia, Calliope, Polyhymnia, and all the others, a kind of endless cleverness, a bloom of ingenuity, that had come into the
world in unexpected ways and left an irreplaceable scent wherever it was found, a sweet, faithful power that fed anyone who
touched it. Art, it was called. Art, Teddy thought. The word was
not worthy of the idea. He could hardly say it aloud. It was
without accent and common. All of it would go with Gus Levi
when he died, would disappear into the New Jersey earth with
him, and that was what Teddy Lewin would mourn for the
rest of his life.

Tears sprang to his eyes. He had buried his mother and father,
his grandfather, and his best friend in Atlantic City, sitting there
in a suite on the eighth floor of the Shelburne, accompanied by
the sound of his aunt's voice. His brother and sister were next.
Benedict and Marion. But Celia was finishing her story. Elsie
Smirnoff. Ovaries . . . He frowned in pain, had a sudden onslaught of familiar, chilling fastidiousness at the sight of his
family facing him in the great square room. Ben was giving him
a queasy look. Celia rested a moment, began to eat her peach.
Two stories, such an effort. Teddy saw Gideon sneak a look at
his watch. Celia's black eyes were shadowed underneath; she
rubbed at them now like a child, hid a yawn with her fist.
"Haskel sent a message," she said, suddenly on the alert again.

They all saw Jack stiffen in his chair. "What kind of message?" he asked.

"It's none of my business, I don't understand any of it, but he asked me to ask you."

"What?"

"He wants to know if you could come home on Friday, so you could take over the yard for him all day Saturday."

"Ah," Jack said.

"He has to go to the Eastern Shore to buy, he says. He has to go to Salisbury."

"No," Ben said. "He can't."

"Just a minute now," Jack said.

"I'm just delivering the message," Celia said, holding up her hand as a sign of innocence. "It's none of my business. I don't understand these things, anyway. My people were never job people."

Hermine gave a little smile, Gideon looked embarrassed.

"For crying out loud, Celia," Jack said.

"What?"

"I mean—" he began.

"You call Haskel and talk to him. It's out of my hands now."

"You're not going to break up your vacation to go home for that?" Ben asked.

"Well, business . . ."

"Dad," Ben said.

"You already paid for the whole week," Teddy said. "You'll lose the money."

Jack looked at him gratefully. "That's right," he said. "I'll lose the money."

"You need the vacation," Teddy said.

Jack hesitated, shifted in his chair. Just then, Gideon rose and walked to the windows. "Too much breeze?" he asked. Celia nodded vaguely to him, mumbled a response. He knew all her signals, they all did. He closed two of the windows, returned to sit alongside Teddy. "Having a good time in Atlantic City?" he asked his cousin amiably. Teddy smiled. It was easy to smile back at Gideon. He had none of his mother's compelling hold on life, none of Hermine's proprietary assumptions. Teddy envied him his patience, his evenness. In the company of his mother and his sister, Gideon walked around with an eyebrow raised in chronic irony and he wasn't even aware of it.

"I like it here," Teddy said.

"You'd have to be crazy not to like it, I guess."

"I like swimming in the ocean. I always like swimming."

"Well, it's certainly better than Baltimore," Gideon said. Teddy laughed. "In this heat," he said, "it sure is."

"It's a relief to be here."

"What's the relief?" Ben asked, interrupting them.

"When you've been here a couple of days," Teddy said, "you'll understand."

"It's Baltimore all over again," Ben said.

Teddy stirred uncomfortably, pretended to ignore Ben.

"What's the difference?" Ben asked "It's just like home."

"You always see things differently from other people," Gideon said mildly.

"True enough," Hermine added. "You see things differently and you always overread. Load everything with too much meaning." Ben shrugged, looking not at all displeased. "It would be interesting," Hermine said, smiling, "to find out what Freud has to say about all that."

"Freud?" Ben said. "Ask Marx, not Freud."

"A-ha," Hermine said. "The classic pattern of evasion."

"Oh, Jesus," Ben muttered.

"Well, it is. It's not my fault that you can't help yourself. It's not yours, either. First you overreact, then you dismiss the evidence."

"What are you talking about?"

"You know what I'm talking about. Don't play dumb."

"Me, dumb?"

"Hey, kids," Gideon said.

Jack and Celia, on the other side of the room, continued their exchange, Celia turning every now and then to observe her children. Her daughter, Hermine. Her nineteen-year-old with the cashmere sweaters and the beautiful bone structure. Her Gideon. Already a little bald. But handsome. Handsome, honest, and genuinely upright. And alongside her children, Bea and Jack's two sons, somewhat less significant. Theodore. Benedict. Where did they all find such names? Celia listened to Jack, Jack listened to his sister-in-law. Half their attention was on the cousins.

"You know what they say about a little learning," Ben said. "One semester of Psych One and you're a dead cuckoo."

"For your information, I'm a Lit major."

"Is that where you picked up all that jargon?"

"Come on, Ben, don't be so touchy. You really do have classic responses. What does it matter what I think about Freud? Who cares? And what's jargon anyway? Just verbal signals that make it easy to recognize concepts. Whatever I feel about psychoanalysis, you can be sure it will have a life far beyond my opinions."

"The analysts will be glad to hear that," Ben said.

"You're smarter than that. Admit for once—"

"A little learning," he repeated.

"I don't claim anything beyond a little learning," Hermine said. She put another cigarette into the holder, twisting it in slowly, then lighting it as though it were an offering of incense. The smoke came at Ben. "But between Freud and Marx . . . near the middle of the twentieth century . . . you do have to admit . . ."

"I don't know which one of you is right," Gideon said in his pleasant voice, "but it seems to me that Hitler is calling the tune today, not Freud or Marx."

"Oh, that's simplistic," Hermine said.

"I agree with Gideon," Teddy said. "Just look at Europe."

There was a silence then and a deep sigh from Celia, who turned her full attention to the children. "Did I hear Hitler?" she said.

"How did we get to this?" Ben asked.

"I'm sorry I brought it up," Gideon said to his mother.

"You're sorry you brought it up," his mother said mindlessly. "What about me?" She turned back to her brother-in-law. "He can't wait to get into the OCS," she said. "Millions are afraid to be drafted and he can't wait to go. He'll be an officer, a volunteer lieutenant in the quartermaster."

"Mother," Gideon said, looking at his feet.

Celia put one hand under her breast. "Another two months and he'll be gone. That's what I have to live with."

"Is that true?" Jack asked. "You're going into the army?"

"Yes," Gideon said, not looking up.

"Why didn't you say anything?" Ben asked.

"Well . . ."

"He's sorry he brought it up," Celia said. "In two months, he'll be gone to Fort Dix, who knows where." She gave a little cry.

"Mother," Hermine said.

"Try and control yourself," Jack said. "It's not good for you, it's not good for Gideon. Besides, you shouldn't exaggerate."

"Listen to Uncle Jack," Hermine said.

"Anyway," Jack said, "there's not going to be a war. It's all bluff. And so what, Gideon will be an officer. It's different for officers."

"Mother," Hermine said. "You promised."

Celia gave them all a look then full of premature grief, something forlorn and bitter. It made Teddy afraid of her for the moment, afraid of her authority, her implacability, afraid that she would do something terrible, to herself or to them. He was afraid, too, of her news, of Gideon's going into the army; he was the first in the family.

"You should not think it's easy," Celia said to Jack. "No father should," she added, lifting a finger ominously in the direction of Teddy and Ben. Then she quieted down, became silent for a moment or two, and finally began to make small talk with

Teddy about his music, about practicing the piano. It was as though the subject of the army had never come up, as though Gideon were not even in the room. It was important that Teddy play every day, she told him calmly, important that he work hard, that he stick to it. That was what everybody told him, even those who had never touched a piano in their lives; that was what he always heard. Teddy began to fidget. Then somehow Celia veered again in midsentence, moved on to the future of their cousins in Warsaw, Teddy's second cousins, or first cousins twice removed, whatever that meant, all those nearly faceless children, cousins and aunts and uncles with unpronounceable last names that filled your mouth with chewy consonants when you tried to say them. They were on Celia's mind these days, she said, they always were.

Why didn't they pay attention? Celia asked the room. Why didn't they listen to her and leave Europe while they could?

It was Celia herself who handled the American correspondence for all of them, responding to the pinched, crotchety handwriting of the one Polish cousin educated enough to do English duty from Warsaw. But Celia never answered in English. She sent them a letter each month in a full, flowing Yiddish that ran across the page in beautiful tiny arcs and circles, filling it with family information, notices of accompanying parcels and money orders, and instructions, endlessly repeated, about coming to America, getting visas, making the applications. None of them listened to her. They were trying to put the old Yiddish behind them, anyway. They were all new Jews, Western liberals and assimilated Europeans, had absolute faith in their world. They accepted the money orders, accepted the parcels of delicacies, sent thank-you letters, letters of good wishes and news of diplomas, marriages, illness, occasional anti-Semitic outbreaks, all, it seemed, hooligan-inspired. The letters were then passed around the family, brother to brother, sister to sister, and sometimes read at Friday night dinner at Sam and Celia's home in Windsor Hills, Celia putting on her delicate wire glasses as she cut off all conversation so that they all could hear the awkward pedantic English in her own rich voice. She could not imagine that they were middle class. She could not understand why they wrote to her in English. She could not forgive them for staying in Warsaw.

Eliezar. Shifra. Bronya, who wrote the letters. Strange names, although not so strange that they took Teddy by surprise. One was an architect. Another taught school. Bronya was a linguist, an expert in Russian, French, German, Polish, and academic English. They were brothers and sisters, Teddy's grandfather's nephews and nieces. Teddy thought of them in Warsaw, thought of his cousins once removed, of the other lives going on at this moment, simultaneously with his own, on the other side of the sea. Their lives were the same as his, the same as Ben's. Only the landscape varied, and the language. One of them, his cousin Halina, who took her vacations on the Riviera, actually existed for Teddy in a photograph, which Bea had pasted in the family album on a page by itself. There she was, in sepia, sitting on a veranda somewhere in the south of France, on a wicker chair exactly like the one at Sloan's, wearing a sailor's outfit with a pomponned beret on her head. It was just like one Hermine had worn when she was twelve. Halina's hands were folded in her lap. She had a look of well-bred curiosity on her face, an indisputable intelligence. She stared straight at the camera. She did not look thin as paste. Teddy found himself returning to that photograph often. Looking like that, prosperous, civilized, at ease, why should she, why should any of them, want to come to Baltimore, Maryland?

Celia had turned back to her brother-in-law. They were talking to each other in low voices now, Jack agreeing with everything Celia said. Affection lay between them like an old pillow. They leaned on it lazily together, letting the time pass. Meanwhile, the cousins had begun to laugh at each other's jokes. The early storm had passed. Hermine had a little gossip from Baltimore to share, passed it along to Ben and Gideon. Now that the news of his enlistment was out, Gideon was already marching quick time in his head, could hardly pay attention to his sister. Teddy eavesdropped on one group, then the other, easily growing impatient, eyeing them for family clues, family links, watching Celia in her beautiful chiffon robe, as liquid as the sea, relaxed now that all urgent conversation was behind them, watching her children, his first cousins, examining their hotel suite, their clothes, their very bodies, Hermine's and Gideon's, which smelled of the heavy, silky smell of money, as clean, as germ-proof, as invulnerable as a bank vault.

All the money came from the wholesaling of ladies' shoes, pumps, oxfords, wedgies, and all the other quick-changing fashions that poured into Sam's loft on Fayette Street and were then dispensed to dozens of retail outlets around town. People had to have shoes. The business was nearly depression-proof. It was almost as sure as being a dentist or a pediatrician. It had brought them a twelve-room house overlooking a valley that had quartered Revolutionary troops in 1777, a colored lady who had a room and bath in the attic, with radio, and an apartment of her own off Pennsylvania Avenue downtown where she blew off steam on Saturday nights, a hunchbacked gardener who grew spectacular roses as big around as cauliflowers, two cars, an irreplaceable Irish harp that Celia loved, along with her gold rococo picture frames from Prague, her cast-iron statues of short-legged German peasants that stood on the terrace, her Meissen China and English crystal, as thin as paper, her thousand yards of damask, all thickly hanging from her windows, her summer suite high up at the Shelburne in which they now all sat, reserved until the High Holy Days, when Sam would send a chauffeur and limousine to carry her and her baggage home. And other things as well, including Bryn Mawr for Hermine and the Wharton School of Finance for Gideon. They were the richest in a family that had its share of riches. Celia had shaped them all, Haskel, Rosa, Saul, Sylvia, Morton, Julius, Jenny, Arthur, and Bea, Bea the youngest, urging Bea upon Goucher

College, until the family's small pile of inherited money ran out, parading her through the antique stores on Howard Street day after day until it had become a habit she could not live without, teaching her what was fine, what was not, lecturing, telling Bea how to do it, teaching her how to be rich. It was an easy lesson for Bea to learn, it was an easy lesson for her brothers and sisters to learn. Willing pupils, all the Sandlers.

Somehow the subject of Haskel arose again, Haskel and his forthcoming trip to Salisbury. Would Jack go home, do his brother-in-law that favor? Celia was asking the question again, was urging Jack to make a decision. She suddenly spoke loud enough for the whole room to hear. Ben turned to listen to her, so did Teddy. Hermine and Gideon grew quiet. "He can't go home," Ben said. "He's got his father here. He's got his two sons. He has to have a vacation too."

Celia shrugged it off, came at the subject another way. She didn't understand such things, she said again, looking bewildered. Her people were not job people, had never been. Gideon bit his lower lip as his mother spoke. Hermine was yawning as though she couldn't keep her eyes open. Jack remained noncommittal. The exchange died down, flared up briefly. They were all running out of conversation. They had nothing more to say to each other. From Sigmund Freud to Johanna R.'s ovaries. It was enough. Who had so much to say to each other as these aunts and uncles, these cousins, these in-laws? Hermine was really yawning loudly now, a high soprano sound escaping her open mouth. It was after nine. While the curtains at the one open window blew in with sudden force, Teddy heard Ben say something about Teddy and Ben hurrying if they were going to make the last show. Ben was already on his feet. What last show, Teddy wondered.

"I've been promising Teddy for days," Ben said, stretching with fatigue. "Will you be able to get back to the hotel without us?" he asked his father. Jack nodded. "You sure you want to go to a movie?" Jack asked. Absolutely sure, Ben promised. Been looking forward to it all day. Right, Teddy? Right. Celia then reminded Jack of his three baths, clucked a bit over his sunburn. She too got to her feet. "What are you going to see?" Hermine asked Teddy. He turned to his brother.

"Uh . . ." Ben said. He stretched again. *"Four Feathers,"* he said. "

"Oh, a horse-and-bugle show," Hermine said.

Four Feathers, Teddy thought. It hadn't even opened in Atlantic City yet. What a pair of liars they were.

"Cost one point eight to make," Ben said. "Been in production two years." He checked his watch. "We'd better hurry, Teddy baby."

Teddy couldn't wait. He had been ready to go ever since he had walked into the enormous room from the soundless corridor outside and showed his fingernails to Aunt Celia. "Come on," he said, suddenly seized by energy. They started out of the room, saying good-by to their cousins.

"Don't be such a stranger," Celia called after them. "You hear me? You know where I am. It won't hurt you to pay a visit. You don't have to wait for your father. . . ."

Her voice still came at them through the closing elevator doors.

9

"He always does that," Ben said, moving along the Boardwalk so fast that Teddy's shins hurt from the effort to keep up.

"What?"

"Kowtows to them. Lets them run him. Does what they say. He always gives in to the Sandlers."

"He didn't give in."

"If we hadn't been there, he would have run back to Baltimore tomorrow, just because Celia brings a message from Haskel."

"She didn't say tomorrow."

"Tomorrow, Friday. What's the difference?"

"But it's his job."

"For Christ's sake, Teddy. You're hopeless."

"What's he supposed to do?"

"It's his vacation. Nobody has any right to interfere with that. The worst part is that it's all academic, anyway. Haskel *has* to ruin his vacation. That's the way it is, that's the way they are together. They both expect it. There is no way that Haskel Sandler could leave Jack Lewin alone to enjoy a few days in the sun. If Haskel really *had* to go to the Eastern Shore this weekend, he'd call. He wouldn't send a message with Celia."

"I bet Dad doesn't go back."

"But only because if he does, we'll make his life more miserable than Haskel will."

They were silent for a few minutes, then Ben began to chew

the bone again. "It drives me nuts," he said. "He's smarter than all of them. He has more intelligence in his little finger than all the Sandlers. And he lets them walk all over him. What's wrong with him, anyway?"

"He's scared of not having a job," Teddy said.

"You think so?"

"What else could it be?"

"Is it worth all that?"

"It's paying for your college, for my music."

"I could work."

"But you don't."

"He should get out and start his own business."

"With what?"

"Other people seem to manage it."

"I'll tell you something. I think Daddy likes it with Haskel. I think he likes to be needed like that."

"Used is more like it."

"I think he likes it. I don't think he'd be happy out on his own. He'd miss all that."

"Your mother's no help, either," Ben said, in a low voice.

"Don't start that now," Teddy said.

"Well, she's not. She's filled with all the Sandler crap."

"Ben."

"It's true."

"I'm not going to listen to all that again. I warn you."

"It doesn't mean I don't love her."

"She just wants to live well, she just wants to have a little money."

"But it's your father who has to come through."

" . . . . . ."

"God, I hate that bitch."

"Ben."

Ben turned to his brother, his face distracted. "Not Mother," he said. "That Hermine."

"Oh, Hermine," Teddy laughed, almost hysterically. "A rat."

"Where is Virginia Avenue, dahling? . . . Sloan's? Never heard of it. Do you have a bath? Have you ever seen a bar of soap? Let me show you what one looks like. Jesus Christ!"

"Who cares about Hermine? You're crazy if you listen to her. The whole family hates her."

"You'd better stay away from them, my friend."

"Who?"

"The family. The Sandlers. They'll get to you."

"Oh, come on, Ben."

"It's the truth."

"What do you think I am, a ninety-pound weakling?"

"I'm warning you. You'll wake up one fine morning and one of your lovely uncles will sidle over to you and offer you a job, with all the same beautiful promises that Haskel made to your father. A piece of the business and all that. And you'll think to yourself, well, why not, look how successful they are, look how much they have, why not me. Just like your father did. Like he still does. The day your father sees a piece of the business, he'll be in his grave."

"You sound so bitter. Don't be like that, Ben."

"You watch out. They'll be after you. They won't be happy until they've got you, until you're just like they are. And your mother will be their ally. She will. She'll want the same thing for you. They'll work on all your guilt feelings about the family and not having money. And on all your doubts about yourself. They'll hold out a golden apple, just within reach. And you won't know how to resist it. They'll make you feel that you won't be able to do anything without them."

"I can take care of myself. I'm no fool."

"You don't know how fierce they can be."

"Don't worry, I know."

"Remember. Be prepared."

"You're making too much of it, Benjy. You're making it sound like the end of the world."

"You're very vulnerable. You should never forget it."

Teddy sighed.

"You are. You're soft, sensitive, full of what they call quivering sensibility."

As Ben neatly ticked him off on his fingers, Teddy began to go slack. It happened every time. His brother was right, his brother really knew him. He was soft, he was sensitive. His skin was as thin as a piece of mica peeled to its last layer. He was vulnerable to everything, without emotional discretion; hidden at the bottom of his soul lay a dusty mound of unhealed wounds. Soft. He hated the mere sound of the word.

"You're an artist, O brother mine. Remember that."

Teddy blushed in the dark. Artist. Another one of those words he shied from. It was for other people, not Teddy Lewin. It was for disheveled people who painted, or sculpted, or wrote four-line poems that were printed in the *Morning Sun*, and never knew where their next meal was coming from. No one took artists seriously. There were no artists on Linden Avenue or in Windsor Hills. They lived elsewhere in Baltimore, clustered together downtown in tiny rebuilt houses on Tyson Alley, quarantined behind the antique shops. The Sandlers wouldn't know what to say to an artist.

"I don't want to be an artist," he said, turning away.

"Unfortunately," Ben said coolly, "you won't have a choice."

"You don't know what you're talking about," Teddy said. But again there was something formidable in Ben's words. He reminded him of his father, of his uncles. They all made the same assumptions about him, as though he had no will, no desires of his own. They all thought they could predict his future. It was as though everything was already decided, ordained by family consensus. He would be ready to disprove them over and over again, every day of his life. He would be what he decided to be.

"Where'd you find that *Four Feathers* business?" Teddy asked, eager to change the subject.

"Not bad, huh?" They both laughed.

"Ben, slow down. My legs hurt. We've got no place to go, anyway." Then they did slow down, began to stroll along like ordinary vacationers, eyeing the concessions, the other visitors, the rolling chairs, the auctions. There was a whole life going on around them, they suddenly noticed, to which they had both been blind for at least a quarter of an hour, striding so purposefully, arguing in its midst. There it was, an infinity of satisfied humans in streaming motion, touched to blissful distraction by the presence of the moon, the sea, and the astringent warmth of familiar saline air. They looked as though they had been enjoying it all forever, as though they had always known it was coming to them. Five minutes passed in silence between the brothers. They walked slowly, shoulder to shoulder, like everyone else. A body jostled them as it passed, another. They jumped out of the path of a rolling chair. They were hawked by a diamond vendor, pursued by the caramel scent of crackerjacks. Everyone was. Walking together in the vast communal slip on the boards: more bliss.

"It's all relative, anyway," Ben finally said. He had Teddy by the elbow. "It all depends where you're looking at it from."

"What's relative?" Teddy asked.

"Life. Everything. It takes as many forms as there are pairs of eyes. Everybody sees it differently. Everybody sees it in terms of themselves. Even time itself is relative."

"What does that mean?"

"Didn't you ever hear of Einstein?" Ben asked, guiding Teddy through the crowd. "Didn't you ever hear of his theory?"

"I see him in the newsreels. A lot of hair."

"He says that time is different down here than it is out there." Ben took in the whole universe with a single, sweeping gesture. "It moves at a different rate of speed in space. You even grow older in a different way. Slower, I think."

"Do you live longer?"

"That's what everyone hopes, I guess. It's something terribly strange. But I have my own theory about time."

"Different from Einstein?"

"Different from everybody."

"Tell me."

"I don't believe that time exists. I believe that man invented it for his own convenience. Know what I mean? After all, why is an hour an hour? Only because we say it is. In itself, a minute has no meaning. And what's a day, a week, a month? All inventions, man-made objects. We pass through space, on a fixed circular route, aging as we go around. But it's only we who move. Time is like a spiral, moving around itself over and over again. Time is a single point, one lousy dot in space, on which we all dance, everybody who ever lived, everybody who ever will live, as though it were the head of a pin."

"Like angels?"

Ben gave him a swift, sharp look. "If you will," he said. "If that's the way you want it. . . . You know, beyond time, even the weather is relative. It depends on where you're looking at it from. They say that up there, on top of the clouds, the sun always shines and the sky stays blue. It's like heaven."

"I don't understand what the weather has to do with time," Teddy said. Ben gave him an impatient look. "I mean," Teddy went on, "that the weather can be proved scientifically. It's a scientific thing that's measurable. It exists outside of us, whether we're here or not. But time doesn't."

Ben didn't answer.

"Doesn't time disappear when we die?" Teddy asked.

"Where'd you get that?"

"Doesn't it?"

"How should I know?"

"Well, you're the one with all the theories."

"I'm not insisting on anything," Ben said. "I'm just speculating."

"Well?"

"Let's think about it for a while," Ben said after a moment. That was how he always signaled that he was tired of the exchange: let's think about it. Teddy shrugged in mild frustration, tried to keep his responses silent. Five minutes on relativity, on time and the weather. It was better than nothing. Ben's mind was always leapfrogging over its own self. Teddy knew all the cues, accepted them, was grateful that he was part of the game. For the moment, it was over, but Ben would return to it another time, and Teddy would make sure to be there for a second exchange. His brother's lectures suited him perfectly.

By now they were walking at a reasonable pace; the conversation had taken some of the energy out of them. They moved one block on, then another; for a few minutes, they peered silently out to sea, leaning side by side on the metal railing that faced the beach. There was nothing out there except a stationary red light somewhere to the south. Then: "Let's go," Ben said, and Teddy, a little chilled, followed him. They came slowly alongside the Convention Hall, pulled up a little short now by the sudden massiveness of it, the nervy grandeur of its vaulting curved roof, its length, breadth, and volume. They approached it tentatively, slightly intimidated. A flood of statistics loosed itself in Teddy's head and was instantly tamped down. So many feet high, so many long, so many wide. Where else was there such a place? Down Georgia Avenue, the brothers could see moving vans being unloaded onto ramps leading into the Hall. Huge scenic flats fluttered in the night breeze against the Convention Hall walls, waiting to be carried inside. A hundred feet away, they could hear the sound of canvas flapping against stone.

"That must all be for Miss America," Teddy said.

"*Kitsch.*"

Teddy threw his brother an offended look, then led the way down Georgia Avenue, pausing with Ben to check out each photo that lined the wall of the Convention Hall. Miss Arizona, in a three-foot-by-three black-and-white. Very foxy looking. Miss Mississippi. Frances Marie Howard from Ohio again, with her snaggle tooth. Gertrude (Trude) Beauchamp. That gang. Pictures that broke up into a thousand dots if you allowed your eyes to go out of focus for an instant. Bathing suits like satin girdles and impeccable smiles out of Ipana ads. Ben ticked them off cynically. "Never make it," he said to Linda Sue Wofford, shaking his head in wonder at her inch-long eyelashes. "Never make it, never make it, never make it." To Grace Monoghan, Anne Troxell, Dorothy Barnes, Margaret Ann Morris. "Never, never, never." He counted off failure on his fingers, one by one. "Never," he said again, to Sally Corner, to Juanita Hemps, to Sara May Johnson, Jeanette Brown, Dorothy Hankel. "What a bunch of dismal bags," he said, with a finality that seemed to foreclose all their futures.

"There are a couple," Teddy said loyally.

"Maybe one. Maybe two."

"A couple."

"What makes them think they're going to win?"

"Everybody tells them. From kindergarten on."

"Dismal," Ben said again. "The whole thing. The whole idea."

"You can fit a thirteen-story apartment house in there," Teddy said, looking up at the building.

Ben rolled his eyes.

"It's four times as big as Madison Square Garden."

"Imagine that."

"The roof shrinks three inches every winter."

"You don't say."

"Oh, come on," Teddy said. "Let's go in. I want to see it."

There was a steady bustle of work going on alongside the loading platforms, trucks backing into position, others pulling away, workmen hoisting flats up onto the platforms, then into the Hall through the open doors. From inside, came the sound of a rehearsal piano, playing a few measures of the same tune over and over again. "A pretty girl is like a melody, That haunts you night and day. Da, da, da, dum . . ." It never got further than that. There would be a pause of a few seconds, the muffled sound of voices, then the pianist would start again. "A pretty girl is like . . ." The brothers stood on the pavement with their hands in their pockets, suddenly shy. "Oh, why not," Ben finally said.

They wandered in slowly, full of wariness, like Teddy and Erich Kessler at the Ritz, through a hallway or two, then self-consciously onto the dark, empty arena floor. It was bigger than a football field, as big as two, a vast plane pocked here and there by mounds of wooden folding chairs piled on top of each other. Along the walls, dim lights burned, red exit signs, tiny clusters of twenty-watt bulbs, the meager sustenance of show business in off-performance time. But up front, a hundred feet away, the Hall's stage was ablaze with light. In front of it sat three men, in total silence, total immobility, arms folded over their chests. Alongside them was a lone woman. The woman carried a clip-board covered with notes, wore sunglasses. On stage sat the rehearsal pianist, in shirt sleeves and suspenders. An unlighted cigar hung from the side of his mouth. Surrounding him, gathered together around the piano like moths warming themselves at a flame, stood a dozen girls, all in bathing suits and high heels. The names of their home states were pinned to their chests. Every now and then, when their chattering grew too loud, the woman in the sunglasses would clap her hands for silence. Meanwhile, below the apron of the stage, a man in sneakers was giving the girls directions, and one by one, as he called them from a list in his hand, they would try to make their way along the apron of the stage, accompanied by the pianist, as though they were out of a Ziegfeld line. The man, who wore a purple neckerchief and a headband to keep his hair out of his eyes, eyed them all dole-fully. Then, as though he were spelling out basic English for a tribe of Hottentots, he would tell them precisely what he wanted them to do, showing them how to walk on high heels, walk, walk, walk slowly, then how to turn without stumbling, turn with grace, without breaking the line, and proceed in the opposite direction, all in time to the music.

"Pull your stomach in," he said, his voice rising. The girl in

front of him made a visible effort to suck in her gut, but it
threw her off balance. She could not walk and think about her
stomach at the same time. The director's nostrils dilated.
"Sweetie," he began, then hoisted himself up on the stage. "This
way, darling, this way." A hand on one hip, he proceeded along
the stage front, turning with ease at stage left and returning.
For a moment, he flirted with the empty auditorium. The girls
watched voraciously. Several of them applauded as he jumped
down onto the floor of the arena. He was better at it than any
of them. By now, Teddy and Ben had unfolded a couple of
chairs for themselves. They sat alone amidst the empty vastness
of the arena floor, while workmen hung scenery on stage and
the girls who wanted to be Miss America learned how to walk
in front of strangers. Teddy's stomach rumbled as Miss Idaho
tried out a few steps and tripped. "For God's sake," the director
called. "How did you make it to the finals?" His voice cut the
air like a hornet's sting. The girl was almost in tears. The three
silent men squirmed in their chairs. Cigar smoke rose in the air.
"A real baked potato," Ben muttered. The woman in the sunglasses comforted Miss Idaho from the floor. Somebody tried a
spotlight on stage center. A few hands began to set up chairs in
the back of the auditorium. Miss Idaho tried it again, then again.
The director sighed, distractedly snapped his headband against
his forehead, called for Miss Oregon. "Or-gon," he said. Miss
Oregon came stage front, chewing gum. There was a moment's
silence. Ben poked Teddy with his elbow. "Never make it," he
whispered. Miss Oregon wore a red bathing suit. "What is that,
sweetie," the director began, "moving up and down inside your
mouth?"

On and on they came, some competent, some better, some
even with a sure sense of themselves, a firm presence that could
not be shaken by a mere hack director from Broadway or a
duenna hired for publicity reasons or two or three silent promoters sitting out front dreaming up ways to drum up business for
the Labor Day weekend. Frances Marie Howard, with her snag-

gle tooth. She clearly didn't give a damn, Teddy saw, as she thrust her long white legs one after the other across the Convention Hall stage, not caring whether she was doing it the show business way or not. When she turned, she gave them all a single, fierce, intelligent look, showed her flawed tooth. The director looked beaten. Then one or two others, caught in the spot, sure of themselves, taking their time. At the sight of them, Ben sighed, Teddy grew agitated. "Whoo," he said under his breath. They looked six feet tall up there, standing on their stiletto heels, swollen pompadours topping their blond heads. They were another race, flesh firmed by their bathing suits, some gift of utter confidence shedding a momentary glow in the bright light on stage. Teddy knew that glow, had known it in one variation or another all his life. Charlotte, with her shining unguents, French cream glistening on her face, hair down her back, staring at herself in a mirror. Thelma Talles, mauve parasol spinning overhead on the beach, listening attentively to Jack Lewin's stories. Barbara Demarest, trim in day-school uniform, soft gray flannel pleats covering her thighs at the piano. F. M. Howard. And Bea, the scent of simple English talc . . . Then three girls, bored with waiting their turn, linked arms and suddenly highstepped across the stage like the Rockettes. Everybody was laughing. "Ladies," the director called. "If you only did what I asked you to do and quit horsing around . . ."

Miss Indiana, Miss Alabama, the girls from Texas, Wyoming, Colorado, Kansas, Vermont. Poor Miss Wyoming could not learn how to make a turn without losing her balance. Miss Kansas kept going over on her ankles; she wasn't used to high heels. The director had begun to sweat. His voice had risen, a New York accent thickening in his throat. His cheeks were flushed. Whenever the lady in sunglasses made an objection or commiserated with a girl, he turned his back on her and began to shout at the pianist. It was getting late. It was after ten. The rehearsal had gone on too long. Some of the girls had gooseflesh from the chill in the air. The stage was white with their legs, white and shining with their bare shoulders and arms, the satin bathing suits gleaming from one wall to another. But they had all been at it for too long. None of them had had dinner, just a glass of milk and an apple. There had been too many mistakes, too much clumsiness, too frequent humiliations. The girls wanted to go back to their hotel, back to a little room service and a warm bath. It was chillier than ever in the Hall. In a couple of days it would be September. When the time came for the girls to walk out along the stage in front of thousands of Atlantic City customers, they would know how to do it. There was no doubt in their minds. For the director, his whole reputation was at stake. His next show depended on the success of this one. He had no faith in any of the girls. He walked again across stage front, hips swiveling, turning, giving classic instructions. Ben watched silently. Teddy rose to his feet momentarily, pulled at the crotch of his white ducks, tucked in the edges of his navy shirt. The family colors. White. Navy. Bea's colors. Teddy's. He stood there while the overhead lights slowly came on in the Hall, one by one, a powerful massing of the auditorium's capabilities, tested for the moment by a careful stagehand who did not want to take any chances. On they came, like the aurora borealis, the girls onstage dimming, returning to lifesize, as the Hall itself brightened, while Ben and Teddy Lewin, Teddy on his feet pulling at himself, were caught in the full illumination of Convention Hall.

There was silence for a moment. Ben froze. Teddy and the director stared at each other. The lady with the clipboard turned in her chair, caught sight of them. She adjusted her sunglasses. Then the other men turned, the three promoters, cigars twisting in their mouths. The pianist struck a light chord. "Who are you?" the director asked, with a pretense at calm. Teddy turned around. There was no one behind him. The question was for him. He had known that. Who was he? "What are you doing here?" the director hissed. His baggy pants rode high over his stomach. His neckerchief absorbed his sweat. He had a sagging-face built on pasty jowls. He suddenly looked old, covered with fleshy folds like Celia or one of Teddy's other aunts. He thrust a finger in the air. "What is that skinny bastard doing in here?"

Teddy considered it a moment. His face was burning. What was he doing in there? "Let's go," he said to Ben. They moved for the door, the one they had come in by, made it across the vast floor without another question being asked. The lights overhead were dimming. No one was chasing them. No one followed. After a moment, the rehearsal returned to itself. They slipped into the corridor, out of sight. Ben was giggling. "Move your ass, you skinny bastard," he whispered happily to his brother. "Make it snappy." Teddy began to giggle, too. By now, they had reached Georgia Avenue. All the trucks were unloaded. A couple of teamsters were eating sandwiches on the platforms, drinking beer. They headed for the Boardwalk, Ben first imitating the director, one hand on his hip, shaking his buttocks, pursing his thin lips, then picking on Miss Wyoming and Miss Kansas. Miss Corn Pone, he called her. He went over on his heels, stumbled on the curb. Teddy was doubled up. Finally, Ben began to strut along the pavement, lifting his knees high in a fake cakewalk he had seen somewhere, like Jimmy Cagney moving fast on his high mick haunches, or a Forest Park cheerleader crisscrossing the football field at half time with a baton held overhead. It was wonderful. Nobody could do it like Ben. His energy was everywhere. It lifted Teddy for the moment, carried him along. God bless Ben, he thought. Bless him. Bless him.

PART THREE

Baltimore, Md., 1930. It is seven thirty in the morning, snow on the ground, six inches of it, twenty-four hours old, sleet-hardened now into ice. The milkman has just pulled up in front of the Lewin house. He jumps out of his wagon, strokes his blanketed horse once or twice on a flank. The horse turns his head to watch him. Old friends. The air is faintly mauve with new morning light, crystallized through thousands of icicles that hang from identical porches up and down the street. In the living room Teddy pulls a curtain aside an inch or two, watches the milkman. This is the milkman's time of day. He is full of spring, full of early morning life. He has ear-muffs on, a green wool cap. As he touches the horse one more time, running his hand along the sweating buttock, the wagon behind them slips a foot on the ice, a real jolt, Teddy can tell, then another, pulling the horse rigidly into the traces. There is a moment's unbearable strain, horse against wagon. The milkman races for the driver's seat, reaches for the brake. By then, the wagon has slipped a third time, and some irresistible combination of gravity, ice, and missed traction has pulled the horse to its knees. Teddy watches him struggle. There is a sudden horse shriek, full of panic, another pulling. The horse goes over, the milkman at its side. An icicle falls from the Benesches' house next door. There is the first glint of sun. Two columns of steam come from the horse's nostrils. His eyes are rolled up into his head. What is it, Teddy's mother asks from behind him. Her voice sounds sleepy. There is a slow unwinding of action then, Bea calling to the milkman from the front door, Ben suddenly standing alongside Teddy. Jack is already at the lumberyard, opening the gates at this precise moment so that the loaded trucks can get an early start to building sites on the other side of town. The milkman is using the Lewins' phone, pleading with someone for help. He has stuffed his earmuffs into his back pocket. Ben rushes out to the porch, rushes back. Three neighbors now stand in the street surrounding the stricken horse. The steam still comes from his nostrils. Five minutes pass. The milkman solaces his horse, pulls at the traces, tries to get it to its feet. Breakfast, Bea calls from the kitchen. Teddy stays at the window. He is going to see a secret revealed, he is going to see magic. Another fifteen minutes go by. A stranger arrives in a car. The horse is suddenly on its feet. The stranger pats its flanks, exactly like the milkman, lets his hand run over the sweating skin under the blanket, looks into the horse's mouth. He pulls the upper lip back, kneels to examine the right front leg. Ben now stands alongside them. Bea calls for breakfast again. Then Ben comes back into the house, shaking his head. Come on, Teddy, Bea says. Before it gets cold. She is imperative. In a minute, in a minute. Come away, she says. He doesn't answer. Ben watches through the window, standing next to Teddy. The stranger stands in front of the milk horse. The milkman weeps without shame. The stranger pulls out a black revolver. The secret is about to unfold, the magic trick will be performed. There is another exchange between the milkman and the stranger. Teddy has never seen a revolver before, cannot take his eyes off it. Then the stranger places the gun against the horse's forehead, visibly counts to three, and pulls the trigger. At the shot, a half-dozen icicles fall from the eaves over Teddy's porch. The horse pulls back its mouth. Huge teeth grit themselves. The horse rises into the air a foot or two, all of it, head to half-silken tail, then slowly settles to the ground. A vast accumulation of gas escapes it, a sound louder, lasting far longer, than the shot itself. Teddy is trembling. Well, Bea says from behind him, you saw. She makes it sound like an accusation. I tried to keep you away from it. That's what happens to horses who break their legs.

Together minutes later, Ben and Teddy eat their breakfast in the tiled kitchen through a kind of nausea that, without their knowledge, begins to take permanent hold of both of them.

1931. Bea and Jack Lewin's friends gather in the living room after a Saturday night movie downtown. Four couples sit around eating delicatessen sandwiches, corned beef and pastrami picked up at Sussman and Lev's. Mustard is everywhere, huge pickles like baseball bats, coffee and ginger ale. Teddy peers down at them from upstairs through the slats of the stairway railing. He is bent over in his pajamas, in Ben's pajamas, passed down for one more season of wear, his feet bare, listening hard. Someone tells a dirty joke. Bursts of giddy, satisfied laughter fill the room. The women laugh louder than the men. Then someone tells another. Teddy hears Bea's light voice murmuring a protest. No one pays attention. The evening wears on. At one point, as someone heads for the stairway to go upstairs to the bathroom, Teddy scurries into bed, holding his breath. When all is clear, he heads for the top of the stairway again. Later, as the evening breaks, Bea Lewin and Mac Seldin stand in the hallway next to the porcelain elephant which serves as a telephone table. Again Bea murmurs something. It is too light, too easy for Teddy to understand. He peers down, makes them out. Bea is looking at the floor. Mac Seldin suddenly reaches out for the zipper at the base of Bea's neck, makes as though he is going to pull it down. Through the slats, Teddy sees a sudden abashed look on Bea's face. It is mixed for the moment with something almost eager, something pleased. She likes what Mac has done, this slight gesture toward her. Nevertheless . . . Mac! The name cracks through the house. It is like a pistol shot. Jack is at their side in a moment, in a split moment, laughing nervously, hustling the guest and his wife, Selma, on their way. In a few minutes, the house is quiet. Everyone is gone. Bea and Jack sit in the living room for a long time, rehashing the evening. Teddy finally goes to sleep. Mac, he hears again inside his head, at one o'clock in the morning. It is his mother's voice, like a whip cracking.

Two years later. They are going to visit Grandfather Sandler at Levindale, Bea's own father, Celia and Haskel's father, master of the Sandler brood. He is eighty-four, with a beard like barbed wire, bloodshot eyes, a back humped with age. It is a Sunday afternoon, nearly spring. Bea carries a box filled with cake and black bread. It is her father's beloved pumpernickel. They edge into the parking space, make their way to the brick buildings without talking. It is like a campus, Teddy thinks, it is like going to visit the University of Maryland in College Park. He is trying to forget where he is. He knows these visits. The Lewins come to Levindale five times a year. So do all the other Sandler brothers and sisters. That makes fifty annual Sunday visits for the old man. The remaining two weeks are catch-as-catch-can. Teddy and Ben wander down the corridor, Bea and Jack behind them. Every now and then, Jack sighs. Jack's own father, Barney, is still young, still clean-shaven. He still has girl friends, a new one every few months. He never visits Levindale. He never goes to see his friends there. A wailing sound comes from down the hall. Teddy turns nervously. Bea gives him a reassuring smile. She is dressed carelessly today, as though her mind were not on it. Someone is beating on a door around a corner. Teddy's heart picks up a beat. He works at pretending he is else-where. He will not think about Levindale. At the door to his grand-father's room, in which there is a spyhole, the family pauses. Bea shapes a wave in her hair. Jack makes a visible effort to pull himself together, hustling the boys out of the way. He touches his fly. They knock, enter. Teddy's grandfather sits on a cot. His hands are folded between his legs. He looks up, says something in Yiddish. Some-one has once told Teddy that his grandfather was a fence in the old days. Stolen goods passed through his hands, on their way elsewhere. It is hard to believe. He looks so emptied sitting on the cot, as though he has never had another life. It is hard to tell even whether he knows who they are. Then he insists that Teddy sit on his lap. Jack gives Teddy a nod of encouragement. His grand-father's thighbones are like knives. Close up, Teddy can see his mouth through his beard, stares at the red and pink gums, covered with white spots, smells the sour breath through his grandfather's words. What is he saying? Ben stands at the window, gazing out at the lawn. He is too old to sit on his grandfather's lap. There is a scream from down the hall, another. Teddy hears the sound of running feet. Bea shows her father the food she has brought. He laughs with pleasure when he sees the pumpernickel. Teddy's grandfather's thighbones slice into Teddy's buttocks. He thinks about something else, thinks about school, about music, thinks about the movies, about going to the Rialto later in the day. His grandfather has him in a grip like iron, as strong as his other grandfather's, Barney's. Where did they all get their strength, these old people? I have to go, Teddy says. Yes, Bea confirms. They talk some more. Teddy's grandfather opens his mouth. It is as ancient as Hades down there, inflamed with dank chronic infection, moist with spittle. I have to go, Teddy says again. Teddy's grandfather begins to croon at him in Yiddish. Ben still gazes out the window. Jack pats the old man on the shoulder, somehow gets Teddy out of his grip. Bea actually kisses her father on the cheek, making an unpleasant face as she pulls away. Good-by, Teddy calls. Relief floods him like warm spring rain. Ben is saying good-by. Bea is talking to a nurse outside the room. Teddy's grandfather folds his hands again between his legs, lets them hang there. Teddy takes one last look at him. He has bloodshot eyes, moist, full lips, His own father had been a horse thief near Lodz, someone told Teddy. A fence. A horse thief. The smell of urine and stained underwear. The family's dirty linen, entombed in a room eight by twelve in an old age home in the greening suburbs of northwest Baltimore.

1934. Baltimore, inside the huge inflammable Barnum and Bailey tent pitched annually in the empty field across the street from Pimlico Race Track. Jack and Teddy Lewin sit in a center box, in the best seats. The tickets cost five dollars apiece. It is Jack's plunge, managed once on behalf of each son. Tonight it is Teddy's turn. Father and son are eating crackerjacks. They are dizzy with the evening's overdose of midget clowns, trapeze artists, elephants who drop massive turds like steaming volcanic rocks wherever they stop, showgirls in bird-feather plumes, the overamplified voice of a ringmaster dizzy himself with reflected glory, a band made up entirely of brass, and danger, too many kinds even to count, danger from Clyde Beatty's lions, from the threat of fire, from a Flying Wallenda missing his footing and falling at Teddy's feet, dead. It is ten minutes before the end of the show. Teddy has been shivering intermittently all evening. Dad, he says, ashamed of his fear. Let's go. Let's beat the crowd. Jack eyes his son. You sure? We'll miss the guy getting shot out of the cannon. I don't care, Teddy says. He cannot bear any more excitement, any more risks. Let's go. Still eyeing Teddy, Jack makes a decision about his son. It is not the first. He gathers his coat, helps Teddy into his lumber jacket, picks up their programs, and while the huge audience settles back in silence for the evening's climax, pulls his son along by the hand, the two of them furtively slipping along the sawdust, toward the exit sign, hunched over. They are out into the chill spring night before the cannon shot is heard.

1

They were beneath the boards again, the four of them, squatting like a line of Eskimos looking out to sea, Teddy Lewin, Erich Kessler, Joseph Talles, and the honeyed Tibor. It was like ice again under there, a move back into a prehistoric era of threatening glaciers. Behind them lay the same broken wastebasket, the same used condom, the lensless sunglasses, and behind that, the mound of sand with the dog shit on top. It was like concrete now, frozen waste, without odor, without power to offend; one good rain would wash it deep into the cold sand. The world never changed, Teddy thought, eyeing the antique turds curled around each other. In front of him, the sea beat in more urgently. Some new force was in the air, some change. It was almost Labor Day. Autumn was coming, the delicious falling into another winter. He thought of snow, listened to the breakers chop the shoreline in quick, thudding strokes. The summer was gone. He would be going home in four days, back to the sweet brick rowhouse near Druid Hill Lake, back to Marion and her one-eyed doll, back to his impeccable Bea. A nostalgia for both of them took sudden hold, memories of their smiles, their voices, Marion's thin hair, Bea's perfect bob. Navy-and-white outfits, spectator shoes. The Chickering in the living room, Celia's choice. They would go back to their old routine, Friday night dinner at Celia's or another aunt's, Charlotte Melnicov on Monday, full of complaints against life, school out in Forest Park, and downtown, twice a week, piano with Mabel Johns, music theory, and the adorable ones from Roland Park. Each night, Ben lectured them at the dinner table about Issues and Principles. His father listened patiently, then snapped back. He knew as much about capitalism as his son, he said. He understood the forces that ruled the world. He would not allow himself to be patronized, told Ben so. Then there would be a sulk and dessert would be eaten in silence. On Monday night, Ben and Charlotte Melnicov flirted with each other. Even Teddy could see that, watching them closely at the table. Once he had caught them playfully grappling for the *Evening Sun* in the living room, pressing into each other while Ben held the paper high over his head out of Charlotte's reach. They had remained like that for a few seconds, averting their eyes, until some hysteria in Bea's voice, objecting, had brought them apart. They had both been red in the face, had avoided each other ever since. Charlotte, the Slavic beauty who couldn't pass the bar. Teddy dreamed of her brushing out her hair, seated nude in front of a mirror.

"Let's play the scariest game," Tibor said. Erich turned to look at him, eyes wide. Joseph chortled. "You guys know the scariest game?"

Teddy stood up, stretched. He had discovered that the nights were boring in Atlantic City. He had paced the lobby at Sloan's, had written his postcards, had had his routine exchange tonight with Gustav Levi. His father was sitting at a bridge table in the cardroom, behind Thelma Talles, his hand resting lightly on her shoulder. Ben had gone off on his own again. Teddy wanted a change. The scariest game. Was that another dirty book?

"What is it?" Teddy asked.

Tibor took a deep breath. "Well, the game is to tell the scariest thing that ever happened to you."

"Who wins?"

"Nobody wins. It's just a game."

Teddy made a face.

"You don't like it?" Tibor asked.

Tibor's features were shadowed in the darkness. But Teddy

could see his face checkered by nervous, changing angles as he shifted on his haunches under the Boardwalk. Neon light from above caught him in split-second motion, a heightened cheekbone over a half smile, the glossy black hair, blacker even than his mother's, brown skin showing a faint pink where the sun had burned it, the honed, muscular arms. He was better-looking than Joseph, more compact, more supple, like a finished sketch for which Joseph was only the preliminary draft.

"I never played it," Teddy said.

"What about the kraut?"

Erich Kessler shrugged. He had no ideas of his own. He was as enclosed as a Rhine castle, as silent and remote, stranded on the shoreline of history. Nevertheless, he offered a suggestion.

"Let's go to the movies," he said.

"Movies?" Tibor was astounded.

"I like the movies."

"Jesus Christ."

"Well, how do you play?" Teddy asked.

"What I said before. Everybody tells the scariest thing that ever happened to him."

"Nothing scary ever happened to me," Teddy said.

"My ass."

Teddy stretched again. "Let me think," he said.

"What about you?" Tibor said to Erich.

Erich turned up the palms of his hands plaintively. "Nothing."

"You mean nothing ever scared you?"

"Nothing."

"Think back."

"Nothing."

"Not even failing something in school, not even being kept back?"

"Nothing."

"What about you?" Teddy asked. They were all shifting position now, moving from side to side, standing, then sitting, rubbing their haunches, stretching neck muscles. Joseph was hug-

ging himself. It was getting colder. The wind whipped the pennants on top of the Steel Pier. Above them, the tourists pounded
up and down the Boardwalk, the midweek crowd. Everyone wore
sweaters tonight.

"Sure," Tibor said. "Plenty of scary things happened to me."

"Me, too," Joseph said.

"Maybe I'll find something," Teddy said.

"I'll start it," Tibor said. "Maybe that'll get you guys going."

"What are you going to tell?" Joseph asked.

"You'll hear." He thought a moment, bit his lip. "Okay," he
finally said. "I got one. Maybe it's not the scariest, but it's bad
enough."

"What?" Joseph said.

"Well," Tibor began. "We used to live over in East Baltimore.
You know where that is, Lewin? Full of Polacks and Wops? We
lived there for twelve years before we moved out to Park Heights.
We lived near Broadway, where the Hopkins Hospital is. Everybody poor. I mean poor. Us too."

"We weren't so poor," Joseph said.

"It wasn't Park Heights," Tibor said. "That I can tell you.
Anyway, everybody was moving out of the neighborhood except
us. The Rudolphs, the Jacobsons, the Blumbergs, all those
people, only a couple of us left. So one day, me and Joseph are
walking home around six o'clock at night, not really dark, not
light either, and we get caught in this vacant lot in the next
block to our house."

"Oh, yeah," Joseph said, smiling. "I remember."

"You remember?" Tibor said. "Well, keep your trap shut, it's
my story. There are these three Polack kids surrounding us.
Laughing at us. You know, high-school kids, big kids we seen
every day of our life. My brother here makes a run for it, just
starts swinging his arms around in the air like a windmill and
he's out and down the street. He doesn't even look back until
he gets to the corner, then he throws me this look, too bad, kid,
and he's running. On your back, kike. That's what I hear. That's

what one of them says. And I knew he meant it as soon as he opened his mouth. I was so scared then that I farted. One of them laughs at me and spits on the ground. On your back, they yell, don't you understand English? They begin to shove at me, you know, hands on the chest, like it's a game, pushing me one to the other, then pulling at my legs. Then I'm on the ground. Like this." Tibor rolled over on his back, cringed in pretended terror. "Then, when I'm laying there like this, alone, all three of them, dumb Polack sons-of-bitches, Jesus, they pull out their Polack cocks and piss all over me, all over my knickers and everything."

"What happened then?" Erich Kessler said.

"That's not enough?" Tibor sat up.

"They leave you alone then?" Teddy asked.

"Sure. They pissed all over me and went home to have dinner." All four boys laughed then. "And I was wearing Joseph's old sweater, too," Tibor added.

Teddy shook his head in disbelief. "Christ," he said.

"Pretty scary, huh?" Tibor asked. "Maybe if you hadn't run off," he said to his brother, pointing accusingly at Joseph.

"They'd have pissed on two of us," Joseph said. They all laughed again.

"Jesus," Teddy said. "Pissed on you."

"Those guys from Southern and Patterson Park don't fool around. They don't like you, they don't like you." There was a sudden mixed note of admiration and anger in Tibor's voice. All the boys heard it. "I mean," he added, "didn't any of you ever have a yen to piss on somebody? Just like that?" He snapped his fingers.

"You mean you thought it was okay?" Teddy asked.

"I didn't say that. Forget it. You uptown guys don't know. All you know is Jews. Rich Jews. What you need is one year in East Baltimore. That'd fix you for life. Now you heard my scary story and I still made you laugh. How about yours? Let's hear."

"Nobody ever pissed on me," Teddy said, with heavy irony.

"There's always the first," Tibor said, flashing anger. "I could manage it."

"Hey," Joseph called.

"Let's hear now," Tibor said.

"Well," Teddy began. "Once my mother took my sister and me and my cousins on the boat to Tolchester."

"That dump," Tibor said.

"That's a beach down the Chesapeake Bay," Teddy said for Erich Kessler's benefit. "Anyway, on the boat ride back they forgot to put the blocks under one of the trucks and halfway there it almost rolled overboard."

The boys were silent, waiting. "I mean it was one of those big ten-wheel monsters and there was this horrible grinding noise that nobody knew what it was, and suddenly the boat lurched over like this"—here Teddy angled his hand precipitously—"and I thought we were going to sink."

Tibor raised an eyebrow.

"It's true," Teddy said.

"I didn't read about any boat sinking in the Bay."

"I didn't say it sank. The driver shoved in the blocks and saved it."

"That's it?"

"Well, when the boat came up right they caught me half-in half-out a lifeboat."

There was a mild uproar then, laughter from the boys, Tibor yelling louder than all of them. "Si-ssy," he yelled, clapping his hands together.

"It was no joke. I thought we were going down."

"Try another one."

"What do you mean?"

"That's not good enough. That's nothing. Find something scary."

"You don't think I was scared?"

"Not like me when they pissed on me. Now, if the boat sank . . ."

"You want blood?"

"Come on, give us another one."

Teddy settled back on his elbows. "Well," he said, after a moment's thought, "a couple of years ago, over on Lanvale Street, there were these two houses at each end of the block. Know what I mean? Anyway, one of them had this bulldog locked up in the back yard behind chicken wire. This ugly bow-legged thing that foamed at the mouth whenever we went by on the way to school."

"Teeth sticking out?" Tibor asked.

"Yes," Teddy said. "Fangs on each side, hanging over his lip. Every time we went by, the dog would throw itself against the chicken wire and foam at us. It scared the hell out of me every day of my life."

"That's the story?" Joseph asked.

"Wait, you'll hear. Anyway, at the other end of the block, there was this huge black police dog. You know the kind? This big thing with a head like a wolf locked up in the back yard on a chain. No chicken wire around him. Just an open back yard. Every time we went by, he'd throw himself at us and the chain would pull him off his feet as though he was shot. It was a tossup, which corner to use."

"Then?"

"Well, that went on for a couple of years. The bulldog down at one end, the German police at the other. Once the neighbors signed a petition to get rid of them both but it didn't work. So one day I'm walking along Lanvale Street with some kids after school and I hear somebody go uh-uh, in that voice, and then I see somebody else freeze dead, like it's the end of the world, and then we're all standing on the curb in a huddle, and down the street from one end, right in the middle, comes the little ugly bulldog, two fangs hanging outside its mouth, just walking slowly down the middle of the street staring straight ahead, but lifting each leg real high, and from the other end comes the German police, sort of sliding along on its belly, close to the ground, both of them coming at each other down Lanvale Street, slow as molasses, off the chain, out of the yard, not making a sound. . . ."

The boys waited. Teddy was silent.

"Don't leave us hanging," Tibor said.

"Come on," Joseph said.

Tibor bit a fingernail, spat it out. "So?" he said urgently.

"That's all I remember," Teddy said. "That and being so scared that I thought I was going to faint there. My heart was so charged up—"

"You mean you don't remember what happened?"

"That's all I remember, the two dogs coming at each other like that."

"Nothing else?" Joseph said.

"You don't remember who won?" Tibor asked.

"I don't even remember the fight. I just stood there. I couldn't move. I was paralyzed."

"Oh, Jesus," Tibor said.

"It's not a bad scary story," Joseph said.

"I talk about it now and my heart's going a mile a minute," Teddy said.

"How can you not remember?" Tibor asked.

"I don't. I swear to you."

"Nothing?"

"Just what I told you."

"It's pretty good anyway," Joseph said. "I bet the German police chewed the hell out of that bulldog."

"They say that when a bulldog gets a hold with its jaws it never lets go until death," Teddy said.

"I bet the German police killed it dead."

"I don't know."

"You know about German police dogs, Kessler," Joseph said. "They could beat a bulldog any day, right?"

"In Germany, they're very gentle, very well-trained."

"But when they have to, they can do it, can't they?"

"They hunt criminals in Germany."

"That's not what he means," Tibor said. "That's Rin-Tin-Tin stuff."

"Bulldogs can beat anything," Teddy said. "That's why they're called bulldogs."

"You really mean you don't remember anything after that?" Tibor asked.

"I must have gone blind," Teddy said.

"I'd have liked to seen that fight." Tibor rested a moment on his elbows, then turned back to Erich Kessler. "How about a story from you."

"I have nothing."

"Everybody has a story."

"I have nothing."

"You were never scared?"

"Nothing."

"Christ."

"What about me?" Joseph asked.

"What about you?"

"Nobody asked me."

"Your stories are the same as mine."

"You think so? You're so sure?"

"You mean, something else happened to you that didn't happen to me?"

"What do you think, I'm your Siamese twin?"

"All right. So what's your story?"

"I'm not sure I can tell it."

"It was your idea, not mine."

"Come on, you guys. I'm freezing," Teddy said.

"Just snuggle up a little," Tibor said. "We'll all get warm."

Teddy hugged himself, sat with his arms wrapped around his knees and body, hunched over. Tibor sat alongside him. He pulled his shirt collar up. "Come on, let's have a little body contact," Tibor said, "it'll keep us from freezing our asses off." Nobody moved. "Hurry up, Joseph," Tibor said, mincing the words. "The uptown kid is going to catch his death."

"You gotta swear you'll never tell this."

"I swear," Tibor said.

"Everybody swear."

"I swear," Teddy and Erich Kessler said together.

"Well, there was this Sunday morning last year. I had the grippe. Tibor was at Sunday school. I guess everybody thought I was too sick to move or something. I had a temperature. Anyway, I was going to the bathroom and I saw that the big bedroom door was opened an inch. I could hear sounds coming out of there." Joseph stopped, peered nervously into the dark.

"That's very scary," Tibor said.

"Wait. After I went to the bathroom, I couldn't help it. I stopped at the door, looked where it was open."

"And you saw Daddy kissing Mommy," Tibor said.

"Don't be so smart."

"Then what'd you see?"

"Well, maybe it doesn't sound like much. But my mother was sitting on her long chair in the bedroom, naked. Nothing on. No clothes. She was crying. Like this." Joseph stretched out, buried his face in his hands. "My old man was standing in front of the mirror, brushing his hair in his BVD's. He was smiling at himself in the glass. There was one button missing on the flap of his BVD's. Part of his hairy ass was hanging out."

"That's the story?" Tibor asked.

"It scared the hell out of me. I swear it did. I never told anybody."

"That's the whole story?"

"Yes."

"But she's always crying with him."

"I know, I know. But I could see everything. It was that she was naked. She didn't cover anything. She didn't even care.

And him smiling at himself like that, bare-assed, brushing his hair, making a beautiful part. And not a word."

"It would scare me," Teddy said.

"You guys scare easy," Tibor said, shaking his head. "I'm really surprised at you, Joseph. That's your big secret?"

"I knew I shouldn't tell you. What the hell."

"I thought you were going to say that you saw something."

"I did see something."

"I mean really something."

Joseph threw Tibor a dark look. "Like what?" he asked.

"You know."

". . . . . ."

"What a bunch of dopes. Didn't any of you guys ever see your parents fucking?"

A look of horror crossed Erich Kessler's face. He glanced vengefully at Tibor, turned quickly again to face the sea, said nothing. Joseph and Teddy were silent, too, flanking Tibor on their haunches. They were excluding Tibor, were excluding each other. Minutes passed. It grew even colder. Underneath the wind, there was a thin slice of frigid air which cut into everything. The sound of footsteps above them returned. There was a weak blast of trumpets from the Steel Pier, the whining end of a set. Teddy stared at the sand beneath him, ran his fingers through it. He had begun to brood. The telling of his two stories had exhausted him. He had others too, if he'd only been asked, if there had been time. Some powerful new mood had overcome him, some sense of himself, of his own presence. He thought of his stories, of Tolchester and the boat, of the German police and the bulldog. There were plenty more where they came from. There was practically a bottomless horde, there was never an end to scary stories. The world would be telling them until Doomsday and beyond. Then he thought of Thelma Talles and her husband. He heard Tibor ask his question again.

"Why don't you just shut up?" Joseph said.

"Yeah?"

"Don't you know when enough's enough?"

"What are you all of a sudden, Mister Goody Two-shoes?"

" . . . . . ."

"I bet you're just like these two guys over here."

"What do you mean?"

"You believe everybody sits around holding hands."

"Don't pull that stuff on me, Tibor."

"These guys don't believe their old men ever sleep with their mothers." Teddy shifted uncomfortably. Erich got to his feet.

"See?" Tibor smiled in triumph.

"See what?" Teddy said.

"See," Tibor said in a whole new voice, phlegmy and flat and slow, "that your gimpy old man is fucking my old lady right now."

As they grappled for each other off balance in the icy sand, a moan came from Teddy. He heard it as though it came from the other side of the world. At the sound, Joseph jumped to his feet. "For Christ's sake," he cried out. "Lay off, both of you." Teddy and Tibor were rolling over onto the beach, Tibor's hard little body slipping from Teddy's hands. They came together once, foreheads colliding, twice, separated for an instant. They were both suddenly sweating in the cold. A peculiar, passionate half-sob escaped the two of them almost at the same moment. Tibor's shirt came out of his pants, the tails hanging over his buttocks. His clear skin caught the moonlight, white on pink. Teddy had him for a moment by the neck, smelling his quick-rising sweat, distracted by it. His hold weakened. Then, a second later, he lost him. It ended with Tibor stretched full-length above Teddy, hugging him in a terrible, insistent grip. Both of them could hardly breathe. They stayed that way for a minute, limb on limb, staring in the dark into each other's eyes. Joseph stirred above them, grunted objections. Erich Kessler shifted uneasily on a sandy mound behind Joseph, kept looking aimlessly over his shoulder. Then Tibor made a move as though he were going to kiss Teddy full on the lips. He brought his own face up an inch or two, then thrust it down to Teddy's, hovering there a split second. Then, as he quickly pulled back, he forced a tight, barking laugh that was meant for Joseph and Erich Kessler. It was like a cough, as bitter as Barney Levin's daily hack. Teddy felt its force, felt Tibor's harsh breath, the moment's insupportable impulse. He discovered that he had his own face twisted violently into the sand. After a moment, sighing, Tibor finally released himself and slowly rose to his feet, the length of his compact body coming up stiffly. He brushed the sand from his pants, made a final forced, disgusted sound. Erich Kessler stood ten feet away, hands in his pockets, shivering silently in the cold. Joseph stepped between Tibor and Teddy.

"You and your scary games," he said to his brother.

Teddy stood up. He had sand in his shoes, sand on his chin and in his hair.

"Everybody all right?" Joseph asked.

"I'm okay," Tibor said. "How about you, kid?" He gave Teddy a sudden curious little smile, intimate and sly, full of a lifetime's satisfied insolence.

"Okay," Teddy said. His voice shook.

"You won't tell, will you? Nobody'll tell, right? I'm depending on you guys."

A few minutes later, full of a sense of mutual complicity, they all started back for Sloan's, single file.

2

It seemed to him that he sleepwalked through the whole next day. When he first awoke, he had a sudden failure of memory. He couldn't surface the night before. It had disappeared into the past, like Jesse Smirnoff into the ground. He lay alongside his father in the double bed, gazing dreamily at Jack's peeling nose, at the triple layer of emerging new skin on his shoulders, thinking about Celia and Hermine and Gideon, his immaculate aunt and cousins, thinking about the Shelburne and their suite, then about Miss America and Frances Marie Howard's intelligent look. She wouldn't get close to Miss America with that snaggle tooth and that snappy walk of hers. Skinny little bastard, the director had cried out in front of everybody in the Convention Hall. Then Ben had high-stepped his way up to the Boardwalk, as determined as Frances Marie Howard, and Teddy had followed happily. But that was another night. That was not the night before.

His father's slim moustache caught the light now. He turned on his side, mumbled a word in his sleep. At the foot of the bed, Ben was snoring. It was another morning. Teddy could see the Surf Hotel silhouetted through the drawn window shades. Nothing moved in the room. Ben's paperback book lay on the floor. So did his pants and shirt. It always drove Bea crazy, his sloppiness, the pile of goods he left behind him everywhere, books, papers, combs in the bathroom thick with accumulated hairs. It was a wonder he could make his way through college.

He thought of Gideon's enlistment. His cousin would be an officer in the U.S. Army, of his own free will. Teddy would share the glory, the whole family would share the glory. It was perfect that Gideon should be an officer. There was nothing else for him. He had the no-nonsense carriage, the square shoulders, the athletic yen and slightly astringent after-shave smell that all the Sandler men aspired to. Erect, balding, looking straight at the world, full face. The cousins were better at it than the uncles. The uncles were still not so sure of how to do it. Full face made them nervous. Erect made them too visible. They handled the world their own way, stubbornly beating it into shape behind everyone's back. But the cousins knew that the world loved them. They knew that everybody loved them. They were rich, educated, and confident, and they shared their generation's fine Sandler features. Among them, only Teddy Lewin and his brother Benjy were not rich. They shared other things.

He couldn't remember for the moment whether or not his father had been in bed when he got back from the beach. The four of them had slipped quietly into the hotel through the ground-floor screen door and made their way upstairs to the lobby. It had been half deserted. Pearl Sloan stood at the counter, chewing on a pencil as she worked on her books. Her husband, Hy, was already asleep. It was dim everywhere. The Talles boys had quickly disappeared, Erich moved somewhere into the background. In the sunroom, Teddy had caught a glimpse of his old friend Gustav Levi. He was writing a letter again, the beautiful black pen flashing in the lamplight. Up and down the pen moved, the golden nib lighting the way, then left to right, combining literate diagrams in rigid horizontal sequence in order to create sense, send a comprehensible message. Lurking in that head, while the pen moved, hiding out in the intricate nooks and crannies that Gustav Levi kept invisible to most of the world, was a set of astounding questions. Teddy knew them all: *Lwh*, *Lewy*, whirling dervishes, Jews who fainted in ecstasy at the thought of God, revolutionary biblical battles, rationales for the destruction of humanity and the world itself. There were no answers to such questions. There was no point in raising them. Everyone seemed to know that but Gustav Levi, who pretended otherwise. In the end, it all came down to a nighttime wrestling match on a cold Atlantic City beach. That was what all the questions amounted to; solve that and everything was solved.

Gustav Levi looked up then, sent Teddy a salute, a finicky gesture that duplicated his finicky manners at the dinner table, his finicky choices of menu, his finicky daily maintenance of himself. Gus Levi was alone. There was no one to think about those things for him. He had to remember everything himself, diet, cleanliness, and all the rest. In that, he was like Charlotte Melnicov. Teddy had returned Gustav Levi's salute, even managed a calm smile. Gustav Levi looked wistful at the sight of him.

He wandered around the lobby, joined Erich Kessler, who had found his father in the same old corner chair. Frederick Kessler had managed several dozen more pages of *The Forty Days of Musa Dagh* tonight. He was tired from the effort and proud. He had had to use the dictionary only four, five times, he told the boys. He urged the book on them, began to give them the plot. "You know Musa Dagh?" Frederick Kessler asked. Armenia and Turkey? He closed the thick red volume, rested the book in his lap. The boys had never heard of Musa Dagh, the massacre was before their time. Then Frederick Kessler began to tell them the life story of Franz Werfel, the author. "A little, fat man," he said, "from Ohstria." Erich sat down on the arm of his father's chair. Together like that they made a double image of displaced bones and nerve. Teddy could hardly separate one from the other. Erich paid careful attention to what his father was saying, at one point cupped his ear in his hand in order to hear better. Every night, they had dinner together in their three-room flat in Washington Heights. From the living room window, they could see the George Washington Bridge and the cliffs of New Jersey. Each week they alternated laundry duty with the new washing machine in the basement, and every night, they listened to each other tell about the day's events, took it all in as though none of it had ever happened before to anyone else, as though they were the first to have to deal with experience. A tough old worker in the millinery loft on Thirty-sixth Street, an old Socialist from Russia, trying to dominate the union shop. A sarcastic public-school teacher with no mercy, who persecuted Erich. A newly discovered compatriot from Düsseldorf, or Essen, or Stuttgart, or Berlin, or Hannover, or Hamburg, or Munich, or near compatriots from Vienna, Salzburg, and other towns from the East Reich. It was all a never-ending wonder to the two of them, part of another life they had never imagined for themselves, had never even considered except when they saw a Hollywood film in the cinema in Frankfurt. Who had thought of coming to America? Teddy left them like that, serenely proceeding with the day's recital, Franz Werfel, Musa Dagh, Turkish villainy, the death of two million Armenians, as though there indeed lay the center of the world, the very meaning of life.

He found his father, as he knew he would, in the cardroom. Jack had hardly changed position since Teddy had left the hotel. He was still sitting behind Mrs. Talles, who was playing a bridge hand with bored authority. Something had happened to her enthusiasm, something had damaged her cheerfulness. She yawned frequently, laid out her cards as though it were a terrific effort. People in Atlantic City grew sleepy in different ways than they did elsewhere. Teddy knew that by now. The air first exhilarated them, then dropped them early in the evening with a powerful fatigue. The sun scorched all energy. The sea lapped at them all day, then invisibly continued the process through the night without any of them even being aware of it. Nobody could resist all that. Nobody wanted to. That was what they paid for. Mrs. Wolf was Thelma Talles' sad-eyed partner, Nurse Chernichowski and a stranger her opponents. Jack leaned over Thelma Talles' shoulder, pointed at a card, whispered in her ear. She shrugged, threw down the card. Teddy watched them for a few minutes. Tibor's white-skinned old lady. Teddy's charred old man. They were simply playing bridge. Teddy too shrugged indifferently, like Thelma Talles, turned around, walked out.

Upstairs, the room was empty. Ben's cot was already unfolded in front of the double bed, the bottom sheet limply hanging out on one side. That was how Ben would sleep, on a half-made bed. Over his slim, long body, he'd toss another sheet, lie curled in it all night long. But by then, Teddy was already asleep, sunk like a smooth stone on his six inches of mattress, twisted on his side so that he would not roll over and touch his father. He stayed that way all night, hardly moving, his body rigid with control, knees drawn up, shoulders hunched, neck tight, arms folded into his chest. When he awoke in the morning, he had to unfurl himself like a flag.

He heard his grandfather cough down the hall, a croupy sound that went on sporadically for five minutes. It was his morning sound, like Tibor Talles' tight laugh, the way he cleared himself for the day. Chronic bronchitis, the family said, and nagged him about his smoking. Every February, he went into Sinai Hospital for three days of testing. When he came out, he had a prescription for special medicine and orders to give up cigarettes. It never varied. What did the doctors say, Jack always asked. I'm fine, I'm fine, Barney answered, and the smoke-filled year would begin again.

His grandfather had been flirting all week with Etta Sukenik. He was paying court to her at every meal, sitting at her right, staring at her pigeon breast, smiling a lot. It all looked somewhat unnatural. At her left, meanwhile, Frederick Kessler was paying her soft compliments. He seemed to smile a lot, too. The two men competed with each other, Barney sharp and aggressive, Frederick Kessler gallant, full of conversation about the opera. It was nothing serious, Teddy recognized, there were no real stakes, it just kept the two aging gentlemen interested at table number five and gave them a feeling of getting their money's worth. Barney Levin had a girl friend wherever he went, uptown, downtown, in East Baltimore, one out in Forest

Park, a stout widow with hair the color of cotton candy. He had once told Teddy's father, in Teddy's presence, that if he didn't have a girl friend every week, he was irritable for the next seven days. They had both glanced at Teddy then. "It's your business," Jack had said to his father and walked off. The old man lived alone in a room just off North Avenue, cooked his meals on a small burner set on top of his bureau, argued with his landlady when the day became unbearably dull. When he visited the Lewins, who lived just a few blocks away, he stayed an hour, no more, barely spoke more than a single sentence to any of them. He liked to turn over the silver pieces in the living room, check the hallmark, examine the china for the stamp of its factory. Wherever he was, he left a pile of ashes. Once a year, he brought them a box of chocolates and every couple of months he asked Jack the same sly question. "Are you making ten thousand yet?" he would say. "Not again, Pa," Jack would snap back, growing red in the face, and that would be that.

Once Barney had brought a girl friend to visit them. It was the lady with the cotton-candy hair. Barney had made the long trip out to Forest Park on the 32 streetcar, had picked up his friend, had then made the long trip back. She had sat in Bea's antique living room, wearing a purple dress with an inch-long split at the waist, fingering fake pearls. That afternoon, both Jack and Bea had turned irascible. Teddy could tell that they couldn't wait for Barney to leave. After a cup of coffee and a piece of cake at the kitchen table, he did, taking his friend sedately down the steep front steps, holding her under the elbow, letting the hand with the missing finger hang at his side. Watching them go, Bea and Jack had turned to stare at each other for a moment, then shrugged. "You don't think?" Bea asked. "You can't tell with him," Jack said. "He claims he likes her. He tells me he's lonely. Who knows?" But nothing had come of it, no proposal, no marriage. She remained one of his weeklies, as Jack called Barney's friends, another widow hatching youthful dreams inside an aging carcass. They all wore too much makeup, spoke too loudly. They all made too much of Ben and Teddy, pinching their cheeks a little harder than was necessary. They thought that would help them land the boys' grandfather.

The room had grown hotter. The sun was up. Jack mumbled in his sleep again. Ben pulled the sheet over his head. Teddy sat up on the edge of the bed, slipped on his bathrobe. He could hear breakfast dishes clattering in the dining room. Voices trailed upward in the alleyway outside. Saul was already on duty down there, flatfooting around sleepily in his white jacket and T-shirt, handling his tables' orders. Teddy made his way down the hall to the bathroom. He heard water running inside, the toilet flush. He leaned against the wall, waiting patiently, a towel over his arm, toothbrush and paste in his hand. His head seemed perfectly clear to him, he seemed to be without feeling this morning. The toilet flushed again. At the sound, Tibor Talles' apparition appeared in front of him, a sudden emergence from the heated morning atmosphere, a pink sunburned face with avid Oriental eyes coming close to his own for a moment, seeking something, a touch, an acknowledgment, then vanishing. It was like his old friend Eddie Glazer, the half-wit prowler. "Hmmm," Teddy said aloud. The door to the bathroom opened. It was Charlotte Melnicov, wearing a long yellow robe, a towel over her arm, like Teddy, toothbrush and paste in her hand. She had cream on her face, no lipstick on. Her hair was piled on top of her head like a great blond bush, a pale, golden honeycomb held in place by a thousand bobby pins. Another apparition, rising in the heat. "I warmed it up for you," she said without expression.

She brushed past him, a familiar fixed look on her face. She was always like that in the morning, always a little behind, slow, still dim and heavy with the night's dreams and what they portended. Teddy watched her over his shoulder. She glided into her room, began to pull bobby pins from her hair one by one. It was a great effort. Teddy caught a glimpse of her book on the night table, face down, marking her place. She was almost finished; she had fewer than fifty pages to go. What would happen to Charlotte Melnicov, he wondered as her hair began to fall to her waist. He slipped into the bathroom, locked the door. Her scent was everywhere, tooth powder, heady unguents from Nice, another, closer body scent mixed with it all, her real self. She had possession of the bathroom, no doubt about it. It was like his mother. She was there whether she was there or not. He could not get away from her. Soon Charlotte would go home to her widowed father in Baltimore, to live off his East Baltimore ground rents. Soon her boyfriend Larry Bernard, a giant among men, would pick up his law practice where he had left it in the Baltimore Trust Building and try to find a nice rich girl whose money would help him run for city council again. Already, Charlotte looked Bea's age. What happens to people? Teddy thought. What will happen to me?

He went through the day like that, full of pretended, prideful composure, floating with fake serenity over the ordinary life around him. He breakfasted alone, finishing his milk just as Gustav Levi showed up with *The New York Times* and seated himself across the table. Gustav Levi tried a few subjects on his friend, made no headway. The news was worse than ever this morning, he said. Teddy didn't seem to care. Gustav Levi quartered the paper then, gave his order to Saul, and began to read the editorials. Occasionally, he glanced over the top of the paper at Teddy.

At lunch, he sat next to Etta Sukenik, who crooned little speeches in perfect diction at everyone, playing with Barney and Frederick Kessler with equal attention. She talked again about music. She was planning to give a recital on Saturday night in the lobby of Sloan's. A few operetta songs, she said. Nothing too heavy. Herbert, Romberg, and a little Rudolph Friml. Pearl Sloan had insisted. She wouldn't leave her alone, Etta Sukenik said, until she said yes. Charlotte sighed again over Etta Sukenik's career. Etta Sukenik brushed it off. Yet it was clear that it was the most important thing in the world to her. She talked about other things, made an effort, but it was the opera, nothing else, that she cared about. As she talked to them, Teddy watched her deep, heavy, professional breathing, a forceful, even progression from diaphragm up through her throat, then out into the world in a trained rhythm. She impressed him. She existed outside Sloan's, beyond the hotel. It was clear that she could do without all of them. Over her tea, she turned to Teddy and said: "Of course, you will accompany me on Saturday night." For a moment, he didn't know what she meant. When he understood, he grew nervous, offered confused objections. She waved it all aside. Nonsense, her manner said. It's all nonsense to resist. He tried again. The idea mildly terrified him. She paid no attention. It was all decided and she had decided it. There was no more to say.

Then he went swimming, lying on the beach most of the afternoon, alternately riding the waves in and drying himself in the sun. Somewhere near the Boardwalk lay the Talles brothers. Joseph looked dead to the world. Tibor was building another castle. Their mother sat under her parasol. Jack watched them all from a bench on the Boardwalk, in slacks and long-sleeve shirt, a tennis hat on his head to protect him from the sun. Alongside Teddy, Charlotte Melnicov read the last pages of *Gone With the Wind*. Larry Bernard was nowhere in sight. Every now and then, Teddy thought of Etta Sukenik. Her imperiousness made him laugh. Who did she think she was? Nevertheless, something in his nerves told him he was trapped, told him he would not escape her, told him he didn't even want to. An accompanist at Sloan's, a Saturday night song recital. "She's really crazy, that Sukenik lady," he said to Charlotte. Charlotte didn't answer.

After dinner, the Talles brothers approached Teddy and Erich Kessler. Tibor thought it would be an interesting project if they all climbed the fire escape outside Sloan's a little later in the evening and sneaked a look at what was going on inside the rooms on each floor. Erich Kessler gave Tibor a long hard look. Teddy went on writing his postcard to Marion. He acted as though he were fiercely concentrating, as though nothing could distract him. Tibor tried again, looked disappointed, looked hurt, then turned away. Joseph followed. In the cardroom, the bridge game began. This time Jack took a hand, playing as Thelma Talles' partner. Over in the corner, Frederick Kessler read *The Forty Days of Musa Dagh*. The old lady Eisen sat on her throne, half asleep. Gustav Levi was upstairs. His dyspepsia was at him again. "Everybody misses you," Teddy wrote to Marion. "The whole hotel asks for you. Please give love to Mother." He drew a circle, put in two eyes, a dot for a nose, a smiling mouth. He made the eyes crossed to remind Marion of Gloria Goldman. But it hardly mattered; he'd be home before the card arrived. Inside the cardroom, there was a burst of laughter. The Talles boys passed by again, on their way to the Boardwalk. They were talking in seductive whispers. It was Thursday. Their father would arrive tomorrow, bringing money he had made off the draft. Tomorrow night they would have a blow-job in Chalfonte Alley. Wherever that was. . . . The hours passed. Night closed on the Surf, on the Cotswold, on Sloan's. For Teddy it was as though he had been asleep all day.

3

It was Friday night again, Teddy's second at Sloan's. They were already through grace-before-dinner, Rabbi Miller's choked voice lamenting its way through the sweet words, the Amens tonight resounding throughout the dining room with fearful somberness. Rabbi Miller took his good time about it, promised a sermon later. "Sermons," Gustav Levi said under his breath. "Too late, too late." The war news had arrived.

The smell of roasted chickens was everywhere, cooked onions, peas from Iowa, potatoes roasted with the chickens, and something else, something imprecise, the accumulated fragrances of a summer's kitchen. Teddy had had enough of it. He discovered that he hated the dining room, hated its constriction, hated sitting day after day with his friends at table number five. It was compulsory service. It was boring. On Friday night, there were prayers. Every night, there was adult conversation. That's what they all pretended. It was like plucked strings, pizzicato words. Nothing connected. Nothing led to anything else. Only Gustav Levi and Ben Lewin and sometimes the opera singer could speak an entire sentence in consecutive order. The rest communicated through a set of brisk gestures, hands and head, and mumbled phrases that were broken in two. Yet gestures were often enough, mumbled phrases sufficed. They all understood each other.

That morning, as the news came through the radio in excited bursts, the same communiqué repeated endlessly all through the afternoon, Erich Kessler, standing next to Teddy, had released a short, sharp, high-pitched gasp that seemed to come from a mechanism hidden at the top of his head. It was almost a scream. Something waiting for just such a moment. The Germans were into Poland, the bombs were already falling. In the morning paper from Philadelphia, lying on the cigar counter in front of the radio, there was a picture of German troops swinging back a Polish boundary gate to make way for the Panzer tanks. All the soldiers were laughing in the picture, making jokes. They looked posed, false, full of counterfeit humor. Teddy had not known what to say to Erich Kessler. Erich Kessler was embarrassed at the sound he had made. He leaned into the radio, blushing, pretending to listen intently, as though he had made a terrible social gaffe, something unforgivable in public, some uncontrollable released flatulence.

Alongside Erich Kessler, Teddy had stood at attention, drumming his fingers on the cigar counter. Pearl Sloan was working at her books again. She hardly seemed to notice the news. Across the lobby, the porter was vacuuming the carpet. His mind was clearly elsewhere. There was calm all around them. Mrs. Wolf left on a shopping expedition with Mrs. Stern. Nurse Chernichowski went out to buy a hot-water bottle for the old lady Eisen. In the dining room, Hy Sloan counted the flatware. It was going to be as hot today as yesterday. The sun struck the porch across the street at the Cotswold at a sleek angle, but it was too strong already for anyone to sit in it. Teddy nervously paced the lobby. He had cousins in Poland. He had aunts, uncles. He began to think of them, to imagine them today, this morning. But it was six hours later in Poland. They were already on to other matters. The news Teddy was hearing was dead before it reached his ears. He checked a map in the Philadelphia paper. He had always thought that Poland was to the north; but there, in black ink, it stretched to the east. There was even a little piece of Germany stuck at the top of it.

The day moved on that way, news reports every half hour, voices already heavy with doom. The English were not in it. The

French were not in it. It was only the Germans and the Poles. There could still be a deal between the great powers. By mid-afternoon, the German border had expanded twenty miles into Poland from two directions. Erich stuck close to Teddy, avoided his father. Frederick Kessler read his book, checked the newspapers, said nothing. Gustav Levi missed lunch, stayed in his room all afternoon. Jack Lewin was off to observe Thelma Talles on the beach. The Talles brothers went swimming. At four o'clock, the husbands began to arrive, Victor Talles churning in with two huge grips and presents for his wife. She was still at the beach, he was told. Ben was off again, on his own expeditions. He didn't get out of bed until eleven o'clock in the morning anyway. By evening, some fever had taken hold of Teddy Lewin, a piercing suspense that started his tic going again, had him reciting baseball statistics to himself when it became unbearable. Home runs, stolen bases, runs batted in, that kind of thing. He wanted to hear more news, but it was always the same stories that came over the radio. He wanted the radio to describe the battles blow by blow. He thought he wanted to be there, in Lodz or Katowice or further north, in Pultusk, where the Germans were coming down from East Prussia in two columns.

At five o'clock, there was a lesson in Slavic pronunciation on the radio. "While many foreigners have conquered Poland in the past," the announcer said from New York, "few have ever conquered the pronunciation of the language." Erich and Teddy stared at each other as though they were sitting in school, waiting to be called on. *L*, they were told, sounded like *W* in Polish. *W* was pronounced like *V*, and sometimes *F*. *CZ* wasn't *CZ* at all but *SH;* and Poles were addicted to adding vowels and consonants to words in an unexpected way. Warsaw became Var-sha-va. Lwow was Voof. Tczew was Cheff and Slawoj-Skladkowski, Swa-voy-skwad-kof-ski. The boys laughed nervously. The announcer made it all sound as though it would be over tomorrow. Swa-voy-skawd-kof-ski, Teddy said. Voof. They laughed again. Then there were the politicians and the generals. Stachiewicz, Sikorski,

Sosnkowski, Smigly-Ridz, Beck, Noscicka, and Pilsudski himself. The names came through the loudspeaker, heavy with Slavic syllables twisted out of shape.

Then Jack had passed by, still wearing his tennis hat. There was a brief, guilty exchange about why Teddy had not been to the beach, a peremptory order for him to take a bath. "See you," Teddy said to Erich Kessler. "See you." Upstairs, he went through all the motions in perfect order, examined his sunburn, lay in the tub while the green water darkened around him, even brushed his teeth, put on his white ducks, navy shirt, saddle shoes. Somewhere else, there was the sound of cannon. His father was deaf to it. Everyone at Sloan's was deaf to it. Yet, whenever Teddy thought of it, his heart went urgent, there was a sharp surge of strident beats that were echoed throughout his body, it was as though life were finally beginning.

"Sermons," Gustav Levi said again at table number five. "The barn door's open. The time for sermons was yesterday. It's too late for that. What we need now is the strength to hold fast to the nature of ordinary things. That's what will console us. A determination not to give up essential matters. Not to let go. No matter how banal they seem, how commonplace. Reject the phenomenal! Let the other side, let the *Deutschen* play with demons. Otherwise, we'll never get through this war."

"Whose war?" Ben said.

"This war. The world's war."

"But we're not in *any* war."

"Don't talk sophistry tonight," Gus Levi said.

"It's only Germany and Poland," Ben said.

"Only?"

"The Russians are out of it, protected by treaty. The French won't fight, and the English can't. There's no self-interest involved for us. It's the end of capitalism, maybe. It's the end of democratic capitalism, but that doesn't necessarily mean the American people will care enough to fight."

"It makes me nervous," Charlotte said. "It scares me. My

father was in the first one. I remember it, too. I remember him in his puttees. My mother died in the flu epidemic. I remember the whole thing."

"It won't be like that one," Ben said.

"It will be unimaginable," Gus Levi said.

"It will all be over in a week," Frederick Kessler said.

Gustav Levi looked at him thoughtfully. Frederick Kessler and Erich sat alongside each other tonight. They had never looked so much alike, erect in their dining chairs, sealed by their glasses, impassive, a double presence full of silent authority. They gazed at the rest of the table. Teddy caught their look, caught Gustav Levi's, waited.

"Why do you say that?" Gustav Levi finally said.

"Because the German Army cannot be defeated."

Again Gustav Levi stared at his new friend. Something passed between them, challenge and response. What would Gustav Levi say to that? But it was Ben Lewin who spoke.

"Could that possibly be a boast?" he asked.

There was a moment's pause while Frederick Kessler had his son translate the word for him. They nodded together a few times, Erich explaining.

"But it's true," Frederick Kessler protested. "Everyone knows that the German Army cannot be defeated. They will not make the same mistakes they made in 1914. This is not the same thing at all. They will conquer Poland in a week and it will all be over."

"Is that what you want?" Ben asked.

Frederick Kessler sat quietly then, looking down at his plate. His hands were folded in his lap. Together, he and his son were at a kind of stubborn attention, a resigned, withdrawn posture that bound them to each other even more strongly and set them apart from the rest. It dominated the table for a few moments. Then it went slack as Etta Sukenik, looking around at them all shrewdly, changed the subject and began to talk about the training and care of musical artists. There was the wrong emphasis on the first and not enough on the second, she said. She enunciated the words slowly, directing her attention to Frederick Kessler. Her own training, she went on, had come from two women, Frieda Ashworth and Marcella Sembrich. Surely, they all remembered Marcella Sembrich, the greatest Marguerite America had ever heard. Both teachers had supported Etta Sukenik just enough, not too much, not too little. Their teaching had been very precise, like Etta's diction. When she gave her first song recital in Aeolian Hall, she was perfectly prepared. The next morning, one critic compared her to Galli-Curci and talked about her intelligence and charm. Those were the words she used, without embarrassment, without self-consciousness. It was all due to the training and care she had received from Frieda Ashworth and Marcella Sembrich. Now, of course, she would not sing in Europe until the war was over. In Europe, opera would be the first casualty. Art always suffered. Wasn't that so? Didn't they all agree?

Dinner proceeded like that, in a stately way, course by course, the heavy disturbance hanging over all of them, an uneasiness that made its way throughout the entire dining room. Occasionally, there would be a burst of laughter from another table. Occasionally, Saul would make a sour joke. Occasionally, Jack Lewin would turn in his chair and stare over a couple of dozen heads at Thelma Talles, who sat next to her husband, Victor, with her back to them all. She was in black again tonight, her skin like white velvet. She hardly spoke. Tibor and Joseph sat on either side of their parents.

Once grace was said, Etta Sukenik was the first to leave. She swept away as though she were going to make an entrance on stage. Barney watched her cross the room, a look of dark disappointment on his face.

"Oh, Pa," Jack said. "Cheer up. There's always another one."

"She teases," Barney said.

"Don't feel bad. There's always the old lady Eisen."

Barney snorted. He turned to Teddy. "You hear that? Your

father thinks I should make love to the old lady Eisen. I'm seventy-three, she's eighty-two. She was nine when I was born. Together, we make one hundred fifty-five. Imagine one hundred fifty-five. In one bed."

The table burst into laughter. Even Frederick Kessler brightened for the moment. His competition with Barney was over, in any case. Etta Sukenik was not interested in either of them. She had made that perfectly clear. All she cared about was her voice and her career. The rest was like a whispered cue coming at her from the wings or the prompter's box, something to sustain her briefly until she had made her entrance and sung the first note of another aria. They all began to fold their napkins, take a last sip of tea. Their chairs scraped the floor of Sloan's dining room as they stood up. Dinner was over.

"Did you enjoy your meal?" Gustav Levi called to Teddy. He sounded more cheerful.

"I like chicken."

"It wasn't chicken tonight. It was another kind of bird." Then he began to march in place, saluting, and singing under his breath. "When the capons go rolling along . . ."

Teddy laughed again. Gustav Levi laughed with him. Something was restored. Gustav Levi was good at that. He always fixed things up, even when he felt most dyspeptic. He couldn't stand unpleasantness, couldn't bear scenes; but he knew how to hold fast to the nature of ordinary things, he knew where everything belonged, in what place, at what level, and what it was all worth.

"I hope I'm not going to lose you after you go home," Gustav Levi said, in front of everybody. He made it sound like a joke. Teddy blushed. "I have a feeling I've lost you already."

No words came.

"I don't want to lose you, you know."

Teddy managed a smile, Gustav Levi returned it. "Honestly," Gustav Levi began, "when you think about it, the accumulated facts of a person's life, anybody's life, are so astounding, so staggering, that they can hardly be assimilated."

"Oh, Gus," Charlotte said, rising from the table. "What does that have to do with the price of eggs?"

"I just thought it was worth mentioning. After all, we won't be together much longer, we'll have all winter to think about it."

Then Saul leaned over Jack's shoulder and said: "There's a telephone call for you outside."

"It's Mother," Teddy said. "Has to be."

All three then scurried for the lobby. "Let me, let me," Teddy said, racing for the phone. "Mom," he called into the mouthpiece. Jack and Ben crowded him through the folding doors. But it was Celia, not Bea. She had just finished her dinner. She was sitting in her room with Hermine, waiting for Sam to arrive. Gideon had gone to Philadelphia for the weekend. She had wondered what they were doing, she had wondered whether they had gone home.

"Home?" Teddy asked. "We're not going home until Sunday. We have two more days."

"I just thought," she said. "Haskel wanted to go to the Eastern Shore. He asked me."

"I'll let you speak to Daddy," Teddy said.

Then Teddy stood outside the folding doors while Jack spoke to his sister-in-law. By then, brother Ben was gone. He was not interested in Celia or Hermine. He didn't care about Haskel Sandler and the Eastern Shore, about kiln-dried pine and two-by-fours. Teddy saw his father say hello, smile, say yes. Then he began to nod at the phone, quick, brusque strokes of his head, up and down. Yes, he said. No, he said. Yes. Yes. Yes. At one point, he glanced at Teddy, rolled his eyes. No, he said. Then yes, yes, yes. A long pause, then a brief reply, some hesitation, a couple of dozen words, Jack expostulating, waving his hands in the enclosed booth. Finally, he hung up. "That's your Aunt Celia for you, all right," he said as he came out. He kept looking behind him as though she might emerge through the mouthpiece. "She'll never change. None of them will."

Then Barney came over to them, rubbing his hands. "I can't even get into the men's room," he said. "It's so crowded."

"So go upstairs," Jack said.

Barney paid no attention. "I never know in a crowded men's room," he said, "whether to stand behind an old man who can't start to piss or a young man who can't stop." He laughed then, kept rubbing his hands together.

"She thought we went home today," Teddy said, watching his father warily.

"I know she did," Jack said. He glanced guiltily at Teddy, turned away.

Then the Talles boys were at his side again, stuffing their dollar bills into their pockets. "No," Teddy said before they had even asked. "Come on," Joseph whispered, "It'll do you good. It's what the doctor ordered." But Tibor had his brother by the arm, pulling at him. He had already discarded Teddy; they had discarded each other; a bargain struck without spoken negotiation.

"Well," Teddy said, suddenly rising on his toes and stretching.

The Talles brothers were gone to Chalfonte Alley. The Kesslers sat in a corner of the lobby, carefully writing a shared letter to the two Mrs. Kesslers in Frankfurt. Ben was off on his own. In another corner, Jack sat and chatted with the Talleses. Victor Talles was telling them stories through his cigar smoke, making points by chopping the air with his hand. Thelma Talles was silent. BVD's, Teddy thought, a mirror and a hairbrush. Scary stories. His own and others. Charlotte Melnicov and her boyfriend, Larry Bernard, were standing nearby, waiting to say good night to the old lady Eisen. Nurse Chernichowski was at her side, making conversation for both of them. Everyone passed by, Mrs. Wolf, the Sterns, Maurice Pearman, fifty-eight others. Half of them didn't know the other half's names. They were familiar, everyday faces that nevertheless remained stubbornly strange to each other. But the room was stirring, turning again on its weekly axis.

Teddy would be going home soon. He had two more days. The world was different tonight than it was the day he arrived. The world had changed. Already, there was a war in another place.

4

Another Atlantic City morning. Saturday, the last.

The same heat hung in their room, the same brilliant morning light that sharpened all outlines, left no shadows. He was the first up, as usual. Lying there tightened on his side, he began to unfold limb by limb. He felt tired, his thighs were heavy. He wasn't getting enough rest. He hadn't slept a night through since he had arrived in Atlantic City. First it was Bea, asleep heavily in this very bed, with her daughter snoring like an insect alongside her. On those mornings, Teddy had hardly moved for fear of awakening them. During the night, his mother came in after he was asleep, whispering her way to the window or the closet or into bed in her Japanese kimono or her light nightgown, which was so thin, so transparent and weightless, that it could be rolled up into a ball to fit the palm of a hand. It was the same with Marion's nightclothes, the same with her faded pink underwear. Cotton candy, all of it. Now, it was Jack, his small-framed body fishbone thin, scarred by the sun, healing itself now through sleep. He moved his upper lip, his moustache shagging the surface like soft moss on a stone. He was as clean-cut as Jack Holt. He looked like a little movie star.

Sounds came from the next room. Hawking, a few murmured words, more hawking. The walls in Sloan's must be one-eighth of an inch thick. Teddy heard the sound of bedsprings. If he wanted, he could step into the closet and hear every word they were saying next door. And smell Bea's scent, that mild, weathered remembrance of olde England and her kempt rose gardens. At the foot of the bed, Ben suddenly turned over in a swift, convulsive movement. He pulled the sheet tight around him. Teddy couldn't tell his head from his foot. What was going on inside his brother, anyway? Teddy would never hear about the New York summer. He knew that now. It was locked away forever. Ben would retain his secrets, nurture them. That was the way he did everything that had to do with himself. He was impenetrable, a human knot, always had been. He could visit his grandfather Sandler at Levindale and never speak to the old man, just stand at the window staring out at the beautiful lawns. He could watch the milkman's horse get shot at the front curb and never seem to bat an eye. He was that way at the dinner table at home, unless he wanted to show them all how smart he was, how provincial their ideas. He was on his way somewhere. Anyone could tell that. He would leave them all soon. Half of him was already gone.

There was another sound from the next room, quiet, argumentative voices. Jack stirred, settled back into deep sleep. Teddy watched him attentively, the clear, small-scaled profile, the tender moustache, closed eyelids like tiny eggshells, wondrous eyebrows perfectly shaped. In sleep, there was some expression of wistfulness around his mouth, something at the corners that suggested needs that had nothing to do with the rest of the family. Teddy lay there for the moment, afraid of moving, unable to take his eyes off his father. He could lie there forever probably and think about his father, Jack Lewin, born Jacob Hersh Levin, and his mother, Beatrice Sandler Lewin, think about them and the lives they had, what they needed and wanted, the dreams they had put behind them, one by one, the dreams they still had, obsessively pursued, what they did every day, how they did it, all those things, things uncountable, the sum of endless, infinite seconds, his father's and mother's ordinary ways with ordinary things. He could think about it all calmly, as though their lives were really their own, as though their lives really belonged to them. But already the sun was rising higher in the room. Ben Lewin threw off his sheet and sat up in bed looking dazed and lost. Jack Lewin, too, awoke, snapping his black eyes in every direction to get himself in focus. Teddy had come back to his own self, had forgotten what he was thinking, what he was looking at, what had distracted him so compellingly just a few minutes before. "You're up," he stated.

Ben yawned. Leaning forward, he began to massage the inside of his thighs. Jack still lay on his back, looked thoughtful. Finally, he sat up and cleared his throat. "Listen," he said.

"What?" Teddy said.

Jack didn't answer for a minute or two. He looked wan now, a little troubled. "Listen," he repeated. "I promised Haskel I'd be back in time for him to leave for the Eastern Shore tomorrow."

". . . . . ."

"We're going back on the four thirty."

"Jesus," Ben said.

"Watch the language."

"Oh, Dad," Teddy said. "I was planning."

"Well, business before pleasure."

"You mean, Haskel can't wait until Monday?" Ben asked.

"We're going back on the four thirty, this afternoon."

"Oh, Dad."

"You've had two weeks, Teddy. You don't have any complaints."

"But there were things I wanted to do."

"Two weeks is enough for anybody."

"You let Celia pull that?" Ben said. He picked up a shoe, dropped it violently.

"Celia had nothing to do with it."

"Yes, she did," Teddy said. "I spoke to her myself."

"I don't want any more discussion. We're going back this afternoon."

"I'm supposed to play for the Sukenik lady tonight."

"She'll get along without you."

"Dad."

"That's enough. Get yourselves packed now. If you plan it right, you'll be able to get a swim in, do everything you wanted to do. I'll tell Grandpa. It won't make any difference to him."

Ben muttered something in his bitter voice. Then he began to fold the sheets in quarters. Teddy got up, put on a bathing suit. "All I have is dirty laundry," he said, looking for his bag. He fingered the mothhole patch in his trunks; he was beginning to open it up again after a couple of weeks of daily probing.

"Is that suit dry?" Jack asked.

"No," Teddy said.

"Don't you think you should put on a dry suit?"

"That'll mean I'll have two wet suits to carry back."

Jack turned to his own packing. "One of you offer to help Grandpa."

"I don't want to go back today."

"I told you the discussion was over, Teddy. You lost your hearing or something?"

"It's not what I planned."

"I'm making the plans around here."

At that Ben gave a cynical little laugh.

"You, too," his father said. "Get yourself ready. We're going to have to leave the hotel around four. Don't give me any last-minute problems."

At least the decision was firm. That much the boys recognized. If Jack wanted to go back, if that was what he thought he had to do, he did it without outward hesitation. But there were the Sandlers again, inside their very lives, turning them this way and that, Celia's taste, Celia's insistence, Haskel's needs, Haskel's demands, and Bea's compromising acquiescence in it all. It was her lifetime of saying yes to them, shared for years now with her husband who, his sons recognized, had been only too willing to accept each obligation, each false hope that was held out to him as the real thing. It was no way to live. They both knew that, Teddy and Ben. It was not for them. They would do it another way when their time came, but, for now, whenever it happened, they turned their backs on their father in helpless embarrassment, and all three knew it, to their shame.

By eleven that morning, Teddy was at the beach, a Hershey bar wrapped up in his towel for lunch. He'd skip Sloan's this noon, had said good-by to Saul at breakfast, taking him a little by surprise, his long lawyer's nose twitching once or twice at the news, had told Etta Sukenik that he would not be able to accompany her at her recital tonight, waiting to be scolded. All she had said was "As you must," and turned away, her mind clearly at work already on an alternative solution. Only Gus Levi had seemed affected by their change in plans. He had given Teddy a steady gaze over *The New York Times* at the news Teddy had volunteered. "A pity," he had then said. "Everything ends." Yes, Teddy had wanted to say, everything ends. I know that. Tell me something new, something I won't forget, something for me alone. But Gustav Levi, pale as the Atlantic City moon, had calmly continued turning the pages in the Saturday edition of the *Times*, reading the long, panic-filled reports from Warsaw and Berlin, absorbed by the *Times*'s editorial position on the conflict, testing the possibilities of England and France coming in before long. Teddy had never seen his friend outside the hotel, never on the beach, never on the Boardwalk, never on the street. Why did he come to Atlantic City in the first place?

Everybody was on the beach, the Talleses in their usual isolated spot, the Kesslers, right in front of Teddy, and a few feet away the two hopeless lovebirds, chirping fruitily to each other this morning, Charlotte Melnicov and the Big L. A high sun opened onto them, a late summer blaze. But there was something definitely cooler in the air, something moving in from the north. A slight shift in the angle of the earth's axis, a mere twist in another direction, and they would all freeze to death in an instant, caught in a massive ice block formed on the split second. Still, this sun could burn. He would turn a deeper tan if he just lay quietly in its path. He had tried the water once a few minutes earlier and the chill in it had taken him by surprise. It was as though a pack of ice floes were sailing a few feet offshore. He settled back now amidst the new weekend crowd, looked into the sky, let the shapeless crowd noises fall around him, dozed for a second. When he awoke, Erich Kessler was sitting on the blanket alongside him. In front of them, his father sat with his bathing cap on, the edges folded up over his ears. Herr Olympic Swimmer, the unsmiling Hessian champ of the Australian crawl. He gazed unhappily across the sea now, straight ahead, an unwavering look filled with unbearable nostalgia and the beginnings of despair.

"When does school begin?" Teddy asked.

"Two weeks," Erich said.

They were silent for a moment, then Teddy said, "Do you ever come to Baltimore?"

"No."

"If you do . . ."

Erich's father turned to him, said something in German. Erich nodded. "My father thinks we'll go back on Monday."

"The summer's over anyway."

"No. He's thinking about my mother."

" . . . . . ."

"He has to find a visa."

"Ah," Teddy said.

"It's very complicated. He has to pull the wires. I found out," Erich went on, without a pause, "that to make the horse jump into the ocean, the man touches his stomach underneath with an electric prod."

"The horse there?" Teddy pointed to the Steel Pier.

"Yes. The horse would never jump into the ocean by itself. They give it electricity to make it jump."

"I wish I had seen it," Teddy said. "I wish we had one rainy day."

"The man trains the horse like that. Sometimes he jumps before the electricity touches him, he's so afraid."

"I thought I was going to try to swim under the Pier, too."

"There are two horses."

"Well," Teddy said.

"French poodles are trained like that to dance on the stage."

"Want some chocolate?" Teddy held out the bar.

Again, Frederick Kessler said something to Erich in German.

"We're going to take a swim," Erich said.

"I'll stay here awhile," Teddy said. He lay back then, stretched. He could feel his pelvic bones jutting just above his thighs. His skin there felt paper thin. He had no chest, ribs like a zoo cage. He had none of Erich Kessler's solidity, the square shoulders, already manly in outline, the full bones above his waist and below the neck. He had none of Tibor Talles' slippery suppleness, that unique compactness in which the body moved as a single limb in itself, as its own beautiful extension. He was skinny, like a marink, knees like doorknobs, thin arms and wrists, only his fingers powerful, like Barney's, long and firm, with ice-blue veins running into them from his hands like sources of energy. Mabel Johns and Miss Eversfield admired his hands. Good for Bach, good for Mozart and Chopin, not yet strong enough for Rachmaninoff. Little Pad-a-roos-ki, he thought, as he turned on his side and caught sight of Charlotte and the Big L nearby. Then he was asleep again.

When he awoke, Larry Bernard was smearing suntan lotion onto Charlotte's back again, up and down, around in huge palmy circles. He was on his knees again behind her, his heavy athlete's buttocks digging into his heels. She sat cross-legged in the sand, her book in her lap. She was on the last chapter. Each morning, she complained that she couldn't put the book down, yet couldn't stand the idea of finishing it. She was terrified of finishing anything, just as terrified of beginning.

"I've been thinking of those two," the Big L finally said in his big voice, swinging his hand from the base of Charlotte's spine up to her shoulders.

"Who?"

"The doctor from Pittsburgh. The doctor and his wife. Doctor Lazarus."

"Why them?"

"Didn't you ever think, what they do together?"

". . . . . ."

"Him so short?"

The question hung slyly in the air for a moment. Charlotte wore a half-smile that flickered in embarrassment. Teddy closed his eyes, thought of Dr. and Mrs. Lazarus. There was no answer from Charlotte Melnicov.

"Don't you ever wonder?" Larry Bernard continued blandly.

". . . . . ."

"Lazarus rises," he suddenly said, falling back on his haunches. "I bet he probably goes up on her." Then he rested his chin on her shoulder.

"Oh, Larry," Charlotte said, feebly waving the words away. But she was laughing with mock indignation, as he locked his chin on her shoulder so that she was unable to move, laughing at the nerve, the unembarrassed crassness of her boyfriend. He knew how to make people pay attention. He knew how to make them listen. Larry Bernard would try to get away with anything and make people laugh at it. He could do it to Teddy Lewin, too. Teddy shared their laughter now, his face buried in the blanket. It really did take nerve to talk like that, and when you did, it turned out that people loved you for it. He probably goes up on her. . . . Teddy blushed, laughed again. Dr. Lazarus and his placid wife with the thick braided hair. One short, the other tall and broad. Still, like Herman and Claire and Mignon, they could sound all the sweet possibilities, in Teddy's head, of flesh on flesh, all the permutations, one with the other, all the lovely private angles of human touch. One wisecrack from Larry Bernard . . . He waited a few minutes, got to his feet, walked over to Charlotte and Larry.

"I'm going," he said.

Charlotte pulled him down alongside her, pecked him on the cheek, stroked his hair once. She started to lecture him dutifully on good manners, checked herself. "I'll call Mother as soon as I get back," she said. "Be sure to tell her that. Be sure to tell her I'm having a wonderful time." Then Larry Bernard shook his hand, gave him his big councilman's smile, and went on comfortably massaging Charlotte's back as she opened her book again for one last go.

There was not much else, just a swirl of last-minute packing and bill paying. By then, forty-five minutes before the train left, Teddy couldn't stand another minute at Sloan's. Let the Atlantic Ocean evaporate into thin air, let the sand disappear, let the whole long, skinny spit sink into the earth, for all he cared. He would go home, with his brother, Benedict, and his father, Jack, and *his* father, Barney. It was time. Bea Lewin was waiting for him. So was his sister, Marion. Let the sun go down, never to rise again. He would settle into his old rowhouse near Druid Hill Lake, into his own small room facing the narrow alleyway out back, where all summer long the watermelon man wandered up and down, calling his wares, with his little broken cart and fly-ridden horse. At the last minute, Ben had strolled into the lobby, looking unconcerned. He thrust a book into Teddy's hand. *Personal History,* by Vincent Sheean. "You can borrow it," he said. Fifty-nine cents, the tag read. A loan from his brother, who gave nothing away, not ice in the winter.

In the street then, as they loaded their bags into the taxi themselves, the driver sitting behind the wheel watching them with a toothpick in his mouth, Gustav Levi finally got out into the open air. He looked different outside, some kind of fugitive, paler than he seemed at table number five, a total stranger to the world. They all shook hands, talked at each other. Across the street, the ladies on the Cotswold veranda eyed them with interest, put down their fans and newspapers, watched the departure as they watched all the departures. Jack caught their look, eyed them back. So did Teddy, looking for the lady in the ginger wig.

"Ah," Jack said in sudden disgust. "Everybody at Sloan's wants to be just like them, wants to be a *goy*."

"No," Gustav Levi said. "You're wrong."

"What then?"

"They just want to be rich."

"Rich?"

"Yes, rich. And they're not even supposed to be alive, not even supposed to be here. Not if the *goyim* had their way all these years."

But the taxi driver was in a hurry. Before he knew it, Teddy was waving at Gus Levi out the back window. His tall, thin, pale figure disappeared down Virginia Avenue. He was gone, so was Sloan's, and the Cotswold and the beach and the Boardwalk, all of it lost in the enormous reflected vault of sunlight overhead. They were really leaving Atlantic City.

At the station, the late-afternoon crowd was trying to get back to Philadelphia. "Don't look for four seats together," Jack said. "It'll never work. You boys gets yourselves a seat and I'll take care of Grandpa." They were all jammed up against the gate, waiting for the stationmaster to open it up. They would go from Atlantic City past the salt marshes, from the sea swamps onto dry Jersey land, going north and west, mile by dusty mile, to North Philadelphia. There they would have to change trains for Baltimore. It would be another jam, another station crush, feeling the edges of other travelers' grips and valises cutting into their knees and thighs, another expectant run for seats for the rest of the hot trip south. In a couple of hours, Teddy would be home. He'd be home for Sunday night hot dogs and the Sunday night radio. Everybody would be back in another two weeks after the long summer vacation. Jack Benny, Eddie Cantor, Joe Penner the fool, Charlie McCarthy, and at nine o'clock the "Ford

Sunday Evening Hour," with W. J. Cameron spilling anti-Semitic intermission bilge all over the living rooms of America while the sixty-piece orchestra opened and closed the program with its lugubrious theme song. Teddy could hardly wait.

"Abends, will ich schlafen geh'n,
vierzehn Engel um mich steh'n:
zwei zu meinen Häupten,
zwei zu meiner Füssen,
zwei zu meiner Rechten,
zwei zu meiner Linken,
zweie, die mich decken,
zweie, die mich wecken," and so on, and so on, every Sunday night, fourteen Humperdinckian angels to the right and left, leading the way to paradise, with Bea Lewin sitting close to the radio, next to Teddy, waiting for the announcement of the next week's guest star. Sunday night.

There was a sudden clang then, a compression of the crowd waiting to board the train. They were already separated, Jack and Barney over there, Ben just behind Teddy. Teddy had Ben's new book under his arm. A whistle blew, once, twice. Teddy's muscles tightened, the sphincter's unmistakable response, the first ring of human resistance. After a moment, the great iron station gates swung back. Everyone wedged forward. Afraid that he would miss the train, afraid that he would not get a seat, would have to stand in the shuddering heated coach all the way to North Philadelphia, Teddy raced on ahead, down the long, roofed station platform, tunneling feverishly through the afternoon crowd for a place on one of the great black iron carriages, out of the airless, sand-flattened shadows that fell now from Absecon Bay and the west.

"Board," the conductor sang over their heads, breaking the word in two as he eyed the thick pocket watch in the palm of his hand.

Teddy hurried on, stumbling a little over his valise. He threw one last look back, for Ben and his father and Barney Levin, missed them for the moment on the platform and then, like everyone else, faced forward, nervously beginning to make his way down the dim curving track of his own future.

A Note About the Author

Robert Kotlowitz was educated in the Baltimore public schools, at the Peabody Conservatory there, and at Johns Hopkins University. For many years he was managing editor of *Harper's* magazine, and in 1971 he joined WNET Channel 13, where he is now vice-president in charge of programing; as executive producer of "The Sleeping Beauty," he was the recipient of a National Emmy in 1972. His first novel, *Somewhere Else,* was published in 1972 and received the Edward Lewis Wallant Prize Novel award as well as the National Jewish Book Award in 1973. Mr. Kotlowitz lives in New York City with his wife and two sons.

A Note About the Type

The main body of the book was set on the Linotype in Fairfield, a type face designed by the distinguished American artist and engraver Rudolph Ruzicka. This type displays the sober and sane qualities of a master craftsman whose talent has long been dedicated to clarity. Rudolph Ruzicka was born in Bohemia in 1883 and came to America in 1894. He has designed and illustrated many books and has created a considerable list of individual prints in a variety of techniques.

This book was composed by Maryland Linotype Composition Co., Baltimore, Maryland. It was printed and bound by The Haddon Craftsmen, Inc., Scranton, Pennsylvania.

Typography and binding design by Joy Chu.